black swan green

blackswangreen

A NOVEL

David Mitchell

alfred a. knopf canada

PUBLISHED BY ALFRED A. KNOPF CANADA

Copyright © 2006 David Mitchell

www.randomhouse.ca

This is a work of fiction. Names, characters, places, and incidents are the products of the
author's imagination or are used fictitiously. Any resemblance to actual events, locales,
or persons, living or dead, is entirely coincidental.

Library and Archives Canada Cataloguing in Publication

Mitchell, David (David Stephen)
  Black swan green : a novel / David Mitchell.

ISBN-13: 978-0-676-97496-6
ISBN-10: 0-676-97496-1

I. Title.

PR6063.I785B53 2006   823'.92   C2005-905424-7

Book design by Casey Hampton

First Edition

Printed and bound in the United States of America

10 9 8 7 6 5 4 3 2 1

blackswangreen

january man

Do not *set foot in my office.* That's Dad's rule. But the phone'd rung twenty-five times. Normal people give up after ten or eleven, unless it's a matter of life or death. Don't they? Dad's got an answering machine like James Garner's in *The Rockford Files* with big reels of tape. But he's stopped leaving it switched on recently. Thirty rings, the phone got to. Julia couldn't hear it up in her converted attic 'cause "Don't You Want Me?" by Human League was thumping out dead loud. *Forty* rings. Mum couldn't hear 'cause the washing machine was on berserk cycle *and* she was hoovering the living room. *Fifty* rings. That's just not normal. S'pose Dad'd been mangled by a juggernaut on the M5 and the police only had this office number 'cause all his other I.D.'d got incinerated? We could lose our final chance to see our charred father in the terminal ward.

So I went in, thinking of a bride going into Bluebeard's chamber after being told not to. (Bluebeard, mind, was waiting for that to happen.) Dad's office smells of pound notes, papery but metallic too. The blinds were down so it felt like evening, not ten in the morning. There's a serious clock on the wall, exactly the same make as the serious clocks on the walls at school. There's a photo of Dad shaking hands with Craig Salt when Dad got made regional sales director for Greenland. (Greenland the supermarket chain, not Greenland the country.) Dad's IBM computer sits on the steel desk. *Thousands* of pounds, IBMs cost. The office phone's red like a nuclear hotline and it's got buttons you push, not the dial you get on normal phones.

So anyway, I took a deep breath, picked up the receiver, and said our number. I can say that without stammering, at least. Usually.

But the person on the other end didn't answer.

"Hello?" I said. "Hello?"

They breathed in like they'd cut themselves on paper.

"Can you hear me? I can't hear you."

Very faint, I recognized the *Sesame Street* music.

"If you can hear me"—I remembered a Children's Film Foundation film where this happened—"tap the phone, once."

There was no tap, just more *Sesame Street*.

"You might have the wrong number," I said, wondering.

A baby began wailing and the receiver was slammed down.

When people listen they make a listening noise.

I'd heard *it*, so they'd heard *me*.

"May as well be hanged for a sheep as hanged for a handkerchief." Miss Throckmorton taught us that *aeons* ago. 'Cause I'd sort of had a reason to have come into the forbidden chamber, I peered through Dad's razor-sharp blind, over the glebe, past the cockerel tree, over more fields, up to the Malvern Hills. Pale morning, icy sky, frosted crusts on the hills, but no sign of sticking snow, worse luck. Dad's swivelly chair's a lot like the Millennium Falcon's laser tower. I blasted away at the skyful of Russian MiGs streaming over the Malverns. Soon tens of thousands of people between here and Cardiff owed me their lives. The glebe was littered with mangled fusilages and blackened wings. I'd shoot the Soviet airmen with tranquilizer darts as they pressed their ejector seats. Our marines'll mop them up. I'd refuse all medals. "Thanks, but no thanks," I'd tell Margaret Thatcher and Ronald Reagan when Mum invited them in, "I was just doing my job."

Dad's got this fab pencil sharpener clamped to his desk. It makes pencils sharp enough to puncture body armor. H pencils're sharpest, they're Dad's faves. I prefer 2Bs.

The doorbell went. I put the blind back to how it was, checked I'd left no other traces of my incursion, slipped out, and flew downstairs to see who it was. The last six steps I took in one death-defying bound.

Moron, grinny-zitty as ever. His bumfluff's getting thicker, mind. "You'll *never* guess what!"

"What?"

"You know the lake in the woods?"

"What about it?"

"It's only"—Moron checked that we weren't being overheard—"gone and froze *solid*! Half the kids in the village're there, right now. *Ace* doss or what?"

"Jason!" Mum appeared from the kitchen. "You're letting the cold in! Either invite Dean in*side*—hel*lo* Dean—or shut the door."

"Um . . . just going out for a bit, Mum."

"*Um* . . . where?"

"Just for some healthy fresh air."

That was a strategic mistake. "What are you up to?"

I wanted to say "Nothing" but Hangman decided not to let me. "Why would I be up to anything?" I avoided her stare as I put on my navy duffel coat.

"What's your new black parka done to offend you, may I ask?"

I still couldn't say "Nothing." (Truth is, black means you fancy yourself as a hard-knock. Adults can't be expected to understand.) "My duffel's a bit warmer, that's all. It's parky out."

"Lunch is one o'clock *sharp*." Mum went back to changing the Hoover bag. "Dad's coming home to eat. Put on a woolly hat or your head'll freeze."

Woolly hats're gay but I could stuff it in my pocket later.

"Good-bye then, Mrs. Taylor," said Moron.

"Good-bye, Dean," said Mum.

Mum's never liked Moron.

Moron's my height and he's okay but *Jesus* he pongs of gravy. Moron wears ankle-flappers from charity shops and lives down Druggers End in a brick cottage that pongs of gravy too. His real name's Dean Moran (rhymes with "warren") but our P.E. teacher Mr. Carver started calling him "Moron" in our first week and it's stuck. I call him "Dean" if we're on our own but name's aren't just names. Kids who're really popular get called by their first names, so Nick Yew's always just "Nick." Kids who're a bit popular like Gilbert Swinyard have sort of respectful nicknames like "Yardy." Next down are kids like me who call each other by our surnames. Below us are kids with piss-take nicknames like Moran Moron or Nicholas Briar, who's Knickerless Bra. It's all ranks, being a boy, like the army. If I called Gilbert Swinyard just "Swinyard," he'd kick my face in. Or if I called Moron "Dean" in front of everyone, it'd damage my own standing. So you've got to watch out.

Girls don't do this so much, 'cept for Dawn Madden, who's a boy gone wrong in some experiment. Girls don't scrap so much as boys either. (That said, just before school broke up for Christmas, Dawn Madden and Andrea Bozard started yelling "Bitch!" and "Slag!" in the bus queues after school. Punching tits and pulling hair and everything, they were.) Wish I'd been born a girl, sometimes. They're generally loads more civilized. But if I ever admitted that out loud I'd get BUMHOLE PLUMMER scrawled on my locker. That happened to Floyd Chaceley for admitting he liked Johann Sebastian Bach. Mind you, if they knew Eliot Bolivar, who gets poems published in *Black Swan Green Parish Magazine,* was *me,* they'd gouge me to death behind the tennis courts with blunt woodwork tools and spray the Sex Pistols logo on my gravestone.

So anyway, as Moron and I walked to the lake he told me about the Scalectrix he'd got for Christmas. On Boxing Day its transformer blew up and nearly wiped out his entire family. "Yeah, sure," I said. But Moron swore it on his nan's grave. So I told him he should write to *That's Life* on BBC and get Esther Rantzen to make the manufacturer pay compensation. Moron thought that might be difficult 'cause his dad'd bought it off a Brummie at Tewkesbury Market on Christmas Eve. I didn't dare ask what a "Brummie" was in case it's the same as "bummer" or "bumboy," which means homo. "Yeah," I said, "see what you mean." Moron asked me what I'd got for Christmas. I'd actually got £13.50 in book tokens and a poster of Middle-earth, but books're gay so I talked about the Game of Life, which I'd got from Uncle Brian and Aunt Alice. It's a board game you win by getting your little car to the end of the road of life first, and with the most money. We crossed the crossroads by the Black Swan and went into the woods. Wished I'd rubbed ointment into my lips 'cause they get chapped when it's this cold.

Soon we heard kids through the trees, shouting and screaming. "Last one to the lake's a *spaz!*" yelled Moron, haring off before I was ready. Straight off he tripped over a frozen tire rut, went flying, and landed on his arse. Trust Moran. "I think I might've got a concussion," he said.

"Concussion's if you hit your head. Unless your brain's up your arse." What a line. Pity nobody who matters was around to hear it.

The lake in the woods was *epic.* Tiny bubbles were trapped in the ice like in Fox's Glacier Mints. Neal Brose had proper Olympic ice skates he hired out for 5p a go, though Pete Redmarley was allowed to use them for free so other kids'd see him speed-skating around and want a go too. Just staying up on the ice is hard enough. I fell over loads before I got the knack of sliding in my trainers. Ross Wilcox turned up with his cousin Gary Drake *and* Dawn Madden. All three're pretty good skaters. Drake and Wilcox're taller than me too now. (They'd cut the fingers off of their gloves to show the scars they'd got playing Scabby Queen. Mum'd *murder* me.) Squelch sat on the humpy island in the middle of the lake where the ducks normally live, shouting, *"Arse over tit! Arse over tit!"* at whoever fell over. Squelch's funny in the head 'cause he was born too early, so nobody ever thumps him one. Not hard, anyway. Grant Burch rode his servant Philip Phelps's Raleigh Chopper actually on the ice. He kept his balance for a few seconds, but when he pulled a wheelie the bike went flying. After it landed it looked like Uri Geller'd tortured it to death. Phelps grinned sickly. Bet he was wondering what he'd tell his dad. Then Pete Redmarley and Grant Burch decided the frozen lake'd be perfect for British Bulldogs. Nick Yew said, "Okay, I'm on for that," so it was decided. I *hate* British Bulldogs. When Miss Throckmorton banned it at our primary school after Lee Biggs lost three teeth playing it, I was *dead* relieved. But this morning any kid who denied loving British Bulldogs'd've looked a total ponce. Specially kids from up Kingfisher Meadows like me.

About twenty or twenty-five of us boys, plus Dawn Madden, stood in a bunch to be picked like slaves in a slave market. Grant Burch and Nick Yew were joint captains of one team. Pete Redmarley and Gilbert Swinyard were the captains of the other. Ross Wilcox and Gary Drake both got picked before me by Pete Redmarley, but I got picked by Grant Burch on the sixth pass, which wasn't embarrassingly late. Moron and Squelch were the last two left. Grant Burch and Pete Redmarley joked, "No, you can have 'em both, we want to *win!*" and Moron and Squelch had to laugh like they thought it was funny too. Maybe Squelch really did. (Moron didn't. When everyone looked away, he had the same face as that time after we all told him we were playing Hide-and-Seek and sent him off to hide. It took an hour for him to work out nobody was looking for him.) Nick Yew won the toss so us lot were the Runners first and Pete Redmarley's team were the Bulldogs. Unimportant kids' coats were put at either end of the lake as goalmouths to reach through and to defend. Girls, apart from Dawn Madden, and the littl'uns were cleared off the ice. Redmarley's Bulldogs formed a pack in the middle and us Runners slid to our starting goal. My heart was drumming now. Bulldogs and Runners crouched like sprinters. The captains led the chant.

"British Bulldogs! One two *three!*"

Screaming like kamikazes, we charged. I slipped over (accidentally on purpose) just before the front wave of Runners smashed into the Bulldogs. This'd tie up most of the hardest Bulldogs in fights with our front Runners. (Bull-dogs have to pin down both shoulders of Runners onto the ice for long enough to shout "British Bulldogs one two three.") With luck, my strategy'd clear some spaces to dodge through and on to our home goalposts. My plan worked pretty well at first. The Tookey brothers and Gary Drake all crashed into Nick Yew. A flying leg kicked my shin but I got past them without com-ing a cropper. But then Ross Wilcox came homing in on me. I tried to wrig-gle past but Wilcox got a firm grip on my wrist and tried to pull me down. But instead of trying to struggle free I got a firmer grip on *his* wrist and flung him off me, straight into Ant Little and Darren Croome. Ace in the *face* or what? Games and sports aren't about taking part or even about winning. Games and sports're really about humiliating your enemies. Lee Biggs tried a poxy rugby tackle on me but I shook him free *no* sweat. He's too worried about the teeth he's got left to be a decent Bulldog. I was the fourth Runner home. Grant Burch shouted, "Nice work *Jacey*-boy!" Nick Yew'd fought free of the Tookeys and Gary Drake and got home too. About a third of the Runners got captured and turned into Bulldogs for the next pass. I hate that about British Bulldogs. It forces you to be a traitor.

So anyway, we all chanted, "British Bulldogs one two THREE!" and charged like last time but this time I had no chance. Ross Wilcox *and* Gary Drake *and* Dawn Madden targeted me from the start. No matter how I tried to dodge through the fray it was hopeless. I hadn't got halfway across the lake before they got me. Ross Wilcox went for my legs, Gary Drake toppled me, and Dawn Madden sat on my chest and pinned my shoulders down with her knees. I just lay there and let them convert me into a Bulldog. In my heart I'd always be a Runner. Gary Drake gave me a dead leg, which might or might not've been on purpose. Dawn Madden's got cruel eyes like a Chinese em-press and sometimes one glimpse at school makes me think about her all day. Ross Wilcox jumped up and punched the air like he'd scored at Old Trafford. The spazzo. "Yeah, yeah, Wilcox," I said, "three against one, well done." Wilcox flashed me a V-sign and slid off for another battle. Grant Burch and Nick Yew came windmilling at a thick pocket of Bulldogs and half of them went flying.

Then Gilbert Swinyard yelled at the top of his lungs, *"PIIIIIILE-ONNNNNN!"* That was the signal for every Runner and every Bulldog on the lake to throw themselves onto a wriggling, groaning, growing pyramid of kids. The game itself was sort of forgotten. I held back, pretending to limp a bit from my dead leg. Then we heard the sound of a chain saw in the woods, flying down the track, straight toward us.

The chain saw wasn't a chain saw. It was Tom Yew on his purple Suzuki 150cc scrambler. Pluto Noak was clinging to the back, without a helmet. British Bulldogs was aborted 'cause Tom Yew's a minor legend in Black Swan Green. Tom Yew serves in the Royal Navy on a frigate called HMS *Coventry*. Tom Yew's got every Led Zep album ever made *and* can play the guitar introduction to "Stairway to Heaven." Tom Yew's actually shaken hands with Peter Shilton, the England goalkeeper. Pluto Noak's a less shiny legend. He left school without even taking his CSEs last year. Now he works in the Pork Scratchings factory in Upton-on-Severn. (There's rumors Pluto Noak's smoked cannabis but obviously it wasn't the type that cauliflowerizes your brain and makes you jump off roofs onto railings.) Tom Yew parked his Suzuki by the bench on the narrow end of the lake and sat on it, sidesaddle. Pluto Noak thumped his back to say thanks and went to speak to Collette Bozard, who, according to Moron's sister Kelly, he's had sexual intercourse with. The older kids sat on the bench facing him, like Jesus's disciples, and passed round fags. (Ross Wilcox and Gary Drake smoke now. Worse still, Ross Wilcox asked Tom Yew something about Suzuki silencers and Tom Yew answered him like Ross Wilcox was eighteen too.) Grant Burch told his servant Phelps to run and get him a peanut Yorkie and a can of Top Deck from Rhydd's Shop, yelling after him, "*Run*, I told yer!" to impress Tom Yew. Us middle-rank kids sat round the bench on the frosty ground. The older kids started talking about the best things on TV over Christmas and New Year's. Tom Yew started saying he'd seen *The Great Escape* and everyone agreed everything else'd been crap compared to *The Great Escape*, specially the bit where Steve McQueen gets caught by Nazis on the barbed wire. But then Tom Yew said he thought it'd gone on a bit long and everyone agreed that though the film was classic it'd dragged on for *ages*. (I didn't see it 'cause Mum and Dad watched the Two Ronnies Christmas special. But I paid close attention so I can pretend to've watched it when school starts next Monday.)

The talk'd shifted, for some reason, to the worst way to die.

"Gettin' bit by a green mamba," Gilbert Swinyard reckoned. "Deadliest snake in the world. Yer organs burst so yer piss mixes with yer blood. *Agony*."

"Agony, sure," sniffed Grant Burch, "but you're dead pretty quick. Havin' yer skin unpeeled off yer like a sock, that's worse. Apache Indians do that to yer. The best ones can make it last the whole night."

Pete Redmarley said he'd heard of this Vietcong execution. "They strips yer, ties yer up, then rams Philadelphia cheese up yer jax. *Then* they locks yer in a coffin with a pipe goin' in. *Then* they send starving rats down the pipe. The rats eat through the cheese, then carry on chewin', into *you*."

Everyone looked at Tom Yew for the answer. "I get this dream." He took a drag on his cigarette that lasted an age. "I'm with the last bunch of survivors, after an atomic war. We're walking up a motorway. No cars, just weeds. Every time I look behind me, there're fewer of us. One by one, you see, the radiation's getting them." He glanced at his brother Nick, then over the frozen lake. "It's not that I'll die that bothers me. It's that I'll be the last one."

Nobody said a lot for a bit.

Ross Wilcox swiveled our way. He took a drag on his cigarette that lasted an age, the poser. "If it wasn't for Winston Churchill *you* lot'd all be speakin' German now."

Sure, like Ross Wilcox would've evaded capture and headed a resistance cell. I was *dying* to tell that prat that *actually*, if the Japanese hadn't bombed Pearl Harbor, America'd never've come into the war, Britain'd've been starved into surrender, and Winston Churchill'd've been executed as a war criminal. But I knew I couldn't. There were swarms of stammer-words in there, and Hangman's bloody merciless this January. So I said I was busting for a waz, stood up, and went down the path to the village a bit. Gary Drake shouted, "Hey, Taylor! Shake your dong more than twice, you're *playing* with it!," which got fat laughs from Neal Brose and Ross Wilcox. I flashed them a V-sign over my shoulder. That stuff about shaking your dong's a craze at the moment. There's no one I can trust to ask what it means.

Trees're always a relief, after people. Gary Drake and Ross Wilcox might've been slagging me off, but the fainter the voices became, the less I wanted to go back. I *loathed* myself for not putting Ross Wilcox in his place about speaking German, but it'd've been *death* to've started stammering back there. The cladding of frost on thorny branches was thawing and fat drops drip-drip-dripping. It soothed me, a bit. In little pits where the sun couldn't reach there was still some gravelly snow left, but not enough to make a snowball. (Nero used to kill his guests by making them eat glass food, just for a laugh.) A robin, I saw, a woodpecker, a magpie, a blackbird, and far off I *think* I heard a nightingale, though I'm not sure you get them in January. Then, where the faint path from the House in the Woods meets the main path to the lake, I heard a boy, gasping for breath, pounding this way. Between a pair of wishbone pines I squeezed myself out of sight. Phelps dashed by, clutching his master's peanut Yorkie and a can of Tizer. (Rhydd's must be out of Top Deck.) Behind the pines a possible path led up the slant. I know *all* the paths in this part of the woods, I thought. But not this one. Pete Redmarley and Grant Burch'd start up British Bulldogs again when Tom Yew left. That wasn't much of a reason to go back. Just to see where the path might go, I followed it.

There's only one house in the woods so that's what we call it, the House in the Woods. An old woman was s'posed to live there, but I didn't know her name and I'd never seen her. The house's got four windows and a chimney, same as a little kid's drawing of a house. A brick wall as high as me surrounds it and wild bushes grow higher. Our war games in the woods steered clear of the building. Not 'cause there're any ghost stories about it or anything. It's just that part of the woods isn't good.

But this morning the house looked so hunkered down and locked up, I doubted anyone was still living there. Plus, my bladder was about to split, and that makes you less cautious. So I peed up against the frosted wall. I'd just finished signing my autograph in steamy yellow when a rusty gate opened up with a tiny shriek and there stood a sour aunt from black-and-white times. Just standing there, staring at me.

My pee ran dry.

"God! Sorry!" I zipped up my fly, expecting an *utter* bollocking. Mum'd flay alive any kid she found pissing against *our* fence, then feed his body to the compost bin. Including me. "I didn't know anyone was living . . . here."

The sour aunt carried on looking at me.

Pee dribbles blotted my underpants.

"My brother and I were born in this house," she said, finally. Her throat was saggy like a lizard's. "We have no intention of moving away."

"Oh . . ." I still wasn't sure if she was about to open fire on me. "Good."

"How noisy you youngsters are!"

"Sorry."

"It was very careless of you to wake my brother."

My mouth'd glued up. "It wasn't me making all the noise. Honestly."

"There are days"—the sour aunt never blinked—"when my brother loves youngsters. But on days like these, my oh my, you give him the furies."

"Like I said, I'm sorry."

"You'll be *sorrier*," she said, looking disgusted, "if my brother gets a hold of you."

Quiet things were too loud and loud things couldn't be heard.

"Is he . . . uh, around? Now? Your brother, I mean?"

"His room's just as he left it."

"Is he ill?"

She acted like she hadn't heard me.

"I've got to go home now."

"You'll be *sorrier*"—she did that spitty chomp old people do to not dribble—"when the ice cracks."

"The ice? On the lake? It's as solid as anything."

"You *always* say so. Ralph Bredon said so."

"Who's he?"

"Ralph Bredon. The butcher's boy."

It didn't feel at all right. "I've got to go home now."

Lunch at 9 Kingfisher Meadows, Black Swan Green, Worcestershire, was Findus ham'n'cheese Crispy Pancakes, crinkle-cut oven chips, and sprouts. Sprouts taste of fresh puke but Mum said I had to eat *five* without making a song and dance about it, or there'd be no butterscotch Angel Delight for pudding. Mum says she won't let the dining table be used as a venue for "adolescent discontent." Before Christmas I asked what not liking the taste of sprouts has to do with "adolescent discontent." Mum warned me to stop being a Clever Little Schoolboy. I should've shut up but I pointed out that Dad never makes her eat melon (which *she* hates) and Mum never makes Dad eat garlic (which *he* hates). She went *ape* and sent me to my room. When Dad got back I got a lecture about arrogance.

No pocket money that week, either.

So anyway, this lunchtime I cut my sprouts up into tiny pieces and glolloped tomato ketchup over them. "Dad?"

"Jason?"

"If you drown, what happens to your body?"

Julia rolled her eyes like Jesus on his cross.

"Bit of a morbid topic for the dinner table." Dad chewed his forkful of crispy pancake. "Why do you ask?"

It was best not to mention the frozen-up pond. "Well, in this book *Arctic Adventure* these two brothers Hal and Roger Hunt're being chased by a baddie called Kaggs who falls into the—"

Dad held up his hand to say *Enough!* "Well, in *my* opinion, Mr. Kaggs gets eaten by fish. Picked clean."

"Do they have piranhas in the Arctic?"

"Fish'll eat anything once it's soft enough. Mind you, if he fell into the Thames, his body'd wash up before long. The Thames always gives up its dead, the Thames does."

My misdirection was complete. "How about if he fell through ice, into a lake, say? What'd happen to him then? Would he sort of stay . . . deep frozen?"

"*Thing,*" Julia mewled, "is being *grotesque* while we're eating, Mum."

Mum rolled up her napkin. "Lorenzo Hussingtree's has a new range of tiles in, Michael." (My abortion of a sister flashed me a victorious grin.) "Michael?"

"Yes, Helena?"

"I thought we could drop by Lorenzo Hussingtree's showroom on our way to Worcester. New tiles. They're ex*quisite.*"

"No doubt Lorenzo Hussingtree charges exquisite prices, to match?"

"We're having workmen in anyway, so why not make a proper job of it? The kitchen's getting embarrassing."

"Helena, why—"

Julia sees arguments coming even before Mum and Dad sometimes. "Can I get down now?"

"*Darling.*" Mum looked really hurt. "It's butterscotch Angel Delight."

"Yummy, but could I have mine tonight? Got to get back to Robert Peel and the Enlightened Whigs. Anyway, Thing has ruined my appetite."

"Pigging on Cadbury's Roses with Kate Alfrick," I counterattacked, "is what's ruined *your* appetite."

"So where did the Terry's Chocolate Orange go, Thing?"

"Julia," Mum sighed, "I *do* wish you wouldn't call Jason that. You've only got one brother."

Julia said, "One too many" and got up.

Dad remembered something. "Have either of you been into my office?"

"Not me, Dad." Julia hovered in the doorway, scenting blood. "Must've been my honest, charming, obedient, younger sibling."

How did he know?

"It's a simple enough question." Dad had hard evidence. The only adult I know who bluffs kids is Mr. Nixon, our headmaster.

The pencil! When Dean Moran rang the doorbell I must've left the pencil in the sharpener. *Damn* Moron. "Your phone was ringing for *yonks*, like, four or five minutes, *honestly*, so—"

Dad didn't care. "What's the rule about not going into my office?"

"But I thought it might be an emergency so I picked it up and there was"—Hangman blocked "someone"—"a person on the other end but—"

"I believe"—now Dad's palm said *HALT!*—"I just asked you a question."

"Yes, but—"

"*What* question did I just ask you?"

" 'What's the rule about not going into my office?' "

"So I did." Dad's a pair of scissors at times. *Snip* snip *snip* snip. "Now, why don't you *answer* this question?"

Then Julia did a strange move. "That's funny."

"I don't see anyone laughing."

"No, Dad, on Boxing Day when you and Mum took Thing to Worcester, the phone in your office went. Honestly, it went on for *aeons*. I couldn't concentrate on my revision. The more I told myself it wasn't a desperate ambulanceman or something, the likelier it seemed it was. In the end it was driving me crazy. I had no choice. I said 'Hello' but the person on the other end didn't say anything. So I hung up, in case it was a pervert."

Dad'd gone quiet but the danger wasn't past.

"That was just like me," I ventured. "But I didn't hang up straightaway 'cause I thought maybe they couldn't hear me. Was there a baby in the background, Julia?"

"*Okay*, you two, enough of the private-eye biz. If some joker *is* making nuisance calls then I don't want *either* of you answering, no matter what. If it happens again, just unplug the socket. Understand?"

Mum was just sitting there. It didn't feel at all right.

Dad's "DID YOU *HEAR* ME?" was like a brick through a window. Julia and me jumped. "Yes Dad."

Mum, me, and Dad ate our butterscotch Angel Delight without a word. I didn't dare even look at my parents. *I* couldn't ask to get down early too 'cause Julia'd already used that card. Why *I* was in the doghouse was clear enough, but God knows why Mum and Dad were giving each other the silent treatment. After the last spoonful of Angel Delight Dad said, "Lovely, Helena, thank you. Jason and I'll do the washing up, won't we, Jason?"

Mum just made this nothing-sound and went upstairs.

Dad washed up, humming a nothing-song. I put the dirty dishes in the hatch, then went into the kitchen to dry. I should've just shut up, but I thought I could make the day turn safely normal if I just said the right thing. "Do you get" — Hangman *loves* giving me grief over this word — "nightingales in January, Dad? I might've heard one this morning. In the woods."

Dad was Brillo-padding a pan. "How should I know?"

I pushed on. Usually Dad likes talking about nature and stuff. "But that bird at granddad's hospice. You said it was a nightingale."

"Huh. Fancy you remembering that." Dad stared over the back lawn at the icicles on the summerhouse. Then this noise came out of Dad like he'd entered the World's Miserablest Man of 1982 Competition. "Just concentrate on those glasses, Jason, before you drop one." He switched on Radio 2 for the weather forecast, then began cutting up the 1981 *Highway Code* with scissors. Dad bought the updated 1982 *Highway Code* the day it came out, and he says old ones could cause accidents if they're not destroyed. Tonight most of the British Isles will see temperatures plunging well below zero. Motorists in Scotland and the North should be careful of black ice on the roads, and the Midlands should anticipate widespread patches of freezing fog.

Up in my room I played the Game of Life, but being two players at once is no fun. Julia's friend Kate Alfrick called for Julia to study together. But they were just gossiping about who's going out with who in the sixth form, and playing Police singles. My billion problems kept bobbing up like corpses in a flooded city. Mum and Dad at lunch. Hangman colonizing the alphabet. At this rate I'm going to have to learn sign language. Gary Drake and Ross Wilcox. They've never exactly been my best mates but today they'd ganged up against me. Neal Brose was in on it too. Last, the sour aunt in the woods worried me. How come?

Wished there was a crack to slip through and leave all this stuff behind. Next week I'm thirteen but thirteen looks way worse than twelve. Julia moans nonstop about being eighteen but eighteen's *epic*, from where *I'm* standing. No official bedtime, twice my pocket money, and for Julia's eighteenth she went to Tanya's Night Club in Worcester with her thousand and one friends. Tanya's's got the *only* xenon disco laser light in *Europe*! How ace is *that*?

Dad drove off up Kingfisher Meadows, alone.

Mum must still be in her room. She's there more and more recently.

To cheer myself up I put on my granddad's Omega. Dad called me into his office on Boxing Day and said he had something very important to give me, from my grandfather. Dad'd been keeping it till I was mature enough to look after it myself. It was a watch. An Omega Seamaster De Ville. Granddad bought it off a real live Arab in a port called Aden in 1949. Aden's in Arabia and once it was British. He'd worn it every day of his life, even the moment he died. That fact makes the Omega more special, not scary. The Omega's face is silver and wide as a 50p but as thin as a tiddlywink. "A sign of an excellent watch," Dad said, grave as grave, "is its thinness. Not like these plastic tubs teenagers strap to their wrist these days to strut about in."

Where I hid my Omega is a work of genius and second in security only to my Oxo tin under the loose floorboard. Using a Stanley knife I hollowed out a crappy-looking book called *Woodcraft for Boys*. *Woodcraft for Boys*'s on my shelf between real books. Julia often snoops in my room, but she's never discovered this hiding place. I'd know 'cause I keep a ½p coin balanced on it at the back. Plus, if Julia'd found it she'd've copied my ace idea for sure. I've checked *her* bookshelf for false spines and there aren't any.

Outside I heard an unfamiliar car. A sky-blue VW Jetta was crawling along the curb, as if its driver was searching for a house number. At the end of our cul-de-sac the driver, a woman, did a three-point turn, stalled once, and drove off up Kingfisher Meadows. I should've memorized the number plate in case it's on *Police* 999.

Granddad was the last grandparent to die, and the only one I have any memories of. Not many. Chalking roads for my Corgi cars down his garden path. Watching *Thunderbirds* at his bungalow in Grange-over-Sands and drinking pop called Dandelion and Burdock.

I wound the stopped Omega up and set the time to a fraction after three.

Unborn Twin murmured, *Go to the lake.*

The stump of an elm guards a bottleneck in the path through the woods. Sitting on the stump was Squelch. Squelch's real name's Mervyn Hill but one time when we were changing for P.E., he pulled down his trousers and we saw he had a nappy on. About nine, he'd've been. Grant Burch started the Squelch nickname and it's been years since anyone's called him Mervyn. It's easier to change your eyeballs than to change your nickname.

So anyway, Squelch was stroking something furry and moon gray in the crook of his elbow. "Finders keepers, losers weepers."

"All right, Squelch. What you got there, then?"

Squelch's got stained teeth. "Ain't showin'!"

"Go on. You can show *us*."

Squelch mumbled, "Kit Kat."

"A Kit Kat? A chocolate bar?"

Squelch showed me the head of a sleeping kitten. "Kitty cat! Finders keepers, losers weepers."

"Wow. A cat. Where'd you find her?"

"By the lake. Crack o' dawn, b'fore anyone else got to the lake. I hided her while we did British Bulldogs. Hided her in a box."

"Why didn't you show it to anyone?"

"Burch and Swinyard and Redmarley and them *bastards*'d've tooked her away's why! Finders keepers, losers weepers. I hided her. Now I come back."

You never know with Squelch. "She's quiet, isn't she?"

Squelch just petted her.

"Could I hold her, Merv?"

"If you don't breathe a *word* to no one"—Squelch eyed me dubiously—"you can stroke her. But take them gloves off. They're nobbly."

So I took off my goalie gloves and reached out to touch the kitten.

Squelch lobbed the kitten at me. "It's *yours* now!"

Taken by surprise, I caught the kitten.

"Yours!" Squelch ran off laughing back to the village. "*Yours!*"

The kitten was cold and stiff as a pack of meat from the fridge. Only now did I realize it was dead. I dropped it. It thudded.

"Finders," Squelch called, his voice dying off, "keepers!"

Using two sticks, I lifted the kitten into a clump of nervy snowdrops.

So still, so dignified. Died in the frost last night, I s'pose.

Dead things show you what you'll be too one day.

Nobody'd be out on the frozen lake, I'd suspected, and there wasn't a soul. *Superman II* was on TV. I'd seen it at Malvern Cinema about two years ago on Neal Brose's birthday. It wasn't bad but not worth sacrificing my own private frozen lake for. Clark Kent gives up his powers just to have sexual intercourse with Lois Lane in a glittery bed. Who'd make such a stupid swap? If you could *fly*? Deflect nuclear missiles into space? Turn back time by spinning the planet in reverse? Sexual intercourse can't be *that* good.

I sat on the empty bench to eat a slab of Jamaican Ginger Cake, then went out on the ice. Without other kids watching, I didn't fall *once*. Round and around in swoopy anticlockwise loops I looped, a stone on the end of a string. Overhanging trees tried to touch my head with their fingers. Rooks *craw* . . . *craw* . . . *craw*ed, like old people who've forgotten why they've come upstairs.

A sort of trance.

The afternoon'd gone and the sky was turning to outer space when I noticed another kid on the lake. This boy skated at my speed and followed my orbit, but always stayed on the far side of the lake. So if I was at twelve o'clock, he was at six. When I got to eleven, he was at five, and so on, always across from me. My first thought was he was a kid from the village, just mucking about. I even thought he might be Nick Yew 'cause he was sort of stocky. But the strange thing was, if I looked at this kid directly for more than a moment, dark spaces sort of swallowed him up. The first couple of times I thought he'd gone home. But after another half loop of the lake, he'd be back. Just at the edge of my vision. Once I skated across the lake to intercept him, but he vanished before I got to the island in the middle. When I carried on orbiting the pond, he was back.

Go home, urged the nervy Maggot in me. *What if he's a ghost?*

My Unborn Twin can't stand Maggot. *What if he* is *a ghost?*

"Nick?" I called out. My voice sounded indoors. "Nick Yew?"

The kid carried on skating.

I called out, "Ralph Bredon?"

His answer took a whole orbit to reach me.

Butcher's boy.

If a doctor'd told me the kid across the lake was my imagination, and that his voice was only words I thought, I wouldn't've argued. If Julia'd told me I was convincing myself Ralph Bredon was there to make myself feel more special than I am, I wouldn't've argued. If a mystic'd told me that one exact moment in one exact place can act as an antenna that picks up faint traces of lost people, I wouldn't've argued.

"What's it like?" I called out. "Isn't it cold?"

The answer took another orbit to reach me.

You get used to the cold.

Do the kids who'd drowned in the lake down the years mind me trespassing on their roof? Do they *want* new kids to fall through? For company? Do they envy the living? Even me?

I called out, "Can you show me? Show me what it's like?"

The moon'd swum into the lake of night.

We skated one orbit.

The shadow-kid was still there, crouching as he skated, just like I was.

We skated another orbit.

An owl or something fluttered low across the lake.

"Hey?" I called out. "Did you hear me? I want to know what it's—"

The ice shrucked me off my feet. For a helterskeltery moment I was in midair at an unlikely height. Bruce Lee doing a karate kick, that high. I knew it wasn't going to be a soft landing but I hadn't guessed how *painful* a slam it'd be. The crack shattered from my ankle to my jaw to my knuckles, like an ice cube plopped into warm squash. No, bigger than an ice cube. A mirror, dropped from Skylab height. Where it hit the earth, where it smashed into daggers and thorns and invisible splinters, *that's* my ankle.

I spun and slid to a shuddery stop by the edge of the lake.

For a bit, all I could do was lie there, basking in that *supernatural* pain. Even Giant Haystacks'd've whimpered. "Bloody bugger," I gasped to plug my tears. "Bloody bloody bloody bugger!" Through the flinty trees I could *just* hear the sound of the main road but there was no *way* I could walk that far. I tried to stand but just fell on my arse, wincing with fresh pain. I couldn't move. I'd die of pneumonia if I stayed where I was. I had no idea what to do.

"You," sighed the sour aunt. "We suspected you'd come knocking again soon."

"I hurt"—my voice'd gone all bendy—"I hurt my ankle."

"So I see."

"It's killing me."

"I daresay."

"Can I just phone my dad to come and get me?"

"We don't care for telephones."

"Could you go and get help? Please?"

"We don't *ever* leave our house. Not at night. Not here."

"Please." The underwatery pain shook as loud as electric guitars. "I can't walk."

"I know about bones and joints. You'd best come inside."

Inside was colder than outside. Bolts behind me slid home and a lock turned. "Down you go," the sour aunt said, "down to the parlor. I'll be right along, once I've prepared your cure. But whatever you do, be *quiet*. You'll be very sorry if you wake my brother."

"All right . . ." I glanced away. "Which way's your parlor?"

But the dark'd shuffled itself and the sour aunt'd gone.

Way down the hallway was a blade of muddy light, so that was the direction I limped. *God* knows how I walked up the rooty, twisty path from the frozen lake on that busted ankle. But I must've done, to've got here. I passed a ladder of stairs. Enough muffled moonlight fell down it for me to make out an old photograph hanging on the wall. A submarine in an arctic-looking port. The crew stood on deck, all saluting. I walked on. The blade of light wasn't getting any nearer.

The parlor was a bit bigger than a big wardrobe and stuffed with museumy stuff. An empty parrot cage, a mangle, a towering dresser, a scythe. Junk, too. A bent bicycle wheel and one soccer boot, caked in silt. A pair of ancient skates, hanging on a coat stand. There was nothing modern. No fire. Nothing electrical apart from a bare brown bulb. Hairy plants sent bleached roots out of tiny pots. *God* it was cold! The sofa sagged under me and sssssssssed. One other doorway was screened by beads on strings. I tried to find a position where my ankle hurt less but there wasn't one.

Time went by, I suppose.

The sour aunt held a china bowl in one hand and a cloudy glass in the other. "Take off your sock."

My ankle was balloony and limp. The sour aunt propped my calf on a footstool and knelt by it. Her dress rustled. Apart from the blood in my ears and my jagged breathing there was no other sound. Then she dipped her hand into the bowl and began smearing a bready goo onto my ankle.

My ankle shuddered.

"This is a poultice." She gripped my shin. "To draw out the swelling."

The poultice sort of tickled but the pain was too vicious and I was fighting the cold too hard. The sour aunt smeared the goo on till it was used up and my ankled completely clagged. She handed me the cloudy glass. "Drink this."

"It smells like . . . marzipan."

"It's for drinking. Not smelling."

"But what is it?"

"It'll help take the pain away."

Her face told me I had no real choice. I swigged back the liquid in one go like you do milk of magnesia. It was syrupy-thick but didn't taste of much. I asked, "Is your brother asleep upstairs?"

"Where else would he be, Ralph? Shush now."

"My name's not Ralph," I told her, but she acted like she hadn't heard.

Clearing up the misunderstanding'd've been a massive effort, and now I'd stopped moving. I just couldn't fight the cold anymore. Funny thing was, as soon as I gave in, a lovely drowsiness tugged me downward. I pictured Mum, Dad, and Julia sitting at home watching *The Paul Daniels Magic Show* but their faces melted away, like reflections on the backs of spoons.

The cold poked me awake. I didn't know where or who or when I was. My ears felt bitten and I could see my breath. A china bowl sat on a footstool and my ankle was crusted in something hard and spongy. Then I remembered everything, and sat up. The pain in my foot had gone but my head didn't feel right, like a crow'd flown in and couldn't get out. I wiped the poultice off my foot with a snotty hanky. Unbelievably at first, my ankle swiveled fine, cured, like magic. I pulled on my sock and trainer, stood up, and tested my weight. There was a faint twinge, but only 'cause I was looking for it. Through the beaded doorway I called out, "Hello?"

No answer came. I passed through the crackly beads into a tiny kitchen with a stone sink and a *massive* oven. Big enough for a kid to climb in. Its door'd been left open, but inside was dark as that cracked tomb under Saint Gabriel's. I wanted to thank the sour aunt for curing my ankle.

Make sure the back door opens, warned Unborn Twin.

It didn't. Neither did the frost-flowered sash window. Its catch and hinges'd been painted over long ago and it'd take a chisel to persuade it open, at least. I wondered what the time was and squinted at my granddad's Omega but it was too dark in the tiny kitchen to see. Suppose it was late evening? I'd get back and my tea'd be waiting under a Pyrex dish. Mum and Dad go *ape* if I'm not back in time for tea. Or s'pose it'd gone midnight? S'pose the police'd been alerted? *Jesus.* Or what if I'd slept right through one short day and into the night of the next? The *Malvern Gazetteer* and *Midlands Today*'d've already shown my school photo and sent out appeals for witnesses. *Jesus.* Squelch would've reported seeing me heading to the frozen lake. Frogmen might be searching for me there, right now.

This was a bad dream.

No, worse than that. Back in the parlor, I looked at my grandfather's Omega and saw that there *was* no time. My voice whimpered, "*No.*" The glass face, the hour hand, and the minute hand'd gone and only a bent second hand was left. When I fell on the ice, it must've happened then. The casing was split and half its innards'd spilt out.

Granddad's Omega'd never once gone wrong in four decades.

In less than a fortnight, I'd killed it.

Wobbly with dread, I walked up the hallway and rasped up the twisted stairs, "Hello?" Silent as night in an ice age. "I have to go!" Worry about the Omega'd swatted off worry about being in this house, but I still daredn't shout in case I woke the brother. "I've got to go home now," I called, a bit louder. No reply. I decided to just leave by the front door. I'd come back in the day-time to thank her. The bolts slid open easily enough, but the old-style lock was another matter. Without the key it wouldn't open. That was that. I'd have to go upstairs, wake the old biddy to get her key, and if she got annoyed that was just tough titty. Something, *something,* had to be done about the catas-trophe of the smashed watch. God knows what, but I couldn't do it inside the House in the Woods.

The stairs curved up steeper. Soon I had to use my hands to grip the stairs above me, or I'd've fallen back. How on *earth* the sour aunt went up and down in that big rookish dress was anybody's guess. Finally, I hauled myself onto a tiny landing with two doors. A slitty window let in a glimmer. One door had to be the sour aunt's room. The other had to be the brother's.

Left's got a power that right hasn't, so I clasped the iron doorknob on the left door. It sucked the warmth from my hand, my arm, my blood.

Scrit-scrat.

I froze.

Scrit-scrat.

A deathwatch beetle? Rat in the loft? Pipe freezing up?

Which room was the *scrit-scrat* coming from?

The iron doorknob made a coiling creak as I turned it.

Powdery moonlight lit the attic room through the snowflake-lace curtain. I'd guessed right. The sour aunt lay under a quilt with her dentures in a jar by her bed, still as a marble duchess on a church tomb. I shuffled over the tipsy floor, nervous at the thought of waking her. What if she forgot who I was and thought I'd come to murder her and screamed for help and had a stroke? Her hair spilt over her folded face like pondweed. A cloud of breath escaped her mouth every ten or twenty heartbeats. Only that proved she was made of flesh and blood like me.

"Can you hear me?"

No, I'd have to shake her awake.

My hand was halfway to her shoulder when that scrit-scrat noise started up again, deep inside *her*.

Not a snore. A death rattle.

Go into the other bedroom. Wake her brother. She needs an ambulance. No. Smash your way out. Run to Isaac Pye in the Black Swan for help. No. They'd ask why you'd been in the House in the Woods. What'd you say? You don't even know this woman's name. It's too late. She's dying, right now. I'm certain. The scrit-scrat's uncoiling. Louder, waspier, daggerier.

Her windpipe bulges as her soul squeezes out of her heart.

Her worn-out eyes flip awake like a doll's, black, glassy, shocked.

From her black crack mouth, a blizzard rushes out.

A silent roaring hangs here.

Not going anywhere.

hangman

Dark, Light, *Dark*, Light, *Dark*, Light. The Datsun's wipers couldn't keep up with the rain, not even at the fastest setting. When a juggernaut passed the other way, it slapped up spumes onto the streaming windscreen. Through this car-wash visibility I only *just* made out the two Ministry of Defence radars spinning at their incredible speed. Waiting for the full might of the Warsaw Pact forces. Mum and me didn't speak much on the way. Partly 'cause of where she was taking me, I think. (The dashboard clock said 16:05. In seventeen hours *exactly* my public execution'd take place.) Waiting at the Pelican crossing by the closed-down beautician's she asked me if I'd had a good day and I said, "Okay." I asked her if she'd had a good day too and she said, "Oh, sparkling creative and deeply fulfilling, thank you." Dead sarky, Mum can be, even though she tells me off for it. "Did you get any Valentine's cards?" I said no, but even if I'd had some I'd've told her no. (I did get one but I put it in the bin. It said "Suck My Dick" and was signed by Nicholas Briar, but it looked like Gary Drake's handwriting.) Duncan Priest'd got four. Neal Brose got seven, or so he reckons. Ant Little found out that Nick Yew'd got *twenty*. I didn't ask Mum if she'd got any. Dad says Valentine's Days and Mother's Days and No-Armed Goalkeeper's Days're all conspiracies of card manufacturers and flower shops and chocolate companies.

So anyway, Mum dropped me at Malvern Link traffic lights by the clinic. I forgot my diary in the glove compartment and if the lights hadn't turned red for me, Mum would've driven off to Lorenzo Hussingtree's with it. ("Jason" isn't exactly the acest name you could wish for but any "Lorenzo" in *my* school'd get Bunsen-burnered to death.) Diary safe in my satchel, I crossed the flooded clinic car park, leaping from dry bit to dry bit like James Bond froggering across the crocodiles' backs. Outside the clinic were a couple of second or third years from the Dyson Perrins School. They saw my enemy uniform. Every year, according to Pete Redmarley and Gilbert Swinyard, all the Dyson Perrins fourth years and all our fourth years skive off school and meet in this secret arena walled in by gorse on Poolbrook Common for a mass scrap. If you chicken out you're a homo and if you tell a teacher you're *dead*. Three years ago, apparently, Pluto Noak'd hit their hardest kid so hard that the hospital in Worcester'd had to sew his jaw back on. He's still sucking his meals through a straw. Luckily it was raining too hard for the Dyson Perrins kids to bother with me.

Today was my second appointment this year so the pretty receptionist in the clinic recognized me. "I'll buzz Mrs. de Roo for you now, Jason. Take a seat." I like her. She knows why I'm here so she doesn't make pointless conversation that'll show me up. The waiting area smells of Dettol and warm plastic. People waiting there never look like they have much wrong with them. But I don't either, I s'pose, not to look at. You all sit so close to each other but what can any of you talk about 'cept the thing you want to talk about least. "So, why are *you* here?" One old biddy was knitting. The sound of her needles knitted in the sound of the rain. A hobbity man with watery eyes rocked to and fro. A woman with coat hangers instead of bones sat reading *Watership Down*. There's a cage for babies with a pile of sucked toys in it, but today it was empty. The telephone rang and the pretty receptionist answered it. It seemed to be a friend, 'cause she cupped the mouthpiece and lowered her voice. *Jesus*, I envy *anyone* who can say what they want at the same time as they think it, without needing to test it for stammer-words. A Dumbo the Elephant clock tocked this: to–mor–row–mor–ning's–com–ing–soon–so–gouge–out–your–brain–with–a–spoon–you–can–not–e–ven–count–to–ten–be–gin–a–gain–a–gain–a–gain. (Quarter past four. Sixteen hours and fifty minutes to live.) I picked up a tatty *National Geographic* magazine. An American woman in it'd taught chimpanzees to speak in sign language.

Most people think stammering and stuttering are the same but they're as different as diarrhea and constipation. Stuttering's where you say the first bit of the word but can't stop saying it over and over. *St-st-st-st*utter. Like that. Stammering's where you get stuck straight after the first bit of the word. Like this. *St . . . . AMmer!* My stammer's why I go to Mrs. de Roo. (That really is her name. It's Dutch, not Australian.) I started going that summer when it never rained and the Malvern Hills turned brown and fires broke out. Miss Throckmorton'd been playing Hangman on the blackboard one afternoon with sunlight streaming in. On the blackboard was

NIGH–ING––E

Any *duh*-brain could work that out, so I put up my hand. Miss Throckmorton said, "Yes, Jason?" and *that* was when my life divided itself into Before Hangman and After Hangman. The word "nightingale" kaboomed in my skull but it just *wouldn't come out.* The *n* got out okay, but the harder I forced the rest, the tighter the noose got. I remember Lucy Sneads whispering to Angela Bullock, stifling giggles. I remember Robin South staring at this bizarre sight. I'd've done the same if it hadn't been me. When a stammerer stammers their eyeballs pop out, they go trembly-red like an evenly matched arm wrestler, and their mouth guppergupperguppers like a fish in a net. It must be quite a funny sight.

It wasn't funny for me, though. Miss Throckmorton was waiting. Every kid in the classroom was waiting. Every crow and every spider in Black Swan Green was waiting. Every cloud, every car on every motorway, even Mrs. Thatcher in the House of Commons'd frozen, listening, watching, thinking, *What's* wrong *with Jason Taylor?*

But no matter how shocked, scared, breathless, ashamed I was, no matter how much of a total flid I looked, no matter how much I *hated* myself for not being able to say a simple word in my own language, I *couldn't* say "nightingale." In the end I had to say, "I'm not sure, miss," and Miss Throckmorton said, "I see." She did see, too. She phoned my mum that evening and one week later I was taken to see Mrs. de Roo, the speech therapist at Malvern Link Clinic. That was five years ago.

It must've been around then (maybe that same afternoon) that my stammer took on the appearance of a hangman. Pike lips, broken nose, rhino cheeks, red eyes 'cause he never sleeps. I imagine him in the baby room at Preston Hospital playing *eeny, meeny, miney, mo.* I imagine him tapping my koochy lips, murmuring down at me, *Mine.* But it's his hands, not his face, that I really feel him by. His snaky fingers that sink inside my tongue and squeeze my windpipe so nothing'll work. Words beginning with N have always been one of Hangman's favorites. When I was nine I dreaded people asking me "How old are you?" In the end I'd hold up nine fingers like I was being dead witty but I know the other person'd be thinking, *Why didn't he just tell me, the twat?* Hangman used to like Y-words, too, but lately he's eased off those and has moved to S-words. This is bad news. Look at any dictionary and see which section's the thickest: it's S. Twenty million words begin with N or S. Apart from the Russians starting a nuclear war, my biggest fear is if Hangman gets interested in J-words, 'cause then I *won't even be able to say my own name*. I'd have to change my name by deed poll, but Dad'd never let me.

The only way to outfox Hangman is to think one sentence ahead, and if you see a stammer-word coming up, alter your sentence so you won't need to use it. Of course, you have to do this without the person you're talking to catching on. Reading dictionaries like I do helps you do these ducks and dives, but you have to remember who you're talking to. (If I was speaking to another thirteen-year-old and said the word "melancholy" to avoid stammering on "sad," for example, I'd be a laughingstock 'cause kids aren't s'posed to use adult words like "melancholy." Not at Upton-on-Severn Comprehensive, anyway.) Another strategy is to buy time by saying "er . . ." in the hope that Hangman's concentration'll lapse and you can sneak the word out. But if you say "er . . ." too much you come across as a right dimmer. Lastly, if a teacher asks you a question directly and the answer's a stammer-word, it's best to pretend you don't know. I couldn't count how often I've done this. Sometimes teachers lose their rag (specially if they've just spent half a lesson explaining something) but *any*thing's better than getting labeled "School Stutterboy."

That's something I've always *just* about avoided, but tomorrow morning at five minutes past nine this is going to happen. I'm going to have to stand up in front of Gary Drake and Neal Brose and my *entire* class to read from Mr. Kempsey's book, *Plain Prayers for a Complicated World.* There will be *dozens* of stammer-words in that reading which I *can't* substitute and I *can't* pretend not to know because there they are, printed there. Hangman'll skip ahead as I read, underlining all his favourite N- and S-words, murmuring in my ear, "*Here,* Taylor, try and spit *this* one out!" I *know,* with Gary Drake and Neal Brose and everyone watching, Hangman'll *crush* my throat and *mangle* my tongue and *scrunch* my face up. Worse than Joey Deacon's. I'm going to stammer worse than I've ever stammered in my life. By nine-fifteen my secret'll be spreading round the school like a poison-gas attack. By the end of first break my life won't be worth living.

The grotesquest thing I ever heard was this. Pete Redmarley swore on his own grave it's true, so I s'pose it must be. This boy in the sixth form was sitting his A levels. He had these parents from hell who'd put him under massive pressure to get a whole raft of A grades and when the exam came, this kid just cracked and couldn't even understand the questions. So what he did was get two Bic Biros from his pencil case, hold the pointy ends against his eyes, stand up, and head-butt the desk. Right there, in the exam hall. The pens skewered his eyeballs so deep that only an inch was left sticking out of his drippy sockets. Mr. Nixon, the headmaster, hushed everything up so it didn't get in the papers or anything. It's a sick and horrible story but right now, I'd rather kill Hangman that way than let him kill me tomorrow morning.

I mean that.

Mrs. de Roo's shoes clop so you know it's her coming to fetch you. She's forty or maybe even older, and has fat silver brooches, wispy bronze hair, and flowery clothes. She gave a folder to the pretty receptionist, tutted at the rain, and said, "My my, monsoon season's come to darkest Worcestershire!" I agreed it was chucking it down, and left with her quick. In case the other patients worked out why I was there. Down the corridor we went, past the signpost full of words like PEDIATRICS and ULTRASCANS. (No ultrascan'd read *my* brain. I'd beat it by remembering every satellite in the solar system.) "February's *so* gloomy in this part of the world," said Mrs. de Roo, "don't you think? It's not so much a month as a twenty-eight-day-long Monday morning. You leave home in the dark and go home in the dark. On wet days like these, it's like living in a cave, behind a waterfall." I told Mrs. de Roo how I'd heard Eskimo kids spend time under artificial sunlamps to stop them getting scurvy, 'cause at the North Pole winter lasts for most of the year. I suggested Mrs. de Roo should think about getting a sunbed.

Mrs. de Roo answered, "I shall think on."

We passed a room where a howling baby'd just had an injection. In the next room a freckly girl Julia's age sat in a wheelchair. One of her legs wasn't there. She'd probably love to have my stammer if she could have her leg back, and I wondered if being happy's about other people's misery. That cuts both ways, mind. People'll look at me after tomorrow morning and think, "Well, my life may be a swamp of shit but at least I'm not in Jason Taylor's shoes. At least I can *talk*."

February's Hangman's favorite month. Come summer he gets dozy and hibernates through to autumn, and I can speak a bit better. In fact, after my first run of visits to Mrs. de Roo five years ago, by the time my hay fever began everyone thought my stammer was cured. But come November Hangman wakes up again, sort of like John Barleycorn in reverse. By January he's his old self again, so back I come to Mrs. de Roo. *This* year Hangman's worse than ever. Aunt Alice stayed with us two weeks ago and one night I was crossing the landing and I heard her say to Mum, "*Honestly*, Helena, when are you going to do something about his *stutter*? It's social suicide! I never know whether to finish the sentence for him or just leave the poor boy dangling on the end of his rope." (Eavesdropping's sort of thrilling 'cause you learn what people really think, but eavesdropping makes you miserable for exactly the same reason.) After Aunt Alice'd gone back to Richmond, Mum sat me down and said it mightn't do any harm to visit Mrs. de Roo again. I said okay, 'cause actually I'd wanted to but I hadn't asked 'cause I was ashamed, and 'cause mentioning my stammer makes it realler.

Mrs. de Roo's office smells of Nescafé. She drinks Nescafé Gold Blend non-stop. There're two ratty sofas, one yolky rug, a dragon's-egg paperweight, a Fisher-Price toy multistory car park, and a giant Zulu mask from South Africa. Mrs. de Roo was born in South Africa but one day she was told by the government to leave the country in twenty-four hours or she'd be thrown into prison. Not 'cause she'd done anything wrong, but because they do that in South Africa if you don't agree that colored people should be kept herded off in mud-and-straw huts in big reservations with no schools, no hospitals, and no jobs. Julia says the police in South Africa don't always bother with prisons, and that often they throw you off a tall building and say you tried to escape. Mrs. de Roo and her husband (who's an Indian dentist) escaped to Rhodesia in a jeep but had to leave everything they owned behind. The government took the lot. (The *Malvern Gazetteer* interviewed her, that's how I know most of this.) South Africa's summer is our winter so their February is lovely and hot. Mrs. de Roo's still got a slightly funny accent. Her "yes" is a "yis" and her "get" is a "git."

"So, Jason," she began today. "How are things?"

Most people only want a "Fine, thanks" when they ask a kid that, but Mrs. de Roo actually means it. So I confessed to her about tomorrow's form assembly. Talking 'bout my stammer's nearly as embarrassing as stammering itself, but it's okay with her. Hangman knows he mustn't mess with Mrs. de Roo so he acts like he's not there. Which is good, 'cause it proves I *can* speak like a normal person, but bad, 'cause how can Mrs. de Roo ever defeat Hangman if she never even sees him properly?

Mrs. de Roo asked if I'd spoken to Mr. Kempsey about excusing me for a few weeks. I already had done, I told her, and this is what he'd said: "We must all face our demons one day, Taylor, and for you, that time is nigh." Form assemblies're read by students in alphabetical order. We've got to *T* for "Taylor," and as far as Mr. Kempsey's concerned that's that.

Mrs. de Roo made an *I see* noise.

Neither of us said anything for a moment.

"Any headway with your diary, Jason?"

The diary's a new idea prompted by Dad. Dad phoned Mrs. de Roo to say that given my "annual tendency to relapse," he thought extra "homework" was appropriate. So Mrs. de Roo suggested that I keep a diary. Just a line or two every day, where I write when, where, and what word I stammered on, and how I felt. Week One looks like this:

Date	place	Word	How I felt
12th Feb, 1982	dining room	normally	Bad
13th Feb 1982	school gym	Simon & Son	stupid
14th Feb, 1982	school bus	swimm-ing	bad and stupid
15th Feb 1982	on telephone	Notting-ham	awful
16th Feb 1982	Mr Rhydd's shop	x newspaper	awful and bad
17th Feb 1982	French lesson	Sur le Pont D'-Avignon	bad.

"More of a chart, then," Mrs. de Roo said, "than a diary in the classical mode, as such?" (Actually, I wrote it last night. It's not lies or anything, just truths I made up. If I wrote *every* time I had to dodge Hangman, the diary'd be thick as the Yellow Pages.) "Most informative. Very neatly ruled, too." I asked if I should carry on with the diary next week. Mrs. de Roo said she thought my father'd be disappointed if I didn't, so maybe I should.

Then Mrs. de Roo got out her Metro Gnome. Metro Gnomes're upside-down pendulums without the clock part. They tock rhythms. They're small, which could be why they're called gnomes. Music students normally use them but speech therapists do too. You read aloud in time with its tocks, like this: here–comes–the–can–dle–to–take–you–to–bed–,–here–comes–the–chop–per–to–chop–off–your–head. Today we read a stack of N-words from the dictionary, one by one. The Metro Gnome *does* make speaking easy, as easy as singing, but I can hardly carry one around with me, can I? Kids like Ross Wilcox'd say, "What's this then, Taylor?," snap off its pendulum in a *nano*second, and say, "Shoddy workmanship, that."

After the Metro Gnome I read aloud from a book Mrs. de Roo keeps for me called *Z for Zachariah*. *Z for Zachariah*'s about a girl called Ann who lives in a valley with its own freak weather system that protects it after a nuclear war's poisoned the rest of the country and killed everyone else off. For all Ann knows she's the only person alive in the British Isles. As a book it's utterly brill but a bit bleak. Maybe Mrs. de Roo suggested I read this to make me feel luckier than Ann despite my stammer. I got a bit stuck on a couple of words but you'd not've noticed if you weren't looking. I know Mrs. de Roo was saying, *See, you* can *read aloud without stammering.* But there's stuff not even speech therapists understand. Quite often, even in bad spells, Hangman'll let me say whatever I want, even words beginning with dangerous letters. This (a) gives me hope I'm cured, which Hangman can enjoy destroying later, and (b) lets me con other kids into thinking I'm normal while keeping alive and well the fear that my secret'll be discovered.

There's more. I once wrote Hangman's Four Commandments.

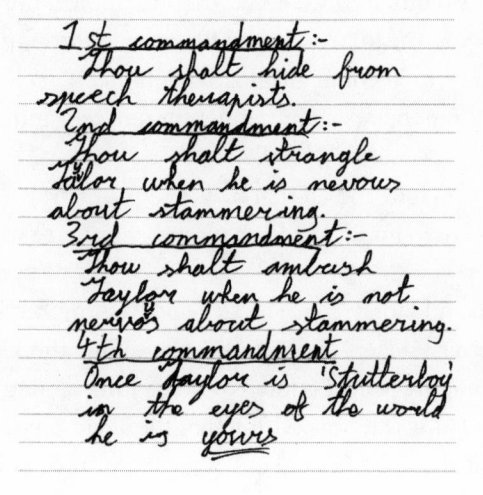

Like I said, the First Commandment kicks in whenever I'm with Mrs. de Roo. Tomorrow morning, Hangman's going for the fourth.

When the session was over, Mrs. de Roo asked me if I felt any more confident about my form assembly. She'd've liked me to say "Sure!" but only if I meant it. I said, "Not a lot, to be honest." Then I asked if stammers're like zits that you grow out of, or if kids with stammers're more like toys that're wired wrong at the factory and stay busted all their lives. (You get stammering adults too. There's one on a BBC1 sitcom called *Open All Hours* on Sunday evenings where Ronnie Barker plays a shopkeeper who stutters so badly, so hilariously, that the audience *pisses* itself laughing. Even knowing *Open All Hours* is on makes me shrivel up like a plastic wrapper in a fire.)

"*Yis,*" said Mrs. de Roo. "That's the question. My answer is, It depends. Speech therapy is as imperfect a science, Jason, as speaking is a complex one. There are seventy-two muscles involved in the production of human speech. The neural connections my brain is employing now, to say this sentence to you, number in the tens of millions. Little wonder one study put the percentage of people with some kind of speech disorder at twelve percent. Don't put your faith in a miracle cure. In the vast majority of cases, progress doesn't come from trying to kill a speech defect. Try to will it out of existence, it'll just will itself back stronger. Right? No, it's a question—and this might sound nutty—of understanding it, of coming to a working accommodation with it, of respecting it, of not fearing it. *Yis,* it'll flare up from time to time, but if you know *why* it flares, you'll know how to douse what makes it flare up. Back in Durban I had a friend who'd once been an alcoholic. One day I asked him how he'd cured himself. My friend said he'd done no such thing. I said, 'What do you mean? You haven't touched a drop in three years!' He said all he'd done was become a teetotal alcoholic. That's my goal. To help people change from being stammering stammerers into nonstammering stammerers."

Mrs. de Roo's no fool and all that makes sense.

But it's sod-all help for 2KM's form assembly tomorrow morning.

Dinner was steak-and-kidney pie. The steak bits're okay, but kidney makes me reach for the vomit bucket. I have to try to swallow the kidney bits whole. Smuggling bits into my pocket is too risky since Julia spotted me last time and grassed on me. Dad was telling Mum about a new trainee salesman called Danny Lawlor at the new Greenland Superstore in Reading. "Fresh from some management course, and he's Irish as Hurricane Higgins, but my word, that lad hasn't kissed the Blarney Stone, he's bitten off chunks of it. Talk about the gift of the gab! Craig Salt dropped by while I was there to instill some God-fearing discipline into the troops, but Danny had him *eating out of his hand* in five minutes flat. Executive material, is that young man. When Craig Salt gives me nationwide sales next year, I'm fast-tracking Danny Lawlor and frankly I don't care whose nose I put out of joint."

"The Irish've always had to live by their wits," said Mum.

Dad didn't remember it was Speech Therapy Day till Mum'd mentioned she'd written a "plumpish" check to Lorenzo Hussingtree in Malvern Link. Dad asked what Mrs. de Roo'd thought about his diary idea. Her comment that it was "most informative" fueled his good mood. " 'Informative'? Indispensable, more like! Smart-Think Management Principles are applicable across the board. Like I told Danny Lawlor, any operator is only as good as his data. Without data, you're the *Titanic*, crossing an Atlantic chock-full of icebergs without radar. Result? Collision, disaster, good night."

"Wasn't radar invented in the Second World War?" Julia forked a lump of steak. "And didn't the *Titanic* sink before the First?"

"The principle, O daughter of mine, is a universal constant. If you don't keep records, you can't make progress assessments. True for retailers, true for educators, true for the military, true for *any* systems operator. One bright day in your brilliant career at the Old Bailey you'll learn this the hard way and think, 'If only I'd listened to my dear wise father. How right he was.' "

Julia snorted horsily, which she gets away with 'cause she's Julia. I can never tell Dad what I really think like that. I can feel the stuff I don't say rotting inside me like mildewy spuds in a sack. Stammerers can't win arguments 'cause once you stammer, H-h-hey p-p-presto, you've l-l-lost, S-s-st-st-utterboy! If I stammer with Dad, he gets that face he had when he got his Black & Decker Workmate home and found it was minus a crucial packet of screws. Hangman just *loves* that face.

After Julia and I'd done the washing up Mum and Dad sat in front of the telly watching a glittery new quiz show called *Blankety Blank*, presented by Terry Wogan. Contestants have to guess a missing word from a sentence and if they guess the same as the panel of celebrities they win crap prizes like a mug tree with mugs.

Up in my room I started my homework on the feudal system for Mrs. Coscombe. But then I got sucked in by a poem about a skater on a frozen lake who wants to know what it's like to be dead so much, he's persuaded himself that a drowned kid's talking to him. I typed it out on my Silver Reed manual typewriter. I love how it's got no number 1 so you use the letter l. My Silver Reed's probably what I'd save if our house ever caught fire, now my grand-dad's Omega Seamaster's busted. The worst thing in a locked house in a bad dream, that was.

So anyway, my radio-alarm suddenly said 21:15. I had less than twelve hours. Rain drummed on my window. Metro Gnomes're in rain and poems too, and breathing, not just tocks of clocks.

Julia's footsteps crossed my ceiling and went downstairs. She opened the living room door and asked if she could phone Kate Alfrick about some Eco-nomics homework. Dad said okay. Our phone's in the hallway to make it un-comfortable to use, so if I creep over the landing to my surveillance position I can catch just about everything.

"Yeah, yeah, I *did* get your Valentine's card, and very sweet it is too, but *lis-ten*, you *know* why I'm calling! Did you pass?"

Pause.

"Just tell me, Ewan! Did you *pass*?"

Pause. (Who's Ewan?)

"*Excellent! Brilliant! Fantastic!* I was going to chuck you if you'd failed, of course. Can't have a boyfriend who can't drive."

("Boyfriend"? "Chuck"?) Muffled laughter plus pause.

"No! *No!* He's *never!*"

Pause.

Julia did the *ohhh!* moany noise she does when she's mega-jealous. "God, why can't *I* have a filthy-rich uncle who gives me sports cars? Can't I have one of yours? Go on, you've got more wealthy relatives than you need . . ."

Pause.

"You *bet*. How about Saturday? Oh, you've got classes all morning, I keep forgetting . . ."

Saturday morning classes? This Ewan must be a Worcester Cathedral School kid. Posh.

". . . Russell and Dorrell's café then. One-thirty. Kate'll drive me in."

A sly Julia laugh.

"No, I certainly will *not* be bringing him. *Thing* spends his Saturdays skulking up trees or hiding down holes."

The sound of the nine o'clock news filled the hallway as the living room door opened. Julia switched to her Kate voice. "Got that bit, yeah, Kate, but I still can't get my head round question nine. I'd better check your answers before the test. Okay . . . okay. Thanks. See you in the morning. G'night."

"Sort it out?" Dad called from the kitchen.

"Pretty much," said Julia, zipping up her pencil case.

Julia's an ace liar. She's applied to do Law at university and she's got several offers of places already. (Lawyer-liar, liar-lawyer. Never noticed that before.) The idea of any boy snogging my sister makes me grab the vomit bucket but quite a few sixth formers fancy her. I bet Ewan's one of these super-confident kids who wears Blue Stratos aftershave and winkle-picker shoes and a wedge like the man from Orchestral Manoeuvres in the Dark. I bet Ewan speaks in well-drilled sentences that march by perfectly, like my cousin Hugo. Speaking well is the same as commanding.

God knows what job *I'm* going to be able to do. Not a lawyer, that's for sure. You can't stammer in court. You can't stammer in a classroom, either. My students'd *crucify* me. There aren't many jobs where speaking isn't a part of it. Miss Lippetts said once nobody buys poetry, so I can't be a professional poet. I could be a monk, but church is more boring than watching the screen-test card. Mum made us go to Sunday school at Saint Gabriel's when we were smaller but it turned every Sunday morning into torture by boredom. Even Mum got bored after a few months. Being trapped in a monastery'd be *murder*. How about a lighthouse keeper? All those storms, sunsets, and Dairylea sandwiches'd make you lonely in the end. But lonely is something I'd better get used to. What girl'd go out with a stammerer? Or even dance with one? The last song at the Black Swan Green Village Hall Disco'd be over before I could spit out D-d-d-you want to d-d-d-d-*dance*. Or what if I stammered at my wedding and couldn't even say "I do"?

"Were you listening in just now?"

Julia'd appeared, leaning on my door frame.

"What?"

"You heard me. Were you eavesdropping on my phone call just now?"

"What phone call?" My reply was too fast and too innocent.

"If you ask me"—my sister's glare made my face begin to smoke—"a little privacy isn't too much to ask. If *you* had any friends to phone, Jason, I wouldn't listen in on you. People who eavesdrop are such *maggots*."

"I wasn't eavesdropping!" How whiny I sounded.

"So how come your door was closed three minutes ago, but now it's wide open?"

"I don't—" (Hangman seized "know" so I had to abort the sentence, spazzishly.) "What's it to you? The room felt stuffy." (Hangman let "stuffy" go unchallenged.) "I went to the bog. A draft opened it."

"A draft? Sure, there's a hurricane blowing over the landing. I can hardly stand upright."

"I *wasn't* listening in on you!"

Julia said nothing for long enough to tell me she knew I was bullshitting. "Who said you could borrow *Abbey Road*?"

Her L.P. was by my crappy record player. "You hardly listen to it."

"Even if that *were* true, it wouldn't make it your property. You never wear Granddad's watch. Does that make it *my* property?" She entered my room to get her record, stepping over my Adidas bag. Julia glanced at my typewriter. Lurching with shame, I hid my poem with my body. "So you agree," she said, her real meaning as subtle as nutcrackers, "a little privacy isn't too much to ask? And if this record has a *single* scratch on it, you're *dead*."

Through the ceiling's coming not *Abbey Road* but "The Man with the Child in His Eyes" by Kate Bush. Usually Julia only plays Kate Bush when she's hyperemotional or when she's got her period. Life must be pretty brill for Julia. She's eighteen, she's leaving Black Swan Green in a few months, she's got a boyfriend with a sports car, she gets twice as much pocket money as me, and she can make other people do whatever she wants with *words*.

Just *words*.

Julia's just put on "Songbird" by Fleetwood Mac.

＊　＊　＊

Dad gets up before it's light on Wednesdays 'cause he's got to drive to Oxford for a midweek meeting at Greenland HQ. The garage is below my bedroom, so I hear his Rover 3500 growl into life. If it's raining, like this morning, its tires *shsssssh* on the puddly drive and the rain shplatterdrangs on the swiveled-up garage door. My radio-alarm glowed 06:35 in numerals of Mekon green. One hundred and fifty minutes of life left, that was all. I could already see the rows and columns of faces in my class, like a screen of space invaders. Guffawing, puzzled, appalled, *pitying*. Who decides which defects are funny and which ones are tragic? Nobody laughs at blind people or makes iron-lung jokes.

If God made each minute last six months I'd be middle-aged by breakfast and dead by the time I got on the school bus. I could sleep forever. I tried to push away what was in store by lying back and imagining the ceiling was the unmapped surface of a G-class planet orbiting Alpha Centauri. Nobody was there. I'd never have to say a word.

"Jason! Up time!" yelled Mum from downstairs. I'd dreamed I'd woken in a gas-blue wood and'd found my granddad's Omega, in one piece, in fiery crocuses. Then came running feet and the thought it was a spook running home to Saint Gabriel's graveyard. Mum yelled again "*Jason!*" and I saw the time: 07:41.

I mustered a muzzy "Okay!" and ordered my legs out of bed so the rest of me'd have to follow. The bathroom mirror, worse luck, showed no signs of leprosy. I thought about pressing a hot flannel to my forehead, drying it, and then complaining to Mum of a temperature, but she's not that easy to fool. My lucky red underpants were in the wash so I settled for my banana-yellow ones. It's not a P.E. day so it won't matter. Downstairs, Mum was watching the new breakfast TV on BBC1 and Julia was slicing a banana into her Alpen.

"Morning," I said. "What's that magazine?"

Julia held up the front cover of *Face*. "If you touch it when I'm gone I'll strangle you."

I *should've been born*, hissed Unborn Twin, *not* you, *you cow.*

"Is that expression supposed to mean something?" Julia hadn't forgotten last night. "You look like you're wetting yourself."

I could've retaliated by asking Julia if she'd strangle *Ewan* if *he* touched her *Face*, but that'd've been admitting I *was* an eavesdropping maggot. My Weetabix tasted like balsa wood. After I'd finished, I cleaned my teeth, put today's books in my Adidas bag and Bic Biros in my pencil case. Julia'd already gone. She goes to the sixth-form site of our school with Kate Alfrick, who's already passed her driving test.

Mum was on the phone telling Aunt Alice about the new bathroom. "Hang on, Alice." Mum cupped the phone. "Have you got your lunch money?"

I nodded. I decided to tell her. "Mum, there's—"

Hangman was blocking "something."

"Hurry up, Jason! You'll miss the bus!"

Outside was blowy and wet, like a rain machine was aimed over Black Swan Green. Kingfisher Meadows was all rain-stained walls, dripping bird tables, wet gnomes, swilling ponds, and shiny rockeries. A moon-gray cat watched me from Mr. Castle's dry porch. *Wished* there was some way a boy could turn into a cat. I passed the bridleway stile. If I was Grant Burch or Ross Wilcox or any of the council-house kids from down Wellington End, I'd just skive off and hop over that stile and follow the bridleway to wherever it went. Even see if it leads to the lost tunnel under the Malvern Hills. But kids like me just can't. Mr. Kempsey'd notice *straight off* that I was absent on my dreaded form-assembly day. Mum'd be phoned by morning break. Mr. Nixon'd get involved. Dad'd be called out of his Wednesday meeting. Truant officers and their sniffer dogs'd be put on my trail. I'd get captured, interrogated, skinned alive, and Mr. Kempsey'd *still* make me read a passage from *Plain Prayers for a Complicated World*.

Once you think about the consequences, you've had it.

Outside the Black Swan girls were clustered under umbrellas. Boys can't use umbrellas 'cause they're gay. ('Cept for Grant Burch, that is, who stays dry by getting his servant Philip Phelps to bring a big golfing umbrella.) My duffel coat keeps my top half dryish but at the corner of the main road a Vauxhall Chevette'd soaked my shins. My socks were gritty and damp. Pete Redmarley and Gilbert Swinyard and Nick Yew and Ross Wilcox and that lot were having a puddle fight but just as I got there, the noddy-eyed school bus pulled up. Norman Bates looked at us from behind his steering wheel like a sleepless slaughterman at a sty of ripe pigs. We got on board and the door hissed shut. My Casio said 8:35.

On rainy mornings the school bus stinks of boys, burps, and ashtrays. The front rows get taken by girls who get on at Guarlford and Blackmore End and just talk about homework. The hardest kids go straight to the back, but even kids like Pete Redmarley and Gilbert Swinyard behave themselves when Norman Bates's driving. Norman Bates is one of those cracked stone men you shouldn't mess with. One time, Pluto Noak opened the emergency exit for a doss. Norman Bates went to the back, grabbed him, dragged him to the front, and literally chucked him off the bus. Pluto Noak cried up from his ditch, "I'm taking you to court I am! You bust me flamin' *arm!*"

Norman Bates's reply was to remove his cigarette from the corner of his mouth, lean down the steps of his bus, stick out his tongue like a Maori, and stub out the still-glowing cigarette, slow and deliberate, actually on his tongue. We heard the hiss. The man flicked the stub at the boy in the ditch.

Then Norman Bates sat down and drove off.

Nobody's touched the fire door on his bus since that day.

Dean Moran got on at the Druggers End stop, just at the edge of the village. "Hey, Dean," I said, "sit here if you want." Moran was so pleased I'd used his real name in front of everyone he grinned and plomped right down. "*Jesus*," said Moran. "If it keeps pissing it down like this the Severn'll burst its banks down at Upton by hometime. And Worcester. And Tewkesbury."

"Definitely." I was being friendly for my benefit as much as his. On the bus home tonight I'd be lucky if the Invisible Man'd want to sit by J-J-J-ason T-T-Taylor the s-*sss*-s-ssschool s-*sss*-s-ssstutterboy. Moran and me played Connect 4 on the steamed-up windows. Moran'd won one game before we even got to Welland Cross. Moran's in Miss Wyche's form at school, 2W, which is the next-to-bottom class. But Moran's no duffer, not really. It's just that everyone'd give him a hard time if his marks were too good.

A black horse stood in a marshy field looking miserable. But not as miserable as I was going to be in twenty-one minutes and counting.

The heater under our seat'd melted my school trousers onto my shins and someone dropped an eggy fart. Gilbert Swinyard roared, "Squelch's dropped a gas bomb!" Squelch grinned his brown grin, blew his nose on a Monster Munch packet, and chucked it. Crisp bags don't fly far and it just landed on Robin South in the row behind.

Before I knew it, the bus swung into our school and we all piled off. On wet days we wait for the bell in the main hall instead of the playground. School was all skiddy floors this morning, damp steaming anoraks, teachers telling kids off for screaming and first years playing illegal tag in the corridors and third-year girls trawling the corridors with linked arms singing some crappy pop song. The clock by the tunnel to the staff room where kids are made to stand as a punishment through their lunchtimes told me I had eight minutes to live.

"Ah, Taylor, splendid." Mr. Kempsey pinched my earlobe. "The very pupil whom I seek. Follow. I wish to deposit words into your auditory organ." My form teacher led me down the gloomy passageway leading to the staff room. The staff room's like God. You can't see it and live. It was ahead, ajar, and cigarette smoke billowed out like fog in Jack the Ripper's London. But we turned off and stepped into the stationery storeroom. The stationery storeroom's sort of a holding cell for kids in the shit. I was wondering what I'd done. "Five minutes ago," Mr. Kempsey said, "a telephone call was channeled to myself. This telephone call was regarding Jason Taylor. From a well-wisher."

You just have to wait with Mr. Kempsey.

"Petitioning me to grant a last-minute act of clemency."

Mr. Nixon, the headmaster, dashed past the doorway, emitting fumes of anger and tweed.

"Sir?"

Mr. Kempsey grimaced at my dim-wittedness. "Am I to understand that you anticipate this morning's form-assembly with a level of trepidation one might describe as 'debilitating dread'?"

I sensed Mrs. de Roo's white magic but didn't dare hope it might save me. "Yes sir."

"Yes Taylor. It seems your dedicated speech therapist holds the opinion that a postponement of this morning's trial by ordeal may be conducive to a longer-term level of self-confidence vis-à-vis the Arts of Rhetoric and Public Speaking. Do you second this motion, Taylor?"

I knew what he'd said but he was expecting me to act confused. "Sir?"

"*Do* you or *don't* you wish to be excused from this morning's reading?"

I said, "Very much, sir, yes."

Mr. Kempsey squished his mouth. People always think that not stammering is about jumping in at deep ends, about baptisms of fire. People see stammerers on TV who're forced, one magic day, to go onto stage in front of a thousand people and lo and behold a perfect voice flows out. *See.* Everyone smiles. *He had it in him all along! All he needed was a friendly push! Now he's cured.* But that's such *utter* bollocks. If it ever actually happens it's just Hangman obeying the First Commandment. Just go back and check up on that "cured" stammerer one week later. You'll see. The *truth* is, deep ends cause drowning. Baptisms of fire cause third-degree burns. "You can't turn tail at the prospect of public speaking your whole life through, Taylor."

Maggot said, *Want to bet?*

"I know, sir. That's why I'm doing my best to master it. With Mrs. de Roo's help."

Mr. Kempsey didn't give in right away, but I sensed I was in the clear. "Very well. But I had you down as having more pluck than this, Taylor. I can only conclude that I had you down wrongly."

I watched him go.

If I was the pope I'd've made Mrs. de Roo a saint. On the spot.

Mr. Kempsey's reading from *Plain Prayers for a Complicated World* was about how in life it can rain for forty days and forty nights but God made a promise to humanity that one day a rainbow will appear. (Julia says it's absurd how in 1982 Bible stories're still being taught like they're historical fact.) Then we sang the hymn that goes *All God's gifts around us are sent from heaven above, so thank the Lord, thank the Lord, for a-a-all his love.* I thought that was that but after Mr. Kempsey'd read the notices and orders from Mr. Nixon, Gary Drake put up his hand. "Excuse me, sir, but I thought it was *Jason Taylor's* turn to read the assembly today. I was really looking forward to hearing him. Is he going to be doing it next week instead?"

Every neck in our classroom swiveled its head my way.

Sweat sprung out in fifty places, all over me. I just stared at the chalk nebulae on the blackboard.

After a few seconds that felt like a few hours Mr. Kempsey said, "Your spirited defense of established protocol is commendable, Drake, and, no doubt, altruistic. However, I possess reliable intelligence that Taylor's vocal apparati are in an unseaworthy condition. Thus, your classmate is excused on quasimedical grounds."

"So will he be doing it next week instead, sir?"

"The Alphabet marches on regardless of human frailties, Drake. Next week is T-for-Michelle Tirley, and Ours Is Not To Wonder Why."

"Doesn't seem very fair, sir, does it?"

What've *I* ever done to Gary Drake?

"Life is regularly *un*fair, Drake." Mr. Kempsey locked the piano. "Despite our best endeavors, and we must face its challenges as they arise. The sooner you learn that"—our teacher shot a stare not at Gary Drake but straight at *me*—"the better."

Wednesdays kick off with Double Maths with Mr. Inkberrow. Double Maths is just about the worst lesson of the week. Normally I sit next to Alastair Nurton in Maths but this morning Alastair Nurton was sitting next to David Ockeridge. The only free seat was next to Carl Norrest, right in front of Mr. Inkberrow's desk, so I had to sit there. It was raining so hard the farms and fields outside were dissolving in whites. Mr. Inkberrow frisbeed us back our exercise books from last week and started the lesson by asking a few dead-easy questions to "engage the brain."

"Taylor!" He'd caught me avoiding his eye.

"Yes sir?"

"In need of a little focusing, *hmm*? If *a* is eleven and *b* is nine and *x* is the product of *a* times *b*, what is the value of *x*?"

The answer's a piece of piss: it's ninety-nine.

But "ninety-nine" is a double-N word. A double stammer. Hangman wanted revenge for my stay of execution. He'd slid his fingers into my tongue and was clasping my throat and pinching the veins that take oxygen to my brain. When Hangman's like that I'd look a *total* flid if I tried to spit the word out. "A hundred and one, sir?"

The brighter kids in the class groaned.

Gary Drake did this loud croak. "The boy's a genius!"

Mr. Inkberrow takes off his glasses, huffs them, and polishes them with the fat end of his tie. "Nine times eleven equals 'A hundred and one,' you say, *hmm*? Let me ask you a follow-up question, Taylor. Why do we bother getting up in the morning? Can you tell me that, *hmm*? Why oh why oh *why* do we flipping *bother*?"

relatives

"They're *here!*" I yelled as Uncle Brian's white Ford Granada Ghia cruised up Kingfisher Meadows. Julia's door closed as if to say, *Big deal*, but a volley of getting-ready noises banged downstairs. I'd already taken down my map of Middle-earth and hidden away my globe and anything else Hugo might think babyish, so I just stayed sitting on my windowsill. Last night's gale'd sounded like King Kong trying to yank our roof off and was only just dying down. Across the road, Mr. Woolmere was hauling off bits of his blown-down fence. Uncle Brian turned into our drive and the Granada came to a rest alongside Mum's Datsun Cherry. First out was Aunt Alice, Mum's sister. Then my three Lamb cousins piled out of the back. First came Alex in a THE SCORPIONS LIVE IN 1981 T-shirt and a Björn Borg headband. Alex is seventeen but he's got bubonic zits and his body's three sizes too large for him. Next was Nigel the Squirt, the youngest, busy solving a Rubik's Cube at high speed. Last came Hugo.

Hugo fits his body like a glove. He's two years older than me. "Hugo" would be a cursed name for most kids but on Hugo it's a halo. (Plus, the Lambs go to an independent school in Richmond where you get picked on not if you're posh but if you're not posh *enough*.) Hugo wore a black zip-up top with no hood and no logo, button-fly Levi jeans, pixie boots, and one of those woven wristbands you wear to prove you're not a virgin. Luck loves Hugo. When Alex, Nigel, and me are still swapping Euston Road for Old Kent Road plus £300 and praying to scoop the kitty from Free Parking, Hugo's already got hotels on Mayfair and Park Lane.

"You *made* it!" Mum crossed the driveway and hugged Aunt Alice.

I opened the window a crack to hear better.

Meanwhile Dad'd come round from the greenhouse all togged out in his gardening gear. "Blustery weather you've brought us, Brian!"

Uncle Brian'd hauled himself out of his car and did a jokey step-back-in-amazement when he saw Dad. "Well, catch a load of the intrepid horticulturist!"

Dad wagged his trowel. "This blooming wind's *flattened* my daffodils! We have 'our man' do the lion's share in the garden, but he can't come until Tuesday, and as the old Chinese proverb—"

"Mr. Broadwas is one of those priceless village characters," said Mum, "who's worth twice what we pay him because he has to undo all the damage Michael wreaks."

"—as the ancient Chinese proverb goes, 'Wise man say, To be happy for week, mally wife. To be happy for month, sraughter pig. To be happy for rifetime, prant garden.' Rather amusing, eh?"

Uncle Brian pretended to find it rather amusing.

"When Michael heard his ancient Chinese proverb on *Gardeners' Question Time* the other day," Mum remarked, "the pig came *before* the wife. But look at you three boys! You've shot up *again*! Whatever are you putting on their corn flakes, Alice? Whatever it is, I should put some on Jason's."

That was a kick in the ribs.

"Well," Dad said, "let's all get inside before we get blown away."

Hugo received my telepathic signal and looked up at me.

I half-waved.

The drinks cabinet is only opened when visitors and relatives come. It smells of varnish and sherry vapors. (Once, when everyone was out, I tried some sherry. Syrupy Domestos, it tastes of.) Mum had me haul a dining room chair into the living room 'cause there weren't enough. These chairs weigh a ton and it banged my shin something *chronic* but I acted like it was no sweat. Nigel flumped on the beanbag and Alex got one of the armchairs. Alex tapped out a drumbeat on the armrest. Hugo just sat on the rug, cross-legged, saying, "I'm fine here, Aunt Helena, thanks" when Mum told me off for not bringing enough chairs. Julia *still* hadn't appeared. "I'll be down in a *minute!*" she'd hollered, twenty hours ago.

As usual, Dad and Uncle Brian kicked off with an argument about the route from Richmond to Worcestershire. (They were both wearing the golf jersey the other'd given him for Christmas.) Dad thought the A40 would've clipped twenty minutes off the A419 route. Uncle Brian disagreed. Then Uncle Brian said when they left later today he planned to drive to Bath via Cirencester and the A417 and Dad's face lit up with horror. "The A417? Crossing the Cotswolds on a bank holiday? Brian, it'll be living hell!"

Mum said, "I'm sure Brian knows what he's doing, Michael."

"The A417? *Purgatory!*" Dad was already leafing through his *AA Book of British Towns* and Uncle Brian'd sent Mum a look that said, *If it makes the old boy happy, let him.* (That look got on my wick.) "We have these innovations in this country, Brian, commonly known as 'motorways' . . . here, you need the M5 down to junction 15 . . ." Dad stabbed the map. "Here! Then just head east. No need to get bogged down in Bristol. M4 to junction 18, then the A46 to Bath. Bob's your uncle."

"Last time we went to see Don and Drucilla"—Uncle Brian didn't look at the *AA Book of British Towns*—"we did that. Took the M4 north of Bristol. Guess what. Stuck, bumper-to-bumper, for two hours! Weren't we, Alice?"

"It certainly was quite a long time."

"Two hours, Alice."

"But," Dad countered, "that was because you got caught in a contraflow when the new lane was being built. You'll zip along the M4 today. Clean as a whistle. Guarantee it."

"Thank you, Michael," Uncle Brian said mewily, "but I'm not really a great 'fan' of motorway driving."

"Well, Brian." Dad clomped shut his *AA Book of British Towns.* "If you're a 'fan' of crawling along at thirty in a convoy of geriatric caravanners, the A417 to Cirencester is the route for you."

"Come and give us a hand, please, Jason."

"Give us a hand" meant "get everything." Mum was showing Aunt Alice her recently souped-up kitchen. Meaty smells leaked out of the oven. Aunt Alice stroked the new tiles, saying, "Ex*quis*ite!" while Mum poured three glasses of Coke for Alex, Nigel, and me. Hugo'd asked for a glass of cold water. Then I poured a bag of Twiglets into a dish. (Twiglets're snacks that adults think kids like but they taste of burnt matches dipped in Marmite.) *Then* I put everything on a tray in the hatch, went round, and carried it to the coffee table. Dead unfair *I* had to do everything. If it'd been me and not Julia who was still in my room, they'd've sent in a SWAT squad by now.

"The memsahibs have got *you* well trained, I see," said Uncle Brian. I pretended to know what a memsahib is.

"Brian?" Dad waved the decanter at him. "Drop more sherry?"

"Why the heck not, Michael? Why the heck not?"

Alex grunted as I gave him his Coke. He scooped up a fistful of Twiglets. Nigel did this perky "Thanks very much!" and grabbed the Twiglets too. Hugo said, "Cheers, Jace" for the water and "No thanks" to the Twiglets. Uncle Brian and Dad'd left Driving and moved on to the Recession.

"No, Michael," Uncle Brian said, "you're mistaken, for once in your life. The accountancy game's more or less immune to economic doldrums."

"But you can't tell *me* your client base isn't feeling the pinch?"

"The 'pinch'? Blimey O'Riley, Michael, they're taking it in the teeth! Bankruptcies and foreclosures, morning, noon, and night! We're rushed off our bloody feet, pardon my French. Swamped! Tell you, I'm grateful to that woman in Downing Street for this financial—what's that latest fad?— anorexia. Us number crunchers are making a killing! And as partners' bonuses are profit-related, yours truly is sitting rather pretty."

"Bankrupts," Dad prodded, "are hardly repeat customers."

"But with a never-ending supply"—Uncle Brian glugged his sherry—"who gives a tinker's cuss? No, no, it's you shopfolk that *my* heart goes out to. This recession'll bleed the high street *dry* before it's finished. Quote me on that."

I think not, said Dad's wagging finger. "The hallmark of switched-on management is success in the lean years, not the years of plenty. Unemployment *may* be up to three million, but Greenland took on ten management trainees this quarter. Customers want quality food at bulk prices."

"Relax, Michael." Uncle Brian did a jokey surrender. "You're not at a seaside sales conference now. But I think you've got your head in the sand. Even Tories are talking about 'tightening belts' . . . Unions dead on their feet, not that that's a bad thing in my book. But we've got British Leyland hemorrhaging jobs . . . the docks dwindling away . . . British Steel imploding . . . Everyone ordering ships from South bloody Korea, wherever that is, instead of the Tyne and the Clyde . . . Comrade Scargill threatening revolution . . . It's difficult to see how it can't have a knock-on effect on frozen crispy pancakes and fish fingers, in the long run. Alice and I do worry, you know."

"Well," Dad said, leaning back, "it's very good of you and Alice to worry, Brian, but the retailing sector is holding its own and Greenland is robust."

"Very glad to hear it, Michael. Very glad indeed."

(So was I. Gavin Coley's dad was laid off by Metalbox in Tewkesbury. His birthday at Alton Towers was canceled, Gavin Coley's eyes sunk into his skull a few millimeters, and a year later his parents got divorced. Kelly Moran told me his dad's still on the dole.)

Hugo wore a thin leather cord around his neck. I wanted one.

When the Lambs visit, salt and pepper magically turn into "the condiments." Dinner was prawn cocktails in wine glasses for starters, lamb chops with chef's hats with duchesse potatoes and braised celery for main, and a Baked Alaska for "dessert," not "afters." We use the mother-of-pearl napkin rings. (Dad's dad brought them back from Burma on the same voyage he got the Omega Seamaster I smashed in January.) Before starting the starters, Uncle Brian opened the wine he'd brought. Julia and Alex got a whole glass, Hugo and me just half, "and a whistle wetter for you, Nigel."

Aunt Alice did her usual toast: "To the Taylor and Lamb dynasties!"

Uncle Brian did *his* usual: "Here's looking at you, kid!"

Dad pretended to find that rather amusing.

We all clinked glasses (except Alex) and took a sip.

Dad is *guaranteed* to hold his wine glass up to the light and say, "*Very* easy to drink!" He didn't let us down today. Mum shot him a look, but Dad never notices. "I'll say this much for you, Brian. You can't half-choose a decent plonk."

"Fabulous to earn your stamp of approval, Michael. Treated myself to a crate of the stuff. Comes from a vineyard near that charming cottage we rented in the lakes last year."

"Wine? The Lake District? Cumbria? Oh, I think you'll find you're mistaken there, Brian."

"No, no, Michael, not the *English* lakes, the *Italian* lakes. Tuscany." Uncle Brian whirlpooled his wine round his glass, snuftered it, and glugged it back. "Nineteen seventy-three. Blackberryesque, melony, oaky. I concur with your expert judgment, though, Michael. Not a bad little vintage."

"Well," said Mum, "dig in, everyone!"

After the first round of *delicious!*es Aunt Alice said, "It's been all go at school this term, hasn't it, boys? Nigel the captain of the chess club."

"President," said Nigel, "actually."

"Beg pudding! Nigel the *president* of the chess club. And Alex is doing incredible things with the school computer, aren't you, Alex? I can't even set the video recordery doo-dah, but—"

"Alex's *streets* ahead of his teachers," said Uncle Brian, "truth be told. What is it you're doing with it, Alex?"

"Fortran. BASIC." Alex spoke like it hurt him. "Pascal. Z-80 Code."

"You must be *ever* so intelligent," said Julia, so brightly I couldn't tell if she'd said it sarkily or not.

"Oh, you *bet* Alex is intelligent," said Hugo. "The Brain of Alexander Lamb's the Final Frontier of British science."

Alex glared at his brother.

"There's a real future in computering." Dad loaded his spoon with prawns. "Technology, design, electric cars. *That's* what schools should be teaching. Not all this 'Wandered lonely as a cloud' guff. Like I was telling Craig Salt—he's our M.D. at Greenland—just the other—"

"Couldn't agree with you more, Michael." Uncle Brian made a face like an evil mastermind announcing his plan for world domination. "Which is why Alex is getting a hot-off-the-press twenty-pound note for every grade A this year, and a ten-pound note for every B—to buy his very own IBM." (My jealousy throbbed like a toothache. Dad says paying your kids to study is "derelict.") "Nothing beats the profit motive, right?"

Mum stepped in. "And how about you, Hugo?"

At last I could study Hugo without pretending not to.

"Mainly," Hugo answered, taking a sip of water, "I've had some lucky races in the canoeing team, Aunt Helena."

"Hugo"—Uncle Brian burped—"has *showered* himself in glory! By rights he should be the head honcho oarsman chappie, but some stuffed fat-arsed governor—oops, pardon my French—who owns half of Lloyd's Insurance threatened to kick up a stink if his own Little Lord Herbert Bonks wasn't appointed. What's that child's name again, Hugo?"

"You might mean Dominic Fitzsimmons, Dad."

" '*Dominic Fitzsimmons*'! Couldn't make it up, could you?"

I *prayed* the spotlight'd swivel its gaze toward Julia. I *prayed* Mum wouldn't mention the poetry prize, not in front of Hugo.

"Jason won the Hereford and Worcester County Libraries Poetry Prize," said Mum. "Didn't you, Jason?"

"I *had* to write it." Shame boiled my earlobes and there was nowhere to look but at my food. "In English. I didn't—" I tested the word "know" a couple of times but saw I was going to stammer spastically on it. "—I didn't *realize* Miss Lippetts was even going to enter it."

"Don't hide your light under a bushel!" cried Aunt Alice.

"Jason won a splendid dictionary," said Mum. "Didn't you Jason?"

Alex the Git fired his sarcasm below adult radar. "I'd really like to hear your poem, Jason."

"Can't. Don't have my exercise book."

"What a pity."

"The *Malvern Gazetteer* printed the winning entries," said Mum. "Along-side Jason's mug shot, in fact! We can dig it out after dinner."

(Even the memory was a torture. They sent a photographer to school and made me pose in the library reading a book, like a complete gaylord.)

"Poets"—Uncle Brian smacked his lips—"so I've heard tell, catch naughty diseases from Parisian ladies of ill repute and die in drafty gavottes by the Seine. Quite a career plan, eh, Mike?"

"Wonderful prawns, Helena," Aunt Alice said.

Dad said, "Frozen, from Greenland in Worcester."

"*Fresh*, Michael. From the fishmongers."

"Oh. Didn't know there were still any fishmongers left."

Alex dug up the poetry prize again. "At least tell us what your poem was about, Jason. The blossoms of spring? Or was it a love poem?"

"Can't see you getting much out of it, Alex," said Julia. "Jason's work lacks the subtlety and maturity of the Scorpions."

Hugo spluttered, to niggle Alex. And to tell me whose side he was on. I could've kissed Julia out of sheer gratitude. Almost.

"Wasn't *that* funny," Alex muttered at Hugo.

"Don't sulk, Alex. It ruins your good looks."

"*Boys*," warned Aunt Alice.

The posh gravy boat was passed around the table. Between my creamed pota-toes and my miniature Yorkshire puds I created a Mediterranean of gravy. Gibraltar was the tip of a carrot. "Dig in!" said Mum.

Aunt Alice was the first to say, "Divine chops, Helena."

Uncle Brian did a crap Italian accent. "Dey melt-a in da mouth!"

Nigel grinned adoringly at his dad.

"The secret's in the marinade," Mum said to Aunt Alice. "I'll let you have the recipe afterwards."

"Oh, but Helena, I'm not leaving without it!"

"A smidgeon more wine, Michael?" Uncle Brian topped up Dad's glass (from the second bottle) before Dad could answer, then his own. "Don't mind if I do, Michael, thanks. Here's looking at you, kid! So Helena, I see your mobile pagoda hasn't gone up to the great Oriental junkyard in the sky yet?"

Mum put on her polite puzzled face.

"Your *Datsun*, Helena! If you weren't such a wonderful cook it'd be difficult to forgive you for breaking the First Law of Automobiles. Don't trust a Jap or the tat he churns out. The Germans've got the right idea for once. Seen the new Volkswagen adverts? There's this pint-sized Nip, running round trying to find the new VW Golf, then it drops from the ceiling and flattens him! *Wet* myself first time I saw it, didn't I, Alice?"

"Isn't your camera"—Julia wiped her mouth with her napkin—"a Nikon, Uncle Brian?"

Hugo said, "Nothing wrong with Japanese hi-fi technology, either."

"Or computer chips," added Nigel.

So I said, "Their motorbikes are pretty classic as well."

Uncle Brian did this disbelieving shrug. "Precisely my point, boys and girls! Japs'll take everyone else's technology, shrink it down to their own size, and then sell it back to the rest of the world, right, Mike? Mike? You're with me on *this* one, at least? What do you expect from the only Axis power that never apologized for the war! They got away with it. Scot-free."

"Two hundred thousand civilians killed by atom bombs," said Julia, "and two million more incinerated by firebombs is hardly what *I* would call 'Scot-free.' "

"But the *fact* of the matter is"—Uncle Brian doesn't hear what he doesn't want to—"the Japs are *still* fighting the war. They own Wall Street. London's next. Walking from the Barbican to my office, you'd need . . . twenty pairs of hands to count all the Fu Manchu look-alikes you pass by. Listen to this, Helena. My secretary bought herself one of those . . . oh, whateverthehelltheycall'ems . . . y'know, those motorized rickshaws . . . a Honda Civic. That's it. A turd-brown Honda Civic. She drove it out of the showroom and at the very first roundabout—I jest not—its exhaust dropped—clean—*off*. There's your reason why they're so competitive. They make tat. See? Can't have it all in this life. Not without picking up a nasty fungal infection, anyway, eh, Mike?"

"Pass me the condiments, please, Julia," Dad said.

Hugo and I caught each other's eye and for one moment we were alone in a roomful of waxworks.

"My Datsun"—Mum offered some braised celery to Aunt Alice, who made a *No thanks* gesture—"passed its MOT with flying colors last week."

"Don't tell me," Uncle Brian sniffed, "you got it MOT'ed at the very same place that sold you your mobile pagoda in the first place?"

"Why ever shouldn't I?"

"Ah, Helena." Uncle Brian shook his head.

"I'm not quite seeing your point, Brian."

"Helena, Helena, Helena."

Hugo asked for "just a sliver" of Baked Alaska, so Mum cut him a wodge as big as Dad's. "You're a growing lad, for heaven's sakes!" (I filed the tactic away for future use.) "Dig in, everyone, before the ice cream melts."

After the first spoonful, Aunt Alice said, "Out of this world!"

Dad said, "Very nice, Helena."

"Mike," Uncle Brian said, "you're not going to let this bottle languish here half-drunk now, are you?" He tipped a fat glug into Dad's glass, then his own, then raised his glass to my sister. " 'Here's looking at you, kid!' But I'm still at a loss to understand why a young lady of your obvious talents isn't aiming for the Big Two. At Richmond Prep, I jest not, it's Oxford this and Cambridge that, morning, noon, and night, isn't it, Alex?"

Alex raised his head ten degrees for a quarter second to say yes.

"Morning, noon, and night," said Hugo, dead seriously.

"Our careers adviser," Julia said, spooning a dribble of ice cream before it got to the tablecloth, "Mr. Williams, has a friend in the radical bar in London, who says that if I want to specialize in environmental law then Edinburgh or Durham are really the places to—"

"Then *I'm sorry.*" Uncle Brian judo-chopped the air. "Sorry sorry sorry, but Mr. Williams—a closet Welshman, doubtless—Mr. *Williams* should be tarred, feathered, tied to a mule, and sent back to Haverfordwest! It's not *what* you learn at university, it's"—Uncle Brian was steamy red now—"it's *who you network with! Only* at Oxbridge can you network with tomorrow's elite! I jest not, with the right college tie I'd've got made partner ten years ago! Mike . . . Helena! Surely you're not going to stand idly by while your firstborn squanders herself at the University of Nowhereshire?"

Annoyance darkened Julia's face.

(I usually retreat to somewhere safe at this point.)

Mum said, "Edinburgh and Durham have good reputations."

"Doubtless, doubtless, but *what you've got to remember* is"—Uncle Brian was now almost shrieking—" 'Are they the best on the market?' and the *an-*

swer is 'Are they *heck*!' Blimey O'Riley, this, *this*, is *precisely* the problem with comprehensive schools. Fabulous for little Jack and Jill Mediocrity, but do they push the brightest and ablest? Do they *heck*! For those teaching unions, 'brighter' and 'abler' are dirty words."

Aunt Alice put her hand on Brian's arm. "Brian, I think—"

"I refuse to be 'Brianned' when our only niece's *future* is at stake! If my concern makes me a snob, then bugger it and 'scuse my French, I'll *be* the bloodiest snob I *know* and wear that badge with pride! Why *anyone* with the brains for Oxbridge would set their sights on Jockland is simply *beyond* my *understanding*." Uncle Brian emptied his glass in one urgent swallow. "Unless perhaps—" My uncle's face turned from Outraged to Pervy in three seconds. "Ah yes—unless there's a young Scottish stallion with a hairy sporan you're not confessing to anyone about, Julia, eh? Eh, Mike, eh? Eh, Helena? Thought of that, eh?"

"*Brian*—"

"Don't worry, Aunt Alice." Julia smiled. "Uncle Brian knows I'd rather be involved in a multiple car crash than discuss my private life with him. I intend to study law in Edinburgh, and all the Brian Lambs of tomorrow will have to do their networking without me."

I'd've never got away with saying that, *ever*.

Hugo raised his glass to her. "Well *said*, Julia!"

"Ah." Uncle Brian did a sort of punctured laugh. "You'll probably go far in the legal game, young lady, even if you *do* insist on a second-class university. You've got the art of the *non secateur* off pat."

"Fabulous to earn your stamp of approval, Uncle Brian."

A cow of an awkward pause mooed.

"Hurrah!" Uncle Brian scoffed. "She insists on the last word."

"You've got a strand of celery stuck to your chin, Uncle Brian."

The coldest place in our house is the downstairs bog. In winter your bum freezes to the seat. Julia'd said good-bye to the Lambs and'd gone to Kate Alfrick's to do some History revision. Uncle Brian had gone up to the spare room "to rest his eyes." Alex'd gone to the bathroom for the third time since he'd arrived. Each time he took over twenty minutes. Don't know *what* he was finding to do in there. Dad was showing Hugo and Nigel his new Minolta. Mum and Aunt Alice were having a stroll round the windy garden. In the mirror above the washbasin I was scanning my face for signs of Hugo. Could I turn myself into him by sheer willpower? Cell by cell. Ross Wilcox is doing it. At primary school he was a thicko nobody, but now he smokes with older kids like Gilbert Swinyard and Pete Redmarley and people're calling him "Ross" instead of "Wilcox." So there must be a way.

I'd sat down and done a good clean crap when I heard voices getting louder. Eavesdropping's wrong, I know, but it was hardly *my* fault if Mum and Aunt Alice chose to natter *right* outside the ventilator flaps, was it?

"*You* shouldn't be apologizing, Helena. Brian was . . . God, I could *shoot* him!"

"Michael brings the worst out in him."

"No, let's just—Helena, your rosemary! It's virtually a tree. I just *can't* get my herbs to thrive. Apart from the mint. The mint's going crazy."

A pause.

"I wonder," Mum said, "what Daddy would make of them. If he could see them now, I mean."

"Brian and Michael?"

"Yes."

"Well, first he'd tell us, 'Told you so!' Then he'd roll up his sleeves, pick up whatever they were arguing the opposite of, and not leave the ring until both of them were battered into mute agreement."

"That's a bit harsh."

"Not as harsh as Daddy! Julia would give him a run for his money, though."

"She can be rather . . . opinionated."

"At least it's CND and Amnesty International she's opinionated about, Helena, and not Meaty Loaf or the Deaf Leopards."

A pause.

"Hugo's turning into a real charmer."

" 'Charmer' is *one* word."

"But look at how he *insisted* on doing the washing up. Of course I couldn't let him."

"Yes, I know, it wouldn't melt in his mouth. Jason's still painfully quiet. How's his speech therapy going?"

(I didn't want to hear this. But I couldn't without flushing the bog. If I did, they'd know they'd been overheard. So I was stuck there.)

"Snail's pace. He sees this South African lady called Mrs. de Roo. She tells us not to expect miracle cures. We don't. She tells us to be patient with him. We are. Not much else to say."

A long pause.

"You know, Alice, even after all these years, I *still* find it hard to believe Mummy and Daddy have gone for *good.* That they are actually . . . dead. Not just on a cruise liner in the Indian Ocean, out of reach for six months. Or— what's funny?"

"Being stuck with Daddy on a cruise liner! That *would* be purgatory."

Mum didn't answer.

A longer pause.

"Helena, I'm not prying"—Aunt Alice's voice'd shifted—"but you haven't mentioned any more of those phantom telephone calls since January?"

A pause.

"I'm sorry, Helena, I shouldn't have stuck my beak into—"

"No, no . . . I mean, God knows, who else can I discuss it with? No. There haven't been any more. I feel a bit guilty for jumping to conclusions. It was just a storm in a teacup, I'm sure. A nonexistent storm, I should say. If it hadn't been for—you know, that 'incident' of Michael's five and a half years ago, or whenever it was, I wouldn't've thought twice. Wrong numbers and crossed lines happen all the time. Don't they?"

("Incident"?)

"Exactly," Aunt Alice answered. "Exactly. You haven't . . . said . . ."

"A 'confrontation' with Michael'd be like digging up a grave."

(My goose bumps actually *hurt.*)

"Of *course* it would," Aunt Alice answered.

"The average Greenland trainee has a better idea of what goes on in the head of Michael Taylor than his own wife, half the time. Mind you, now I know why Mummy was so down, half the time."

(I didn't understand. I didn't want to. I wanted to. I don't know.)

"You're getting morbid, Big Sister."

"You're my morbid-mop, Alice. *You*'ve got glamour. *You* get to meet Chinese violinists and swarthy Aztec panpipe ensembles. Who's at the theater this week?"

"The Basil Brush *Boom-Boom* Bonanza."

"See?"

"Their agent is notoriously prickly. You'd think Liberace was in town, not some down-on-his-luck TV actor with his hand up a fox's bum."

"No business like show business."

A pause.

"Helena, I know I've told you this twenty *thousand* times, but you need challenges bigger than Baked Alaskas. Julia's flying the nest this year. Why *don't* you think about going back to work?"

Short pause. "One, there's a recession on and people are firing, not hiring. Two, I'm a morbid housewife. Three, I don't live near London, I live in darkest Worcestershire, and opportunities are thinner on the ground. Four, I haven't worked since Jason was born."

"So *what* if your maternity leave went on for thirteen years longer than planned?"

Mum did that single laugh people who don't want to laugh do.

"Even *Daddy* used to boast about your designs to his golf club cronies. All I ever heard was Helena this, Helena that."

"All *I* ever heard was *Alice* this, *Alice* that."

"Well, that was Daddy all over, wasn't it? Come on. Show me where you're thinking of putting that rockery . . ."

I flushed the bog and sprayed the sicky air freshener, holding my breath.

Dad's Rover 3500 lives in one garage, but Mum usually parks her Datsun Cherry on the drive, so the second garage is spare. The bikes live along one wall. Dad's tools live in neat racks above his workbench. Potatoes live in a bottomless sack. The spare garage is sheltered, even on blowy days like today. Dad smokes in there, so there's often a whiff of cigarettes. I even like the oil stains on the concrete floor.

The best thing's the dartboard, mind. Darts is ace. I love the thud as the spike sinks into the board. I love tugging the darts out. When I invited Hugo for a game, he said, "Sure." But then Nigel said he'd come too. Dad said, "Brilliant idea," so the three of us were in the garage playing Round the Clock. (Aim at 1 till you get a 1, then a 2 till you get a 2, then a 3, and so on. First to 20 wins.)

We threw one dart each to see who'd go first.

Hugo got 18, I got 10, Nigel got 4.

"So," Nigel asked me as his brother got a 1 with his first dart. "Have you read *The Lord of the Rings*?"

"No," Maggot lied, so Hugo wouldn't think I was being pally.

Hugo missed 2 with his next dart, but got it with his third.

Nigel told me, "It's *epic*."

Hugo got the three darts and passed them to me. "Nigel, *nobody* says 'epic' anymore."

(I tried to remember if I'd said it since the Lambs came.)

I missed 1 with my first two darts, but got it with my third.

"Nice throw," said Hugo.

"We had to do *The Hobbit* at school." Nigel got the darts. "But *The Hobbit*'s basically just a fairy tale."

"I tried *The Lord of the Rings,*" Hugo said, "but it's *laughable*. Everyone's called Gondogorn or Sarulon and runs about saying, 'These woods'll be *swarming* with Orcs by nightfall.' And as for that Sam, and his '*Oh Master Frodo, what a bootiful dagger you've got' — well!* They shouldn't let that sort of homoerotic porn *near* children. Maybe that's the appeal, Nigel?"

Nigel missed the board and his dart bounced off the brick.

"*Do* be careful, Nigel," Hugo sighed. "You're blunting Jace's darts."

I should've said "It doesn't matter" to Nigel. Maggot didn't.

Nigel's second dart hit the outside rim of the board. A miss.

"Did you know, Jace," said Hugo, casually, "it's a scientific fact that homosexuals can't throw straight?"

To my alarm, I realized Nigel was close to tears.

Hugo has a way of affecting other peoples' luck.

Nigel's third dart hit the rim of the board and pinged off. Nigel snapped. "You're *always* turning people against me!" Red and furious. "I *hate* you, you bloody *bastard*!"

"Not a nice word, Nigel. Do you know what a bastard is, or are you parroting your playmates in your chess club again?"

"Yes I do *actually*!"

"*Yes* you know what a bastard is? Or *yes* you're parroting your playmates?"

"*Yes* I know what a bastard is and *you*'re one!"

"So if *I*'m a bastard, you're saying our mother shagged another man to conceive me, right? So you're accusing her of Playing Away, are you?"

Tears brimmed in Nigel's eyes.

This'd bring trouble crashing down, I knew it.

Hugo did an amused tut. "Dad won't be best pleased to hear your accusation either. Look, why don't you just run along and fiddle with your Rubik's Cube in a quiet corner somewhere? Jason and I will do our best to forget the whole business."

"Sorry about Nigel." Hugo got 3, a miss, and a 4. "Such a space cadet. He has to learn how to detect hints, and act on them. One day he'll thank me for my tutelage. Alex the Neanderthal dork is beyond help, I fear."

I did a sort of laugh, wondering how Hugo makes words like "tutelage" and "alas" sound powerful and not prattish. I threw a miss, then a 2, a 3.

"Ted Hughes came to our school last term," Hugo mentioned.

Now I *knew* he didn't hold my poetry prize against me. "Yeah?"

Hugo threw a 5, a 6, a miss. "He signed my copy of *Hawk in the Rain*."

"*Hawk in the Rain*'s brilliant." A 4, a miss, a miss.

"I'm more into the First World War poets, myself." Hugo threw a 7, an 8, a miss. "Wilfred Owen, Rupert Brooke, and that lot."

"Yeah." I threw a 5, a miss, a 6. "I prefer them too, if I'm honest."

"But George Orwell's the man." A 9, a miss, a miss. "I've got everything he ever wrote, including a first edition *1984*."

A miss, a miss, a 7. "*1984*'s just *incredible*." (Actually I'd got bogged down in O'Brien's long essay and never finished it.) "And *Animal Farm*." (We'd had to read that at school.)

Hugo threw a 10. "If you don't read his journalism"—a near miss—"you can't say you know Orwell." Another near miss. "Damn. I'll post you this collection of essays, *Inside the Whale*."

"Thanks." I fluked an 8, a 9, a 10, and acted like it was nothing special.

"*Brilliant* throwing! Tell you what, Jace, let's liven things up a bit. Got any money on you?"

I had 50p.

"Okay, I'll match that. First to twenty wins fifty pence off the other."

All my pocket money was a bit of a risk.

"Go on, Jace." Hugo grinned like he really liked me. "Don't be a Nigel. Tell you what, you can have your turn again, to start. Three free throws."

Saying yes'd make me more like Hugo, I told myself. "Okay."

"Good man. But best not mention it to"—Hugo nodded through the garage wall—"the maters and the paters, or we'll spend the rest of the afternoon playing Ludo or the Game of Life under strict supervision."

"Sure." I missed, hit the wall, and missed.

"Bad luck," said Hugo. He missed, got an 11, missed.

"What's rowing like, then?" I got my 11, missed, got 12. "All I've been on are the pedalos at Malvern Winter Gardens."

Hugo laughed like I'd made a really funny joke, so I grinned like I had. He missed 12 three times in a row.

"Hard luck," I said.

"Rowing's phenomenal. All rushing, muscles, rhythm, and speed, but only the odd splash, or grunt, or crewmates' breathing. Like sex, now that I think about it. Annihilating your opponents is fun, too. Like our sports master says, 'Boys, it's not the taking part that matters. It's the winning that counts!' "

I threw a 13, 14, then 15.

"My God!" Hugo made a blowing, impressed face. "Not suckering me here, are you, Jace? Tell you what, how about fleecing me for one pound?" Hugo slipped a sleek wallet from his Levis and waved a £1 note at me. "The way *you're* playing today, this smacker'll be yours in five throws. What does your piggy bank say?"

If I lost I wouldn't have any money until next Saturday.

"Oooooo," crooled Hugo. "Don't chicken out on us *now*, Jace."

I heard Hugo talking about me to other Hugos in his rowing club. *My cousin Jason Taylor is such a space cadet.* "Okay."

"*Okay!*" Hugo slipped the pound note into his top pocket. He then threw a 12, a 13, and a 14. He made a surprised noise. "Wonder if my luck might be turning?"

My first dart hit the brick. My second pinged off the metal. My third missed.

Without hesitating, Hugo threw a straight 15, 16, and 17.

Footsteps clopped from the back door to the garage door. Hugo cursed under his breath and flashed me a look that said, *Leave it to me.*

I couldn't've done anything else.

"Hugo!" Aunt Alice stormed into the spare garage. "Would you care to tell me why Nigel's in floods of tears?"

Hugo's reaction was Oscar winning. "*Tears?*"

"Yes!"

"*Tears?* Mum, that boy is *unbelievable* sometimes!"

"I'm not asking you to *believe* anything! I want you to *explain!*"

"What's there *to* explain?" Hugo did this lost, sorry shrug. "Jason invited Nigel and me for a nice game of darts. Nigel kept missing. I gave him a couple of pointers, but he ended up storming off in a tizzy. Spouting foul-mouthed 'French,' too. Why's that boy so com*pet*itive, Mum? Remember how we caught him making up words just to win at Scrabble? Do you think it's growing pains?"

Aunt Alice turned to me. "Jason? What's your version of events?"

Hugo could sell Nigel to a glue factory and Maggot would still say, "It's just like Hugo said, really, Aunt Alice."

"He's welcome back," Hugo assured her, "once his tantrum's blown over. If you don't mind, Jace? Nigel didn't *mean* what he called you."

"I don't mind at all."

"Here's another idea." Aunt Alice knew she'd been stalemated. "Your Aunt Helena's low on coffee, and your father'll need a strong mug when he wakes up. I'm volunteering you to go and get some. Jason, perhaps you'd show your nonstick cousin the way, since you're obviously such allies."

"We've *almost* finished this game, Mum, so—"

Aunt Alice set her jaw.

Isaac Pye, the landlord of the Black Swan, came into the games room at the back to see what the fuss was about. Hugo stood at the Asteroids console, surrounded by me, Grant Burch, Burch's servant Philip Phelps, Neal Brose, Ant Little, Oswald Wyre, and Darren Croome. None of us could believe it. Hugo'd been on for twenty minutes on the *same* 10p. The screen was *full* of floating asteroids and I'd've died in three seconds flat. But Hugo reads the whole screen at once, not just the one rock that's most dangerous. He almost never uses his thrusters. He makes every torpedo count. When the zigzagging UFO comes he lays in a salvo of torpedoes only if the asteroid storm isn't too heavy. Otherwise, he ignores it. He only uses the hyperspace button as a last resort. His face stays calm, like he's reading a quite interesting book.

"That's never three *mill'yun!*" said Isaac Pye.

"Almost three an' a *half* million," Grant Burch told him.

When Hugo's last bonus life *finally* erupted in a shower of stars, the machine did bleepy whoops and announced that the All-Time Top Score'd been topped. That stays on even if the machine's switched off. "I spent a fiver getting up to two and a half mill'yun the other night," grunted Isaac Pye, "an' *that* were the bullock's bollocks, I thought. I'd stand you a pint, lad, but there's two off-duty coppers in the bar."

"That's good of you," Hugo told Isaac Pye, "but I daren't get caught on a drunk-in-charge-a-spacecraft rap."

Isaac Pye did a wurzel snigger and ambled back to the bar.

Hugo entered his name as JHC.

Grant Burch asked it. "What's that stand for, then?"

"Jesus H. Christ."

Grant Burch laughed, so everyone else did. God, I felt proud. Neal Brose'd tell Gary Drake how Jason Taylor hung out with Jesus Christ.

Oswald Wyre said, "How many years did it take you to get that good?"

"Years?" Hugo's accent'd gone just a *bit* less posh and just a *bit* more London. "Mastering an arcade game shouldn't take that long."

"Must've taken a pile of dosh, though," said Neal Brose. "To get that much practice, I mean."

"Money's *never* a problem, not if you've got half a brain."

"No?"

"Money? Course not. Identify a demand, handle its supply, make your customers grateful, kill off the opposition."

Neal Brose memorized every word of that.

Grant Burch got out a pack of cigarettes. "Smoke, mate?"

If Hugo said no he'd damage the impression he'd made.

"Cheers." Hugo peered at the box of Players No. 6. "But anything except Lambert and Butler makes my throat feel like shit for *hours*. No offense."

I memorized every word of that. What a way to get out of smoking.

"Yeah," Grant Burch said, "Woodbines do that to me."

From the bar we heard Isaac Pye repeat, " 'I daren't get caught on a drunk-in-charge-a-spacecraft rap'!"

Dawn Madden's mum peered at Hugo from the smoke-fogged bar.

"Are that woman's boobs for *real?*" Hugo hissed at us. "Or are they a pair of spare heads?"

Mr. Rhydd sticks Lucozade-yellow plastic sheets over his windows to stop the displays from fading. But his "displays" are only ever pyramids of canned pears, and the plastic sheets make the inside of his shop feel like a photograph from Victorian times. Hugo and I read the notices on the board for second-hand Legos, kittens needing homes, good-as-new washing machines for £10 OBO, and ads promising you hundreds of extra pounds in your spare time. The cold-soapy, rotting-orangey, newsprinty smell of Mr. Rhydd's hits you the moment you're inside. There's the Post Office booth in one corner, where Mrs. Rhydd, the postmistress, sells stamps and dog licenses, though not today 'cause today's Saturday. Mrs. Rhydd's signed the Official Secrets Act but she looks quite normal. There's a rack of greetings cards showing men dressed like Prince Philip fishing in rivers saying "On Father's Day" or foxgloves in a cottage garden saying "For My Dearest Grandmother." There are shelves of alphabet spaghetti, Pedigree Chum, and Ambrosia Rice Pudding. There are packs of toys like blow-football and play-money that never sell 'cause they're too crap. A Slush Puppie machine makes cups of snow in felt-pen colors, but not in March. Behind the counter are cigarettes and shelves of beer and wine. On high shelves are jars of Sherbet Bombs, Cola Cubes, Cider Apples, and Army and Navy Tablets. These come in paper bags.

"Wow," said Hugo. "Thrillsville. I've died and gone to *Harrods*."

Just then Kate Alfrick, Julia's best friend, breezed in, and got to the counter at the same time as Robin South's mum. Robin South's mum let Kate go first 'cause Kate just wanted a bottle of wine. She can buy alcohol 'cause she's turned eighteen.

"Ta very much." Mr. Rhydd handed Kate her change. "Celebrating?"

"Not really," said Kate. "Mum and Dad are coming back from Norfolk tomorrow evening. Thought I'd have a nice dinner ready to welcome them home. This"—she tapped the bottle—"is the finishing touch."

"Jolly good," Mr. Rhydd said. "Jolly good. Now then, Mrs. South . . ."

Kate passed us on her way out. "Hello, Jason."

"Hello, Kate."

"Hi, Kate," said Hugo. "I'm his cousin."

Kate studied Hugo through her Russian-secretary glasses. "The one called Hugo."

"Only three hours in Black Swan Green"—Hugo did a funny stagger of amazement—"and I'm being discussed *already*?"

I told Hugo it was to Kate's house Julia'd gone to study.

"Oh, so you're *that* Kate." He gestured at the wine. "Liebfraumilch?"

"Yes," Kate said, in a what's-it-to-you? voice. "Liebfraumilch."

"Bit sweet. You look drier. More the chardonnay type."

(The only wines *I* know are Red, White, Fizzy, and Rosé.)

"Could be you don't know your types as well as you think you do."

"Could be, Kate." Hugo combed his hair with his hand. "Could be. Well, we mustn't keep you away from your revision any longer. Doubtless you and Julia are hard at it. Hope we'll bump into each other again, sometime."

Kate did a frowning smile. "I shouldn't pin your hopes on it."

"Not *all* my hopes, Kate, no. That would be rash. But the world can surprise you. I am a younger man, but this much I do know."

At the door Kate looked over her shoulder.

Hugo had this cocky *See?* expression ready.

Kate left, cross.

"How," Hugo said, reminding me of Uncle Brian, "*appe*tizing."

I paid Mr. Rhydd for the coffee. Hugo said, "That's never *real* crystallized ginger you have in that jar, right up at the top?"

"Certainly is, Blue." Mr. Rhydd calls all us kids "Blue" so he doesn't have to remember our names. He blew his cracked Mr. Punch nose. "Mrs. Yew's mother was partial to it, so I'd order it in for her. She passed away with a new jar barely touched."

"Fascinating. My Aunt Drucilla, who we're staying with in Bath, *adores* crystallized ginger. I'm sorry to send you up your ladder again, but . . ."

"No bother, Blue." Mr. Rhydd stuffed his hanky into his pocket. "No bother at all." He dragged his ladder over, climbed up, and groped for the far jar.

Hugo checked that nobody else was in the shop.

Hugo eeled forward on his chest, over the counter, reached between the rungs of the ladder, just six *inches* under Mr. Rhydd's Hush Puppies, took a box of Lambert & Butler cigarettes, and eeled back.

Numb, I mouthed at him, *What are you doing?*

Hugo stuffed the cigarettes down his pants. "Jason, are you okay?"

Mr. Rhydd shook the jar down at us. "This'd be the badger, Blue?" His nostrils were sockets stuffed with hairy darkness.

"That would indeed be the badger, Mr. Rhydd," said Hugo.

"Jolly good, jolly good."

I was *shitting* myself.

And *then*, as Mr. Rhydd eased himself down the ladder, Hugo snatched two Cadbury's Creme Eggs from the tray and dropped them in my duffel coat pocket. If I'd struggled *now* or even tried to put them back, Mr. Rhydd'd've noticed. To top it all, in the moment between Mr. Rhydd's foot touching the ground and Mr. Rhydd turning round to face us, Hugo swiped a packet of Fisherman's Friends and stuffed *that* in with the Creme Eggs. The packet rustled. Mr. Rhydd wiped dust off the jar. "What'll it be, Blue? Quarter of a pound do you?"

"A quarter of a pound would be *excellent*, Mr. Rhydd."

"Why d'you"—Hangman blocked "nick," *then* "steal," so I had to use the naff "pinch"—"pinch the fags?" I wanted to scarper away from the crime scene as quick as possible, but a slow queue of traffic'd built up behind a tractor, so we couldn't cross the crossroads yet.

"Plebs smoke 'fags.' *I* smoke cigarettes. I don't 'pinch.' Plebs 'pinch.' I 'liberate.' "

"Then why did you 'liberate' the—" (Now I couldn't say "cigarettes.")

"Ye-es?" prompted Hugo.

"The Lambert and Butlers."

"If you mean 'Why did you liberate the cigarettes?' it's because smoking is a simple pleasure, with no proven side effects except lung cancer and heart disease. I intend to be long dead by then. If you mean, 'Why choose Lambert and Butlers in particular?' it's because I wouldn't be seen *homeless* smoking anything *else*, except for Passing Cloud. Which that Tragic Old Dipso doesn't stock in his Village Grocery, of course."

I still didn't get it. "Haven't you got enough money to buy them?"

This amused my cousin. "Do I *look* like I haven't got enough money?"

"But why take the risk?"

"Ah, the liberated cigarette is the sweetest."

Now I knew how Aunt Alice felt in the garage earlier. "But why'd you take the Fisherman's Friends and the Creme Eggs?"

"The Fisherman's Friends are insurance against Mr. Tobacco Breath. The Creme Eggs were insurance against you."

"Insurance against me?"

"You'll hardly grass on me if you also had liberated contraband on you, would you?"

An oil tanker inched past, puking out fumes.

"I didn't grass you off when you made Nigel cry earlier, did I?"

"Make Nigel cry? Who made Nigel cry?"

Then I noticed Kate Alfrick's house, or rather a silver MG parked round the side. This guy who definitely wasn't Julia opened the front door for Kate as she walked up her drive, carrying her wine. The upstairs curtains twitched. "Hey look—"

"Let's cross." Hugo edged toward an oncoming gap. "Hey look what?"

We dashed across the road, to the path to the lake in the woods.

"Nothing."

"No no no no no, you're holding it like a Hollywood Nazi. Relax! Just hold it like it's a fountain pen. There. Now, let there be light . . ." My cousin reached inside his jacket. "Of course, it takes a lighter to impress the quality quim, but lighters do give the game away if found in your blazer pocket by prying Nigels. So Swan Vestas will have to do for this afternoon's lesson."

The lake was nervous with riplets and counterriplets.

"I didn't see you liberate those at Mr. Rhydd's."

"I took them from that grebo in the pub who called me 'mate.' "

"You pinched Grant Burch's matches?"

"Don't look so appalled. Why would 'Grant Burch' suspect me? I'd turned down his mucky cigarette. Yet another perfect crime."

Hugo lit a match, cupped it, and leaned toward me.

A sudden jostle of wind snatched the Lambert & Butler from my fingers. It fell between the slats of the bench. "Oh bum," I said, bending down to retrieve it. "Soz."

"Take a new one and don't say 'Soz.' I'll have to donate the surplus tobacco to the local wildlife, anyway." My cousin held out the pack of Lambert & Butler's. "The wise dealer *never* risks getting caught in possession."

I looked at the offered packet. "Hugo, I'm grateful to you for—y'know, showing me, and everything, but, to be honest, I'm not sure if—"

"Jace!" Hugo did a jokey-amazed face. "Don't say you're backing out *now*? I thought we'd decided to strip you of this shameful virginity of yours?"

"Yeah . . . but maybe . . . not today."

Blind boars of wind crashed through the nervy woods.

" 'Not today,' huh?"

I nodded, worried he'd be pissed off.

"Your choice, Jace." Hugo did the gentlest face. "I mean, we're friends, aren't we? I'd hardly twist your arm into doing something against your will."

"Thanks." I felt stupid with gratitude.

"But"—Hugo lit his own cigarette—"it's my duty to point out, this isn't just about smoking a humble cancer stick."

"How do you mean?"

Hugo grimaced in a Should-I-or-shouldn't-I? quandary.

"Go on. Say it."

"You need to hear some hard truths, cousin." Hugo took a deep drag. "But first I have to know *you* know I'm telling you them for your own good."

"Okay. I"—Hangman gripped "know"—"understand."

"Promise me?"

"Promise."

The green or gray of Hugo's eyes depends on the weather. "This 'Not Today' attitude of yours *is* a cancer. Cancer of the character. It stunts your growth. Other kids sense your Not-Todayness, and despise you for it. 'Not Today' is why those plebs in the Black Swan make you nervous. 'Not-Today'—I would *bet*—is at the root of that speech defect of yours." (A shame bomb blew my head off.) " 'Not Today' condemns you to be the lapdog of authority, *any* bully, *any* shitehawk. They sense you won't stand up to them. Not today, not ever. 'Not Today' is the blind slave of every petty rule. Even the rule that says"—Hugo did this bleaty voice—" *'No, smoking is BAD! Don't listen to naughty Hugo Lamb!'* Jason, you *have* to kill 'Not-Today.'"

This was so appallingly true I could only try to smile.

Then Hugo said, "I was you myself, Jace, once. Just the same. Always afraid. But there's another reason why you *must* smoke this cigarette. Not because it's the first step to becoming someone your turkey-shagging schoolmates will respect instead of exploit. Not because a Young Blood with a mature cigarette is a better proposition to the ladies than a boy with a Sherbert Dip. It's this. Come here. I'll whisper it." Hugo leaned so close his lips touched my ears and ten thousand volts sang through my nervous system. (For a split second I had a vision of Hugo the Oarsman out on the water, cathedrals and riverbanks blurring by, biceps stiffening and loosening under his vest, with girlfriends lining the river. Girlfriends ready to lick him where he told them.) "If you *don't* kill 'Not Today' "—Hugo did a horror-movie-trailer voice—"*One day you'll wake up, look in the mirror, and see Uncle Brian and Uncle Michael!*"

"*Att*aboy . . . breathe in . . . through your mouth, not your nose . . ."

The mouthful of gassy dirt left my mouth.

Hugo was stern. "You didn't suck it into your lungs, did you, Jace?"

I shook my head, wanting to spit.

"You have to *inhale*, Jace. Into your lungs. Otherwise it's like sex without an orgasm."

"Okay." (I don't actually know what an orgasm is, apart from what you call someone who's done something stupid.) "Right."

"I'm just going to pinch your nose," said Hugo, "to stop you cheating." His fingers closed off my nostrils. "Deep breath—not too deep—and let the smoke go down with the air." Then his other hand sealed my mouth shut. The air was cold but his hands were warm. "One, two . . . three!"

In came the hot gassy dirt. My lungs flooded with it.

"Hold it there," urged Hugo. "One, two, three, four, five, and"—he released my lips—"*out.*"

The smoke leaked out, a genie from its bottle.

The wind atomized the genie.

"And that," said Hugo, "is all there is to it."

Vile. "Nice."

"It'll grow on you. Finish the cigarette." Hugo perched himself on the back of the bench and relit his own Lambert & Butler. "As aquatic spectacles go, I am a trifle underwhelmed by your lake. Is this where the swans are?"

"There aren't any actual swans in Black Swan Green." My second drag was as revolting as my first. "It's a sort of village joke. The lake was *classic* in January, mind. It froze over. We played British Bulldogs actually on the ice. Though I found out afterwards there's about twenty kids who've drowned in this lake, down the years."

"Who could blame them?" Hugo did a weary sigh. "Black Swan Green might not be the arsehole of the world, but its got a damn good view of it. You've gone a bit pale, Jace."

"I'm fine."

The first torrent of vomit kicked a *GUUURRRRRR* noise out of me and poured on the muddy grass. In the hot slurry were shreds of prawn and carrot. Some'd got on my splayed fingers. It was warm as warm rice pudding. More was coming. Inside my eyelids was a Lambert & Butler cigarette sticking out of its box, like in an advert. The second torrent was a mustardier yellow. I guppered for fresh oxygen like a man in an airlock. *Prayed* that was the last of it. Then came three short, boiling subslurries, slicker and sweeter, as if composed of the Baked Alaska.

Oh *Jesus*.

I washed my puke-stained hand in the lake, then wiped away the tears from my puke-teared eyes. I'm *so* ashamed. Hugo's trying to teach me how to be a kid like him, but I can't even smoke a single cigarette.

"I'm really"—I wipe my mouth—"really sorry."

But Hugo's not even looking at me.

Hugo's squirmed out on the bench, facing the churned-up sky.

My cousin's sobbing with laughter.

bridle path

My eye spidered over my poster of black angelfish turning into white swans,
across over my map of Middle-earth, around my door frame, into my curtains, lit fiery mauve by my spring sun, and fell down the well of dazzle.

Listening to houses breathe makes you weightless.

But a lie-in's less satisfying if other people aren't up and about, so I
jumped out of bed. The landing curtains were still drawn 'cause Mum and
Julia'd left for London when it was dark. Dad's away on another weekend conference in Newcastle-under-Lyme or Newcastle-on-Tyne. Today, the house is
all mine.

First I pissed, leaving the bathroom door wide open. Next, in Julia's bedroom I put on her Roxy Music L.P. Julia'd go *ape*. I turned up the volume,
dead loud. Dad'd go so *mental* his head'd blow up. I sprawled on Julia's
stripey sofa, listening to this kazookering song called "Virginia Plain." With
my big toe, I flicked the shell-disk wind chime Kate Alfrick'd given her a couple of birthdays ago. Just 'cause I could. Then I went through my sister's chest
of drawers looking for a secret diary. But when I found a box of tampons I felt
ashamed and stopped.

In Dad's chilly office I opened his filing cabinets and breathed in their
metal-flavored air. (A duty-free pack of Benson & Hedges has appeared since
Uncle Brian's last visit.) Then I twizzled on Dad's Millennium Falcon office
chair, remembered it's April Fool's Day, picked up Dad's untouchable telephone, and said, "Hello? Craig Salt? Jason Taylor here. Listen, Salt, you're

sacked. What do you *mean*, why? 'Cause you're a fat orgasm, that's why. Put me through to Ross Wilcox this instant! Ah, Wilcox? Jason Taylor. Listen, the vet'll be around later to put you out of our misery. Bye-bye, scumbag. Been nasty knowing you."

In my parent's creamy bedroom I sat at Mum's dressing table, spiked my hair with L'Oréal hair mousse, daubed an Adam Ant stripe across my face, and held her opal brooch over one eye. I looked through it at the sun for secret colors nobody's ever named.

Downstairs, a wafer of light from where the kitchen curtains didn't quite meet sliced through a gold Yale key and this note:

> Dear Jason
> Here's your front door key—
> DON'T LOSE IT. I've left
> a spare with Mrs. Woolmere
> incase you do. Aunt Alice's
> phone number is on the
> pad. If you're poorly you
> can go to Mrs. Woolmere's.
> You can make yourself a
> sandwich for lunch, but
> put the bread back in

> the bin or it will go
> stale. Quiche Lorraine in
> the fridge for dinner.
> Eat the bowl of fruit
> salad. Will be back by
> 10 this evening. Switch
> everything off when you
> go out. LOCK THE DOOR.
> Don't invite anyone in.
> Don't watch too much
> T.V.   love Mum

Wow. My very own door key. Mum must've decided to leave it for me at the last minute this morning. Normally we hide a spare in a Welly in the garage. I dashed upstairs and chose a key ring Uncle Brian gave me one time, of a rabbit in a black bow tie. I hung it on my belt loop and slid down the banister. For breakfast I ate McVitie's Jamaican Ginger Cake and a cocktail of milk, Coke, and Ovaltine. Not bad. Oh, better than not bad! Every *single* hour of today is a Black Magic chocolate, waiting in its box for me. I retuned the kitchen radio from Radio 4 to Radio 1. That *fab* song with the dusty flute in it by Men at Work was on. *Three* Marks & Spencer's French Fancies, I ate, straight out of the packet. V's of long-distance birds crossed the sky. Mermaid clouds drifted over the glebe, over the cockerel tree, over the Malvern Hills. God, I *ached* to follow them.

What was stopping me?

Mr. Castle stood in a pair of green Wellies, washing his Vauxhall Viva with a garden hose. His front door was open, but the hallway was dead dark. Mrs. Castle could've been in that dark, watching me. You hardly ever see Mrs. Castle. Mum calls her "that poor woman" and says she suffers from Nerves. Is Nerves infectious? I didn't want to dent the morning's shine by stammering, so I tried to slip by Mr. Castle without being seen.

"Morning, young fella!"

"Good morning, Mr. Castle," I answered.

"Off anywhere special?"

I shook my head. Mr. Castle somehow makes me nervous. Once I heard Dad telling Uncle Brian he's a Freemason, which is something to do with witchcraft and pentangles. "It's just it's a"—Hangman blocked "nice"—"a—pleasant morning, so . . ."

"Oh, isn't it just. Isn't it *just!*"

Liquid sunshine streamed down the car windscreen.

"So how old *are* you now, Jason?" Mr. Castle asked this like he'd been discussing it with a panel of experts for days.

"Thirteen," I said, guessing he thought I was still twelve.

"Thirteen, are you? That a fact?"

"Thirteen."

"Thirteen." Mr. Castle looked through me. "Ancient."

The stile at the mouth of Kingfisher Meadows is the source of the bridle path. A green sign saying PUBLIC BRIDLE PATH with a picture of a horse proves it. Where the bridle path officially *ends* is miles less clear. Mr. Broadwas says it fizzles out in Red Earl Wood. Pete Redmarley and Nick Yew said they went rabbiting with their ferrets up the bridle path one time, and that it's blocked by a new estate in Malvern Wells. But best is the rumor that the bridle path leads you to the foot of Pinnacle Hill, where, if you pick your way through toothy brambles and dark ivy and vicious stingers, you'll find the mouth of an old tunnel. Go through that tunnel, and you come out in Herefordshire. Near the Obelisk. The tunnel's been lost since olden times, so its discoverer'd make the front page of the *Malvern Gazetteer.* How cool'd *that* be?

I would track the bridle path to its mysterious end, wherever it might be.

The very first stretch of the bridle path is no mystery at all. Every kid in the village's been down that neck a million times. It just leads past some back gardens to the footy field. The footy field's actually a scrap of ground behind the village hall that belongs to Gilbert Swinyard's dad. When Mr. Swinyard's sheep aren't on it, we're allowed to play footy there. We use coats for goals and don't bother with throw-ins. The scores climb as high as rugby scores, and one game can last *hours,* until the last-but-one kid goes home. Sometimes all the Welland and Castlemorton lot come over on their bikes and then the games are more like battles.

Not a soul was on the footy field this morning, only me. Later on, chances were, a game'd start up. None of the players'd know Jason Taylor'd already been there before them. I'd be fields and fields away by then. Maybe deep under the Malvern Hills.

Oily flies fed on curry-colored cowpats.

New leaves oozed from twigs in the hedges.

Seeds thickened the air, like sweet gravy.

In the copse, the bridle path joined up with a moon-cratered track. Trees knitted overhead, so only knots and loops of sky showed. Dark and cool, it was, and I wondered if I should've brought my coat. Down a hollow, round the bend, I came across a thatched cottage made of sooty bricks and crooked timber. Martins were busy under its eaves. PRIVATE said a sign hung on the slatted gate, where the name should go. Newborn flowers in the garden were licorice allsorts blue, pink, and yellow. Maybe I heard scissors. Maybe I heard a poem, seeping from its cracks. So I stood and listened, just for a minute, like a hungry robin listening for worms.

Or two, or three.

Dogs *hurled* themselves at me.

I hurled *myself* back, across the track, clean onto my arse.

The gate shrieked but, thank *God,* stayed shut.

Two, no, three, Dobermans jostled and slammed, standing on their back legs, barking in*sane*ly. Even when I got up they were still as tall as me. I should've just gone while I had the chance, but the dogs had prehistoric fangs, deranged eyes, gammon tongues, and steel chains round their necks. Their brown-polish-on-black-suede skins wrapped not just dogs' bodies, but something else too, something that needs to kill.

I was scared but I still had to look at the dogs.

Then I got a savage poke in that bone that's the stump of a tail.

"You're goadin' my boys on!"

I whirled round. The man's lip was gnarled and his sooty hair had a streak of white like combed-in bird crap. In his hand was a walking stick strong enough to stave in a skull. "You're *goadin'* my boys!"

I swallowed. Laws down the bridle path are different to main-road laws.

"I don't appreciate that." He glanced at the Dobermans. "SHUT IT!"

The dogs fell quiet and got down from the gate.

"Oh, a whole yard o' guts *you've* got," the man added, studying me some more, "goadin' my boys from *this* side o' the gate."

"They're . . . beautiful animals."

"Oh aye? My boys'd turn you into *mincemeat* if I gave 'em the nod. Still call 'em *beautiful animals* then, would you?"

"I s'pose not."

"I s'pose not. Live down them fancy new houses, don't you?"

I nodded.

"Knew it. Locals have more respect for my boys than some *townie*. You come here, come traipsin' about, leavin' gates open, puttin' up your little toy mansions on land *we've* been workin' for generations. Makes me sick. Just lookin' at you."

"I didn't mean any harm. Honest."

He twizzled his stick. "You can bugger off now."

I began walking, fast, just looking over my shoulder once.

The man hadn't taken his eyes off me.

Faster, warned Unborn Twin. *Run!*

I froze, watching the man open the gate. His wave was almost friendly. *"GET THE BUGGER, BOYS!"*

The three black Dobermans were galloping straight at me.

I ran full pelt but I knew thirteen-year-old boys can't outrun three snarling Dobermans. A snatch of turfy drumming, then I went flying over a ruck and the ground booted the air out of me and I got a glimpse of a leaping dog's flank. I screamed like a girl and scrunched up into a ball and waited for the fangs to sink into my side and ankles and slaver and rip and tear and pluck and for the snarling bagsnatchers to run off with my scrote and liver and heart and kidneys.

A cuckoo'd started up, very near. Surely a minute'd already passed?

I opened my eyes and raised my head.

No sign of the dogs or their master.

A butterfly not from England fanned open and shut, inches away. Cautiously, I got up.

I'd have a couple of glorious bruises, and my pulse was still fast and broken. But otherwise I was okay.

Okay, but a bit poisoned. The dog man despised me for not being born here. He despised me for living down Kingfisher Meadows. That's a hate you can't argue with. No more than you can argue with mad Dobermans.

I carried on up the bridle path, out of the copse.

Dewy cobwebs snaptwanged cross my face.

The big field was full of wary ewes and spanking new lambs. The lambs tiggered up close, bleeping like those crap Fiat Noddy cars, idiotically pleased to see me. The poison of the Dobermans and their master began to thin, a little. A couple of the mother sheep edged closer. They didn't quite trust me. Just as well for sheep they can't work out why the farmer's being so nice to them. (Human beings need to watch out for reasonless niceness too. It's never reasonless and its reason's not usually nice.)

So anyway, I was halfway over the field when I spotted three kids up on the old railway embankment. Up on the Hollow Log, by the brick bridge. They'd already seen me, and if I changed course they'd know I was chickening out of meeting them. So I lay in a course straight for them. I chewed a stick of Juicy Fruit I found in my pocket. Here and there I penalty-shot a poking-up thistle, just to look a bit hard.

Lucky I did. The three kids were Grant Burch, his servant Philip Phelps, and Ant Little, passing round a fag. From inside the log crawled out Darren Croome, Dean Moran, and Squelch.

Grant Burch called down from the log. "All right, Taylor?"

Phelps said, "Come to see the scrap?"

From the foot of the embankment I called up, "What scrap?"

"Me" — Grant Burch squished one nostril and torpedoed a bolt of hot snot out the other — "stick Ross Wankstain Wilcox the Third."

Good news. "What's the scrap about?"

"Me and Swinyard were playin' Asteroids at the Black Swan yesterday evenin', right. Wilcox comes in, actin' like King Hard Knock, sayin' nothin', then he goes an' *drops his fag in my shandy*. Couldn't fuckin' believe it! I says, 'D'you do that on purpose?' Wilcox says, 'What d'*you* reckon?' I says, 'You're gonna fuckin' regret that, *Piss Flaps*.'"

"*Classic!*" Philip Phelps grinned. "'Piss Flaps'!"

"Phelps." Grant Burch frowned. "Don't interrupt me when I'm talking."

"Sorry, Grant."

"So anyway, *I* says, 'Yer gonna fuckin' regret that, *Piss Flaps*.' Wilcox says, 'Make me.' I says, 'Wanna step outside then?' Wilcox says, 'Trust you to pick a place Isaac Pye can come and pull me off yer.' I says, 'Okay *Prick Cheese, you* say where.' Wilcox says, 'T'morrer mornin'. The Hollow Log. Nine-thirty.' I says, 'Better order an ambulance, *Turd Burglar*. I'll be there.' Wilcox just says, 'Good' and walks out."

Ant Little said, "Wilcox's *crazy*. You're gonna *cream* him, Grant."

"Yeah," said Darren Croome. "Course you are."

Great news. Ross Wilcox's building up a sort of gang at school and he's made it pretty clear he's got it in for me. Grant Burch is one of the hardest kids in the third year. Wilcox getting his face kicked in'd label him as a loser and a leper.

"What's the time now, Phelps?"

Phelps checked his watch. "Quarter to ten, Grant."

Ant Little said, "Chickened out, I reckon."

Grant Burch flobbed again. "We'll stay till ten. Then we're off down Wellington Gardens to invite Wilcox out to play. Nobody gets away with being that arsey to *me*."

Phelps said, "What about his dad, Grant?"

"What about his dad, Phelps?"

"Didn't he put Wilcox's mum in hospital?"

"I ain't scared of a bent mechanic. Give us another fag."

Phelps mumbled, "Only Woodbines left, Grant, sorry."

"Woodbines?"

"They're all my mum had in her handbag. Sorry."

"What about your old man's Number Sixes?"

"'Fraid there weren't any. Soz."

"God! All *right*. Gi'us the Woodbines. Taylor, want a smoke?"

" 'Given up,' " Ant Little said sneerily, "ain't yer, Taylor?"

"Started up again," I told Grant Burch, scrambling up the embankment.
Dean Moran helped me over the muddy lip. "All right?"

I told Moran "All right" back.

"Yee-*HAAAAAAR!*" Squelch straddled the Hollow Log like a horse and
whipped his own bum with a whippy stick. "Gonna kick dat boy's *ass* to da
middle o' next week!" He must've got it off some film.

A middle-ranking kid like me shouldn't refuse an invitation from an older
kid like Grant Burch. I held the Woodbine like my cousin'd shown me, and
pretended to take a deep drag. (Actually I kept the smoke in my mouth.) Ant
Little was hoping I'd cough my guts up. But I just breathed out the smoke like
I'd done it a million times before, and passed the cigarette to Darren Croome.
(Why does something as forbidden as smoking taste so foul?) I glanced at
Grant Burch to see how impressed he was but he was looking toward the kiss-
ing gate over by Saint Gabriel's. "Look who it flamin' isn't."

The fighters sized each other up in front of the Hollow Log. Grant Burch's
got an inch or two over Ross Wilcox, but Ross Wilcox is knucklier. Gary
Drake and Wayne Nashend'd come as his lieutenants. Wayne Nashend used
to be one of the Upton Punks, briefly became an Upton New Romantic, but
now he's firmly an Upton Mod. He's an utter thicko. Gary Drake's no thicko,
though. He's in my form at school. But Gary Drake's Ross Wilcox's cousin so
they're always dossing about together.

"Fuck off home to Mummy," Grant Burch told Ross Wilcox, "while you
still can." (A dirty opener, that. Everyone knows about Ross Wilcox's mum.)

Ross Wilcox gobbed at Grant Burch's feet. "*Make* me fuck off."

Grant Burch looked at the gob on his trainers. "You're gonna be cleaning
that off with your fucking tongue, *Piss Flaps*."

"*Make* me."

"Don't make shit, it comes natural."

"Really original line, that, *Burch*."

Hate smells of burnt dead fireworks.

At school, scraps are ace fun. We all scream, "SCRAAAAAAAAAAAAAA-
AAAAAPPP" and rush to the epicenter. Mr. Carver or Mr. Whitlock wades
in, tossing aside members of the audience. But this morning's scrap was more

cold-blooded. My own body flinched under the punches, automatically, like how your leg hoists itself when you're watching a high jumper on TV. Grant Burch body-tackled Ross Wilcox low and fast.

Ross Wilcox got in a weak punch, but had to squirm sideways to not get toppled.

Grant Burch clawed at Ross Wilcox's throat. *"Cunt!"*

Ross Wilcox clawed at Grant Burch's throat. *"Cunt* yer*self!"*

Ross Wilcox punched Grant Burch's head. That *hurt*.

Grant Burch got Ross Wilcox in a headlock. That *really* hurt.

Ross Wilcox was swung one way, swung the other, but Grant Burch couldn't deck him so he punched Ross Wilcox's face. Ross Wilcox managed to twist his hand up and sink his fingers into Grant Burch's face.

Grant Burch shoved Ross Wilcox and booted him in the ribs.

Straightaway they head-butted each other, like rams.

They grapplewrapped each other, garking through clenched teeth.

A crimson streak'd appeared from Grant Burch's nose. It smeared Ross Wilcox's face.

Ross Wilcox tried to trip Grant Burch.

Grant Burch countertripped Ross Wilcox.

Ross Wilcox countercountertripped Grant Burch.

By now, they'd three-legged themselves to the lip of the embankment.

"Watch it!" Gary Drake shouted. "You're right at the edge!"

Knotted round each other, they teetered, clutched, swayed.

Over they went.

At the foot of the embankment, Ross Wilcox'd already got to his feet. Grant Burch was half-sitting up, cradling his right hand in his left and squinting with agony. *Shit*, I thought. Blood and soil clotted Grant Burch's face.

"Aw," mocked Ross Wilcox. "Had enough, now, have we?"

"My wrist's *bust*." Grant Burch grimaced. "Yer fuckin' *wanker!*"

Ross Wilcox flobbed, dead casual. "Looks to me like you've lost then, ain't yer?"

"I've not fuckin' *lost*, yer fuckin' wanker, it's a fuckin' *draw!*"

Ross Wilcox grinned up at Gary Drake and Wayne Nashend. "Grant *Piss Flaps* Burch calls *this* a 'draw'! Well, let's carry on with Round Two then, shall we, hey? Settle this 'draw' shall we, eh?"

Grant Burch's only hope was to turn his defeat into an accident. "Oh, *sure* Wilcox, yeah, with a bust wrist, *course* I will."

"Want me to bust yer other wrist, then, do yer?"

"Oh that'd be *rock* hard of yer!" Grant Burch managed to get up. "Phelps! We're *leaving*!"

"Yeah, yeah, off yer go. Home to Mummy."

Grant Burch didn't risk saying, *At least I've got one.* Instead, he glared up at his frozen, pale servant. "PHELPS! I just *told* yer, yer deaf-aid, WE'RE LEAVING!"

Philip Phelps jerked into life and slid down the embankment on his arse. But Ross Wilcox blocked his path. "Don't you get *tired* of that pillock ordering you about, Phil? He doesn't *own* yer. You *can* tell him to fuck off. What's he going to do?"

Grant Burch yelled, "PHELPS! I ain't tellin' yer *again!*"

Phelps thought about it for a moment, I'm sure. But then he dodged round Ross Wilcox and jogged off after his master. With his good hand, Grant Burch flashed Ross Wilcox a V over his shoulder.

"Oy!" Ross Wilcox picked up a clod of earth. "Forgot yer breakfast, yer bumboys!"

Grant Burch must've ordered Phelps not to turn round.

The soil bomb's trajectory looked perfect.

It was. It exploded on the back of Phelps's neck.

It'd been a risky fight for Ross Wilcox, but it'd gone brilliantly. Burch's scalp makes Wilcox *the* hardest kid in the second year. He'll get invited to be a member of Spooks, most like. He settled on his throne on the Hollow Log. Ant Little said, "I *knew* you'd have Grant Burch, Ross!"

"Me too," said Darren Croome. "We was saying, on our way here."

Ant Little got out a packet of No. 6's. "Smoke?"

Ross Wilcox swiped the entire pack.

Ant Little looked pleased. "Where'd yer get yer ear stud put in, Ross?"

"Did it myself. Needle, candle to sterilize it. Hurts like shit but it's a piece o' piss."

Gary Drake stabbed a Swan Vespa against the bark to light it.

"You two . . ." Wayne Nashend squinted down at Dean Moran and me. "You was here with Burch, wasn't yer?"

"I didn't even *know* about the scrap," Dean Moran protested. "I'm off to White-Leaved Oak, me. To stay with my gran."

"*Walking?*" Ant Little squinted. "White-Leaved Oak's over the Malverns. It'll take ages. Why doesn't yer old man drive yer?"

Moran looked awkward. "He's ill."

"He's on another of his benders," Wayne Nashend said, "ain't he?"

Moran looked down.

"Then why can't yer mum drive yer?"

"Can't leave my dad, can she?"

"What about *you*," Gary Drake asked snakishly, "President Jason Taylor of the Grant Burch Arse-Slurpers Association. What are *you* doing here?"

You can't just say, "I'm out for a walk" 'cause walks are gay.

"Yee-*HAAAAAR!*" Squelch straddled a limb of the Hollow Log like a horse and whipped his own bum with a whippy stick. "Gonna kick dat boy's *ass* to da middle o' next week!"

"*You*"—Darren Croome flobbed—"should be in Little Malvern Loony-bin, Squelch."

"Well, Taylor?" Ross Wilcox isn't so easily distracted.

I spat out my flavorless Juicy Fruit, desperate for a way out. Hangman was gripping the root of my tongue and every letter in the alphabet was a stammer-letter.

"He's coming to my nan's too," said Dean Moran.

"You didn't tell *us* that, Taylor," accused Ant Little, "not *before* Ross kicked the shit out of that wankstain Burch."

I managed to say, "You didn't *ask*, Little."

"Me and Taylor were meeting here." Moran began heading off. "That was the plan all along. He's comin' to my gran's too. C'mon, Jason, better be off now."

The Christmas-tree plantation was dark as eclipses and whiffed of bleach. Armies of them in endless rows and files. Flies, titchy as commas, got into our eyes and nostrils. I should've thanked Moran for the lifeline he'd thrown me back by the Hollow Log, but that would've meant admitting how badly I'd needed it. Instead, I told him about the Dobermans. But it wasn't news to Moran. "Oh, Kit Harris? I knows *'im* all right. Divorced the *same* woman, three times. She must need her bloomin' *head* examinin'. Kit Harris loves one thing only and that's them dogs. He's a teacher, believe it or not."

"A *teacher*? But he's a psycho."

"Yep. At a Borstal, out Pershore way. His nickname's 'Badger,' 'cause o' that streak o' white hair. Not that anyone calls him that to his face. Once one o' the Borstal kids took a dump on the bonnet of his car. Guess how Badger found out who done it."

"How?"

"*Squeezing bamboo needles up every kid's fingernails,* one by one, till someone grassed on the kid who done it."

"No way!"

"God's honest, that is. My sister Kelly told me. Discipline's tougher at Borstals, that's why they're Borstals. At first, Badger tried to get the kid who done it expelled. But the headmaster of the Borstal wouldn't do it, 'cause if yer get expelled from a Borstal that means automatic prison. So a few weeks later, Badger organized a wide-game on Bredon Hill. At night."

"What's a wide-game?"

"Like an army game, a war game. They do 'em in the Scouts too. One side has to capture the other side's flag, stuff like that. So anyway, the next morning, the kid who'd crapped on Badger's car'd *disappeared.*"

"Where to?"

"Exactly! The headmaster told Interpol and that, the kid'd run away during the wide-game. Happens all the time at Borstals. Kelly got to the bottom of it, though. But you have to swear on your own grave you'll never tell anyone."

"I swear."

"On yer own grave."

"On my own grave."

"Kelly was in Rhydd's shop when Badger comes in. This was *three weeks* after the kid'd disappeared, okay? So. Badger buys bread and stuff. Badger's just leaving when Mr. Rhydd asks him, 'What about your Pedigree Chum for your dogs, Mr. Harris?' Badger just says, 'My boys're on a diet, Mr. Rhydd.' Dead evil, like that. 'My boys're on a diet.' Then when he's gone, Kelly over-hears Mr. Rhydd telling Pete Redmarley's old biddy that Badger hadn't bought his usual cans of Pedigree Chum for *three weeks.*"

"Uh-*huh,*" I said, not quite getting it.

"Yer don't need to be Brain of Britain to work out what Badger's Dober-mans was eating for those three weeks, right?"

"What?"

"Badger was feeding his dogs the missing kid!"

"Jesus." I actually shivered. "*Christ.*"

"So if all Badger did was put the shits up yer"—Moran slapped my shoul-der—"yer got off lightly."

A farty ditch'd flooded the bridle path and we both took a running jump. My superior athletic powers got me over. Moran soaked one foot up to his ankle.

"So where *were* you on yer way to, then, Jace?"

(Hangman blocked "Nowhere.") "Just out. For a doss."

Moran's trainer squished. "Must be heading somewhere."

"Well," I confessed, "I've heard the bridle path might lead to a tunnel, through the Malverns. Thought I might go and see if I can find it."

"The tunnel?" Moran stopped and sort of slapped my arm in disbelief. "That's where *I*'m going!"

"What happened to staying with your nan in White-Leaved Oak?"

"I'm going *there* by rediscovering the lost tunnel, see? The one the Romans built to invade Hereford."

"Romans? Tunnels?"

"How else could they kick out the blinkin' Vikings? Done my research, I have, see. Got a torch and a roll of string, and everything. *Three* tunnels go through the Malverns. One's the British Rail one for the train to Hereford. It's haunted by an engineer in orange overalls with a black stripe where the train ran over him. The second tunnel's a Ministry of Defence tunnel."

"A *what?*"

"A tunnel the Ministry of Defence dug for a nuclear bomb shelter. The entrance is in the garden center at Woolworth's in Great Malvern. Gospel. One of the garden center walls is a fake wall what hides a vault door, like in a bank. When the four-minute warning goes off, the Ministry of Defence lot at the RSRE'll be ferried up to Woolies by the military police. Councillors from Malvern Council'll be allowed in, so will Woolworth's manager and assistant manager. Then the military police — who've kept out all the panicking shoppers with their guns — they'll be allowed in. They'll grab one or two of the prettier shop assistants for breeding. Which rules my sister out, don't it? Then that door'll close and all of us'll get blown to kingdom come."

"Kelly didn't tell you all this, did she?"

"Nah, the bloke my dad buys horse shit off of for the garden, his mate's the barman at the RSRE."

It must be true then. "Jesus."

In a drift of khaki pine needles I saw antlers, like Herne the Hunter's. But it was only a branch. "S'pose we may as well join forces," I said. "Hunting the third tunnel. The lost one."

"But" — Moran kicked a pinecone but missed — "who'll do the interview with the *Malvern Gazetteer?*"

I booted a pinecone way up the gloomy path. "Both of us."

Run across a field of daisies at warp speed but keep your eyes on the ground. It's ace. Petaled stars and dandelion comets streak the green universe. Moran and I got to the barn at the far side, dizzy with intergalactic travel. I was laughing more than Moran 'cause Moran's dry trainer wasn't dry anymore, it was glistening in cow shit. Bales of straw made a ramp up to the griddly barn roof, so up we climbed. The cockerel tree you can see from my bedroom wasn't running left to right now, it was running right to left. "Skill place for a machine-gun nest, this barn," I said, displaying my military expertise.

Moran squidged off his shitty trainer and lay back.

I lay back, too. The rusty iron was warm as a hotty.

"This is the life," sighed Moran, after a bit.

"You can say that again," I said, after a bit.

"This is the life," said Moran, straight off.

I *knew* he would. "That's *so* original."

Sheep and lambs were bleating, fields behind us.

A tractor was chuntering, fields ahead.

"Does *your* old man ever get pissed?" Moran asked.

If I said yes I'd be lying, but if I said no it'd look gay. "He has a drink or two, when my Uncle Brian visits."

"Not a drink or two. I mean does he get so *fucking plastered* he . . . he can hardly speak?"

"No."

That *no* turned the three feet between us into three miles.

"No." Moran'd shut his eyes. "Don't look the type, your dad."

"But yours doesn't, either. He's really friendly and funny . . ."

An airplane glinted, mercury bright in the dark high blue.

"Maxine calls it like this, she calls it 'Daddy's going dark.' She's right. He goes dark. He starts . . . y'know, on a few cans, and gets loud and makes shite jokes we have to laugh at. Shouts and stuff. The neighbors bang on the wall to complain. Dad bangs back, call's 'em all the names under the sun . . . then he locks himself in his room but he's got bottles in there. We hear them smash. One by one. Then he sleeps it off. Then afterwards, when he's all so sorry, it's all, '*Oh, I'm never touchin' the stuff again . . .*' That's almost worse . . . Tell you what it's like, it's like this whiny shitty nasty weepy man who isn't my dad takes my dad over for however long the bender lasts, but only I—and Mum and Kelly and Sally and Max—know that it *isn't him*. The rest of the world doesn't know that, see. They just say, *Frank Moran's showing his true colors that is.* But it ain't." Moran twisted his head at me. "But it is. But it *ain't.* But it is. But it *ain't.* Oh, how am *I* s'posed to know?"

A painful minute went by.

Green is made of yellow and blue, nothing else, but when you *look* at green, where've the yellow and the blue gone? Somehow this is to do with Moran's dad. Somehow this is to do with everyone and everything. But too many things'd've gone wrong if I'd tried to say this to Moran.

Moran sniffed, "Fancy a nice cool bottle of Woodpecker?"

"Cider? You've brought cider?"

"No. My dad drunk 'em all. *But—*" Moran fumbled in his bag. "I've got a can of Irn-Bru."

Irn-Bru's fizzy liquid bubble gum, but I said, "Sure" 'cause I hadn't brought any drink myself and Irn-Bru's better than nothing. I'd imagined I could drink from fresh springs but the only water I'd seen so far was that farty ditch.

The Irn-Bru exploded in Moran's hand like a grenade. "Shit!"

"Watch out with that Irn-Bru. It'll be all shaken up."

"You don't flamin' say so!" Moran gave me first swig, as he licked his hand clean. In return, I gave him some Cadbury's Caramel. It'd oozed out of its wrapper, but we picked off the bits of pocket fluff and it tasted okay. I got a hay fever attack and sneezed ten or twenty times into a nuggety hanky.

A vaportrail gashed the sky.

But the sky healed itself. Without fuss.

CRAAAAAAWWWKKK!

I'd slid halfway down the curve of the barn roof, clattering between dreaming and waking, before I got my balance back.

Three monster crows sat in a row, where Moran had last been.

Of Moran there was no sign.

The crows' beaks were daggers. Their oily eyes had cruel plans.

"Piss off!"

Crows know when they're a match for you.

Saint Gabriel's bell rang eleven or twelve times; the crows made me too uneasy to keep count. Tiny darts of water hit my face and neck. The weather had turned while I'd been sleeping. The Malverns'd disappeared behind wings of rain, beating just fields away. The crows hang-glided up and off.

Moran wasn't inside the barn, either. Obviously he'd decided not to share the front page of the *Malvern Gazetteer*. What a traitor! But if he wanted to play Scott of the Antarctic versus Amundsen the Norwegian, that was fine by me. Moran's never beaten me at anything in his *life*.

The barn smelt of armpits, hay, and piss.

Rain began its blitz, tranging bullets off the roof and strafing the puddles round the barn. (Serve Moran the Deserter right if he got a drenching and caught pneumonia.) Rain erased the twentieth century. Rain turned the world to whites and grays.

Over the sleeping giant of the Malvern Hills, a double rainbow linked the Worcestershire Beacon with the British Camp. Ancient Britons got massacred by the Romans there. The melony sun dripped steamy brightness. I set off at a fast yomp, jogging fifty, walking fifty. I decided, if I passed Moran, I wouldn't say a word to him. Cut the traitor dead. The wet turf squeaked beneath my trainers. I climbed a shaky gate and crossed a paddock with jumps for horses made from police cones and stripey poles. Past the paddock was a farmyard. Two silage towers shone like Victorian Apollo spacecraft. Trombone flowers snaked up trellises and a flaky sign read, HORSE MANURE FOR SALE. A cocky rooster eyed its hens. Rain-soggy sheets and white pillowcases hung on a washing line. Frilly panties and bras too. A mossy track disappeared over the rise, toward the main road to Malvern. Passing a stable, I peered into the hot, manure-reeky dark.

Three horses, I made out. One tossed its head, one snorted, one stared at me. I hurried on. If a bridle path goes through a farmyard it can't be private but farmyards definitely don't feel public. I'm afraid of hearing *Trespasser! I'm going to give you a prosecutin' you'll never forget!* (I used to think trespassing was about heaven and hell, because of the Lord's Prayer.)

So anyway, over the next gate was this medium-sized field. A John Deere tractor was plowing it into slimy furrows. Seagulls hovered behind the plow, plucking easy fat worms. I hid till the tractor was headed away from the bridle path.

Then began legging it across, like an SAS agent.

"TAYLOR!"

I'd got noosed before I'd even reached a sprint.

Dawn Madden sat in the cockpit of an ancient tractor, whittling a stick. She wore a bomber jacket and mud-starred Doc Martens with red laces.

I steadied my breath. "All right"—I meant to call her "Madden" 'cause she'd called me "Taylor"—"Dawn."

"Where's"—her knife shaved stringy loops of wood—"the fire?"

"Huh?"

Dawn Madden mimicked my *Huh?* "Why're you running?"

Her oil-black hair's sort of punky. She must use gel. I'd love to gel her gel in for her. "I like to run. Sometimes. Just because."

"Oh aye? And what brings *you* so far up the bridle path then?"

"No reason. I'm just out. For a doss."

"Then"—she pointed to the bonnet of the tractor—"you can doss there."

I badly wanted to obey her. "Why?" I badly didn't want to obey her.

Her lipstick was Wine Gum red. "'Cause I'm telling you to."

"So." I scrambled up the front tire. "What are *you* doing here?"

"I *do* live here, y'know."

The wet bonnet of the tractor made my arse wet. "That farmhouse? Back there?"

Dawn Madden unzipped her bomber jacket. "That farmhouse. Back there." Her crucifix was chunky and black like a Goth's and nestled between her subtle breasts.

"Thought you lived in that house by the pub."

"Used to. Too noisy. And Isaac Pye, the landlord, he's a total slimeball. Not that *he*"—Dawn Madden nodded at the tractor plowing the field—"is much of an improvement."

"Who's he?"

"Official stepfather. That house is his house. Don't you know *anything*, Taylor? Mum and I live there now. Got married last year."

Actually now I remembered. "What's he like?"

"Brains of a bull." She peered at me round an invisible curtain. "Not only the brains, judging by the racket *they* make some nights." Stewy air stroked Dawn Madden's white chocolate throat.

"Are those ponies in the stable yours?"

"Have a good snoop round, did we?"

Her stepfather's tractor was heading back this way.

"I only looked into the stable. Honest."

She got back to her knife and stick. "Horses cost a fortune to keep." Whittle, whittle, whittle. "*That man's* letting the riding school keep them there while they're doing some rebuilding. Anything else you want to know?"

Oh, five hundred things. "What are you making?"

"An arrow."

"What do you want an arrow for?"

"To go with my bow."

"What do you want a bow and arrow for?"

"What-what-*what*, what-*what*-what-what?" (For one horrifying moment I thought she was taking the piss out of my stammer but I think it was more general.) "All questions with you, ain't it, Taylor? My bow and arrow's to hunt boys and kill them. The world's better off without them. Spurty scum, that's what little boys are made of."

"Gee, thanks."

"You're welcome."

"Can I see your knife?"

Dawn Madden tossed her knife, right at me. It was a sheer fluke that it was the blade's handle that hit my rib and not its fang.

"Madden!"

Her stare said, *What?* Dawn Madden's eyes are dark honey.

"That could've stuck right into me!"

Dawn Madden's eyes are dark honey. "Oh, poor Taylor."

The clackering tractor reached us and began a slow turn. Dawn Madden's stepfather beamed hate rays my way. Rusty earth sluiced round the blades of the plow.

Dawn Madden did a spazzo yokel voice at the tractor. " '*Made o' moy flesh an' blood or not, young missy, we're going to have more* respect *in this 'ouse or you'll be out on your bony arse an' don't you go thinkin' Oi'm bluffin' yer 'cos I never bluff no one!*' "

Her knife's handle was warm and a sticky from her grip. The blade was sharp enough to hack off a limb. "Nice knife."

Dawn Madden asked, "Hungry?"

"Depends."

"Pic*ky.*" Dawn Madden unpeeled a squashed Danish pastry from a paper bag. "Won't turn your snout up at a bit of this, though, right?" The girl tore a bit off and waved it at me.

Its icing glistened. "Okay then."

"Here, Taylor! Here, doggy! *Come!* Good boy!"

I crawled over the bonnet toward her, on all fours. Not doggily, but carefully, in case she swatted me into the nettles. You never know with Dawn

Madden. As she leaned toward me I saw the bumplets of her nipples. No bra. My hand moved toward her.

"Paws down! In your teeth, doggy!"

She fed me like that. Arrow to mouth.

Lemony icing, cinnamony dough, raisins sweet and sharp.

Dawn Madden ate too. I saw the cud pulp on her tongue. Closer now, on her crucifix I saw a skinny Jesus. Jesus'd be warmed by her body. Lucky guy. Pretty soon the Danish was all gone. Delicately, she spiked the cherry on the tip of her arrow. Delicately, I lifted it off with my teeth.

The sun went in.

"Taylor!" Dawn Madden peered at her arrow's tip. Her voice went furious. "You *stole* my cherry!"

It stuck in my throat. "You . . . gave it to me."

"You *stole* my fucking cherry and now you've got to *pay* for it!"

"Dawn, you—"

"Since when've *you* been allowed to call me *Dawn?*"

The same game, a different game, or no game?

She pricked my Adam's apple with her arrow. Dawn Madden leaned in so close I could smell the sugar on her breath. "Do I *look* like I'm joking, Jason Taylor?"

That arrow was *really* sharp. I probably could've swatted it off before she could puncture my windpipe. Probably. But it wasn't that simple. For one thing, I had a boner as big as a Doberman.

"You've got to *pay* for what you've taken. That's the *law.*"

"I don't have any money."

"Then think hard, Taylor. How else can you pay me?"

"I—" One dimple. Tiny hairs velvet the groove above her lip. Imp's nose. Petaled lips. Hook smile. A reflected pair of me looking out from her bad doe eyes. "I—I've got a pack of fruit Polos in my pocket. But they're all glued to-gether. You'd have to smash them with a rock."

A spell broke. The arrow fell from my throat.

Dawn Madden climbed back into the tractor's driving seat, bored.

"What?"

Her answer was this disgusted gaze, like I'd turned into a pair of flares on a reject rack in Tewkesbury Market.

I wanted the arrow back, now. "*What?*"

"If you're not off our land by the time I count to twenty"—Dawn Madden crumpled a stick of Wrigley's Spearmint into her beautiful mouth—"I'll tell my stepfather you groped me. If you're not off by the time I count to thirty, I'll tell him you"—her tongue licked the word—"touched me up. Swear to God."

"But I never *touched* you!"

"My stepfather keeps a shotgun above the kitchen dresser. He might mistake *you* for a wickle fwuffy wabbit, Taylor. One—two—three—"

The bridle path wandered into this once-upon-a-time orchard. Brittle thistles and fluffy grass'd grown elbow-high, so you waded rather than walked. I was still thinking about Dawn Madden. I didn't understand. She must sort of fancy me. She wouldn't've given her only Danish pastry to just any kid who happened along. And I sure as hell fancied Dawn Madden. Fancying girls's dangerous, though. Not dangerous, but not simple. It *can* be dangerous. Kids at school *rip* the piss out of you, at first. "Ooh, a *baby*'s on its way," they say, if they see you holding hands in the corridor. Boys who fancy the girl might pick a scrap with you to show her she's going out with a squirt. Then, once you're an official couple like Lee Biggs and Michelle Tirley, you've got to endure her friends writing both your initials plus "4 ever" in arrowed hearts all over their rough books. Teachers join in. When Mr. Whitlock was doing hermaphroditic reproduction in worms last term, he called one worm "Worm Lee" and the other "Worm Michelle." Us boys thought it was a bit funny but the girls *screamed* with laughter like the TV audience on *Happy Days*. 'Cept for Michelle Tirley herself, who turned *beetroot*, hid her face in her hands, and wept. Mr. Whitlock took the piss out of her for that, too.

There're gaps between me and Dawn Madden. Kingfisher Meadows's the poshest estate in Black Swan Green, most kids reckon. Her stepfather's farmhouse is the opposite of posh. I'm in 2KM, the top class at school. She's in 2LP, second from bottom. These gaps aren't easy to ignore. There are rules.

Then there's sexual intercourse. You don't do it in Biology till the third year. A diagram in a textbook of an erect penis in a vagina is one thing, but actually *doing* it, that's another. The only actual vagina I've seen was on a greasy photo Neal Brose charged us 5p to look at. It was a baby kangaroo-prawn in its mother's hairy pouch. I almost vommed up my Mars bar and Outer Spacers.

I've never even kissed anyone.

Dawn Madden's eyes are dark honey.

A conker tree'd erupted out of the earth and'd flexed out millions of strong arms and strong legs. Someone'd hung a tire swing off one bough. The tire spun gently as the earth spun under it. Rainwater'd pooled inside but I tipped it out and had a go. Weightlessness orbiting Alpha Centauri'd be best, but weightlessness on a swing isn't bad. If Moran'd been there too it'd've been an ace laugh. After a bit I shimmied up the frayed rope to see how climbable the tree was. Once you were up, it was *dead* climbable. I even found the ruins of a treehouse. Donkey's yonks'd gone by since it'd seen active service, mind. Higher up, I crawled along a branch and peered out of the green bell. You could see for *miles*. Back toward Black Swan Green, Dawn Madden's farm silos, a spiral staircase of smoke, the Christmas-tree plantation, Saint Gabriel's spire, and its two nearly-as-tall redwoods.

With my Swiss Army knife I carved this in the ribbly bark.

The sap on my blade smelt green. Miss Throckmorton used to tell us that people who carve things on trees are the wickedest sorts of vandals 'cause they're not only making graffiti, they're hurting living beings too. Miss Throckmorton might be right but she can't've ever been a thirteen-year-old boy who met a girl like Dawn Madden. *One day,* I thought, *I'll bring her up to show her this.* I'd do my first kiss with her. Right here. She'd touch me. Right here.

Round the other side of the conker tree, I looked at what lay up the bridle path. A lane snaking to Marl Bank and Castlemorton, fields, more fields, a glimpse of an old gray turret rising above the firs. Line of pylons. You could pick out details on the Malvern Hills now. Sun flashed off cars on the Wells Road. Termite-sized walkers crossing Perseverance Hill. Underneath, some-where, ran the third tunnel. I ate my block of Wensleydale and broken Jacob's crackers, wishing I'd brought some water. I climbed back to the tire-swing rope and was just about to shimmy down when I heard a man's voice and a woman's voice.

"See?" Tom Yew, I recognized straight off. "*Told* you it was just a bit further."

"Yeah, Tom," answered the woman, "about twenty times."

"*You* said you wanted somewhere private."

"I didn't mean halfway to Wales." Now I saw Debby Crombie. Debby Crombie I've never spoken to, but Tom Yew's Nick Yew's older brother, on leave from the Royal Navy. I could've just called out "Hi!" and come down the rope and it'd've been fine. But being invisible was fun. I retreated back along the bough to a fork in the trunk and waited till they'd gone.

But they didn't. "This is it." Tom Yew stopped right by the swing. "The Yew Boys' Very Own Horse Chestnut Tree."

"Won't there be ants and bees and things here?"

"It's called 'nature,' Debs. You get it a lot in the countryside."

Debby Crombie unspread a rug in a dell between two roots.

Even now I could've (should've) let them know I was there.

I tried to. But before I'd worked out an excuse without a stammer-word, Tom Yew and Debby Crombie'd lain down on the rug and started snogging. His fingers undid the buttons up her lavender dress, one at a time, from her knees to her sunburnt neck.

If I said anything *now*, I'd be dead meat.

The conker tree swished, creaked, and rocked.

Debby Crombie stuck her finger into Tom Yew's fly and murmured, "Hello, Sailor." That made them giggle so much they had to stop snogging. Tom Yew reached for his backpack, got out two bottles of beer, and flipped off their caps with his Swiss Army knife. (Mine's red. His is black.)

They clinked bottles. Tom Yew said, "Here's to—"

"—me, gorgeous me."

"*Me*, wonderful me."

"I said it first."

"Okay. You."

They swigged their brown beery sunshine.

"And," Debby Crombie added, seriously, "a safe tour of duty."

"*Course* it's safe, Debs! Five months cruising round the Adriatic, the Aegean, the Suez, and the Gulf? Worst that'll happen to *me* is sunburn."

"Ah, but once you're on board the *Coventry*"—Debby Crombie pouted, or pretended to—"you'll forget all about your pining sweetheart back in boring old Worcestershire. You'll go out on the razz in Athens and pick up V.D. from some floozy Greek temptress called . . ."

"Called what?"

". . . Iannos."

" 'Iannos' is a boy's name. It's Greek for 'John.' "

"Yeah, but you'd only find that out *after* he'd filled you full of ouzo and strapped you to his bed frame."

Tom Yew lay back grinning and looked up *straight* at me.

Thank God he wasn't looking at what he was looking at. Cobras can spot prey moving from half a mile away. But if you don't move a *muscle*, they can't see you, even from five feet. It was that that saved me this afternoon.

"Used to climb this very tree, y'know, when Nick was a wee nipper. One summer, we built a tree house. Wonder if it's still up there . . ."

Debby Crombie was already stroking his groin. "Nothing wee about *this* nipper, Thomas William Yew." Debby Crombie unpeeled Tom Yew's Harley-Davidson T-shirt and flung it away. His back's glazed and muscly like Action Man's. He's got a blue swordfish tattooed on one shoulder.

She squirmed out of her unbuttoned lavender dress.

If Dawn Madden's breasts were a pair of Danishes, Debby Crombie's got two Space Hoppers. Each armed with a gribbly nipple. Tom Yew kissed them in turn and his saliva glistened in the April sun. I *know* watching was wrong but I couldn't not. Tom Yew slipped off her red panties and stroked the cressy hair there.

"If you want me to stop, Madam Crombie, you have to say now."

"Oooh, Master Yew," she crooed, "don't you *dare*."

Tom Yew got on her and sort of jiggled there and she gasped like a Chinese burn and wrapped her legs round him, froggily. Now he moved up and down, Man-from-Atlantisishly. His silver chain jiggled on his neck.

Now her grubby soles met like they were praying.

Now his skin was glazed in roast-pork sweat.

Now she made a noise like a tortured Moomintroll.

Now Tom Yew's body jerkjerked judderily jackknifed and a noise like a ripping cable tore out of him. Once more, like he'd been booted in the balls.

Her fingernails'd sunk salmony welts into his arse.

Debby Crombie's mouth made a perfect O.

A chime from Saint Gabriel's for one o'clock, or maybe two, eddied this far. Moran the Deserter'd be *miles* up the bridle path by now. My only hope was if he got his leg caught in a rusty badger trap. He'd *beg* me to go and get help. I'd say, "Well, Moran, why don't I *think* about it?"

Debby Crombie and Tom Yew *still* hadn't unglued themselves. She was just drowsing, but Tom Yew was snoring. A red admiral fluttered onto the small of his back to drink from the puddle of sweat there.

I felt hungry and nervy and sick and jealous and sluggy and shamed and many things. Not proud and not pleased and not like I ever wanted to do *that*. The noises they'd made weren't quite human. The breeze lullabied the conker tree and the conker tree lullabied me.

"*GaaaAAA!*" Tom Yew shouted. "*FAAAAAAAAA!*"

Debby Crombie shrieked too. Her eyes were open and white.

He'd jumped off her and'd fallen onto his side.

"Tom! Tom! It's okay it's *okay* it's OKAY!"

"Fuck fuck fuck fuck fuck fuck *fuck*."

"Darling! It's Debs! It's okay! It's a nightmare! Only a nightmare!"

Nuddy sunbaked Tom Yew shut his scared eyes, nodded that he understood, crouched against a tentacle-root and gripped his throat. That shout must've *torn* his vocal cords.

"It's all right." Debby Crombie shuffled her lavender dress on and hugged Tom Yew like a mother. "Darling, you're trembling! Put some clothes on. It's all right now."

"Debs, I'm sorry." His voice was crumpled. "Must've scared you."

She spread his shirt over his shoulders. "What was it, Tom?"

"Nothing."

"Oh like hell it was nothing. Tell me!"

"I was on the *Coventry*. There was enemy fire . . ."

"Go on. Go on."

Tom Yew clenched his eyes shut and shook his head.

"Go *on*, Tom!"

"No more, Debs. It was too . . . too fucking real."

"But Tom. I *love* you. I want to know."

"Yeah, and I love *you* too much to *tell* you and that's that. C'mon on. Let's get back to the village. Before some kid sees us."

Cauliflowers grew in neat rows between pointy ridges. I was halfway across when the planes came roaring, demolishing the sky over the Severn Valley. Tornados fly over our school several times a day, so I was ready to cover my ears with my hands. But I *wasn't* ready for *three* Hawker Harrier Jump Jets, close enough to the ground to hit with a cricket ball. The slam of noise was *incredible*! I bent into a tight ball and peeped out. The Harriers curved before they smashed into the Malverns, just, and flew off toward Birmingham, screaming under Soviet radar height. When World War III comes, it'll be MiGs stationed in Warsaw or East Germany screaming under NATO radar. Dropping bombs on people like us. On English cities, towns, and villages like Worcester, Malvern, and Black Swan Green.

Dresden, the Blitz, and Nagasaki.

I stayed curled up till the roar of the Harriers *finally* sank under the hum of distant cars and nearby trees. The earth's a door, if you press your ear against it. Mrs. Thatcher was on TV yesterday talking to a bunch of schoolkids about Cruise Missiles. "The only way to stop a playground bully," she said, as sure of her truth as the blue of her eyes, "is to show to the bully that if *he* thumps *you*, then *you* can jolly well *thump him back* a lot harder!"

But the threat of being thumped back never stopped Ross Wilcox and Grant Burch scrapping, did it?

I brushed straw and dirt off me, and carried on walking till I came to an old-style bathtub in the corner of the next field. From all the hoofed-up mud, I guessed it was used as a feeding trough. In the tub a giant fertilizer bag was covering something. Curious, I pulled the fertilizer bag away.

Here was the dirt-smeared corpse of a boy my age.

This corpse then sat up and lunged at my throat.

"ASHES TO ASHES!" it gibbered. "*DUST TO DUST!*"

One *whole* minute later, Dean Moran was *still* pissing his pants. "Should o' seen yer face!" he wheezed through his laughter. "Should o' *seen* it!"

"Okay, okay," I said, yet again. "Congratulations. You're a genius."

"Looked like you *cacked yer cacks*!"

"Yeah, Moran. You got me really well. *Okay.*"

"*Best* April Fool I *ever* done!"

"So why did you bugger off? I thought we were s'posed to be looking for the tunnel together?"

Moran calmed down. "Ah, y'know . . ."

"No. I don't. Thought we had a deal."

"I didn't want to wake you up," Moran said, awkwardly.

This is about his dad, said Unborn Twin.

Moran'd saved me from Gary Drake, so I let it go. "So are you still on for it? The tunnel? Or are you going to sneak off again on a solo run?"

"I waited here for yer to catch us up, didn't I?"

The unused field had a scrubby rise hiding its far side. "You'll never guess who *I* saw back there," I began telling Moran.

Moran answered, "Dawn Madden, on a tractor."

Oh. "You saw her too?"

"Flamin' nutcase, is that girl. Made me climb up her tractor."

"Did she?"

"Yeah! Made me arm-wrestle her. My Danish for her knife."

"Who won?"

"*I* did! She's only a girl! But then she took my Danish anyway. Told me to bugger off her stepfather's land or she'd get him to turn his shotgun on me. Flamin' nutcase, that girl."

Say if you hunt for Christmas presents in mid-December, find what you're hoping to get, but then on Christmas Day there's no sign of it in your pillowcase. That's how I felt. "Well, *I* saw something better than Dawn Madden on a tractor, *any* day of the week."

"Oh aye?"

"Tom Yew and Debby Crombie."

"Don't tell me!" Moran's got toothy gaps. "She got her tits out?"

"Well—"

The chain of gossip laid itself out link by link. I'd tell Moran. Moran'd tell his sister Kelly. Kelly'd tell Pete Redmarley's sister Ruth. Ruth Redmarley'd tell Pete Redmarley. Pete Redmarley'd tell Nick Yew. Nick Yew'd tell Tom Yew. Tom Yew'd come round to my house this evening on his Suzuki 150cc, tie me in a sack, and drown me in the lake in the woods.

" 'Well' what?"

"Actually, they just snogged."

"Should've sticked around, yer should've." Moran performed his tongue-up-his-nostril trick. "Might've seen a bit o' crump."

Bluebells swarmed in pools of light where the sun got through the trees. The air smelt of them. Wild garlic smelt of toasted phlegm. Blackbirds sang like they'd die if they didn't. Birdsong's the thoughts of a wood. Beautiful, it was, but boys aren't allowed to say "beautiful" 'cause it's the gayest word going. The bridle path narrowed to single file. I let Moran go ahead as a body shield. (I didn't read *Warlord* for all those years without learning something about survival techniques.) So when Moran suddenly stopped I walked smack into him.

Moran had his finger on his lip. Here was a pruney man in a turquoise smock, about twenty paces up the bridle path. The pruney man gazed up from the bottom of a well of brightness and buzzing that, we saw, was made of bees.

"What's he doing?" whispered Moran.

Praying, I nearly said. "No idea."

"A wild hive," Moran whispered, "above him. On that oak. See it?"

I didn't. "Is he a beekeeper, d'you reckon?"

Moran didn't answer at first. The bee man didn't have a beekeeper's mask, though bees coated his smock and face. Just watching made my skin itch and twitch. His scalp'd been shaved and had sort of socket-scars. His torn shoes were more like slippers. "Dunno. Think we can get past him?"

"S'pose," I asked, remembering a horror film about bees, "they swarm?"

This half path snaked off the bridle path right where we were. Moran and I both had the same idea. Moran went first, which isn't as brave as it looks when the danger's behind you. And after a couple of twists and turns he spun around, anxious, and hissed, "Listen!"

Bees? Footsteps? Growing louder?

Definitely!

We ran for our lives, crashing through wave after wave of waxy leaves and clawed holly. The rooty ground rocked and tilted and rose and fell.

In a boggy pocket smothered by drapes of ivy and mistletoe, me and Moran collapsed, too knackered to take another step. I didn't like it there. A strangler'd take someone there to strangle and bury, it was that sort of edgy hollow. Me and Moran listened for sounds of pursuit. It's hard to hold your breath when you've got a stitch.

But the bees weren't following us. Neither was the bee man.

Maybe it'd just been the wood, scaring us for its own amusement.

Moran snorted the phlegm back from his nose and swallowed it. "Reckon we lost him."

"Reckon so. But where's the bridle path gone?"

Squeezing through a missing slat in a mossy fence, we found ourselves at the bottom of a lumpy lawn. Molehills mounded up here and there. A big, silent mansion with turrety things watched us from the top of the slope. A peardrop sun dissolved in a sloped pond. Superheated flies grandprixed over the water. Trees at the height of their blossom bubbled dark cream by a rotted bandstand. On a sort of terrace running round the mansion were jugs of lemon and orange squash just left there, on trestle tables. As we watched, the breeze flicked over a leaning tower of paper cups. Some bowled across the lawn in our direction. Not a soul moved.

Not a soul.

"God," I said to Moran, "I'd *die* for a cup of that squash."

"Me too. Must be a spring fête or somethin'."

"Yeah, but where're all the people?" My mouth was salty and crusted as crisps. "It can't've started yet. Let's just go and help ourselves. If someone sees us we can act like we were going to pay. It'll only be two pence or five pence."

Moran didn't like the plan either. "Okay."

But we were so parched. "Come on then."

Druggy pom-pom bees hovered in the lavender.

"Quiet, ain't it?" Moran's murmur was too loud.

"Yeah." Where were the fête stalls? The spinning wheel to win Pomagne? The eggshell-in-sand-tray treasure hunt? The lob-the-Ping-Pong-ball-into-the-wine-glass stall?

Up close, the mansion windows showed us nothing but ourselves in the mirrored garden. The jug of orange squash had ants drowning, so Moran held the paper cups while I poured the lemon. The jug weighed a ton and its ice cubes clinked. It froze my hands. There're tons of stories where bad things happen to strangers who help themselves to food and drink.

"Cheers." Moran and I pretended to clink our cups before we drank.

The squash turned my mouth cold and wet as December and my body went *Ah*.

The mansion cracked its sides open and men and women spilt through the doors after their own babble. Already our escape route was being cut off. Most of the mansion were dressed in turquoise smocks, same as the bee man. Some crunched-up ones were being pushed in wheelchairs by nurses in nurse uniforms. Others moved by themselves, but jerkily, like broken robots.

With a shudder of horror, I got it.

"Little Malvern Loonybin!" I whispered at Moran.

But Moran wasn't next to me. I just glimpsed him, across the lawn, as he squeezed back through the missing slat. Maybe he thought I was right behind him, or maybe he'd left me in the lurch. But if *I* tried to scarper and got caught, it'd mean we'd nicked the squash. Mum and Dad'd be told I was a thief. Even if I didn't get caught, they might send men with dogs after us.

So I had no choice. I had to stay to find someone to pay.

"Augustin Moans has run away!" A nurse with broomy hair ran slap-bang into me. "The soup was piping hot, but he couldn't be found!"

"Are you talking about"—I swallowed—"the man in the woods? The man with the bees? He's over there." I gestured in the right direction. "Back on the bridle path. I can show you if you want."

"Augustin Moans!" Now she looked at me properly. "How *could* you?"

"No, you're mistaking me for someone else. My"—Hangman stopped me from saying "name"—"I'm called Jason."

"Do you think *I'm* one of the crazy ones? I know ex*actly* who you are! *You*, who ran off on your infantile quest, the very day after our *wedding*! For that idiot Ganache! For a playground promise! You *swore* you'd *loved* me! But then you hear an owl hoot in the firs so off you go, leaving me with child and—and—and—"

I backed off. "I can pay for the squash, if—"

"No you don't! Look!" This nightmarish nurse clasped my arm, tight. "Consequences!" The woman shoved her wrist in my face. "Consequences!" Hideous scars, *really* hideous scars, crissedcrossed the veins. "Is *this* 'love'? Is *this* cherish, honor, and obey?" Her words spattered spittle on my face, so I shut my eyes and looked away. "What—gave—you—the right—to inflict *this*—on *anyone*?"

"Rosemary!" Another nurse walked up. "Rosemary! I've *told* you about borrowing our uniforms a *hundred* times if I've told you *once*, haven't I?" She had a reassuring Scottish accent. "Haven't I?" She gave me a calm nod. "He's a bit young for you, Rosemary, and I doubt he's on our official guest list."

"And I've told *you*," Rosemary snapped, "ten *thousand* times if I've told you *never*. My name is Y*vonne*! I am Y*vonne de Galais*!" This real live lunatic of Little Malvern Towers turned back to me. "Listen to me." Rosemary's breath was Dettol and lamb. "There's no such thing as *some*thing! Why? Because *every*thing's *already* turning into something *else*!"

"Come on now," the real nurse coaxed Rosemary like you'd coax a scared horse. "Let the laddie loose now, shall we? Or shall we have to call the big fellas? Shall we, Rosemary?"

I don't know what I expected to happen next, but it isn't this. Up wells a wail from inside Rosemary, cracking her jaw open, wider and *louder* than any human cry I've ever heard *ever*, rising like a police siren, but much slower and so much sadder. Instantly, every nutter, nurse, and doctor on the lawn stands still, turned into statues. Rosemary's wail soars blastier, scorchier, lonelier. People'll be hearing it a mile away, two miles most like. Who is she howling for? For Grant Burch and his broken wrist. For Mr. Castle's wife and her huddled Nerves. For Moran's dad on his poison bender. For that Borstal kid Badger fed to his dogs. For Squelch, who came out of his mum too soon. For the bluebells the summer'll demolish. And even *if* you'd torn through massy brambles, clawed loose crumbly bricks, and'd clambered into the lost tunnel, in that booming hollowness, deep beneath the Malvern Hills, even there, for sure, this tail-chasing wail'll find you, absolutely, even there.

rocks

Nobody can *believe* it.

The newspapers weren't allowed to say which of our warships'd been hit at first, 'cause of the Official Secrets Act. But now it's on BBC and ITV. HMS *Sheffield*. An Exocet missile from a Super Étendard smashed into the frigate and "caused an unconfirmed number of serious explosions." Mum, Dad, Julia, and me all sat in the living room together (for the first time in ages) watching the box in silence. There was no film of a battle. Just a mucky photo of the ship belching smoke while Brian Hanrahan described how survivors were rescued by HMS *Arrow* or Sea King helicopters. The *Sheffield* hasn't sunk yet but in the South Atlantic winter it's just a matter of time. Forty of our men are still missing, and at least that many're badly burnt. We keep thinking about Tom Yew on the HMS *Coventry*. Terrible to admit it, but everyone in Black Swan Green felt relief that it was only the *Sheffield*. This is horrible. Till today, the Falklands's been like the World Cup. Argentina's got a strong football team, but in army terms they're only a Corned-Beef Republic. Just watching the Task Force leave Plymouth and Portsmouth three weeks ago, it was obvious Great Britain was going to *thrash* them. Brass bands on the quayside and women waving and a hundred thousand yachts and honkers and arcs of water from the fireships. We had the HMS *Hermes*, HMS *Invincible*, HMS *Illustrious*, the SAS, the SBS. Pumas, Rapiers, Sidewinders, Lynxes, Sea Skuas, Tigerfish torpedoes, Admiral Sandy Woodward. The Argie ships are tubs named after Spanish generals with stupid mustaches. Alexander

Haig couldn't admit it in public in case the Soviet Union sided with Argentina, but even Ronald Reagan was on our side.

But now, we might actually *lose*.

Our Foreign Office've been trying to restart negotiations, but the junta are telling us to get stuffed. We'll run out of ships before they run out of Exocets. That's what they're gambling on. Who's to say they're wrong? Outside Leopoldo Galtieri's palace in Buenos Aires, thousands of people are chanting, "We feel your greatness!" over and over. The noise is stopping me from sleeping. Galtieri stands on the balcony and breathes it in. Some young men jeered at our cameras. "Give up! Go home! England is sick! England is dying! History says the Malvinas are Argentina's!"

"Pack of hyenas," Dad remarked. "The British'd show a bit of decorum. People have been *killed*, for heaven's sake! That's the difference between us. Will you just *look* at them!"

Dad went to bed. He's sleeping in the spare room at the moment, 'cause of his back, though Mum told me it's 'cause he tosses and turns so much. It's probably both. They had a right barney this evening, actually over the dinner table. With me and Julia both there.

"I've been thinking—" Mum began.

"Steady now," Dad interrupted, jokily, like he used to.

"—now's rather a good time to build that rockery."

"That whattery?"

"The *rockery*, Michael."

"You've already got your shiny new Lorenzo Hussingtree kitchen." Dad used his *Be reasonable* voice. "Why do you need a mound of dirt with rocks on?"

"Nobody's talking about a mound of dirt. *Rockeries* are made of rocks. And a water feature, I was thinking of."

"*What*"—Dad did a fake laugh—"is a 'water feature' when it's at home?"

"An ornamental pond. A fountain or miniature cascade, perhaps."

"Oh." Dad made a *Fancy that* noise.

"We've been talking about doing something with that scrap of ground by the roses for *years*, Michael."

"You might have. I haven't."

"No, we discussed it before Christmas. *You* said, 'Next year maybe.' Like the year before, and the year before. Besides, *you* said yourself how nice Brian's rockery looks."

"When?"

"Last autumn. And Alice said, 'A rockery would look enchanting in your back garden' and *you* agreed."

"Your mother," Dad said to Julia, "is a human Dictaphone."

Julia refused to be enlisted.

Dad took a gulp of water. "Whatever I said to Alice, I didn't *mean* it. I was being polite."

"Pity you can't extend the same courtesy to your wife."

Julia and me looked at each other.

"What sort of scale," Dad asked wearily, piling peas on his fork, "do we have in mind? A life-sized model of the Lake District?"

Mum reached for a magazine on the sideboard. "Something like this . . ."

"Oh, I get it. *Harper's Bazaar* does a special on rockeries so of course *we* have to have one too."

"Kate's got a nice rockery," Julia said, neutrally. "With heathers."

"Lucky old Kate." Dad put his glasses on to study the magazine. "Very nice, Helena, but they've used real Italian marble here."

Mum's "That's right" meant *And I'm having marble too.*

"Do you have any *inkling* about how much marble costs?"

"More than an inkling. I called a landscape gardener in Kidderminster."

"Why should *I* shell out money"—Dad tossed the magazine on the floor—"for a pile of rocks?"

Mum normally backs down at this point, but not today. "So it's all right for you to spend six hundred pounds on a golf-club membership you hardly *ever* use, but it *isn't* all right for me to improve our property?"

"The golf course," Dad said, trying not to shout, "as I've *tried* to tell you, over and over and over and over, is where deals get cut. Including key promotions. I may not like it, you may not like it, but there it is. And Craig Salt does not play his golf on public links."

"Don't wave your fork at me, Michael."

Dad didn't put his fork down. "I *am* the breadwinner in this family, and I don't think it's unreasonable for me to spend at least a portion of my salary however the hell I see fit."

My mashed potatoes'd gone cold.

"So in effect"—Mum folded her napkin—"you're telling me to stick to jam making and leave the grown-up decisions to the one in the trousers?"

Dad rolled his eyes. (I'd get *killed* for doing that.) "Save the female libber stuff for your Women's Institute friends, Helena. I'm asking you nicely. I've had a very long day."

"Patronize your underlings in your supermarkets as much as you want, Michael." Mum noisily stacked the plates and took them to the kitchen hatch. "But don't try it at home. I'm asking you nicely. *I've* had a very long day." She went into the kitchen.

Dad stared at her empty chair. "So, Jason, how was school?"

My stomach granny-knotted up. Hangman blocked "Not so bad."

"Jason?" Dad's voice went hot and red. "I asked you how school was."

"Fine, thanks." (Today'd been crap. Mr. Kempsey bollocked me for cake crumbs in my music book and Mr. Carver told me I was as "useful as a spastic" at hockey.)

We heard Mum scrape plates into the kitchen bin.

Knife on china, a whooshy thud.

"Excellent," said Dad. "How about you, Julia?"

Before my sister could say a word a plate smashed on the kitchen floor. Dad jumped out of his seat. "Helena?" His breeziness'd gone.

Mum's answer was to slam the back door.

Dad jumped up and went after her.

Rooks crawked round Saint Gabriel's steeple.

Julia blew out her cheeks. "Three stars?"

Miserably, I held up four fingers.

"Just a rocky patch, Jace." Julia's got this brave smile. "That's all. Most marriages have them. Really. Don't worry."

✻ ✻ ✻

Mrs. Thatcher *frazzled* this twerpy prat in a bow tie on BBC1 this evening. He was saying sinking the *General Belgrano* outside the Total Exclusion Zone was morally and legally wrong. (Actually we sunk the *Belgrano* some days ago but the papers've just got hold of the pictures and since the *Sheffield*

we've got *zero* sympathy for the Argie bastards.) Mrs. Thatcher fixed her stained-glass blue eyes on that pillock and pointed out that the enemy cruiser'd been zigzagging in and out of the zone all day. She said something like, "The fathers and mothers of our country did not elect me the prime minister of this country to gamble with the lives of their sons over questions of legal niceties. Must I remind you that *we* are a country at *war?*" The whole studio cheered and the whole country cheered too, I reckon, 'cept for Michael Foot and Red Ken Livingstone and Anthony Wedgwood Benn and all those Loony Lefters. Mrs. Thatcher's bloody *ace.* She's *so* strong, *so* calm, *so* sure. Loads more use than the queen, who hasn't said a dickie bird since the war began. Some countries like Spain are saying we shouldn't've fired on the *Belgrano,* but the only reason so many Argies drowned was that the other ships in its convoy scarpered off instead of saving their own men. Our Royal Navy'd *never ever ever* leave Britons to drown like that. And anyway, when you join the army or navy in *any* country, you're paid to risk your life. Like Tom Yew. Now Galtieri is trying to get *us* back to the negotiating table, but Maggie's told him the only thing *she*'ll discuss is the United Nations' Resolution 502. Argentina's unconditional withdrawal from British soil. Some Argie diplomat in New York, still harping on about the *Belgrano* being outside the zone, said Britain no longer rules the waves, it just waives the rules. The *Daily Mail* says it's typical of a tinpot Latin paper pusher to make stupid quips about life and death. The *Daily Mail* says the Argies should've thought about the consequences *before* they stuck their poxy blue-and-white flag on our sovereign colony. The *Daily Mail*'s dead right. The *Daily Mail* says that Leopoldo Galtieri only invaded the Falklands to distract attention from all his own people he's tortured, murdered, and pushed out of helicopters over the sea. The *Daily Mail*'s dead right again. The *Daily Mail* says Galtieri's brand of patriotism is the last refuge of the scoundrel. The *Daily Mail*'s as right as Margaret Thatcher. All England's turned into a dynamo. People are queueing up outside hospitals to donate blood. Mr. Whitlock spent most of our Biology lesson saying how *certain* patriotic young men cycled to Worcester hospital to give blood. (Everyone knows he was talking about Gilbert Swinyard and Pete Redmarley.) They were told by a nurse that they're too young. So Mr. Whitlock's writing to Michael Spicer, our member of Parliament, to complain that the children of England are being denied the right to contribute to the war effort. His letter's already in the *Malvern Gazetteer.*

Nick Yew is a school hero 'cause of Tom. Nick said the *Sheffield* was just an unlucky fluke. Our antimissile systems'll be modified to knock out the Exocets from now on. So we should be getting our islands back pretty soon. The *Sun*'s paying £100 for the best anti-Argie joke. I can't do jokes, but I'm keeping a scrapbook about the war. I'm cutting out stuff from the newspapers and magazines. Neal Brose is keeping one too. He reckons it'll be worth a fortune twenty or thirty years from now, when the Falklands War has turned into history. But all this excitement'll *never* turn dusty and brown in archives and libraries. No way. People'll remember *everything* about the Falklands till the end of the world.

Mum was at the dining room table surrounded by bank papers when I got back from school. Dad's fireproof document box was out and open. Through the kitchen hatch I asked if she'd had a good day.

"Not a 'good day' exactly." Mum didn't take her eyes off her calculator. "But it's certainly been a real revelation."

"That's good," I said, doubting it. I got a couple of Digestives and a glass of Ribena. Julia'd snaffled all the Jaffa Cakes 'cause she's at home all day revising for her A levels. Greedy moo. "What're you doing?"

"Skateboarding."

I should've just gone upstairs. "What's for dinner?"

"Toad."

One unsarky answer to one simple question, that's all I wanted. "Doesn't Dad usually do all the bank statements and stuff?"

"Yes." Mum finally looked at me. "Isn't your lucky old father in for a pleasant surprise when he comes home?" Something vicious'd got into her voice. It pulled the knot in my guts *so* tight I still can't loosen it.

Wish it *had* been toad for dinner, not tinned carrots, baked beans, and Heinz meatballs in gravy. A plate of browny orange. Mum *can* cook real food, when relatives visit, say. She's on a work-to-rule till she gets her rockery, I reckon. Dad said it was "utterly delicious." His sarcasm didn't bother with camouflage. Neither did Mum's. "I *am* glad you think so." (What Mum and Dad say to each other's half a world away from what they mean, these days. Ordinary polite words shouldn't be so toxic, but they can be.) That was all they said, just about, for the entire meal. Pudding was apple sponge. The syrup trail from my spoon was the path of our marines. To forget the atmosphere, I bravely led our lads yomping over custard snow to ultimate victory in Port Stanley.

It was Julia's turn to do the dishes but we've become sort of allies in the last couple of weeks, so I dried for her. My sister's not totally revolting all the time. She even spoke a bit about her boyfriend, Ewan, while we did the dishes. His mum's in the Birmingham Symphony Orchestra. She's the percussionist and gets to crash the cymbals and play the thundery kettle drums, which sounds an ace laugh. But Hangman's been giving me a hard time since Mum and Dad's last barney, when Mum smashed the plate. So I let Julia do most of the talking. The war's become the first thing I think about in the morning and the last thing at night, so it's nice to hear about something else. Evening sunshine flooded the valley floor between our garden and the Malverns.

The tulips are black plum, emulsion white, and yolky gold.

Mum and Dad must've called a weird cease-fire while we'd been in the kitchen 'cause after the washing up they sat at the table and seemed to be talking normally about the day and stuff. Julia'd asked if they'd like a cup of coffee and Dad'd said, "That'd be lovely, darling" and Mum said, "Thank you, sweetheart." I told myself I'd misread the signs completely when I got back from school, and my gut knot unworried itself a bit looser. Dad was telling Mum a funny story about how his boss Craig Salt'd let Dad's trainee Danny Lawlor drive Craig Salt's DeLorean sportscar round a go-karting track on a team-building weekend. So instead of sloping off upstairs I went into the living room to watch *Tomorrow's World* on TV.

That's how I heard Mum launch her ambush. "By the way, Michael. Why did you take out a second mortgage with NatWest Bank for five thousand pounds in January?"

Five *thousand* pounds! Our house only cost twenty-two!

In the future, according to *Tomorrow's World,* cars will drive themselves along strips implanted in roads. We'll just punch in our destination. There'll never be another traffic accident again.

"Been sifting through my accounts, have we?"

"If I *hadn't* looked at the finances, I'd still be in a state of pristine ignorance, wouldn't I?"

"So. You just went into my office and helped yourself."

Dad, I thought, *Dad! Don't say that to her.*

"Are you *honestly"*—Mum's voice turned quivery—"telling me—*me,* Michael, *me*—that I'm not allowed into your office? That your filing cabinets are out of bounds for *me* as well as the children? Are you?"

Dad said nothing.

"Call me old-fashioned, but I think a wife who discovers her husband is in hock to the tune of five thousand pounds is entitled to some pretty bloody straight answers."

I felt sick, cold, and old.

"And where," Dad finally said, "did this sudden interest in accountancy spring from?"

"Why have you remortgaged our house?"

The *Tomorrow's World* presenter was gluing himself to the ceiling of the studio. "British brains dream up a chemical bond stronger than gravity!" The presenter grinned. "You can bet your *life* on it!"

"Right. Then I'll *tell* you why, shall I?"

"I do wish you would."

"Rescheduling."

"Are you trying," Mum said with a half laugh, "to dazzle me with jargon?"

"It's not jargon. It's rescheduling. *Please* don't go all hysterical on me because—"

"How am I *supposed* to respond, Michael? Using *our house* as security! Then the money gets paid out in tidy parcels to God Knows Where. Or is it to God Knows Who?"

Dad went quiet as death. "What do you mean by that?"

"I *politely* ask you *what* is going on"—Mum'd backed off from some sort of brink—"and all I get is evasion. Can *you* tell me what I'm supposed to think? Please? Because I don't understand what's—"

"*Exactly*, Helena! Thank *you*! You just put your finger on it! You *don't* understand! I took out the loan because *there was a shortfall*! I *know* money is for *the little people* to sort out, but as you may have noticed while you did your Sherlock Holmes act this afternoon, we've got *thumping* great ruddy mortgage payments to keep up on the *first* mortgage! Insurance premiums on all this junk you insist on buying! Utility bills! Your blessed kitchen and your new Royal ruddy Doulton dinner service—that we'll use to impress your sister and Brian twice a year at most—to pay for! Your car to be replaced whenever the ashtray's gone out of fashion! And now, *now*, you've decided life isn't worth living without . . . new adventures in landscape gardening!"

"*Voice*, Michael. The kids'll hear."

"That never seems to worry *you*."

"Now *you're* getting hysterical."

"Right. 'Hysterical.' Fine. You *asked* for a suggestion, *Helena*, so *here we go*. I suggest that *you* spend *your* waking life in meetings, more . . . *bloody* meetings, get blamed for staff shortages, for stock leakages, for disappointing balance sheets. I suggest *you* bugger up *your* back clocking up twenty, twenty-five, thirty thousand road miles *per* year! Then, *then*, you are welcome to call me hysterical. *Until* then, I'd be *grateful* if you didn't give *me* the third bloody degree on how *I* choose to juggle *your* bills. That's *my* suggestion."

Dad stomped upstairs.

He's slamming his filing cabinets drawers.

Mum hasn't left the dining room. I hope to *God* she isn't crying.

Wish *Tomorrow's World* would open up and swallow me.

✵ ✵ ✵

War's an auction where whoever can pay the most in damage and still be standing wins. The news is bad. Brian Hanrahan said the landing at San Carlos Bay was the bloodiest day for the Royal Navy since the Second World War. The hills blocked our radar, so we didn't see the warplanes coming till they were right on top of us. The clear morning was a gift to the Argentinians. They attacked the main ships, not the troop transporters, 'cause once the Task Force is sunk, our land forces'll be easy to pick off. HMS *Ardent* was sunk. HMS *Brilliant* is crippled. HMS *Antrim* and HMS *Argonaut* are out of the war for good. TV's been showing the same pictures, all day. An enemy Mirage III Es sharks through a skyful of Seacats and Seawolfs and Sea Slugs. Waterspouts kerboom in the bay. Black smoke pours from the hull of the *Ardent*. For the first time we saw the Falkland Islands themselves. Treeless, houseless, hedgeless, no colors bar grays and greens. Julia said it's like the Hebrides and she's right. (We went to Mull three years ago for the rainiest holiday in Taylor history, but the best one. Me and Dad played Subbuteo the entire week. I was Liverpool, he was Nottingham Forest.) Brian Hanrahan reported that only the Sea Harriers' counterattack prevented an outright catastrophe. He described an enemy plane downed by a Harrier, cartwheeling right over his head till it crashed into the sea.

HMS *Coventry* wasn't in the report.

God knows who's winning and who's losing now. There's a rumor the Soviet Union's feeding the Argentinians satellite pictures of our fleet, which is why they always know where to find us. (Brezhnev's dying or dead, so nobody knows what's going on in the Kremlin.) Neal Brose said if *that's* true then Ronald Reagan'll *have* to get involved 'cause of the NATO alliance. Then World War III might start.

The *Daily Mail* listed all the lies the junta are telling their people. It made me livid. John Nott, our Minister of Defence, would never lie to *us*. Julia asked how I *knew* we weren't being lied to? "We're British," I told her. "Why *would* the government lie?" Julia replied, To assure us that our wonderful war is going swimmingly when in fact it's going down the toilet. "But," went my answer, "we're winning." Julia said that's exactly what Argentinian people'll be saying right now.

Right now. That's what freaks me. I dip my fountain pen into a pot of ink, and a Wessex helicopter crashes into a glacier on South Georgia. I line up my protractor on an angle in my Maths book and a Sidewinder missile locks onto a Mirage III. I draw a circle with my compass and a Welsh Guard stands up in a patch of burning gorse and gets a bullet through his eye.

How can the world just go on, as if none of this is happening?

I was changing out of my school uniform when this *dream* of a silver MG cruised down Kingfisher Meadows. Into our driveway it swung, and parked under my bedroom window. Rain'd been spitting all afternoon, so the top was up. My first view of my sister's boyfriend, then, was via aerial surveillance. I'd expected Ewan to look sort of Prince Edwardish, but he's got exploding red hair, sooty freckles, and a bouncy walk. He wore a peach shirt under a baggy indigo sweater, black drainpipes, one of those studded belts that sags loose off your hips, and winkle-pickers with white tube socks, like everyone's wearing recently. I yelled up to Julia's attic that Ewan was here. Thumps thumped, a bottle was knocked over, and Julia muttered, "*Bugger.*" (What *is* it that girls *do* before they go out? Julia takes *aeons* to get ready. Dean Moran says his're just the same.) Then she yelled, "MUM! Will you get it?" Mum was already hurrying down the hall. I took up my sniper's-nest position on the landing.

"Ewan, I presume!" Mum used the voice she uses to put nervous people at ease. "A pleasure to meet you, at long last."

Ewan didn't look at all nervous. "Real pleasure to meet you too, Mrs. Taylor." His voice was poshish but not as posh as Mum's put-on posh.

"Julia's told us oodles about you."

"Oh, dear." Ewan has a froggy smile. "That's torn it."

"Oh no no no." Mum laughed like confetti. "It's all good."

"She's told me 'oodles' about you, too."

"Good, good. Well. Jolly good. Won't you step inside while milady's finishing her—well, while she's finishing."

"Thanks."

"So." Mum closed the door. "Julia tells us you're at the Cathedral School? Upper Sixth?"

"That's right. Same as Julia. A levels just around the corner."

"Yes, yes. And do you, er, enjoy it?"

"The Cathedral School? Or the A levels?"

"Er . . ." Mum did a smiley shrug. "The school."

"It's a bit set in its ways. But I wouldn't knock it. Too much."

"A lot to be said for tradition. Far too easy to throw the bathwater out with the baby."

"I'd agree with you wholeheartedly, Mrs. Taylor."

"Right. Well." Mum glanced at the ceiling. "Julia's just getting her things together. Perhaps I could offer you a tea or coffee?"

"That's very kind, Mrs. Taylor"—Ewan's excuse was seamless—"but my mother's birthday dinners run to military precision. If she suspects me of dawdling, it'll be the execution squad at dawn."

"Oh, I can sympathize with her! Julia's brother won't grace the dinner table until everything's stone cold. Drives me to distraction. But I *do* hope you'll eat with us one of these evenings. Julia's father's dying to meet you." (News to me.)

"I'm afraid I'd make a dreadful nuisance of myself."

"Not at all!"

"I might—I'm a vegetarian, you see."

"That's a jolly good excuse to get out the cookery books and try something adventurous. You'll promise to share a meal with us soon?"

(Dad calls vegetarians "the Nut Cutlet Brigade.")

Ewan did a polite smile that wasn't exactly a yes.

"Well. Jolly good. I'll just—pop up and check that Julia knows you're here, why don't I? Will you be okay waiting here, just for a minute or two?"

Ewan inspected the family photos above the telephone. (The Baby Jason one makes me *cringe,* but my parents won't take it down.) I inspected Ewan, the mysterious being who actually *chooses* to spend free time with Julia. He even spends money on necklaces and L.P.s and stuff like that for her. Why?

Ewan didn't look surprised as I came downstairs. "Jason, right?"

"No. I'm *the Thing.*"

"She only calls you that when she's *really* angry with you."

"Yeah, like every minute of every hour of every day."

"Not true. Promise you. And God, you should've heard what she called *me* when she spent the whole morning in the hairdresser's"—Ewan pulled this funny guilty face—"and I didn't even notice."

"What?"

"If I repeated it verbatim," Ewan lowered his voice, "chunks of plaster would come crashing down from the ceiling, in shock. The wallpaper would unpeel itself. A pretty grim first impression *that* would make on your parents, don't you think? Very sorry, but some things must remain veiled in secrecy."

Must be *ace* being Ewan. Being able to talk like that. I could think of much worse kids to have as a brother-in-law. "Can I sit in your MG?"

Ewan glanced at his chunky Sekonda (with metal strap). "Why not?"

"So, do you like it?"

Suede steering wheel. Oxblood leather, walnut and chrome finishings. Gear-stick knob snug in my palm. Sleek lowness, the tilt and hug of the squelky seats. Ghostly glow on the dashboard when Ewan put the key in the ignition. Needles afloat in gauges. Tarry-smelling hood muffling out the wind. An in*cred*ible song filled the car from four hidden speakers. (" 'Heaven,' " Ewan told me, breezy but proud. "Talking Heads. David Byrne's a genius." I just nodded, still taking it all in.) Bitter orange scent from a crystally air freshener. CND sticker next to the tax disk. *God*, if *I* had a car like Ewan's MG, I'd get out of Black Swan Green faster than a Super Étendard. Far away from Mum and Dad and their three-, four-, and five-star arguments. Far from school and Ross Wilcox and Gary Drake and Neal Brose and Mr. Carver. Dawn Madden could come with me, but *nobody* else. I'd do an Evel Knievel off the White Cliffs of Dover, over the English Channel, over the spotless stainless sunrise. We'd land on the Normandy beaches, drive south, lie about our ages, and work in vineyards or ski chalets. My poems'd get published by Faber & Faber with a sketch of me on the cover. Every fashion photographer in Europe'd want to shoot Dawn. My school'd boast about us in their prospectus but I'd never, ever, *ever* come back to muddy Worcestershire.

"Do you a swap," I told Ewan. "My Big Trak for your MG. You can program in up to twenty commands."

Ewan pretended to agonize over this tempting offer. "Not sure if I could navigate the Worcester one-way system, even on a Big Trak." His breath smelt of spearmint Tic Tacs and I caught a whiff of Old Spice. "Sorry."

Julia tapped on my window with an amused *Oy!* in her eyes. I realized that my annoying sister's a woman. Dark lipstick, Julia had on, and a necklace of bluish pearls that'd belonged to our grandma. I wound down the window. Julia peered in at Ewan, then me, then Ewan. "You're late."

Ewan turned Talking Heads down. "*I'm* late?"

That smile's nothing to do with me.

Were Mum and Dad like this, once upon a time?

※　※　※

Our dining room sort of juddered like a silent bomb'd gone off. Me, Mum, and Julia froze as Radio 4 told us which ship'd been sunk. HMS *Coventry*'d been anchored at her usual station north of Pebble Island with the frigate HMS *Broadsword*. At approximately 1400 hours a pair of enemy Skyhawks came flying in at deck level out of nowhere. The *Coventry* launched her Sea Darts, but missed, allowing the Skyhawks to drop four of their one-thousand-pound bombs at point-blank range. One fell astern, but the other three tore into the ship's port side. All three detonated deep within the ship, knocking out the power systems. The fire-control crews were soon overwhelmed, and in a matter of minutes the *Coventry* was listing badly to port. Sea Kings and Wessex helicopters flew over from San Carlos to get the men out of the freezing water. Unhurt men were transferred to the field tents. More serious cases were flown to the hospital ships.

I don't remember what the news moved on to after.

"Nineteen out of how many?" Mum spoke through her fingers.

I knew the answer 'cause of my scrapbook. "About three hundred."

Julia calculated, "Better than ninety percent chance that Tom's okay, then."

Mum'd gone pale. "His *poor* mother! She must be having *kittens*."

I thought aloud: "Poor Debby Crombie, too."

Mum didn't know. "What's Debby Crombie got to do with anything?"

Julia told her, "Debby's Tom's girlfriend."

"Oh," said Mum. "Oh."

War may be an auction for countries. For soldiers it's a lottery.

The school bus still hadn't come by quarter past eight. Birdsong strafed and morsed from the oak on the village green. Upstairs curtains at the Black Swan twitched open and I think I glimpsed Isaac Pye in a kite of sunshine, giving us all the evil eye. There was no sign of Nick Yew yet, but he's always one of the last to arrive 'cause he walks all the way from Hake's Lane.

"My old bid tried to call Mrs. Yew," John Tookey said, "but her phone was busy. Nonstop."

"Half the village was trying to get through," Dawn Madden told him. "That'd be why nobody could."

"Yeah," I agreed. "The lines'd've got jammed."

But Dawn Madden didn't even acknowledge I'd spoken.

"Boomy boom-*boom*," chanted Squelch, "boomer-*ker*-boomer *BOOM!*"

"Shut yer neck, Squelch," Ross Wilcox snapped, "or I'll shut it for yer."

"Don't pick on Squelch," Dawn Madden told Ross Wilcox. "Ain't *his* fault he's soft in the head."

"Shut yer neck, Squelch," Squelch said with a twitch, "or I'll shut it for yer."

"Tom'll be okay," Grant Burch said. "We'd've heard if he weren't."

"Yeah," said Philip Phelps. "We'd've heard if he weren't."

"Is there an echo round here?" grunted Ross Wilcox. "How would *you* two know, anyway?"

"How I'd *know* is that the instant the Yews know," Grant Burch flobbed, "through navy channels, they'd phone *my* old man 'cause Tom's old man and my old man grew up together. *That's* how I know."

"*Sure*, Burch," Wilcox mocked.

"Yeah." Grant Burch's wrist was still in plaster so he couldn't do much about Wilcox's sarcasm. But Grant Burch remembers stuff. "I *am* sure."

"Hey!" Gavin Coley pointed. "Look!"

Gilbert Swinyard and Pete Redmarley appeared in the far distance, way over the crossroads.

"Must've gone down Hake's Lane," guessed Keith Broadwas, "dead early. To the Yews' place. To make sure Tom's okay."

We saw Gilbert Swinyard and Pete Redmarley were almost running.

I tested "Why isn't Nick with them?" but Hangman blocked "Nick."

"How come," Darren Croome said, "Nick ain't with them?"

Birds detonated out of the oak without warning and we jumped but didn't laugh about it. Incredible to see, it was. Countless hundreds of birds, orbiting the village green once, elasticking longer, twice, winging shorter, three times, then, as if following an order, vanishing inside the tree again.

"Maybe," Dawn Madden guessed, "Nixon's given Nick permission not to come to school today. Considering, like."

It was a reasonable guess, but now we could see the looks on Swinyard's and Redmarley's faces.

"Oh . . ." Grant Burch muttered, *"fuck* no."

"By now"—Mr. Nixon coughed to clear his throat—"you are all doubtless aware that Thomas Yew, an old boy of our school, has, in the last twenty-four hours, been killed in the conflict over the Falkland Islands." (Our headmaster was right, we all knew. Norman Bates, the school bus driver, had Radio Wyvern on and Tom Yew's name was on that.) "Thomas was not the most studious boy ever to grace the classrooms of our school, nor the most obedient. Indeed, my register of crimes and punishments informs me I was obliged to administer the slipper on no less than four occasions. But neither Thomas nor myself are"—bleak silence—*"were"*—another one—"the type of man to bear a grudge. When the Royal Navy's recruitment officer approached me for a character reference regarding Thomas, I felt able to recommend this spirited young man, unreservedly and unconditionally. Thomas returned the courtesy some months later, by inviting my wife and myself to his passing-out ceremony in Portsmouth some months later. Rarely have"—a flutter of amazement that anyone'd ever married Mr. Nixon swept round the hall. One glare from Mr. Nixon and the flutter dropped dead—*"rarely* have I accepted an invitation to an official function with such pleasure, and such personal pride. Thomas had clearly flourished under military discipline. He had matured into a worthy ambassador for our school and a credit to Her Majesty's Forces. This is why the grief I feel this morning, upon learning of his death"—surely that wasn't a crack in Nixon's voice?—"aboard HMS *Coventry* is as bitter as it is heartfelt. The mood of depression both in the staff room and in this hall tell me that this grief is shared by all of us." (Mr. Nixon took off his glasses and for a moment he looked not like an SS commandant but just somebody's tired dad.) "I will be sending a telegram of condolence to Thomas's family after assembly, on behalf of the school. I hope that those of you who are close to the Yews will lend them your support. Life can inflict few cruelties—perhaps no cruelty—more acute than the death of a son—or brother. However, I also hope that you will give Thomas's family sufficient space in which to grieve." (A few of the third-year girls were weeping now. Mr. Nixon looked in their direction, but he'd turned his Death Ray off. He said nothing for five, ten, fifteen seconds. A bit of shuffling started. Twenty, twenty-five, thirty seconds. I intercepted a look from Miss Ronkswood to Miss

Wyche that said, *Is he okay?* Miss Wyche shrugged, very slightly.) "I hope," Mr. Nixon finally went on, "that, as you consider Thomas's sacrifice, you will think about the consequences of violence, be it military or emotional. I hope you will note who initiates violence, who conducts the violence, and who must pay the price of violence. Wars do not simply appear from nowhere. Wars come, over a long period of time, and believe me, there is always plenty of blame to be shared out between all those who failed to prevent its bloody arrival. I also hope you will consider what is truly precious in your own lives, and what is merely . . . flimflam . . . grandstanding . . . froth . . . posturing . . . egotism." Our headmaster looked spent. "That is all." Mr. Nixon nodded at Mr. Kempsey at the piano. Mr. Kempsey told us to turn to the hymn that goes, *Oh hear us when we cry to thee for those in peril on the sea.* We all stood up and sang it for Tom Yew.

Normal assemblies have mile-high messages carved into them, like *Helping People Is Good* or *Even Dimmest Dimmers Can Succeed If They Never Give Up.* But I'm not sure if even the teachers were sure what Mr. Nixon meant this morning.

✳   ✳   ✳

Tom Yew's death killed the thrill of the war. There was no way to get his body back to Worcestershire so he's been buried out there, on those rocky islands still being fought over. Nothing's got back to normal yet. Make-believe grief is fun. But when someone really dies, there's just this horrible draggingness. Wars go on for months, or years. Vietnam did. Who says this won't be one of them? The Argentinians've got thirty thousand men on the Falklands, all in dug-in positions. We've got just six thousand trying to scramble out of our bridgehead. Two of our *only* three Chinook helicopters were lost when the *Atlantic Conveyor* was sunk, so our soldiers're having to advance toward Port Stanley on foot. Surely even Luxembourg's got more than three decent helicopters? There's rumors of the Argentinian navy breaking out of its ports and cutting off our sea lines to Ascension Island. We're running out of petrol, too. (Like the armed forces of Great Britain just add up to this crap family car.) Mount Kent, Two Sisters, Tumbledown Mountain. The names're friendly but the terrain isn't. Brian Hanrahan says the only cover for the marines are giant boulders. Our planes can't give air cover 'cause of the mist, snow, hail, gales. Like Dartmoor, he said, in midwinter. Our paras can't dig foxholes 'cause the ground's too hard and some've even been crippled with trench foot. (My granddad once said how *his* dad'd got trench foot in Passchendaele in 1916.) East Falkland's one massive minefield. The beaches, the bridges, the gulleys, everywhere. At night, enemy snipers call for star shells so the landscape's lit pale like fridgelight. Bullets rain down. The Argentinians are using ammunition, one expert says, like they've got an unlimited supply. Plus, our men can't just bomb the buildings or we'd end up killing the same civilians we're s'posed to be saving. And there's not that many of them. General Galtieri knows the winter's on his side. From the balcony of his palace, he said Argentina will fight until the very last man, dead or alive.

Nick Yew hasn't come back to school. Dean Moran saw him in Mr. Rhydd's shop buying a box of eggs and Fairy Liquid, but Moran didn't know what to say. Moran said Nick's face was dead.

Last week the *Malvern Gazetteer* had Tom Yew on its front page. He was smiling and saluting at the camera in his ensign's uniform. I pasted it in my scrapbook. I'm running out of pages.

When I got home on Monday there were about ten lumps of granite blocking the driveway, plus five sacks labeled CRUSHED SHELL FILLER. *Plus* a giant turtle shell that turned out to be a precast fiberglass pond lining. Mr. Castle was on a pair of stepladders clipping his hedge that divides his front garden from ours. "Dad's re-creating the Hanging Gardens of Babylon, is he?"

"Something like that."

"I hope he's got a JCB stashed away in his garage."

"Sorry?"

"Over a ton of rock you've got there. Nobody's going to be shifting *that* little lot on a wheelbarrow. Cracked the tarmac something chronic, too, they have." Mr. Castle smiled and winced at the same time. "I was here, watching the men dump it."

Mum got home twenty minutes later, absolutely *apeshit*. I was watching the war on TV, so across the hallway I heard her phone up the landscapers. "You were supposed to bring the rocks *tomorrow*! You were supposed to lay them in the *garden*! *Not* just dump the things in the middle of our drive! A 'mix-up'? A 'mix-up'? No. *I'm* calling it *criminal stupidity*! Where are we supposed to *park*?" The call ended with Mum shrieking the words "*instructing my solicitors!*" and hanging up.

When Dad came home at gone seven o'clock he didn't mention the rocks on the driveway. Not a word. But the *way* he said nothing was masterly. Mum didn't mention the rocks either, so we had a standoff. You could hear the strain in the room, like the squeak of cables. Mum boasts to visitors and relatives how, no matter what, we sit round as a family to share an evening meal. She'd've done us all a favor if she'd given this tradition a night off. Julia did her best to spin out a story about today's World Affairs A-level paper (she'd got all the questions she'd studied for) and Mum and Dad paid polite attention, but I sort of *felt* the rocks outside, waiting to be referred to.

Mum served up the treacle tart and vanilla ice cream.

"I don't want to be accused of nagging, Helena," Dad began, "but I was wondering when I might be able to park my car in my garage?"

"The workmen will be putting the rockery in place *tomorrow*. There was a misunderstanding about delivery times. They'll be finished by tomorrow evening."

"Ah, good. It's just our insurance policy clearly states we're covered for *off-road* parking only, so if—"

"*Tomorrow*, Michael."

"That's fantastic. This is a lovely treacle tart, by the way. Is it from Greenland?"

"Sainsbury's."

Our spoons scraped on our dishes.

"I don't want to be accused of interfering, Helena—"

(Mum's nostrils actually went stiff, like a cartoon bull's.)

"—but I hope you haven't actually *paid* these people, yet?"

"No. I've paid a deposit."

"A deposit. I see. I only ask because you *do* hear horror stories about people handing over quite large sums of money to cowboys in these fly-by-night businesses. Then before you can even phone a lawyer, the director's done a Ronnie Biggs off to Costa del Chips or wherever. And the poor old customer never gets to see a single penny of his hard-earned money again. Distressing, how these con men can swindle the gullible."

"You *said* you'd 'washed your hands of the whole affair,' Michael."

"I did, yes." Dad can't hide satisfaction to save his life. "But I didn't count on not being able to park my own car on my own drive. That's all I wanted to say."

Something silent smashed without being dropped.

Mum left the table. Not angry, and not tearful, but worse. Like none of us were there.

Dad just stared at where she'd been sitting.

"In my exam today"—Julia twisted a strand of her hair—"this term I'm not totally sure about, 'Pyrrhic victory,' came up. Do you know what a 'Pyrrhic victory' is, Dad?"

Dad gave Julia a very complicated stare.

Julia didn't flinch.

Dad got up and went to the garage, for a smoke, most like.

The wreckage of dessert lay between me and Julia.

We watched it for a bit. "A *what* victory?"

" 'Pyrrhic.' Ancient Greece. A Pyrrhic victory is one where you win, but the cost of winning is so high that it would've been better if you'd never bothered with the war in the first place. Useful word, isn't it? So, Jace. Looks like we're doing the dishes again. Wash or dry?"

* * *

Ceasefire agreed in the Falklands

white flag of half months after the entire invasio

The whole of Great Britain's like it's Bonfire Night and Christmas Day and Saint George's Day and the Queen's Silver Jubilee all rolled into one. Mrs. Thatcher appeared outside 10 Downing Street, saying, "Rejoice! Just rejoice!" The photographers' flashbulbs and the crowds went *crazy*; she wasn't a politician at all, but all four members of Bucks Fizz at the Eurovision Song Contest. Everyone sang *Rule Britannia, Britannia rules the waves, Britons never never never shall be slaves*, over and over. (Has that song got any verses or is it just one neverending chorus?) This summer isn't green; this summer is the red, white, and blue of the Union Jack. Bells've been rung, beacons lit, street parties've broken out up and down the country. Isaac Pye had an all-night happy hour at the Black Swan last night. In Argentina riots're being reported in the major cities, with lootings and shootings, and some people're saying it's just a matter of time before the junta's toppled. The *Daily Mail's* full of how Great British guts and Great British leadership won the war. No prime minister's *ever* been more popular than Premier Margaret Thatcher in the entire history of opinion polls.

I *should* be really happy.

Julia reads the *Guardian*, which's got all sorts of stuff not in the *Daily Mail*. Most of the thirty thousand enemy soldiers, she says, were just conscripts and Indians. Their elite troops all raced back to Port Stanley as the British paratroopers advanced. Some of the ones they left behind got killed by bayonets. Having your intestines pulled out through a slit in the belly! What a 1914 way to die in 1982. Brian Hanrahan said he saw one prisoner being interviewed who said they didn't even know what the Malvinas were or why they'd been brought there. Julia says the main reasons we won were (a) the Argentinians couldn't buy any more Exocets; (b) their navy stayed holed up in mainland bases; (c) their air force ran out of trained pilots. Julia says it would've been cheaper to set every Falkland Islander up with their own farm in the Cotswolds than to've gone to war. She reckons nobody'll pay to clean up the mess, so that much of the farmland on the islands'll be off-limits until the mines've rusted.

A hundred years, that might take.

Today's big story in the *Daily Mail*'s about whether Cliff Richard the singer's having sex with Sue Barker the tennis player, or whether they're just good friends.

Tom Yew wrote a letter to his family the day before the *Coventry* was sunk. The letter made it back to Black Swan Green, just a few days ago. Dean Moran's mum read it, 'cause she was Tom Yew's godmother, and Kelly Moran got the details out of her. Our navy men thought the Falkland Islanders were a bunch of inbred bumblers ("Honest," Tom wrote, "some of these guys are their own fathers"), like Benny the dimwit handyman from *Crossroads* on TV. They even started calling the islanders "Bennies." ("I'm not making this up—I met a Benny this morning who thought a silicon chip was a Sicilian crisp.") Soon everyone in the lower ranks was saying "Benny" this and "Benny" that. When the officers found out, an order was issued to get the men to stop using this name. The men stopped. But a day or two later, Tom was hauled over by his lieutenant, who demanded to know why the crew were referring to the locals not as "Bennies" but as "Stills." "So I told the lieutenant, 'Because they're still Bennies, sir.' "

Dad was half wrong, half right about the landscape gardener doing a runner. When the company stopped answering their phone, Mum drove to Kidderminster, but there was only a broken chair in an empty office. Wires stuck out of the walls. Two men loading a photocopier onto the truck told her the firm'd gone bankrupt. So the rockery rocks stayed on our driveway for two more weeks, until Mr. Broadwas got back from his holiday in Ilfracombe. Mr. Broad-was does some gardening work for my parents. Dad sort of elbowed Mum out of the rescue operation. At eight o'clock this morning (today's Saturday) a big truck carrying a forklift truck pulled up outside our house. Out of the cab got Mr. Broadwas, and his sons Gordon and Keith. Mr. Broadwas's son-in-law Doug drove the forklift truck. First, Dad and Doug took down the side gate so the machine could lug the granite to the back. Next, we all got stuck in digging the hole for the pond. Hot and sweaty work, it was. Mum sort of hovered in the shade, but men with spades put up an invisible wall. She brought a tray of cof-fee and Dutch butter biscuits. Everyone thanked Mum politely and Mum said, "You're welcome" politely too. Dad sent me to Mr. Rhydd's on my bike to get 7UP and Mars bars. (Mr. Rhydd told me it was the hottest day of 1982 so far.) When I got back me and Gordon carted the buckets of topsoil to the end of the garden. I didn't know what to say to Gordon Broadwas. Gordon's in my year at school (in a dimmer's class) and here was my dad *paying* his dad. How embar-rassing's *that*? Gordon didn't speak much either, so maybe he felt embarrassed too. Mum was looking stonier and stonier as the rockery in the garden and the rockery in her blueprint got more and more different. After the pond's shell was lowered and we stopped for toasted sandwiches, Mum announced she was going into Tewkesbury to do some shopping. As her car pulled out and we got back to work, Dad did a jokey sigh. "Women, eh? Banging on about this rock-ery for *years*, and now it's off to the shops . . ."

Mr. Broadwas did a gardener's nod. Not an ally's nod.

By the time Mum came home, Mr. Broadwas, his sons, Doug, and the fork-lift truck'd gone. Dad'd let me fill the pond with water from the hosepipe. I was playing Swingball by myself. Julia'd gone out to celebrate the end of the A levels at Tanya's Night Club in Worcester with Kate, Ewan, and some of his friends. Dad was nestling little ferny claw plants into the chinks between the rocks. "So"—he waved his trowel—"what's the verdict?"

"Very nice," said Mum.

Right away, I knew she knew something we didn't.

Dad nodded. "The boys didn't do a bad job, eh?"

"Oh, not bad at all."

"Best garden pond in the village it'll be, Mr. Broadwas said, once my shrubbery's got a grip. Have a pleasant tootle round Tewkesbury, did we?"

"Very pleasant, thank you," said Mum, as a tubby man with joke-shop sideburns trundled a large, white, lidded wheely bucket round from the front of the house. "Mr. Suckley, this is my husband, and that's my son, Jason. Michael, this is Mr. Suckley."

Mr. Suckley gave me and Dad a "How do."

"That's the pond," Mum said to him. "Please, Mr. Suckley."

Mr. Suckley wheeled his bucket to the edge of the pond, balanced it there, and raised a sort of gate. Water sluiced out, slooshing with it a pair of enormous fish. Not the tiddlers you get in plastic bags from the Goose Fair. These beauts'd've cost a *packet.* "The Japanese revere carp as living trea-sures," Mum told us. "They're symbols of a long life. They live for decades. They'll probably outlive us."

Dad's nose looked very, *very* out of joint.

"Oh, I *know* your forklift gizmo was an unexpected expense, Michael. But think what we saved by using granite instead of marble. And surely the best pond in the village should have the best fish? What's the Japanese name for them again, Mr. Suckley?"

Mr. Suckley emptied the last dribbles into the pond. "Koi."

"*Koi.*" Mum peered into the pond like a mother. "The long gold one's 'Moby.' The mottled one we can call 'Dick.' "

Today'd been so full of stuff, so Mr. Suckley should've been the end. But after tea I was playing darts in the garage when the back door slammed open. "Get *a—way*!" Mum's shriek was *mangled* with anger. "GET AWAY you dirty great BRUTES!"

I ran to the back garden in time to catch Mum *hurling* her Prince Charles and Princess Diana mug at a *gigantic* heron, perched on the rockery. Tea floated out like liquid in zero gravity as the missile passed through a belt of sunlit gnats. The mug exploded when it hit the rockery. The heron raised its angel's wings. Quite unhurriedly, one mighty flap at a time, it climbed into the air. Moby was flapping in its beak. "*PUT* my FISH *DOWN!*" yelled Mum. "You *damn* BIRD!"

Mr. Castle's puppety head popped over the garden fence.

Mum's staring at the heron, appalled, as it shrinks into the lost blue.

Moby's flipping in the Day of Judgment light.

Dad watches all this through the kitchen window. Dad isn't laughing. He's won.

Me, *I* want to bloody kick this *moronic bloody* world in the bloody *teeth* over and over till it bloody *understands* that *not hurting people* is ten bloody *thousand* times more bloody important than being *right.*

spooks

So here I was, tying cotton to Mr. Blake's door knocker, *cacking* myself. The knocker was a roaring brass lion. *Here be the fumbler who should be in bed, and here be the beast who bites off his head.* Behind me, in the playground, Ross Wilcox was *willing* me to balls it up. Dawn Madden sat next to him on the climbing frame. Her beautiful head was haloed by the streetlamp. Who knows what *she* was thinking. Gilbert Swinyard and Pete Redmarley spun on the witch's hat, slowly, assessing my performance. On the high end of the seesaw perched Dean Moran. Pluto Noak weighed down the low end. His fag glowed. Pluto Noak's why I was where I was. When Mr. Blake'd confiscated the football after Gilbert Swinyard'd booted it into his front garden, Noak'd said, "If you ask *me*, that old git deserves a"—he'd licked the words—"a *cherry knocking.*" "Cherry knocking" sounds a pretty word but prettiness often papers over nastiness. Knocking on a door and running off before the victim answers sounds a harmless prank, but cherry knocking says, *"Are we the wind, or kids, or have we come to murder you in your bed?"* It says, *"Of all the houses in the village, why* you?"

Nasty, really.

Or maybe it was Ross Wilcox's fault. If he hadn't snogged Dawn Madden *so* tonguily, I might've sloped off home when Pluto Noak mentioned cherry knocking. I might not've bragged how Hugo my cousin does it by tying one end of a reel of cotton to the knocker and then drives his victim *crazy* by knocking from a safe distance.

Wilcox'd tried to snuff the idea out. "They'd see the thread."

"No," I counterattacked, "not if you use black, and let it go slack after knocking so it's lying along the ground."

"How'd *you* know, Taylor? *You*'ve never done it."

"I bloody have. At my cousin's. In Richmond."

"Where the fuck's Richmond?"

"Virtually London. *Ace* laugh, it was, too."

"Should work." Pluto Noak spoke. "Trickiest part'd be tyin' the thread in the first place."

"It'd take balls." Dawn Madden wore snakeskin jeans. "Would that."

"Nah." *I*'d started it all. "It's a piece of piss."

Tying a thread to a knocker when one fumble means *death* is no piece of piss, however. Mr. Blake had the nine o'clock news on. Through the open window wafted fried onion fumes and news about the war in Beirut. Rumor has it, Mr. Blake's got an air rifle. He worked at a factory in Worcester that makes mining equipment but he got laid off and hasn't worked since. His wife died of leukemia. There's a son called Martin who'd be about twenty now, but one night (so Kelly Moran told us) they had a fight and Martin's never been seen since. Someone'd got a letter from a North Sea oil rig, another from a canning factory in Alaska.

So anyway, Pluto Noak, Gilbert Swinyard, and Pete Redmarley hid it but they were *pretty* damn impressed when I said *I*'d loop the thread. And that's why I found myself fumbling one simple granny knot.

Done.

My throat'd gone dry.

Dead carefully, I lowered the knocker onto the brass lion.

The crucial thing was not to flunk it now, not to panic, not to think what Mr. Blake and my parents'd do to me if I got caught.

I backtracked, trying not to scuff grit on the path, unspooling the cotton.

Mr. Blake's prehistoric trees cast tigery shadows.

The gate's rusty hinges squeaked like glass about to shatter.

Mr. Blake's window snapped open.

An air rifle went off and a pellet hit my neck.

Only when the TV noise'd deadened did I realized that the window'd snapped *shut*. The bullet must've been a flying beetle or something. "Should of seen your face when the window went," snarled Ross Wilcox as I got back to the climbing frame. "Shat your cacks, it looked like!"

But no one else joined in.

Pete Redmarley flobbed. "Least he did it, Wilcox."

"Aye." Gilbert Swinyard gobbed. "Took guts, did that."

Dean Moran said, "Nice one, Jace."

By telepathy I told Dawn Madden, *Your spazzo boyfriend hasn't got nerve to do that.*

"Playtime, kiddiwinkies." Pluto Noak swiveled off the seesaw and Moran crashed to earth and rolled into the dirt with a squawk. "Gi'us the thread, Jason." (The first time he'd called me anything but "Taylor" or "you.") "Let's pay wankchops a call."

Warm with this praise, I handed him the spool.

"Let us go first, Ploot," asked Pete Redmarley, "it *is* my cotton."

"Yer lyin' thief, it ain't yours, yer nicked it off yer old biddy." Pluto Noak unspooled more slack as he climbed up the slide. "Anyway, it takes technique, does this. Ready?"

We all nodded, and took up innocent stances.

Pluto Noak wound the thread in, then delicately tugged.

The brass lion knocker answered. *One, two, three.*

"*Skill,*" mumbled Pluto Noak. That *skill* splashed on me.

A blunt axe of silence'd killed every noise in the playground.

Pluto Noak, Swinyard, and Redmarley looked at each other.

Then they looked at me too, like I was one of them.

"Yeah?" Mr. Blake appeared in a rectangle of yellow. "Hello?"

This, I thought as my blood went hotter and waterier, *could backfire* so *shittily.*

Mr. Blake stepped forward. "Anyone there?" His gaze settled on us.

"Nick Yew's dad's"—Pete Redmarley spoke like we were in the middle of a discussion—"selling Tom's old Suzuki scrambler to Grant Burch."

"Burch?" Wilcox snorted. "What's he sellin' it to *that* cripple for?"

"Breakin' an arm," Gilbert Swinyard told him, "don't make *no one* a cripple, not in my book."

Wilcox didn't quite dare answer back. To my delight.

All through this, Mr. Blake'd been firing us this evil stare. Finally he went back in.

Pluto Noak snorted as the door closed, "Fuckin' *fierce* or what?"

"*Fierce,*" echoed Dean Moran.

Dawn Madden bit her bottom lip and sneaked me this naked smile.

I'll tie fifty threads, I thought-telegrammed her, *to fifty door knockers.*

"Dozy old fucker," mumbled Ross Wilcox, "must be blind as a bloody bat. He treaded on the thread, most like."

"Why," Gilbert Swinyard answered, "would he even be *lookin'* for a thread?"

"Gi'us a go now, Ploot," asked Pete Redmarley.

"Nokey-dokey Sneaky Pete. Too much of a laugh, this. Round Two?"

Mr. Blake's knocker knocked once, twice—

Immediately the door flew open and the cotton reel was jerked out of Pluto Noak's hand. It clattered over the tarmac under the swing.

"*Right* you—" Mr. Blake snarled at the nonexistent cherry knocker who wasn't cowering, terrified, on his doorstep or anywhere else.

I had one of those odd moments when now isn't now.

Mr. Blake marched round his garden, trying to flush out a hiding kid.

"So how much," Gilbert Swinyard asked Pete Redmarley in a loud, innocent voice, "are the Yews askin' Old Burcher for that scrambler?"

"Dunno," said Pete Redmarley. "Couple of hundred, prob'ly."

"Two hundred and fifty," Moran piped up. "Kelly heard Isaac Pye tell Badger Harns in the Black Swan."

Mr. Blake walked up to his gate. (I tried to keep my face half-hidden and hoped he didn't know me.) "*Giles Noak*. Might have known. Want to spend another night in Upton cop shop, do you?"

Wilcox'd grass me off, for sure, if the police got involved.

Pluto Noak leaned over the side of the slide and dropped a spit bomb.

"You cocky little *shite*, Giles Noak."

"Talkin' to me? *I* thought *yer* wanted that kid who just banged yer knocker and ran off."

"Bullshit! It was *you*!"

"Flew back up here from yer door in one giant leap, did I?"

"So *who* is it?"

Pluto Noak did a *Fuck you* chuckle. "Who is it what?"

"Right!" Mr. Blake took one step back. "I'm calling the police!"

Pluto Noak did this *devastating* imitation of Mr. Blake. " 'Officer? Roger Blake here, yes, well-known unemployed child beater of Black Swan Green. Listen, this boy keeps knocking on my door and running away. No, I don't know his name. No, I haven't actually seen him, but come and arrest him anyway. He needs a good *ramming* with a *shiny hard truncheon*! I *insist* on doing it myself.' "

That my cherry knocking'd led to *this* was horrifying.

"After what happened to your *waster* of a father"—Mr. Blake's voice'd turned poisonous—"*you* should know where *human sewage* ends up."

A sneeze exploded out of Moran.

Here's a true story about Giles "Pluto" Noak. Last autumn his then girlfriend Collette Turbot'd been invited by our art teacher Mr. Dunwoody to Art Club. Art Club's after school and it's only open to kids Dunwoody invites. Collette Turbot went and found it was just her and Dunwoody. He told her to pose topless in his darkroom so he could photograph her. Collette Turbot said, I don't think so, sir. Dunwoody told her if she squandered her gifts she'd waste her life marrying pillocks and working at checkouts. Collette Turbot just left. Next day Pluto Noak and another mate from Upton Pork Scratchings factory appeared at lunch in the staff car park. Quite a crowd gathered. Pluto Noak and his mate each got a corner of Dunwoody's Citroën and *rocked it over onto its roof.* "YOU TELL THE PIGS WHAT I DONE," he yelled at the staff-room window at the top of his voice, "AND *I'LL* TELL THE PIGS *WHY* I DONE IT!"

Loads of people *say*, "I don't *give* a toss." But for Pluto Noak, not giving a toss's a religion.

So anyway, Mr. Blake'd taken a cautious step or two back before Pluto Noak reached his gate. "Talk about someone's father like *that*, yer've gotta see it through, Roger. So let's sort this out like men. You and me. Right now. You ain't scared, right? Martin said you've got quite a talent for smashin' up disobedient teenagers."

"*You.*" When Mr. Blake found his voice it'd gone crackly and sort of hysterical. "*You* don't know what you're damn well *talking* about."

"Martin knew well enough, though, didn't he?"

"I never laid a *finger* on that boy!"

"Not a finger." It took me a moment to realize that the next voice belonged to Dean Moran. "Pokers wrapped in pillowcases's more *your* style, weren't it?" You never know with Dean Moran. "So it didn't leave any marks."

Pluto Noak pushed his advantage. "Glory days, eh? *Rog?*"

"Poisonous little crappers!" Mr. Blake marched back to his house. "All of you! The police'll mop *you* up quickly enough . . ."

"*My* old man's got his faults and I ain't sayin' he ain't," Pluto Noak called out, "but he *never* done *nothin'* to me like what you done to Martin!"

Mr. Blake's door slammed loud as a shotgun.

Wished I'd never opened my stupid gob about the cotton now.

Pluto Noak strolled back, all perky. "Nice shot, Moran. Fancy a zap on the old Asteroids up the Swan, me. Comin'?"

The invitation was for Redmarley and Swinyard only. Both answered, "Okay, Ploot." As they left, Pluto Noak nodded me a *Well done.*

"But," Ross Wilcox *had* to say, "Blake'll find the cotton in the morning."

Pluto Noak spat at the polished June moon. "*Good.*"

✳   ✳   ✳

Breaks at school're normally pretty grim. Spend your break alone, you're a No-Friends Loser. Try to enter a ring of high-rank kids like Gary Drake or David Ockeridge, you risk a withering "What d'*you* want?" Hang out with low-rank kids like Floyd Chaceley and Nicholas Briar, that mean's you're one of them. Girls, like Avril Bredon's cloakroom huddle, aren't much of a solution. True, you don't have to prove yourself so much with girls, and they definitely smell better. But pretty soon someone'll start a rumor that you fancy one of them. Hearts and initials'll appear on blackboards.

I try to spend my breaks on journeys between changing destinations, so at least I always look like I've got somewhere to be.

But today was different. Kids came seeking *me* out. They wanted to know if I'd *really* tied cotton to *the* Roger Blake's front door. A certain reputation as a bit of a hard-knock's useful, but not if teachers notice. So I told each kid, "Ah, you can't believe everything you hear, you know." A skill answer, that. It meant *Of course it's true* as well as *Why'd I want to talk to you about it?*

"Far *out*," they told me. Saying that's a craze right now.

At the tuckshop Neal Brose was with the sixth-form prefects behind the counter. (Neal Brose managed to get special permission by persuading Mr. Kempsey he wanted to learn about the business world.) Neal Brose's been giving me the cold shoulder this term, but today he called out, "What'll it be, Jace?"

His friendliness made my mind go blank. "Double Decker?"

A Double Decker flew at my face. I raised a hand to stop it. The chocolate bar landed there, molded to my hand, *perfectly.*

Loads of kids saw it.

Neal Brose jerked his thumb to tell me to pay round the side. But when I held out my 15p he just did this sly grin and closed my fingers round my coins so it *looked* like he'd taken them. He shut the door before I could argue. No

Double Decker ever tasted so good. No nougat *ever* so snowy. No curranty-clag ever so crumbly and sweet.

Then Duncan Priest and Mark Badbury appeared with a tennis ball. Mark Badbury asked, "Game of slam?" Like we'd been best mates for years.

"Okay," I said.

"O*kay!*" said Duncan Priest. "Slam's better with three."

Art was with the same Mr. Dunwoody whose car Pluto Noak'd turtled over last year. Mr. Nixon'd stepped in to save his bacon — to avoid a scandal, so Julia reckons. Nothing happened to Pluto Noak and Mr. Dunwoody came to school with Miss Gilver until his Citroën was repaired. They'd make a good husband and wife, we reckon. They both hate humans.

So anyway, Mr. Dunwoody's face is fitted around his gi*normous* conk. He reeks of Vicks nasal inhaler. Only a fellow stammerer'd notice his tiny slips on *T*-words. His art room's got a clayey smell, for some reason. We never use clay. Mr. Dunwoody uses the kiln as a cupboard, and the darkroom's a twilight zone only Art Club members get to see. From the art-room window you've got a view over the playing fields, so high-ranking kids bag those seats. Alastair Nurton saved me one. A solar system of hot-air balloons hung over the Malverns, over the perfect afternoon.

Today's lesson was on the golden mean. A Greek called Archimedes, Mr. Dunwoody said, worked out the correct place to put a tree and the horizon in any picture. Mr. Dunwoody showed us how to find the golden mean using proportions and a ruler, but none of us really got it, not even Clive Pike. Mr. Dunwoody did this *Why am I wasting my life?* expression. He pinched the bridge of his nose and massaged his temples. "Four years at the Royal Academy for *this*. Out with your pencils. Out with your rulers."

In my pencil case I found a note that sent the art room spinning.

tHE GRAveYarD 8 tOniTe SPOOkS

One number and four words'd just changed my life.

By the time you're thirteen, gangs're babyish, like dens or Legos. But Spooks is more a secret society. Dean Moran's dad said Spooks started years ago as a sort of secret union for farmhands. If a landowner didn't pay what he owed, say, the Spooks'd all go round to get justice. Half the men in the Black Swan'd've been members in those days. It's changed since then, but it's still dead secret. Actual Spooks *never* talk about it. Pete Redmarley and Gilbert Swinyard were in it, me and Moran reckoned, and Pluto Noak *had* to be a leader. Ross Wilcox boasted he's a member, which means he isn't. John Tookey is. One time he got pushed about by some skinheads at a disco in Malvern Link. Next Friday about twenty Spooks, including Tom Yew, rode up there on bikes and motorbikes. All the versions of what happened end with the same skinheads being made to lick John Tookey's boots. That's just one story. There's a hundred others.

My bravery last night obviously must've impressed the right people. Pluto Noak, most like. But who'd delivered the note? I put it in my blazer pocket and scanned the class for a knowing look. Nothing from Gary Drake, or Neal Brose. David Ockeridge and Duncan Priest're popular, but they live out Castlemorton and Corse Lawn way. Spooks is a Black Swan Green thing.

Some second-year girls jogged below the window in training for Sports Day. Mr. Carver shook his hockey stick at a passing pack like Man Friday. Lucy Sneads's tits bounced like twin water balloons.

Who cares who slipped me the note? I thought, watching Dawn Madden's coffee-cream calves. *It got there.*

"Pearls before swine!" Mr. Dunwoody snorted on his Vicks Inhaler. "Pearls before swine!"

Mum was on the phone to Aunt Alice when I got home but she gave me this sunny wave. Wimbledon was on TV with the sound turned down. Summer gusted through the open house. I made a glass of Robinson's Barley Water and made one for Mum too. "Oh," she said when I put it by the phone, *"what a thoughtful son I've raised!"* Mum'd bought Maryland Chocolate Chip Cookies. They're new and totally lush. I grabbed five, went upstairs, changed, lay on my bed, ate the biscuits, put on "Mr. Blue Sky" by ELO and played it five or six times, guessing what test the Spooks'd set me. There's always a test. Swim across the lake in the woods, climb the quarry down Pig Lane, go nightcreeping across some back gardens. Who cares? I'd do it. If I was a Spook, *every* day'd be as epic as today.

The record stopped. I sifted through the afternoon's sounds.

Spaghetti Bolognese is mince, spaghetti, and a blob of ketchup, normally. But Mum did a proper recipe this evening, and it wasn't even anyone's birthday. Dad, Julia, and me guessed the ingredients in turn. Wine, aubergines (rubbery but not pukesome), mushrooms, carrot, red pepper, garlic, onions, toe-flake cheese, and this red dust called paprika. Dad talked about how spices used to be like gold or oil nowadays. Clippers and schooners brought them back from Jakarta, Peking, and Japan. Dad said how in those days Holland was as powerful as the USSR is today. Holland! (Often I think boys don't *become* men. Boys just get papier-mâchéd inside a man's mask. Sometimes you can tell the boy is still in there.) Julia talked about her afternoon in the solicitor's office in Malvern. Julia's doing a summer job there, filing, answering the phone, and typing letters. She's saving to go on holiday with Ewan in August on an InterRail. You pay £175 and can go *anywhere* on the trains in Europe for free for a month. Acropolis at dawn. Moon over Lake Geneva.

Jammy thing.

So anyway, it was Mum's turn. "You won't *believe* who was at Penelope Melrose's today."

"I *completely* forgot to ask." Dad's trying harder to be nice these days. "How was it? Who was it?"

"Penny's fine—but she'd only invited *Yasmin Morton-Bagot* along."

" 'Yasmin Morton-Bagot'? That's *got* to be a made-up name."

"Nobody made her name up, Michael. She was at our wedding."

"Was she?"

"Penny and Yasmin and I were in*sep*arable, during our college days."

"The fairer sex, Jason"—Dad gave me a crafty nod—"hunt in packs."

It felt all right to smile back.

"Right, Dad," Julia remarked, "unlike the *un*fairer sex, you mean?"

Mum pushed on. "Yasmin gave us the Venetian wine glasses."

"Oh, *those* things! The spiky ones without a base so you can't put them down? Are they *still* taking up loft space?"

"I'm rather surprised you don't remember her better. She's very striking. Her husband—Bertie—was a semiprofessional golfer."

"Was he?" Dad was impressed. " 'Was'?"

"Yes. He celebrated going professional by shacking up with a physiotherapist. Cleared out the joint bank accounts. Didn't leave poor Yasmin a bean."

Dad went all Clint Eastwood. "What sort of a man does that?"

"It was the *making* of her. She went into interior design."

Dad sucked air through his teeth. "Risky venture."

"Her first shop in Mayfair was such a hit, she opened another one in Bath within a year. She's not one to name-drop, but she's done work for the *royals*. She's staying with Penny at the moment, to open a third shop in Cheltenham. This one has a big gallery space, too, for exhibitions. But she's been let down by the manageress she'd originally hired to manage it."

"Staff! *Always* the tricky part of the equation. I was telling Danny Lawlor just the other day, if—"

"Yasmin offered *me* the job, you see."

A very surprised silence.

"Fan*tastic*, Mum." Julia beamed. "That's just *brilliant!*"

"Thank you, sweetheart."

Dad's lips smiled. "Certainly, it's a very flattering offer, Helena."

"I ran Freda Henbrook's boutique in Chelsea for eighteen months."

"That funny little place where you worked after college?"

"Mum's got a *fabulous* eye," Julia told Dad, "for colors and textiles and stuff. And she's *great* with people. She'll charm them into buying anything."

"Nobody's denying it!" Dad did a jokey surrender gesture. "I'm sure this Yasmin Turton-Bigot person wouldn't have—"

"Morton-Bagot. Yasmin Morton-Bagot."

" —wouldn't have floated the idea if she had any doubts, but—"

"Yasmin's a born entrepreneur. She handpicks her staff."

"And . . . you said . . . *what*, to her?"

"She's calling Monday for my decision."

The bell ringers in Saint Gabriel's began their weekly practice.

"Only, it's not in any way a pyramid selling thing, is it, Helena?"

"It's a gallery and interiors thing, Michael."

"And you *did* discuss terms? It isn't all commission?"

"Yasmin pays salaries, just like Greenland Supermarkets. I thought you'd be pleased at the prospect of me having an income. You won't have to shell out *hills of money* on my whims anymore. I can afford them myself."

"I am. I'm pleased. Of course I am."

Black cows'd gathered in the field, just over our fence, past the rockery.

"So, you'd be traveling to and from Cheltenham every day, would you? Six days a week?"

"Five. Once I've hired an assistant, it'd be four. Cheltenham's a lot closer than Oxford or London or all the places *you* manage to get to."

"It'll mean pretty major adjustments to our lifestyles."

"They're happening anyway. Julia's off to university. Jason's not a baby anymore."

My family chose this moment to look at me. "I'm pleased too, Mum."

"*Thank* you, darling."

(Thirteen is too old to be a "darling.")

Julia urged her, "You *are* going to take it, right?"

"I'm tempted." Mum did this shy smile. "Being stuck in the house every day is—"

" 'Stuck'?" Dad did an amused squeak. "Believe you *me*, there's no 'stuck' like being stuck to a shop, day in, day out."

"A gallery, *with* a shop. And at least I'd meet people."

Dad looked genuinely puzzled. "You know *dozens* of people."

Mum looked genuinely puzzled. "Who?"

"*Dozens!* Alice, for one."

"Alice has a house, a family, and a part-time business. In Richmond. Half a day away by glorious British Rail."

"Our neighbors are nice."

"Certainly. But we haven't the blindest thing in common."

"But . . . all your friends in the village?"

"Michael, we have lived here since just after Jason was born, but we are *townies*. Oh, they're *polite*, for the most part. In front of us. But . . ."

(I checked my Casio. My appointment with Spooks was soon.)

"Mum's right." Julia toyed with the Egyptian ankh necklace Ewan'd given her. "Kate says if you haven't lived in Black Swan Green since the War of the Roses, you'll never be a local."

Dad wasn't sure what to say.

Mum took a deep breath. "I'm lonely. It's that simple."

The cows swished their tails at the fat flies around their dungy arses.

Graveyards're sardined with rotting bodies, so of course they're scary places. A bit. But few things're only one thing if you think about them long enough. Last summer on sunny days I cycled as far as Ordnance Survey Map 150'd let me. Even Winchcombe, one time. If I found a Norman (rounded) or Saxon (stumpy) church with no one else around, I'd hide my bike round the back and lie down in the graveyard grass. Invisible birds, the odd flower in a jam jar. No Excalibur stuck in a stone, but I did find a tombstone from 1665; 1665 was the Plague Year. That was my record. Gravestones mostly flake away after a couple of centuries. Even death sort of dies. The saddest sentence I *ever* found was in a graveyard on Bredon Hill. HER ABUNDANT VIRTUES WOULD HAVE ADORNED A LONGER LIFE. Burying people's a question of fashion, too, like flares and drainpipe trousers. Yew trees grow in graveyards 'cause the Devil hates the smell of yew, Mr. Broadwas told me. I don't know if I believe that, but Weejee boards're definitely real. There're *stacks* of stories where the glass spells out something like

S - A - T - A - N - I - S - Y - O - U - R - M - A - S - T - E - R,

shatters, then the kids have to call a vicar. (Grant Burch got possessed one time and told Philip Phelps he's going to die on August 2, 1985. Philip Phelps won't go to sleep now unless there's a Bible under his pillow.)

People're always buried facing west, so at the end of time when the Last Trumpet blows, all the dead people'll claw their way up and walk due west to the Throne of Jesus to be judged. From Black Swan Green that means the Throne of Jesus'll be in Aberystwyth. Suicides, mind, get buried facing north. They won't be able to find Jesus 'cause dead people only walk in straight lines. They'll all end up in John O'Groats. Aberystwyth's a bit of a dive, but Dad says John O'Groats's just a few houses where Scotland runs out of Scotland.

Isn't *no* god better than one who does that to people?

In case Spooks were spying on me, I did an ace SAS roll. But Saint Gabriel's graveyard was deserted. Bell-ringing practice was still going on. Close up, bells don't really peal but tip, trip, dranggg, and baloooooom. Quarter past eight came and went. A breeze picked up and the two giant redwoods creaked their bones. Half past eight. The bells stopped and didn't start again. Quietness rings loud as ringing at first. I began worrying about time. Tomorrow's a Saturday, but if I wasn't home in an hour or so, I'd be getting a *hell* of a *What time do you call* this? Nine or ten bell ringers left the church, talking about someone called Malcolm who'd joined the Moonies and'd last been seen giving away flowers in Coventry. The bell ringers drifted through the lych-gate, and their voices floated off toward the Black Swan.

I noticed a kid sitting on the graveyard wall. Too small for Pluto Noak. Too scrawny for Grant Burch or Gilbert Swinyard or Pete Redmarley. Silent as a ninja, I sneaked up on him. He wore an army baseball cap with the flap turned back, like Nick Yew.

I *knew* Nick Yew'd be a Spook.

"All right, Nick."

But it was Dean Moran who went, *Gaaa!* and dropped off the wall.

Moran jumped up from a pond of nettles, swatting his arms, legs, and neck. "These bastard stingers've stinged me like bastards!" Moran knew he looked too much of a tit to get ratty. "What're *you* doing here?"

"What're *you* doing here?"

"Got a note, didn't I? Invitation to join—" You can see Moran think. "Eh. *You*'re never a Spook, are yer?"

"No. I thought . . . *you* were."

"Then this note in my pen case?"

He unscrumpled a note identical to mine.

Moran read my confusion right. "You got a note too?"

"Yeah." This development was confusing, disappointing, and worrying. Confusing 'cause Dean Moran's just not Spooks material. Disappointing 'cause what was the point of joining the Spooks if losers like Moran're being recruited too? Worrying 'cause this smelt like a windup.

Moran grinned. "That's *brilliant*, Jace!" I pulled him back onto the wall. "Spooks havin' *both* of us, at the same time, like."

"Yeah," I said. "Brilliant."

"They must reckon we're a natural team. Like Starsky and Hutch."

"Yeah." I looked round the graveyard for signs of Wilcox.

"Or Torvill and Dean. I knows yer like those little spangly skirts."

"Bloody hilarious."

Venus swung bright from the ear of the moon.

"D'you think," Moran asked, "they're really comin'?"

"Told us to be here, didn't they?"

A muffled trumpet sounded from one of the tithe cottages.

"Yeah, but . . . yer don't think it's a windup?"

Making us wait might be some sort of secret test. *If Moran gives up,* pointed out Maggot, *you'll look a better Spook.* "Go home, if you think so."

"No, I didn't mean that. I just meant . . . hey! Shooting star!"

"Where?"

"There!"

"Nope." If you have to learn it from a book, Moran doesn't know it. "It's a satellite. It isn't burning out. See? Just going in a straight line. Might be a satellite like Skylab, losing altitude. No one knows where it'll crash."

"But how come—"

"*Shush!*"

There's a wilder corner where broken slabs're stacked under corkscrewed holly. Mutterings there, I heard, for sure. Now I smelt cigarettes. Moran followed me, saying, "What is it?" (*God*, Moran can be a pillock.) I stooped to enter this tent of dark green. Pluto Noak sat on one stack of old headstones, Grant Burch on a pile of roof tiles, John Tookey on a third. Wished I could've told them it was *me* and not Moran who'd spotted them. Even saying "Hello" to hard kids is gay so I just said, "All right?"

Pluto Noak, Lord of Spooks, nodded back.

"Ooops." Stooping Moran head-butted my arse and I stumbled forward. "Soz, Jace."

I told Moran, "Don't say 'soz.' "

"So you knows the rules?" Grant Burch flobbed. "Yer gets a leggy over this wall, then yer've got fifteen minutes to get across the six back gardens. Once yer done, yer legs it to the green. Swinyard 'n' Redmarley'll be waitin' under the oak. If yer in time, welcome to the Spooks. If yer late, or if yer don't show, yer ain't no Spook and yer never will be."

Moran and me nodded.

"And if yer *caught*," added John Tookey, "yer ain't no Spook."

"And." Grant Burch pointed a warning finger. "*And*, if yer caught, you ain't never even *heard* of Spooks."

I defied my nerves and Hangman to say, "What's 'Spooks,' Ploot?"

Pluto Noak granted me an encouraging snort.

The holly shivered just as Saint Gabriel's chimed a quarter to nine. "Starting positions!" Grant Burch looked at me and Moran. "Who's first?"

"Me," I said, without glancing at Moran. "I ain't chicken."

The back garden of the first cottage was just a marsh of triffidy weeds. Straddling the wall, I gave the four faces in the graveyard one last glance, swung over, and plummeted into long grass. The house said, *They've gone.* No lights, an unfixed drainpipe, slack net curtains. All the same, I crept low.

Some squatter might be watching, with the lights turned off. With a cross-
bow. (That's the difference between me and Moran. Moran'd just tromp
across like he owned the place. Moran never takes snipers into account.) I
climbed up the plum tree that grew by the next wall.

A coat rustled, just above my head.

Idiot. Just a placky bag, flapping in the branches. That trumpet started up
again, *dead* close now. I slithered off a knobbly branch and balanced on the
next wall. A doddle so far. Better yet, the flat roof of the next garden's oil tank
was just a foot below me, and screened by coal-blue conifers.

The tank *boooooo*med, thunder underfoot.

The second back garden was miles dodgier. The curtains and even half the
windows were open. Two fat ladies sat on a sofa watching Asterixes and
Obelixes on the European *It's a Knockout.* The TV commentator Stuart
Hall was laughing like a Harrier jump jet taking off. The garden had no
cover. A badminton net drooped over the threadbare lawn, that was it. Plas-
ticky bats, bowls, an archery target, and a paddling pool lay littered, all dead
cheap and Woolworth's-looking. Worse, a camper van was parked round the
side. This roly-poly guy with an upside-down face was playing his trumpet in
it. His cheeks swelled bullfroggishly but his gaze was fixed down his garden.

Notes went up.

Notes went down.

Three whole minutes must've gone by. I didn't know what to do.

The back door opened and a fat lady trotted over to the van. As she opened
the door, she said, "Vicky's sleepin'." The trumpeter pulled her in, threw
down his trumpet, and they started snogging hungrily as two dogs attacking a
box of Milk Tray. The camper van began to wobble.

I dropped off the oil tank, slipped on a golf ball, got up, dashed over the
lawn, fell over an invisble croquet hoop, got up, then misjudged my jump
onto the fence beam. My foot made a splintering *whack!*

You're bacon, stated Unborn Twin.

I swung myself over the fence and fell to the earth like a sack of logs.

The third cottage was where Mr. Broadwas lives. If Mr. Broadwas saw me,
he'd phone my dad and I'd be dismembered by midnight. Sprinklers *swsss-
swwsss-swwwsss*ed. Drops swept my face where I sat. Most of the garden was
hidden by a screen of runner beans.

I had another problem. In the garden behind me, a woman's voice called out. "Come *back*, Gerry! It's only them foxes again!"

"'Tain't no fox!" That'd be the trumpeter. "It's one o' them kids!"

Two hands, *right above my head*, gripped the fence.

I sprinted to the end of the runner beans. I froze.

Mr. Broadwas sat on the doorstep. Water chundered into a metal watering can from a tap.

Panic swarmed up me like wasps in a tin.

The woman's voice behind me said, "It's a *fox*, Gerry! Ted shot one last week what he thought was the Beast o' Dartmoor first off."

"Oh aye?" The hands left the top of the fence. One hand appeared in a hole my foot'd punched through the fence. "A fox did *this*, did it?"

Once again, the trumpeter's fingers appeared on top. The fence groaned as he prepared to heave himself up.

Mr. Broadwas hadn't heard 'cause of the water noise, but now he put down his pipe on the step, and stood up.

Trapped, trapped, trapped. Dad'd *murder* me.

"*Mandy?*" A new voice came from the garden behind me. "Gerry?"

"Oh, Vicks," said the first woman. "We heard a strange noise."

"I was practicin' my trumpet," said the man, "and I heard a funny sound, so I came out to take a gander."

"Oh aye? Then what's this?"

Mr. Broadwas turned his back to me.

The fence ahead was too high to jump over, with no fingerholds.

"I CAN SMELL HIM ON YER! I CAN SEE YER LIPPY!"

Mr. Broadwas closed off the tap.

"IT'S NOT LIPSTICK, YER CRAZY BINT," screamed the trumpeter over the fence, "IT'S JAM!"

My dad's gardener walked up to where I crouched, water sloshing in his can. His eyes met mine but he didn't look remotely surprised.

"I came in to find a tennis ball," I blurted.

"The easiest way is down behind the shed."

This didn't sink in at first.

"You're wasting precious time," added Mr. Broadwas, turning to his row of onions.

"Thanks," I gulped, realizing that he knew I'd lied but was letting me off scot-free anyway. I dashed down the path and around the corner of the shed.

The air in the gap was heavy with fresh creosote fumes. Mr. Broadwas must've been a Spook when he was younger too, then.

"I WISH MUM'D DROWNED YER IN WORCESTER CANAL!" The second woman's scream sliced the cool murk. "BOTH OF YER! IN A SACK FULL O' STONES!"

The moon-rocky fourth garden was a spillage of concrete meringue and gravel. Ornaments *everywhere*. Not just gnomes, but Egyptian sphinxes, Smurfs, fairies, sea otters, Pooh Bear and Piglet and Eeyore, Jimmy Carter's face, you name it. Himalayas divided the garden down the middle at shoulder height. This sculpted garden'd once been a local legend and so had its creator, Arthur Evesham. The *Malvern Gazetteer*'d printed photos with the headline THERE'S NO PLACE LIKE GNOME. Miss Throckmorton'd brought our class to have a look. A smiley man'd served us all Ribena and iced biscuits with pin men doing sports on them. Arthur Evesham'd died of a heart attack a few days after our visit, in fact. That was the first time I'd heard "heart attack" and I thought it meant your heart suddenly went crazy and attacked the rest of your body, like a ferret down a rabbit warren. You sometimes see Mrs. Evesham in Mr. Rhydd's, buying old people's shopping like Duraglit and that toothpaste that tastes of Germolene.

So anyway, Arthur Evesham's kingdom'd uglified since his death. A Statue of Liberty lay like a dropped murder weapon. Pooh Bear looked like an acid attack victim. The world unmakes stuff faster than people can make it. Jimmy Carter's nose'd fallen off. I pocketed it, just because. The one sign of life was a candle in an upstairs window. I walked up the Great Wall of China and almost debagged myself on Edmund Hilary and Sherpa Tensing, pointing up to the evening moon. Beyond was a tiny square of lawn set in a bed of mint imperial pebbles. Feet first, I jumped onto this grass.

And sank up to my dick in cold water.

You prat, laughed Unborn Twin, *you ponce you pillock you plonker*.

Water sluiced out of my trouser legs as I scrambled out of the pond. Tiny leaves clung to me like globules of sick. Mum'll go *apeshit* when she sees. But I had to put that out of my mind, 'cause over the very next fence waited the most dangerous garden of all.

The good news was, Mr. Blake's garden was empty of Mr. Blake and the far side had monkey puzzle trees and sword plants. Excellent cover for a

Spook. The bad news was, a greenhouse ran the *entire* length of the garden, right under the fence. A ten-foot high, unstable fence, quivering under my weight. I'd have to inch along the fence in a sitting position, till I was right at Mr. Blake's living room window. If I *fell*, it was *smash* through a glass pane and *slam* on a concrete floor. Unless I got impaled on a tomato cane, like the priest in *The Omen* who gets spiked by a falling lightning conductor.

I had no choice.

The splintery fence-top sawed my bum and palms as I inched along it. My pond-soaked jeans were clammy-heavy. I nearly fell. If Mr. Blake's face appeared in any of the windows, I was dead meat. I nearly fell again.

I cleared the greenhouse and jumped down.

The slab made a ker*klon*ky noise. Luckily for me, the only person in Mr. Blake's lounge was Dustin Hoffman in *Kramer vs. Kramer*. (We'd seen it on holiday in Oban. Julia'd sobbed all the way through and called it the greatest film ever made.) Mr. Blake's lounge was sort of womanly, for a man who lives alone. Lacy lamps, pottery milkmaids, and paintings of African grasslands you buy on the stairs at Littlewoods, if you really want to. His wife must've bought it all before she caught leukemia. I crept under the kitchen window and then down the garden in the far shrubbery till I got to a water butt. I don't know why I looked back at the house right then, but I did.

Mr. Blake, gazing out of an upstairs window. Sixty seconds before there'd've been no *way* he wouldn't've seen me balancing on his fence. (Winning needs luck *and* bravery. I hoped Moran had fat reserves of both.) A Rolling Stones tongue sticker on the window pane'd resisted all attempts to scrape it off. Ghosts of other stickers surrounded that one. It must've been his son Martin's room, once upon a time.

Creased Mr. Blake just stared out. What at?

Not me. I was hidden by leaves.

Into his own reflected eyes?

But Mr. Blake's eyes were holes.

The last garden was Mervyn Hill's. Squelch's dad's only a dustman but his garden's like a National Trust property. 'Cause it was the end tithe cottage, it spread out more. A crazy paving path climbed up to a bench under a trellisy arch of roses. Through the French windows I saw Squelch playing Twister with two younger kids and a man I guessed was their dad. Must be visitors. Squelch's dad spun the spinner. Past the sofa was a TV showing the very end of *Kramer vs. Kramer*, where the kid's mum comes to take him away. I plotted my route. A cinch. A compost heap on the far side'd let me vault over the wall. Crouching, I ran to the trellisy arch. The roses brewed the air.

"Shush up." A shadow-woman sat on the bench five feet away from me. "Ooh, yer little *tyke!*"

"Aw," said her shadow-friend, "littl'un kicking again, love?"

(I couldn't *believe* they hadn't heard me.)

"Ow, ow, ow . . ." Huff. "She's excited to hear yer, Mum. Here, touch the bump . . ."

"*You* was a proper little acrobat, too, love," said the older shadow, "now I think back." (I recognized Squelch's mum.) "Cartwheels and kung fu it was. Merv was always quieter, truth be told, even before he was out."

"Shan't be sorry when *this* little miss decides it's time. I ain't half fed up of bein' a whale on legs."

(Oh *God*. A pregnant woman. One thing *everyone* knows about *them* is if you give them a shock the baby pops out too early. Then the kid might be a retard like Squelch and it'd be my fault.)

"So you're still sure she's a girl?"

"Eleanor in Accounts, right, she did her test. Looped my weddin' ring through a strand of my hair and hung it over my palm. If it swings, yer baby's a boy. Mine loop-the-looped, so she's a girl."

"So *that* old one's still doing the rounds, is it?"

"Eleanor says she's never been wrong yet."

(My Casio said my time was nearly up.)

The game of Twister collapsed into a mound of crushed bodies, bent arms, and wriggling feet. "Look at that rabble!" Squelch's mum tutted, pleased.

"Ben's *so* sorry his mate in the warehouse at Kays Catalogues said no, Mum. About when Merv leaves school, I mean."

"Can't be helped, love. Nice of Ben to try."

(*Time*, throbbed my Casio. *Time*. I care too much, that's my problem. The whole *point* about being a Spook is that you're so hard you don't *care*.)

"I do worry what'll become of Merv, though. Specially when Bill and I, y'know, well, aren't around any longer."

"Mum! Will you listen to yourself?"

"*Merv* can't think of his future, can he? Merv can't think past the day after tomorrow."

"He's always got me and Ben, if it comes to it."

"You'll have three of yer own to look after soon, won't yer? Merv's gettin' *more* of a handful as time goes by, not less. Did Bill say? Found him in his bedroom one day last week flickin' through one o' them *Penthouses*. Bare-naked ladies and that. *That* stage."

"I s'pose it's only natural, Mum. All boys do it."

"I know, Jacks, but in, y'know, an *ordinary* boy, that sort of thing, it finds an outlet. Courtin' girls and that. I love Merv but what girl'll want to walk out with a lad like him? How'd he support a family? Merv's neither fish nor fowl, see. Ain't backward enough when it comes to allowances and what-not, ain't quick enough on his pegs for jobs like shuntin' boxes in Kays Cat-alogues."

"Ben said that's only 'cause they ain't hirin'. The recession and that."

"Tragic part is, Merv's craftier by half than what he makes out he is. It *suits* Merv to act the village idiot, 'cause all the other kids expect it."

A moon-gray cat crossed the lawn. The chimes'd start any second.

"Ben says the Pork Scratchings factory down Upton'll have *anyone*. They even took Giles Noak, *after* his old man got sent down."

(I'd never thought of that. Squelch was just this kid you laugh at. But think about Squelch aged twenty, or thirty? Think about what his mum does for him, every single *day*? Squelch aged fifty, or seventy? What'd happen to him? What's so funny about that?)

"I daresay the Pork Scratchings might, love, but that don't change—"

"Jackie?" The young dad called out from the French windows. "Jacks!"

I squeezed between the trellis and the wall.

"What is it, Ben? We're up here! On the bench."

Roses, thorny as orcs, sank their teeth into my chest and face.

"Is Wendy with yer? Merv got too excited again. Had one of his little acci-dents . . ."

"An whole ten minutes," mumbled Squelch's mum. "Must be a record. All right, Ben!" She got to her feet. "I'm comin'!"

When Squelch's mum and his pregnant sister were halfway to the house, Saint Gabriel bonged the first chime of nine o'clock. I dashed to the wall and bounded onto the compost heap. Instead of springboarding up, I sank into the rotting mush right up to my middle. There's a type of nightmare where the ground's your enemy.

The second chime bonged.

I struggled out of the compost heap and over the last wall, dangled in limbo as the third chime bonged, then dropped onto the drive that runs down the side of Mr. Rhydd's shop. Then, in my soggy compost-covered jeans, I legged it over the crossroads and qualified for Spooks with not two *minutes* to spare but two *chimes*.

As I knelt at the feet of the oak, my breathing grated like a rusty saw. I couldn't even pick the thorns from my socks. But right there, right then, I felt happier than I could remember being. Ever.

"*You*, my son"—Gilbert Swinyard slapped my back—"are one *boney fider* Spook!"

"No one *ever* cut it that fine, mind!" Grant Burch did a goblin cackle. "Ten seconds to spare!"

Pete Redmarley sat cross-legged, smoking. "Thought you'd bottled out." Pete Redmarley is never shocked and he's already got a half-decent mustache. He's never told me he thinks I'm a gay snob but I know that's what he thinks.

"You was wrong, then," stated Gilbert Swinyard. (Being stuck up for by a kid like Gilbert Swinyard's *exactly* the point of being in Spooks.) "Christ, Taylor! What happened to yer trousers?"

"Stepped into . . ." I gasped, still desperate for oxygen. "Arthur Evesham's bastard pond . . ."

Even Pete Redmarley smirked at that.

"Then . . ." I began laughing too. "Fell into Squelch's compost heap . . ."

Pluto Noak jogged up. "Did he do it?"

"Aye," said Gilbert Swinyard, "by the skin of his teeth."

"Ten *seconds* to spare," said Grant Burch.

"There were—" I just stopped myself saluting Pluto Noak. "There was loads of people still around in their gardens."

"Course there are. It ain't dark yet. *Knew* you'd do it, though." Pluto Noak slapped my shoulder. (Dad did that when I learnt to dive, just the once.) "*Knew* it. A celebration is in order." Pluto Noak stuck his arse out, like he was sitting on a phantom motorbike. His right foot kicked it into life. As Pluto Noak's hand revved up, this *stunning* Harley-Davidson fart roared out of his arse. Fraping up through four gears for three, five, *ten* seconds.

Us Spooks *pissed* ourselves.

The noise of a fence collapsing and a kid falling through glass carries a long way at twilight. Gilbert Swinyard's joke about a baby in a microwave died on his lips. The other Spooks looked at me as if I'd know what the noise meant, which I did. "Blake's greenhouse."

"Moran?" Grant Burch sniggered. "He's *broken* it?"

"Fallen through it." (Burch's snigger died.) "Ten, twelve foot."

The bell ringers now came swaying out of the Black Swan singing about a cat who crept into a crypt and crapped and crept out again.

"Moron Moran," rhymed Pluto Noak, "hide up yer warren."

"That *dozy* fuckup," said Pete Redmarley. "I *knew* he was a mistake." He scowled at the other Spooks. "We didn't *need* any new Spooks." (That meant me, too.) "Might as well invite Squelch in, next."

"Better be off, any road." Gilbert Swinyard got up. "All of us."

A fact sunk a hook into me. If *I'd* fallen through Mr. Blake's greenhouse and not Moran, Moran wouldn't be abandoning me to that psycho. He just wouldn't.

Keep your fat trap shut, ordered Maggot.

"Ploot?"

Pluto Noak and the Spooks turned round.

"Isn't anyone going to . . ." Saying this was miles more difficult than running across people's back gardens. ". . . Make sure Moran's"—Hangman jammed "not hurt"—"I mean, what if he's bust a leg or . . . cut to bits on glass?"

"Blake'll call an ambulance," said Grant Burch.

"But shouldn't we . . . y'know . . ."

"No, Taylor." Pluto Noak looked thuggish now. "I do not know."

"That *dildo* knew our rules." Pete Redmarley spat. "Yer gets caught, yer on yer own. You go knockin' on Blake's door after *this*, Jason Taylor, and it'll be *what* and *why* and *who* and the third fuckin' degree and Spooks'll get named and we *ain't* havin' that. We was here long before *you* ever set foot in this village."

"I wasn't going to—"

"*Good.* 'Cause Black Swan Green ain't London or Richmond or wherever the fuck. Black Swan Green ain't got space for secrets. You go knockin' on Roger Blake's door, we'll *know* about it."

The wind riffled the ten thousand pages of the oak tree.

"Yeah, sure," I protested, "I just—"

"You ain't clapped *eyes* on Moran tonight." Pluto Noak jabbed a stubby finger at me. "You ain't seen *us*. You ain't heard of Spooks."

"Taylor." Grant Burch gave me my last warning. "Go home, okay?"

So here I am, two doubled-back minutes later, eye to eye with Mr. Blake's door knocker, *cacking* myself. Mr. Blake is shouting inside the house. He's not bollocking Moran. He's on the phone, shouting about an ambulance. This is just the beginning. I realize something about all the suicides traipsing north, north, north to a nowhere place where the Highlands melt into the sea.

It's not a curse or a punishment.

It's what they *want*.

solarium

"OPEN UP! OPEN UP!" holler door knockers. "OR I'LL BLOW YOUR HOUSE DOWN!" Bells're shyer. Bells're "Hello? Anyone home?" The vicarage had a knocker and a bell and I'd tried both, but still nobody answered. I waited. Perhaps the vicar was putting his quill in his inkpot, huffing, "Gracious, three o'clock already?" I pressed my ear to the door but the big old house gave nothing away. Sunshine flooded the thirsty lawn, flowers blazed, trees drowsed in the breeze. A dusty Volvo Estate sat in the garage needing a wash and wax. (Volvos're the only famous Swedish thing 'cept for ABBA. Volvos've got roll bars so you don't get Garibaldi-biscuited if a juggernaut slams you down a motorway embankment.)

I was half-hoping nobody'd answer. The vicarage's a serious place, the opposite of where kids should be. But when I'd crept here under cover of darkness last week, an envelope'd been Sellotaped over the letter box. FOR THE ATTENTION OF ELIOT BOLIVAR, POET. Inside was a short letter written in lilac ink on slate-gray paper. It invited me to come to the vicarage to discuss my work at three o'clock on Sunday. "Work." Nobody's *ever* called Eliot Bolivar's poems "work."

I kicked a pebble down the drive.

A bolt slid like a rifle and an old man opened up. His skin was blotched as a dying banana. He wore a collarless shirt and braces. "Good afternoon?"

"—Hi, uh, hello." (I meant to say "Good afternoon" but Hangman's keen on G-words lately.) "Are you the vicar?"

The man glanced round the garden, as if I might be a decoy. "I am certainly not a vicar. Why?" A foreign accent, sourer than French. "Are you?"

I shook my head. (Hangman wouldn't even let me say "No.") "But the vicar invited me." I showed him the envelope. "Only, he didn't sign his"—I couldn't even say "name"—"he didn't sign it."

"*Yah*, aha." The nonvicar hasn't been surprised by anything for years. "Come to the solarium. You may remove your shoes."

Inside smelt of liver and soil. A velvet staircase sliced sunlight across the hall. A blue guitar rested on a sort of Turkish chair. A bare lady in a punt drifted on a lake of water lilies in a gold frame. The "solarium" sounded ace. A planetarium for the sun instead of stars? Maybe the vicar was an astronomer in his spare time.

The old man offered me a shoehorn. I'm not sure how to use them, so I said, "No thanks" and prized my trainers off the usual way. "Are you a butler?"

"Butler. *Yah*, aha. A good description of my role in this house, I think. Follow me, please."

I thought only archbishops and popes were posh enough for butlers, but vicars can obviously have them too. The worn floorboards ribbled the soles of my feet through my socks. The hallway wound past a boring lounge and a clean kitchen. The high ceilings had cobwebby chandeliers.

I nearly bumped into the butler's back.

He'd stopped, and spoke around a narrow door. "A visitor."

This solarium didn't have any scientific apparatus in it, though its skylights were big enough for telescopes. The huge window framed a wild garden of foxgloves and red-hot pokers. Bookcases lined the walls. Midget trees stood in mossy pots round the unused fireplace. Cigarette smoke hazed everything like in a TV flashback.

On a cane throne sat an old toady lady.

Old but grand, like she'd stepped out of a portrait, with silver hair and a royal purple shawl. I guessed she was the vicar's mother. Her jewels were big as Cola Cubes and sherbet lemons. Maybe she was sixty, maybe seventy. With old people and little kids you can't be sure. I turned to look at the butler but the butler'd gone.

The old lady's rivery eyeballs chased the words across the pages.

Should I cough? That'd be stupid. She knew I was there.

Smoke streamed upward from her cigarette.

I sat down on an armless sofa till she was ready to talk. Her book was called *Le Grand Meaulnes*. I wondered what *Meaulnes* means and wished I was as good at French as Avril Bredon.

The clock on the mantelpiece shaved minutes into seconds.

Her knuckles were as ridged as Toblerone. Every now and then her bony fingers swept ash off the page.

"My name is Eva van Outryve de Crommelynck." If a peacock had a human voice, that'd be hers. "You may address me as Madame Crommelynck." I guessed her accent was French without being sure. "My English friends, an endangered species in these days, they say to me, 'Eva, in Great Britain your "Madame" is too onions-and-béret. Why not simply "Mrs." Crommelynck?' And I say, 'Go to the hell! What is wrong with onions-and-béret? I am Madame and my *e* is strongly attached!' *Allons donc.* It is three o'clock, a little after, so you are Eliot Bolivar the poet, I presume?"

"Yes." ("Poet!") "Very pleased to meet you, Madame Crommylenk."

"Crom-*mel*-ynck."

"Crom*mel*ynck."

"Bad, but better. You are younger than I estimated. Fourteen? Fifteen?" It's ace being mistaken for an older kid. "Thirteen."

"*Ackkk*, a wonderful, miserable age. Not a boy, not a teenager. Impatience but timidity too. Emotional incontinence."

"Is the vicar going to get here soon?"

"Pardon me?" She leaned forward. "Who"—it came out as "Oo"—"is this 'vicar'?"

"This *is* the vicarage, right?" I showed her my invitation, uneasy now. "It says so on your gatepost. On the main road."

"Ah." Madame Crommelynck nodded. "Vicar, vicarage. You miscomprehend a thing. A vicar lived here once upon a time, doubtless; before him, two vicars, three vicars, many vicars"—her scrawny hand mimed a *poof* of smoke—"but no more. The Anglican church becomes bankrupter and bankrupter, year by year, like British Leyland Cars. My father said, Catholics know how to run the business of religion. Catholics and Mormons. Propagate customers, they tell their congregation, or is the Inferno for you! But your Church of England, no. Consequences is, these en*chant*ible rectory houses are sold or rented, and vicars must move to little houses. Only the *name* 'vicarage' is remaining."

"But." I swallowed. "I've been posting my poems through your letter box since January. How come they're printed in the parish magazine every month?"

"This"—Madame Crommelynck took such a mighty drag on her cigarette I could see it shrink—"should be no mystery to an agile brain. *I* deliver your poems to the real vicar in his real vicarage. An ugly bungalow near Hanley Castle. I do not charge you for this service. Is gratis. Is a fine exercise for my not-agile bones. But in payment, I read your poems first."

"Oh. Does the real vicar know?"

"I *too* make my deliveries in darkness, anonymous, so I am not apprehended by the vicar's *wife*—oh, she is an hundred times worst than he is. An harpy of tattle-tittle. She asked to use *my* garden for her Saint Gabriel's Summer Fête! 'It is tradition,' says Mrs. Vicar. 'We need space for the human bridge. For the stalls.' I tell her, 'Go to the hell! I pay you rent do I not? Who has need of a divine creator who must sell inferior marmalade?' " Madame Crommelynck smacked her leathery lips. "But at least her husband publishes your poems in his funny magazine. Perhaps he is redeemable." She gestured at a bottle of wine standing on a pearly table. "You will drink a little?"

A whole glass, said Unborn Twin.

I could hear Dad saying, *You drank* what? "No thanks."

Madame Crommelynck shrugged: *Your loss.*

Inky blood filled her glass.

Satisfied, she rapped on a small pile of *Black Swan Green Parish Magazines* by her side. "To business."

"A young man needs to learn when a woman wishes her cigarette to be lit."

"Sorry."

An emerald dragon wraps Madame Crommelynck's lighter. I was worried the smell of cigarette smoke'd stick to my clothes and I'd have to make up a story for Mum and Dad about where I'd been. While she smoked, she murmured my poem "Rocks" from May's magazine.

I felt giddy with importance that *my* words'd captured the attention of this exotic woman. Fear, too. If you show someone something you've written, you give them a sharpened stake, lie down in your coffin, and say, "When you're ready."

Madame Crommelynck did a tiny growl. "You imagine blank verse is a liberation, but no. Discard rhyme, you discard a parachute . . . Sentimentality you mistake for emotion . . . You love words, yes"—a pride bubble swelled up in me—"but your words are still the master of *you*, *you* are not yet master of *them* . . ." (The bubble popped.) She studied my reaction. "But, at least, your poem is robust enough to *be* criticized. Most so-called poems disintegrate at one touch. Your imagery is here, there, fresh, I am not ashamed to call it so. Now *I* wish to know a thing."

"Sure. Anything."

"The domesticity in this poem, these kitchens, gardens, ponds . . . is not a metaphor for the ludicrous war in the South Atlantic in this year?"

"The Falklands was on while I was writing the poem," I answered. "The war just sort of seeped in."

"So these demons who do war in the garden, they symbolize General Galtieri and Margaret Thatcher. I am right?"

"Sort of, yes."

"But they are *also* your father and your mother, however. I am right?"

Hesitations're yeses or nos if the questioner already knows the answer. It's one thing writing about your parents. Admitting it's another matter.

Madame Crommelynck did a tobaccoey croon to show her delight. "You are a polite thirteen-year boy who is too timid to cut his umbilical cords! Except"—she gave the page a nasty poke—"*here. Here* in your poems you do what you do not dare to do"—she jabbed at the window—"*here.* In reality. To express what is *here.*" She jabbed my heart. It hurt.

X-rays make me queasy.

Once a poem's left home it doesn't care about you.

" 'Back Gardens.' " Madame Crommelynck held up the June edition.

I was sure she thought the title was a killer.

"But why is this title so atrocious?"

"Uh . . . it wasn't my first choice."

"So why you christen your creation with an inferior name?"

"I was going to call it 'Spooks.' But there's this actual gang who're called that. They go nightcreeping round the village. If I called the poem *that* they might suspect who'd written it and sort of . . . get me."

Madame Crommelynck sniffed, underimpressed. Her mouth chanted my lines at quarter volume. I hoped at least she'd say something about the poem's descriptions of dusk and moonlight and darkness.

"There are many beautiful words in here . . ."

"Thanks," I agreed.

"Beautiful words ruin your poetry. A *touch* of beauty enhances a dish, but you throw a hill of it into the pot! No, the palate becomes nauseous. You belief a poem must be beautiful, or it can have no excellence. I am right?"

"Sort of."

"Your 'sort of' is annoying. A yes, or a no, or a qualification, please. 'Sort of' is an idle *loubard*, an ignorant *vandale*. 'Sort of' says, 'I am ashamed by clarity and precision.' So we try again. You belief a poem must be beautiful, or it is not a poem. I am right?"

"Yes."

"*Yes*. Idiots labor in this misconception. Beauty is *not* excellence. Beauty is distraction, beauty is cosmetics, beauty is ultimately fatigue. Here"—she read from the fifth verse—" 'Venus swung bright from the ear of the moon.' The poem has a terminal deflation. *Ffffffffft!* Dead tire. Automobile accident. It says, 'Am I not a pretty pretty?' I answer, 'Go to the hell!' If you have a magnolia in a moonlight courtyard, do you paint its flowers? Affix the flashy-flashy Christmas lights? Attach plastic parrots? No. You do not."

What she said sounded true, but.

"You think"—Madame Crommelynck snorted smoke—" 'This old witch is crazy! A magnolia tree exists already. Magnolias do not need poets to exist. In the case of a poem, a poem, *I* must create it.' "

I nodded. (I *would*'ve thought that if I'd've had a few minutes.)

"You *must* say what you think, or else spend your Saturday with your head in a bucket and not in conversation with me. You understand?"

"Okay," I said, nervous that "okay" wasn't okay.

"Good. I reply, verse is 'made.' But the word 'make' is unsufficient for a true poem. 'Create' is unsufficient. All words are insufficient. Because of this. *The poem exists before it is written.*"

That, I didn't get. "Where?"

"T. S. Eliot expresses it *so*—the poem is a raid on the inarticulate. I, Eva van Outryve de Crommelynck, agree with him. Poems who are not written yet, or not written ever, exists here. The realm of the inarticulate. Art"—she put another cigarette in her mouth, and this time I was ready with her dragon lighter—"fabricated of the inarticulate *is* beauty. Even if its themes is ugly. Silver moons, thundering seas, clichés of cheese, poison beauty. The amateur thinks *his* words, *his* paints, *his* notes, makes the beauty. But the master knows his words is just the *vehicle* in who beauty sits. The master knows he does *not* know what beauty is. Test this. Attempt a definition now. What is beauty?"

Madame Crommelynck tapped cigarette ash into a blobby ruby ashtray. "Beauty's . . ."

She relished my stumpedness. I wanted to impress her with a clever definition, but I kept crashing into *Beauty's something that's beautiful.*

Problem was, all this is new. In English at school we study a grammar book by a man named Ronald Ridout, read *Cider with Rosie,* do debates on foxhunting, and memorize "I Must Go Down to the Sea Again," by John Masefield. We don't have to actually think about stuff.

I admitted, "It's difficult."

"Difficult?" (Her ashtray was in the shape of a curled girl, I saw.) "Impossible! Beauty is *immune* to definition. When beauty is present, you know. Winter sunrise in dirty Toronto, one's new lover in an old café, sinister magpies on a roof. But is the beauty of these *made*? No. Beauty *is* here, that is all. Beauty *is.*"

"But . . ." I hesitated, wondering if I should say this.

"My one demand," she said, "is you say what you think!"

"You just chose natural things. How about paintings, or music. We say, 'The potter makes a beautiful vase.' Don't we?"

"We *say,* we *say.* Be careful of *say.* Words *say,* 'You have labeled this abstract, this concept, therefore you have captured it.' No. They lie. Or not lie, but are maladroit. *Clumsy.* Your potter has made the vase, yes, but has *not* made the *beauty.* Only an object where beauty *resides.* Until the vase is dropped and breaks. Who is the ultimate fate of every vase."

"But—" I still wasn't satisfied. "Surely *some* people, *some*where know what beauty is? At a university?"

"University?" She made a noise that might've been laughter. "Imponderables *are* ponderable, but answerable, no. Ask a philosopher, but be cautious. If you hear, 'Eureka!,' if you think, 'His answer has captured my question!,' then here is *proof* he is a counterfeit. If your philosopher has *truly* left Plato's cave, if he has stared into that sun of the blind . . ." She counted the three possibilities on her fingers. "He is lunatic, or his answers are questions who is only masquerading as answers, or he is silent. Silent because you can *know* or you can *say,* but both, no. My glass is empty."

The last drops were the thickest.

"Are you a poet?" (I'd *nearly* said "too.")

"No. That title is hazardous. But I had intimacy with poets when I was young. Robert Graves wrote a poem of me. Not his best. William Carlos Williams asked me to abandon my husband and"—she uttered the word like a pantomime witch—"'elope'! Very romantic, but I had a pragmatic head and he was destitute as . . . *épouvantail*, a—how you say the man in a field who frights birds?"

"Scarecrow?"

"Scarecrow. Exactly. So I tell him, 'Go to the hell, Willy, our souls eat poetry, but one has seven deadly sins to feed!' He consented my logic. Poets are listeners, if they are not intoxicated. But *novelists*"—Madame Crommelynck did a *yuck* face—"is schizoids, lunatics, liars. Henry Miller stayed in our colony in Taormina. A pig, a perspiring pig, and Hemingway, you know?"

I'd heard of him so I nodded.

"Lecherousest pig in the entire farm! Cinematographers? *Fffffft. Petits Zeus* of their universes. The world is their own film set. Charles Chaplin also, he was my neighbor in Geneva, across the lake. A charming *petit Zeus*, but a *petit Zeus*. Painters? Squeeze their hearts dry to make the pigments. No heart remains for people. Look at that Andalusian goat, Picasso. His biographers come for my stories of him, beg, offer money, but I tell them, 'Go to the hell, I am not an human *juke*box.' Composers? My father was one. Vyvyan Ayrs. His ears was burnt with his music. I, or my mother, he rarely listened. Formidable in his generation, but now he is fallen from the repertory. He exiled at Zedelgem, south of Brugge. My mother's estate was there. My native tongue is Flemish. So you hear, English is not an adroit tongue for me, too many *-lesses* and *-lessness*es. You think I am French?"

I nodded.

"Belgian. The destiny of discreet neighbors is to be confused with the noisy ones next door. See an animal! On the lawn. By the geraniums . . ."

One moment we were watching the twitch of a squirrel's heart.

The next, it'd vanished.

Madame Crommelynck said, "Look at me."

"I am doing."

"No. You are not. Sit here."

I sat on her footstool. (I wondered if Madame Crommelynck's got a butler 'cause something's wrong with her legs.) "Okay."

"Do not hide in your 'okay.' Closer. I do not bite off the heads of boys. Not on a full stomach. Look."

There's a rule that says you don't gaze too intently at a person's face. Madame Crommleynck was ordering me to break it.

"Look closer."

Those parma violets, I smelt, fabrics, an ambery perfume, and something rotting. Then something weird happened. The old woman turned into an It. Sags ruckused its eye bags and eyelids. Its eyelashes'd been gummed into spikes. Deltas of tiny red veins snaked its stained whites. Its irises misty like long-buried marbles. Makeup dusted its mummified skin. Its gristly nose was subsiding into its skull hole.

"You see beauty here?" It spoke in the wrong voice.

Manners told me to say yes.

"Liar!" It pulled back and became Madame Crommelynck again. "Forty, thirty years ago, yes. My parents created me in the customary fashion. Like your potter making your vase. I grew to a girl. In mirrors, my beautiful lips told my beautiful eyes, 'You are me.' Men made stratagems and fights, worshipped and deceived, burnt money on extravagances, to 'win' this beauty. My age of gold."

Hammering started up in a far-off room.

"But human beauty falls leaf by leaf. You miss the beginning. One tells one, *No, I am tired* or *The day is bad, that is all.* But later, one cannot contradict the mirror. Day by day by day it falls, until this *vieille sorcière* is all who remains, who uses cosmetician's potions to approximate her birth gift. Oh, people say, 'The old are *still* beautiful!' They patronize, they flatter, maybe they wish to comfort themselves. But no. Eating the roots of beauty is a—" Madame Crommelynck sank back into her creaky throne, tired out. "An, how you say, the snail who has no house?"

"A slug?"

"Insatiable, undestructible slug. Where in the hell are my cigarettes?"

The box'd slipped to her feet. I passed them to her.

"Leave now." She looked away. "Return next Saturday, three o'clock, I tell you more reasons why your poems fail. Or do not return. An hundred other works are waiting." Madame Crommelynck picked up *Le Grand Meaulnes*, found her place, and started reading. Her breathing'd got whistlier and I wondered if she was ill.

"Thanks, then . . ."

My legs'd got pins and needles.

As far as Madame Crommelynck was concerned, I'd already left the solarium.

✽   ✽   ✽

Druggy pom-pom bees hovered in the lavender. The dusty Volvo was still in the drive, still needing its wash. I didn't tell Mum or Dad where I was going today, either. Telling them about Madame Crommelynck'd mean (a) admitting I was Eliot Bolivar; (b) twenty questions about who she is I can't answer 'cause she's an unnumbered dot-to-dot; (c) being told not to pester her. Kids aren't s'posed to visit old ladies if they're not grandmothers or aunts.

I pressed the bell.

The vicarage took *ages* to swallow up the chime.

Nobody. Had she gone out for a walk?

The butler hadn't taken this long last week.

I banged the knocker, sure it was useless.

I'd pedaled like mad over here 'cause I was thirty minutes late. Madame Crommelynck'd have a field marshal's attitude to punctuality, I reckoned. All for nothing, it appeared. I'd got *The Old Man and the Sea* by Ernest Hemingway from the school library, just 'cause Madame Crommelynck'd mentioned him. (The introduction said the book'd made Americans burst into tears when it was read on the radio. But it's just about an old guy catching a monster sardine. If Americans cry at that, they'll cry at anything.) I rubbed some lavender in my palms and snuffed. Lavender's my favorite smell, after Wite-Out and bacon rind. I sat down on the steps, not sure where to go next.

A July afternoon yawned.

Mirage puddles'd shimmered on the Welland road as I rode here.

I could've gone to sleep on the baked doorstep.

Little naked ants.

A bolt slid like a rifle and the old butler opened up. "You are back for more." Today he wore a golf jersey. "You may remove your shoes."

"Thanks." As I prized off my trainers I heard a piano, joined by a quiet violin. I hoped Madame Crommelynck didn't have a visitor. Once you have three people you may as well have a hundred. The stairway needed fixing. A knacked blue guitar'd been left on a broken stool. In the gaudy frame a shivery woman sprawled in a punt on a clogged pond. Once again, the butler led me to the solarium. (I looked "solarium" up. It just means "an airy room.") The sequence of doors we passed made me think of all the rooms of my past and future. The hospital ward I was born in, classrooms, tents, churches, offices, hotels, museums, nursing homes, the room I'll die in. (Has it been built yet?) Cars're rooms. So are woods. Skies're ceilings. Distances're walls. Wombs're rooms made of mothers. Graves're rooms made of soil.

That music was swelling.

A Jules Verne hi-fi, all silvery knobs and dials, occupied one corner of the solarium. Madame Crommelynck sat on her cane throne, eyes shut, listening. As if the music was a warm bath. (This time I knew she wouldn't be speaking for a while, so I just sat down on the armless sofa.) A classical L.P. was playing. Nothing like the *rumpty-tump-tump* stuff Mr. Kempsey plays in Music. Jealous *and* sweet, this music was, sobbing *and* gorgeous, muddy *and* crystal. But if the right words existed the music wouldn't need to.

The piano'd vanished. Now a flute'd joined the violin.

(I can still hear it, hours later.)

An unfinished letter going on for *pages* lay on Eva Crommelynck's desk. She'd put on this L.P. when she couldn't think of its next sentence.

A fat silver pen rested on the page she'd stopped writing. I batted off an urge to pick it up and read it.

The stylus clunked in its cradle. "The inconsolable," Madame Crommelynck said, "is so consoling." She didn't look very pleased to see me. "What is that advertisement you are wearing on your chest?"

"What advertisement?"

"*That* advertisement on your sweater!"

"This is my Liverpool F.C. top. I've supported them since I was five."

"What signifies 'Hitachi'?"

"The F.A.'ve changed the rules so football teams can wear sponsors' logos. Hitachi's an electronics firm. From Hong Kong, I think."

"So you *pay* an organization to be their advertisement? *Allons donc.* In clothes, in cuisine, the English have an irresistible urge to self-mutilation. But today you are late."

Explaining the ins and outs of the Mr. Blake Affair would've taken too long. I've lost count of how many times Mum and Dad and even Julia (when she's feeling vicious)'ve said *We'll say no more about it*, then dredge it up five minutes later. So I just told Madame Crommelynck I've got to do the washing up on my own for a month to pay for something I'd broken, and it'd been a late lunch 'cause Mum'd forgotten to defrost the leg of lamb.

Madame Crommelynck got bored before I finished. She gestured at the bottle of wine on her pearly table. "Today you drink?"

"I'm only allowed a thimbleful, on special occasions."

"If an audience with me does not qualify as 'special,' pour my glass."

(White wine smells of Granny Smiths, paint-stripper, and tiny flowers.)

"Always pour so the label is visible! If the wine is good, your drinker should know so. If the wine is bad, you deserve shame."

I obeyed. A drop dribbled down the bottle's neck.

"So. Do I learn today your true name, or do I still give hospitality to a stranger who hides behind a ridiculous pseudonym?"

Hangman was *even* stopping me from saying "Sorry." I got so het up and desperate and angry I blurted out "Sorry!" anyway, but so loud it sounded really rude.

"Your elegant apology does not answer my question."

I mumbled, "Jason Taylor" and wanted to cry.

"Jay *Who*? Pronounce it clearly! My ears are as old as me! I do not have microphones hidden to collect every little word!"

I *hated* my name. "Jason Taylor." Flavorless as chewed receipts.

"If you are an 'Adolf Coffin,' or a 'Pius Broomhead,' I comprehend. But why hide 'Jason Taylor' under an inaccessible symbolist and a Latin American revolutionary?"

My *huh?* must've shown.

"Eliot! T. S.! Bolívar! Simón!"

" 'Eliot Bolivar' just sounded more . . . poetic."

"What is more *poetic* than 'Jason,' an Hellenic hero? Who foundationed European literature if not the ancient Greeks? Not Eliot's coterie of thiefs of graves, I assure you! And what is a poet if he is not a tailor of words? Poets and tailors join what nobody else can join. Poets and tailors conceal their craft *in* their craft. No, I do not accept your answer. I believe the truth is, you use your pseudonym because your poetry is a shameful secret. I am correct?"

" 'Shameful' isn't the exact word, exactly."

"Oh, so *what* is the exact word, exactly?"

"Writing poetry's"—I looked around the solarium, but Madame Crommelynck's got a tractor beam—"sort of . . . gay."

" 'Gay'? A merry activity?"

This was hopeless. "Writing poems is . . . what creeps and poofters do."

"So you are one of these 'creeps'?"

"No."

"Then you are a '*pooof*-ter,' whatever one is?"

"No!"

"Then your logic is eluding me."

"If you're dad's a famous composer and your mum's an aristocrat, you can do things that you can't do if your dad works at Greenland Supermarkets and if you go to a comprehensive school. Poetry's one of those things."

"*Aha!* Truth! You are afraid the hairy barbarians will not accept you in their tribe if you write poetry."

"That's more or less it, yeah . . ."

"More? Or less? Which is the exact word, exactly?"

(She's a pain sometimes.) "That's it. Exactly."

"And you *wish* to become an hairy barbarian?"

"I'm a *kid.* I'm thirteen. *You* said it's a miserable age, being thirteen, and you're right. If you don't fit in, they make your life a misery. Like Floyd Chaceley or Nicholas Briar."

"*Now* you are talking like a real poet."

"I don't *understand* it when you say stuff like that!"

(Mum'd've gone, *Don't talk to* me *in that tone of voice!*)

"I *mean*"—Madame Crommelynck almost looked pleased—"you are entirely of your words."

"What does *that* mean?"

"You are being quintessentially truthful."

"Anyone can be truthful."

"About superficialities, Jason, yes, is easy. About pain, no, is not. So you want a double life. One Jason Taylor who seeks approval of hairy barbarians. Another Jason Taylor is Eliot Bolivar, who seeks approval of the literary world."

"Is that so impossible?"

"If you wish to be a versifier," she answered, whirlpooling her wine, "very possible. If you are a true artist"—she schwurked wine round her mouth—"absolutely *never.* If you are not truthful to the world about who and what you are, your art will stink of falsenesses."

I had no answer for that.

"Nobody knows of your poems? A teacher? A confidant?"

"Only you, actually."

Madame Crommelynck's eyes've got this glint. It's nothing to do with outside light. "You hide your poetry from your lover?"

"No," I said. "I, uh, don't."

"Don't hide your poetry or don't have a lover?"

"I don't have a girlfriend."

Quick as a chess-clock thumper, she said, "You prefer boys?"

I still can't believe she said that. (Yes I can.) "I'm normal!"

Her drumming fingers on the pile of parish magazines said, *Normal?*

"I do like this one girl, actually," I blurted out, to prove it. "Dawn Madden. But she's already got a boyfriend."

"*Oho?* And the boyfriend of Dawn Madden, he is a poet or a barbarian?" (She *loved* how she'd tricked Dawn Madden's name out of me.)

"Ross Wilcox's a prat, not a poet. But if you're going to suggest that I write a poem to Dawn Madden, no *way*. I'd be the village *laughing*stock."

"Absolutely, if you compose derivative verses of cupids and cliché, Miss Madden will remain with her '*prat*' and you will justly earn derision. But if a poem is beauty and *truth*, your Miss Madden will treasure your words more than money, more than certificates. Even when she is as old as I. *Especially* when she is as old as I."

"But." I ducked the subject. "Don't heaps of artists use pseudonyms?"

"Who?"

"Um . . ." Only Cliff Richard and Sid Vicious came to mind.

A phone started ringing.

"True poetry *is* truth. Truth is not popular, so poetry also is not."

"But . . . truth about what?"

"Oh, the life, the death, the heart, memory, time, cats, fear. Anything." (The butler didn't seem to be anwering the phone either.) "Truth is everywhere, like seeds of trees; even deceits contain elements of truth. But the eye is clouded by the quotidian, by prejudice, by worryings, scandal, predation, passion, ennui, and, worst, television. Despicable machine. Television was here in my solarium. When I arrived. I throwed it in the cellar. *It* was watching *me*. A poet throws all but truth in the cellar. Jason. There is a matter?"

"Er . . . your phone's ringing."

"I know a phone is ringing! It can go to the hell! I am talking to *you!*" (My parents'd run into a burning asbestos mine if they thought there was a phone in there ringing for them.) "One week before, we agreed 'What is beauty?' is a question unanswerable, yes? So today, a greater mystery. If an art is *true*, if an art is *free of falsenesses*, it is, a priori, beautiful."

I tried to digest that.

(The phone finally gave up.)

"Your best poem in here"—she rifled through the parish magazines—"is your 'Hangman.' It has pieces of truth of your speech impediment, I am right?"

A familiar shame burnt from my neck, but I nodded.

Only in my poems, I realized, do I get to say *exactly* what I want.

"Of course I am right. If 'Jason Taylor' was the name here, and not 'Eliot Bolivar Ph.D., O.B.E., R.I.P., B.B.C.' "—she biffed the page with "Hangman" on it—"the truth will make the greatest mortification with the hairy barbarians of Black Swan Green, yes?"

"I might as well hang myself."

"*Pfff!* Eliot Bolivar, *he* can hang. You, *you* must *write*. If you still fear to publish in your name, is better not to publish. But poetry is more resilient than you think. For many years I assisted for Amnesty International." (Julia's often on about them.) "Poets survive in gulags, in detention blocks, in torture chambers. Even in that misery hole there is poets working, *Merde*gate, no, where in the hell, on the Channel, I always am forgetting . . ." (She rapped her forehead to shake free the name.) "*Mar*gate. So believe me. Comprehensive schools are not so infernal."

"That music, when I came in. Was that your dad's? It was beautiful. I didn't know there *was* music like that."

"The sextet of Robert Frobisher. He was an amanuensis for my father, when my father was too old, too blind, too weak to hold a pen."

"I looked up Vyvyan Ayrs in the *Encyclopaedia Britannica* at school."

"Oh? And how does this authority venerate my father?"

The entry'd been short enough to memorize. " 'British composer, born 1870 Yorkshire; died 1932 Neerbeke, Belgium. Noted works: *Matruschyka Doll Variations, Untergehen Violinkonzert*, and *Todonvogel*—' "

"*Die TODtenvogel! TODtenvogel!*"

"Sorry. 'Critically respected in Europe during his lifetime, Ayrs is now rarely referred to outside the footnotes of twentieth-century music.' "

"That is all?"

I'd expected her to be impressed.

"A majestic encomium." She said it flat as a glass of Coke left out.

"But it must've been *ace* having a composer for a father."

I held the dragon lighter steady as she lowered the tip into the flame. "He made great unhappinesses for my mother." She inhaled, then blew out a quivery sapling of smoke. "Even today, to forgive is difficult. At your age, I went to school in Brugge and saw my father at weekends only. He had his ill-ness, his music, and we did not communicate. After his funeral, I wished to ask him one thousand things. Too late. Old story. Next to your head is a pho-tographic album. Yes, that one. Pass it."

A girl Julia's age sat on a pony under a big tree, before color was invented. A strand of hair curled against her cheek. Her thighs clamped the pony's flanks.

"God," I thought aloud, "she's gorgeous."

"Yes. Whatever beauty is, I had it, in those days. Or it had me."

"You?" Startled, I compared Madame Crommelynck with the girl in the photo. "Sorry."

"Your habit with that word diminishes your stature. Néfertiti was my finest pony. I entrusted her to the Dhondts—the Dhondts were family friends—when Grigoire and I escaped to Sweden seven, eight years after this photo-graph. The Dhondts were killed in 1942, during occupation by the Nazis. You imagine they are Resistance heroes? No, it was Morty Dhondt's sports car. His brakes failed, *boom*. Néfertiti's destiny, I do not know. Glue, sausages, stews for black-market men, for Gypsies, for SS officers, if I am realistic. This photograph was taken in Neerbeke in 1929, 1930 . . . Behind that tree is Zedelgem Château. My ancestors' home."

"Do you still own it?"

"It no longer exists. The Germans built an airfield where you see, so the British, the Americans . . ." Her hand made a *boom* gesture. "Stones, craters, mud. Now is all little boxes for houses, a gasoline station, a supermarket. Our home who survived half a millennium exists now only in a few old heads. And a few old photographs. My wise friend Susan has written this. 'By slicing out *this* moment and freezing it . . .'" Madame Crommelynck studied the girl she'd once been and tapped ash from her cigarette. "'. . . all photographs testify to time's relentless melt.'"

A bored dog barked a garden or two away.

A bride and groom pose outside a flinty chapel. Bare twigs say it's winter. The groom's thin lips say, *Look what I've got.* A top hat, a cane, half fox. But the bride's half lioness. Her smile's the idea of a smile. She knows more about her new husband than he knows about her. Above the church door a stone lady gazes up at her stone knight. Flesh-and-blood people in photographs look at the camera, but stone people look through the camera straight at you.

"My producers," announced Madame Crommelynck.

"Your parents? Were they nice?" That sounded stupid.

"My father died of syphilis. Your encyclopedia did not say that. Not a 'nice' death, I recommend you avoid. You see, the era"—"era" was a long sigh—"was different. Feelings were not expressed so incontinently. Not in our class of society, anyhow. My mother, oh, she was capable of great affection, but tem*pest*uous anger! She exerted power over all who she chose. No, I think not 'nice.' She died of an aneurysm just two years later."

I said, "I'm sorry," like you're s'posed to, for the first time in my life.

"It was a mercy she did not witness the destruction of Zedelgem." Madame Crommelynck raised her glasses to peer closer at the wedding photo. "How young! Photographs make me forget if time is forwards or backwards. No, photographs make me wonder if there *is* a forwards or backwards. My glass is empty, Jason."

I poured her wine, with the label showing properly.

"I never comprehended their marriage. It's alchemy. Do you?"

"Me? Do I understand my parents' marriage?"

"That is my question."

I thought hard. "I've"—Hangman gripped "never" and wouldn't let it go—"I haven't thought about it before. I mean . . . my parents're just there. They argue quite a lot, I s'pose, but they do a lot of their talking when they're arguing. They *can* be nice to each other. If it's Mum's birthday and Dad's away he gets Interflora to bring flowers. But Dad's working most weekends 'cause of the recession, and Mum's opening this gallery in Cheltenham. There's like this cold war over *that* at the moment." (Talking with some people's like moving up higher screens of a computer game.) "If I'd been more like an ideal son like a kid from *Little House on the Prairie*, if I'd been less sulky, then maybe Mum and Dad's marriage might've been"—the true word was "sunnier," but Hangman was active today—"friendlier. Julia, my"—Hangman teased me over the next word—"sister, she's ace at poking fun at Dad. Which he loves. And she can cheer Mum up just by rabbiting on. But she's off to university in the autumn. Then it'll just be the three of us. I can never get the right words out, not like Julia." Stammerers're usually too stressed to feel sorry for themselves, but a few drops of self-pity fell on me. "I can never get *any* words out."

Far off, the butler switched on his Hoover.

"*Ackkk*," Madame Crommelynck said, "I am an inquisitive old witch."

"No you're not."

The old Belgian lady gave me a pointy glare over her glasses.
"Not *all* the time."

A young pianist sat on his piano stool, relaxed, smiling, smoking. His hair was quiffed waxy like hair on old-fashioned film stars, but he didn't look toffish. He looked like Gary Drake. Nails in his eyes, wolf in his grin.

"Meet Robert Frobisher."

"He's the one," I asked, checking, "who wrote that incredible music?"

"Yes, he is the one who wrote that incredible music. Robert revered my father. Like a disciple, a son. They shared a musical empathy, who is an empathy more intimate than the sexual." (She said "sexual" like it was any other word.) "It is thanks to Robert, my father could compose his final masterpiece, *Die Todtenvogel*. In Warsaw, in Paris, in Vienna, for a brief summer, the name of Vyvyan Ayrs was restored to glory. *Oh*, I was a jealous *demoiselle!*"

"Jealous? Why?"

"My father praised Robert without respite! So my behavior was disgracious. But such reverences, such empathies that existed between them, they are very combustible. Friendship is a calmer thing. Robert left Zedelgem in winter."

"Back to England?"

"Robert had no home. His parents had uninherited him. He accommodated in an hotel, in Brugge. My mother forbidded me to meet him. Fifty years ago, reputations were important passports. Ladies of pedigree had a chaperone every minute. Anyhow, I did not wish to meet. Grigoire and I were engaged and Robert was sickness in his head. Genius, sickness, flash-flash, storm, calm, like a lighthouse. An isolated lighthouse. He could have eclipsed Benjamin Britten, Olivier Messiaen, all of them. But after he completed his sextet he blew his brains out in his hotel bathroom."

The young pianist was still smiling.

"Why did he do it?"

"Has suicide only one cause? His family's rejection? Despondency? Too much he read my father's Nietzsche? Robert was obsessed of recurrence eternal. Recurrence is the heart of his music. We live *exactly* the same life, Robert believed, and die *exactly* the same death again, again, again, to the *same* demisemiquaver. To eternity. Or else"—Madame Crommelynck relit her gone-out cigarette—"we can blame the girl."

"What girl?"

"Robert loved a silly girl. She did not love him in return."

"So he killed himself just because she wouldn't love him?"

"A factor, perhaps. How big, how small, only Robert can tell us."

"But *killing* himself. Just over a girl."

"He was not the first one. He will not be the last one."

"*God.* Did the girl, y'know, know about it?"

"Of course! Brugge is a city who is a village. She knew. And I assure you, fifty years later, the conscience of that girl *still* hurts. Like rheumatism. She would pay any price for Robert not to die. But what can she do?"

"You've kept in touch with her?"

"It is difficult for us to avoid, yes." Madame Crommelynck kept her eyes on Robert Frobisher. "This girl wants my forgiveness, before she dies. She begs me, 'I was eighteen! Robert's devotions were just a . . . a . . . flattery game for me! How could I *know* a famished heart will eat its mind? Can *kill* its body?' Oh, I pity her. I *want* to forgive her. But here is the truth." (Now she looked at me.) "I *abhor* that girl! I abhorred her all my life and I do not know how to *stop* to abhor her."

When Julia's *really* got on my wick, I vow I'll *never* talk to her again. But by teatime, often as not, I've forgotten it. "Fifty years's a long time to stay angry with someone."

Madame Crommelynck nodded, glum. "I do not recommend it."

"Have you tried *pretending* to forgive her?"

" 'Pretending' "—she looked at the garden—"is not the truth."

"But you said *two* true things, right? One, you *hate* this girl. Two, you *want* her to feel better. If you decided that the wanting truth's more important than the hating truth, just *tell* her you've forgiven her, even if you haven't. At least she'd feel better. Maybe that'd make you feel better too."

Madame Crommelynck studied her hands, moodily, both sides. "Sophistry," she pronounced.

I'm not sure what "sophistry" means so I kept schtum.

Far away the butler switched off the Hoover.

"Robert's sextet is now impossible to buy. You encounter his music only by serendipity in vicarages in July afternoons. This is your one chance in your life. You can work this gramophone?"

"Sure."

"Let us listen to the other side, Jason."

"Great." I turned the record over. Old L.P.s're as thick as plates.

A clarinet woke up and danced around the cello from side A.

Madame Crommelynck lit a new cigarette and shut her eyes.

I lay back on the armless sofa. I've never listened to music lying down. Listening's reading if you close your eyes.

Music's a wood you walk through.

A thrush warbled on a starry bush. The turntable gave a dying *ahhh* and the stylus clunked home. Madame Crommelynck's hand told me to stay where I was when I got up to light her cigarette. "Tell me. Who are your teachers?"

"We've got different teachers for different subjects."

"I mean, what are the writers you revere most greatly?"

"Oh." I mentally scanned my bookshelf for the really impressive names. "Isaac Asimov. Ursula Le Guin. John Wyndham."

"*Assy-smurf? Ursular Gun? Wind-'em?* These are modern poets?"

"No. Sci-fi, fantasy. Stephen King, too. He's horror."

" 'Fantasy'? *Pffft!* Listen to Ronald Reagan's homilies! 'Horror'? What of Vietnam, Afghanistan, South Africa? Idi Amin, Mao Tse-Tung, Pol Pot? Is not enough horror? I *mean*, who are your *masters*? Chekhov?"

"Er . . . no."

"But you have read *Madame Bovary*?"

(I'd never heard of her books.) "No."

Each name climbed up the octave. "Hermann Hesse?"

"No." Unwisely, I tried to dampen Madame Crommelynck's disgust. "We don't really do Europeans at school—"

" 'Europeans'? England is now drifted to the Caribbean? Are you African? Antarctican? You *are* European, you illiterate monkey of puberty! Thomas Mann, Rilke, Gogol! Proust, Bulgakov, Victor Hugo! This is your culture, your inheritance, your *skeleton*! You are ignorant even of *Kafka*?"

I flinched. "I've heard of him."

"This?" She held up *Le Grand Meaulnes*.

"No, but you were reading it last week."

"Is one of my bibles. I read it every year. So!" She frisbeed the hardback book at me, hard. It hurt. "Alain-Fournier is your first true master. He is nostalgic and tragic and enchantible and he aches and you will ache too and best of everything, he is *true*."

As I opened it up a cloud of foreign words blew out. *Il arriva chez nous un dimanche de novembre 189* . . . "It's in French."

"Translations are incourteous between Europeans." She detected the guilt in my silence. "*Oho*? English schoolboys in our enlightened 1980s cannot read a book in a foreign language?"

"We *do* do French at school . . ." Madame Crommelynck made me go on. ". . . But we've only got up to *Youpla boum! Book 2*."

"*Pfffffffffffft!* When *I* was thirteen I spoke French and Dutch fluently! I could converse in German, in English, in Italian! *Ackkk*, for your schoolmasters, for your minister of education, execution is too good! Is not even arrogance! It is a baby who is too *primitive* to know its nappy is stinking and bursting! You English, you *deserve* the government of Monster Thatcher! I curse you with *twenty years* of Thatchers! Maybe *then* you comprehend, speaking one language only is *prison*! You have a French dictionary and a grammar, anyhow?"

I nodded. Julia does.

"So. Translate the first chapter of Alain-Fournier from French to English, or do not return next Saturday. The author needs no parochial schoolchildren to disfigure his truth, but *I* need you to proof you do not waste my time. Go."

Madame Crommelynck turned to her desk and picked up her pen.

Once again, I saw myself out of the vicarage. I stuffed *Le Grand Meaulnes* under my Liverpool F.C. top, in case I ran into any kids.

*   *   *

It thundered during Religious Education the day school broke up for the summer. By the time we got to Black Swan Green it was *pissing* it down. Getting off the bus, Ross Wilcox shoved me between my shoulder blades. I arse-flopped into this ankle-deep puddle where the gutter'd flooded. Ross Wilcox and Gary Drake and Wayne Nashend *shat* themselves laughing. Goosey-goosey girls turned and tittered under their brollies. (Mysterious how girls can always conjure up umbrellas.) Andrea Bozard saw, so of course she nudged Dawn Madden and pointed. Dawn Madden shrieked with laughter like girls do. (*Bitch*, I didn't quite dare say. The rain'd gummed a loop of her beautiful hair to her smooth forehead. I'd've *died* if I could've taken that loop of hair in my mouth and sucked the rain out.) Even Norman Bates, the driver, barked one bark of amusement. But I was *soaked* and humilated and *furious*. I wanted to tear random bones out of Ross Wilcox's mutilated body, but Maggot reminded me he's the hardest kid in the second year and he'd probably just twist both hands off my wrists and lob them over the Black Swan. "Oh re-

ally blinking funny Wilcox"—Maggot stopped me from saying "fucking funny" in case Wilcox demanded a scrap—"that's pathetic—" But on "pathetic" my voice squeaked like my balls haven't dropped. Everyone heard. A fresh bomb of laughter blew me into tiny bits.

I knocked a rhythm on the vicarage knocker and finished with the doorbell. Wormcasts pitted the bubbling lawn like squeezed blackheads and slugs were climbing up walls. The porch roof was dripping. My parka hood was dripping. Mum's gone to Cheltenham today to speak with builders, so I'd told Dad I'd probably go and play electronic battleships at Alastair Nurton's. ("Probably" is a word with an emergency ejector seat.) Dean Moran's considered a bad influence since the Mr. Blake Affair. I'd come on my bike 'cause if anyone'd been out I could've just said "All right?" and cycled on. If you're caught on foot you might face an interrogation. But today everyone was watching Jimmy Connors versus John McEnroe on TV. (It's wet here but it's sunny in Wimbledon.) *Le Grand Meaulnes* was wrapped inside two Marks & Spencer placky bags stuffed inside my shirt, with my translation. I spent *hours* on it. Every other word, I'd had to look up in the dictionary. Even Julia noticed. She said yesterday, "Things slackened off towards the end of term, I thought." I answered that I wanted to get my summer homework over and done with. The weird thing is, doing the translation didn't *feel* like hours, not once I got going. *Bags* more interesting than *Youpla boum! Le français pour tous (French Method) Book 2* about Manuel, Claudette, Marie-France, Monsieur *et* Madame Berri. I'd liked to've asked Miss Wyche, our French teacher, to check my translation. But getting creepstained as a model student in a subject as girly as French'd sink what's left of my middle-ranking status.

Translating's half poem and half crossword and no doddle. Loads of words aren't actual words you can look up, but screws of grammar that hold the sentence together. It takes *yonks* to find out what they mean, though once you know them you know them. *Le Grand Meaulnes* is about this kid Augustin Meaulnes. Augustin Meaulnes's got an aura, like Nick Yew, that just has an effect on people. He comes to live with a schoolmaster's son called François as a boarder. François tells the story. We hear Meaulnes's footsteps, in the room above, before we even see him. It's brilliant. I'd decided to ask Madame Crommelynck to teach me French. Proper French, not French at school. I'd even started daydreaming about going to France, after my O levels or A levels. French kissing's where you touch with your tongues.

The butler was taking *forever*. Even longer than last week.

Impatient for my new future to come, I pressed the doorbell again.

Immediately, a pinky man in black opened up. *"He*llo."

"Hello."

The rain turned up a notch or two.

"Hel*lo.*"

"Are you the new butler?"

"Butler?" The pinky man laughed. "Gracious, no! That's a first! I'm Francis Bendincks. Vicar of Saint Gabriel's." Only now did I see his dog collar. "And you are?"

"Oh. I've come to see Madame Crommelynck . . ."

"Francis!" Footsteps *cronk cronk cronk*ed down the wooden stairs. (Outdoor shoes, not slippers.) A woman's voice snipped at high speed. "If that's the television-license people, tell them I've looked *high* and *low* but I think they must've carted the thing off—" She saw me.

"This young chap's come to visit Eva, apparently."

"Well, this young chap had better step inside, hadn't he? Till the rain lets up, at least."

Today the hallway had a behind-a-waterfall gloominess. The guitar's blue paint'd flaked off like a skin disease. In her yellow frame a dying woman in a boat trailed her fingers in the water.

"Thanks," I managed to say. "Madame Crommelynck's expecting me."

"Why that would be, I wonder?" The vicar's wife poked her questions rather than asked them. "Oh! Are you Marjorie Bishampton's youngest, here for the sponsored spelling bee?"

"No," I said, unwilling to tell her my name.

"So?" Her smile looked grafted on. "You *are*?"

"Er, Jason."

"Jason . . . ?"

"Taylor."

"That rings a *bell* . . . Kingfisher Meadows! Helena Taylor's youngest. Poor Mrs. Castle's neighbors. Father a big cheese at Greenland Supermarkets, right? Sister off to Edinburgh this autumn. I met your mother at the Art Exhibition last year, in the village hall. She was taken with an oil painting of Eastnor Castle, though I'm sorry to say she never came back. Half the profits went to Christian Aid."

She wasn't getting a "Sorry" from *me*.

"Well, Jason," said the vicar. "Mrs. Crommelynck has been called away. Rather unexpectedly."

Oh. "Will she be back anytime—" (The wife brought on my stammer like an allergy. I was stuck on "soon.")

" 'Soon'?" The wife gave me a *can't pull the wool over* my *eyes* smile that mortified me. "Hardly! They're gone as in *Gone!* It happened—"

"Gwendolin." The vicar raised his hand like a shy kid in class. (I recognized the name Gwendolin Bendincks from the parish magazine. She writes half of it.) "I'm not sure if it's appropriate to be—"

"Nonsense! It'll be all round the village by teatime. Truth will out. We have some perfectly *dreadful* news, Jason." Gwendolin Bendincks eyes'd lit up like fairy lights. "The Crommelyncks have been *extradited!*"

I wasn't too sure what that meant. "Under arrest?"

"I'll jolly well say so! Goose-stepped back to Bonn by the West German police! Their lawyer contacted us this morning. He refused to tell me *why* they'd been extradited, but, putting two and two together—the husband retired from the Bundesbank six months ago—it's some sort of financial scam. Embezzlement. Bribery. *Lots* of that goes on in Germany."

"Gwendolin." The vicar had a wheezy smile. "Perhaps it's premature to—"

"Mind you, *she* once mentioned a few years spent in Berlin. Suppose she was spying for the Warsaw Pact? I *told* you, Francis, I always *felt* they kept themselves to themselves more than was natural."

"But perhaps they're—" (Hangman choked the "not" of "not guilty.")

" 'Not guilty'?" Gwendolin Bendincks's lips twitched. "The home secretary wouldn't let Interpol whisk them away if he wasn't jolly well sure of his facts, would he? But it's an ill wind, I always say. Now we can use the lawn for our fête, after all."

"What," I asked, "about their butler?"

For two whole seconds Gwendolin Bendincks was stopped in her tracks. "*Butler?* Francis! What's this about a *butler?*"

"Grigoire and Eva," said the vicar, "didn't have a butler. I assure you."

I saw it. What a dildo I am.

The butler was the *husband.*

"I made a mistake," I said, sheepishly. "I'd better go now."

"Not *yet!*" Gwendolin Bendincks hadn't finished. "You'll get soaked to your skin! So tell us, what *was* your connection with Eva Crommelynck?"

"She was sort of teaching me."

"Is that a fact? And what might she have been teaching you about?"

"Er . . ." I couldn't admit to poetry. "French."

"How *cozy*! I remember *my* first summer in France. Nineteen, I would have been. Or twenty. My aunt took me to Avignon, you know, where there's the song about dancing on the bridges. The English mademoiselle caused *quite* a stir amongst the local bees . . ."

The Crommelyncks will be in German police cells, right now. A stammering thirteen-year-old kid in deathliest England'll be the last thing on Mrs. Crommelynck's mind. The solarium's gone. My poems are crap. How could they not be? I'm thirteen. What do *I* know about Beauty and Truth? Better bury Eliot Bolivar than let him carry on churning out shite. *Me? Learn French?* What was I *thinking*? God, Gwendolin Bendincks talks like fifty TVs all on at once. Her mass and density of words is bending space and time. A brick of loneliness is reaching terminal velocity inside me. I'd like a can of Tizer and a Toblerone, but Mr. Rhydds's shop's shut on Saturday afternoons.

Black Swan Green's shut on Saturday afternoons.

All pissing England's shut.

souvenirs

"So while *I'm* slaving away" — Dad pulled a face to shave round his lips — "in a sweaty conference room, covering in-store promotions with this year's crop of" — Dad jutted out his chin to shave a tricky bit — "Einsteins, *you* get to swan round Lyme Regis in the sun. All right for *some*, eh?" He unplugged his shaver.

"Guess so."

Our room looked over roofs down to where this funny quay crooks into the sea. Gulls dived and screamed like Spitfires and Messerschmitts. Over the English Channel the sticky afternoon was as turquoise as Head and Shoulders shampoo.

"Ah, you'll have a *whale* of a time!" Dad hummed a bendy version of "I Do Like to Be Beside the Sea Side." (The bathroom door'd opened by itself, so I could see Dad's chest reflected in the mirror as he put on a string vest and the shirt he'd just ironed. Dad's chest's hairy as a cress experiment.) "Wish *I* could be thirteen again."

Then, I thought, *you've obviously forgotten what it's like.*

Dad opened up his wallet and took out three pound notes. He hesitated and took out two more. He leaned through the doorway and put it on the chest of drawers. "A little spending money."

Five quid! "*Thanks*, Dad!"

"Don't spend it on fruit machines, though."

"Course not," I answered before the ban spread to arcade games. "They're a total waste of money."

"Glad to hear you say so. Gambling's for mugs. Right, it's now"—Dad looked at his Rolex—"twenty to two?"

I checked my Casio. "Yes."

"You never wear your granddad's Omega, I've noticed."

"I, er"—my secret bit my conscience for the millionth time—"don't want to accidentally damage it."

"Quite right. But if you *never* wear it, Granddad might as well've donated it to the Oxfam shop. Anyway, my session winds up at five, so I'll meet you back here then. We'll have dinner somewhere nice, and then, if the girl in reception isn't mistaken, *Chariots of Fire* is showing at the local fleapit. Perhaps you can track the cinema down this afternoon? Lyme's smaller than Malvern. If you get lost, just ask for the Hotel Excalibur. As in King Arthur. Jason? Are you listening to me?"

Lyme Regis was a casserole of tourists. Everywhere smelt of suntan oil, hamburgers, and burnt sugar. My jean pockets corked with a crusty hanky to foil the pickpockets, I waded along the high street. I looked at the posters in Boots and bought the summer edition of *2000 AD* in W. H. Smiths for 40p. I rolled it up and stuck it in my back pocket. I sucked Mint Imperials in case I met a suntanned girl who'd take me upstairs to one of those saggy houses with seagulls screaming on the ridges, and draw her curtains and lie me on her bed and teach me how to kiss. Mint Imperials're hard as pebbles at first but they distintegrate into sugary mush. I looked in jewelers for an Omega Seamaster but as usual there weren't any. A man in the last one told me I should be looking in antique shops. I spent ages in a stationery shop in a trance conjured up by all the perfect pads. I bought a packet of Letraset and a TDK C-60 cassette to tape songs off the radio. Nearer the harbor were clumps of mods, bags of rockers, a chain of punks, and even a few teds. Teds're extinct in most towns, but Lyme Regis's famous for fossils 'cause of the shale cliffs. The Fossil Shop's fab. It sells conch shells with titchy red bulbs inside, but they were £4.75 and blowing all my money on one souvenir'd've been daft. (Instead I bought a series of thirteen dinosaur postcards. Each one's got a different dinosaur, but if you put them end to end in order, the background landscape joins up and forms a frieze. Moran'll be pretty jealous.) The trinketty shops're full of inflatable octopuses, stunt kites, buckets, and spades. There were these pens. If you tilted them, a strip of color slid away to reveal a naked lady whose bosoms're two sawn-off missiles. The strip'd slid down to her belly button when a voice said, "You gonna buy that or what, sonny?"

I was concentrating on what the strip'd show next.

"*Oy!* You gonna buy that?" The shopkeeper meant *me*. I could see his blob of gum rolling round his mouth as his jaws opened and shut. His T-shirt had a picture of a giant dick with legs chasing something that looked like a hairy oyster on legs and the slogan IT'S JUST ONE THING AFTER ANOTHER. (I still don't get that.) "Or just stand there getting turned on?"

I fumblingly jabbed the pen back in its hole and scooted out, deep-frying in embarrassment.

The shopkeeper tossed "Mucky little bugger!" after me. "Buy yourself a dirty mag!"

Lyme Regis Wildest Dreams Amusement Arcade's sort of built into the hillside park, on the seafront. Pudgy grim smoking men played this horse-racing game where you bet real money on plastic horses that move round a track. The track's under a glass shield to stop you nobbling the horses. Pudgy grim smoking women played bingo in a closed-off bit where a spangle-jacketed man calls out numbers and smiles like a bee. The arcade game part was darker so the screens glow brighter and Jean Michel Jarre music was on. I watched kids playing Pac-Man, Scrambler, Frogger, and Grand Prix Racer. The Asteroids was out of order. There's a new game where you fight the giant robot horses from *The Empire Strikes Back*, but that was 50p a go. I changed a £1 note into 10p coins from a grebo in the booth reading the heavy metal magazine *Kerrang!*

The coins in my caged fist rattled like magic bullets.

Space Invaders first. The Taylor Method's to zap out a duct through my shelter and kill the aliens from safety. It worked for a while but then an alien torpedoed me through my own duct. That's never happened before. My strategy collapsed and I didn't even clear the first screen.

Next I had a go on a Kung Fu game. I was MegaThor. But MegaThor just danced around like an electrocuted spazzo while Rex Rockster kicked the shit out of him. Kung Fu games'll never catch on. I hurt my thumbnail more than I'd hurt Rex Rockster.

I wanted a go on Air Hockey, where a plastic disk floats on a cushion of air. American kids're always playing it on TV. But you need another human. So I figured I'd get the money I'd wasted on MegaThor back from Eldorado Cascade. Eldorado Cascade's a sort of console where you roll 10p coins onto mirrored ledges. Moving walls push the coins teetering on the ledges onto the next ledge down, and 10p coins falling off *that* ledge fall into your scoop. Loads of coins were ready to avalanche into my scoop.

Those teetering coins're glued on, I reckon. I lost 50p!

Then I saw this lush girl.

Three girls spilled out of the photo booth after the fourth nuclear flash. From Eldorado Cascade I'd been watching their six legs and thirty painted toes. Like Charlie's Angels, one was dark (but chinless), one was straw-blond (extra chin), and one was coppery-freckly. The dark one and the blond one had a dribbly Cornetto each. (There was an ice-cream stall right by the photo booth.) They pressed their mouths against the slot where the photos come out and yelled unfunny orders into the machine, like "Get a move on!" When they got bored of that they ducked back into the booth, shared the earphones of a Sony Walkman, and sang to "The Tide Is High" by Blondie. But the copper one licked a sharp Zoom ice lolly and studied the ice-cream chart. Her top showed her belly button.

She wasn't as lush as Dawn Madden but I drifted over to study the ice-lolly chart too. Magnets don't need to understand magnetism. She smelt of warm sand. Just standing near her made the tiny hairs on my arms riffle.

I untucked my shirt to let it drape over my accelerating boner.

"Is that a Zoom?" God. I'd apparently *spoken* to the girl.

She looked at me. "Yeah." I fell a thousand feet up. "Zooms're the best thing they've got here." Her accent was like off *Coronation Street* in Manchester. "Unless you're, like, into choc ices."

"Okay. Thanks."

I bought a Zoom off a person I remember absolutely nothing about.

"You on holiday too"—*she* spoke to *me*—"or d'you live here, like?"

"Holiday."

"We're from Blackburn." She nodded at the other two, who hadn't noticed me yet. "Where're you from?"

"Uh . . . Black Swan Green." I was so nervous that even Hangman'd run off to hide somewhere. It makes no sense but it happens.

"You what?"

"It's a village. In Worcestershire."

"Worcestershire? Is that in the middle somewhere?"

"Yeah. It's the most boring county, so no one ever knows where it is. Blackburn's up north, isn't it?"

"Yeah. So, is Black Swan Green famous for black swans or green swans or something?"

"No." What could I say that'd *really* impress her? "There aren't even any white swans there."

"So there're no swans in Black Swan Green?"

"Yeah. It's a sort of a local joke."

"Oh. That's pretty funny, really, isn't it?"

"Thanks." Sweat pinpricked out from fifty places on my body.

"Dead nice here, in't it?"

"Oh yeah." I wondered what to say next. "Dead nice."

"You going to eat that lolly, or what?"

The icy Zoom'd stuck to my fingertips. I tried to peel the paper wrapper off but it just shredded dead crappily.

"You need a bit of technique, like." Her ruby fingertips took my Zoom and tore the end off the wrapper. She placed the torn end in her mouth and blew. The wrapper ballooned up, then just slid off. My hidden boner was about to explode, killing everyone in Wildest Dreams Amusement. She let the wrapper drop to the floor and handed me back my Zoom. "Is that *Smash Hits*?" She meant the 2000 AD summer special, still rolled up in my pocket.

Wished to hell it was.

"Our Sally!" The black-haired chinless girl came up and I hated her till the end of time. "Don't tell me you've started your fishing trip *already*?" (The straw girl giggled from her stool in the booth and I hated her too.) "You're only one hour off the coach. What's this one called then?"

I had to answer. "Jason."

" 'Jason'!" She did this toffee-nosed accent. "I *say*! Se*bas*tian's playing *polo* with *Jason* on the *croquet* lawn! Rath-*er*! I *say*! *Jason*'s sucking a Zoom too, just like *Sally*! How Mr. and Mrs.! So have you got your rubber johnnies, *Jason*, 'cause at the rate Our Sally's going you'll need 'em in the next thirty minutes."

I floundered for a killer put-down line without any stammer words in it. And floundered, and floundered.

"Or don't they teach you biology at schools like yours?"

"Stick your fat gob into *everything*," Sally snapped, "don't you?"

"Untwist your knickers, Our Sal! Only asking your new *boyfriend* if he knows the facts of life, like. Or is his thing bending over in the showers for prefects after a *jolly* good game of *rugger*?"

All the girls watched me to see how the boy'd defend himself.

My Zoom was dribbling down my wrist.

"*Why* Tim put up with your fat, nasty, dirty *trap*"—Sally folded her arms and jutted her hips out—"for so long before *dumping* you, I'll never know."

I was turning invisible and there was nothing I could do.

"I dumped *him*, for *your* information. And at least *my* boyfriend didn't go munching up Wendy Lench the *day after* splitting up with *me*!"

"That's a lie, Melanie Pickett, and you know it!"

"Under the coats," Melanie Pickett almost sang, "at Shirley Poolbrook's party! Ask *anyone* who was there!"

The photo machine buzzed.

The straw one giggled. "I think the photos are done . . ."

A battalion of old ladies marched by from the bingo enclosure. I jumped into their ranks before the three girls noticed, and hurried back to the Hotel Excalibur. Boys are bastards, but they're predictable bastards. You never know *what* girls're thinking. Girls're from another planet.

The beehive receptionist gave me the message that Dad's seminar was running over so he'd be a bit late. Greenland trainees were in the lobby, joking and comparing notes. I felt like a teacher's kid in a staff room, so I went up to our room. It smells of net curtains, toast, and toilet cleaner. The wallpaper's got eggy daffodils and the carpet's all melted flowers. The only things on TV were cricket where nobody scored and a western where nobody shot anyone.

I read *2000 AD* on my bed.

But I kept thinking about the three girls. Girls and girlfriends're worrying. Sex education's only about how to make babies and how not to make babies. What *I* need to know is what you do to turn ordinary girls like Sally from Blackburn into girlfriends you can snog and be seen snogging. I'm not sure if I really want to have sexual intercourse and I *definitely* don't want babies. Babies just poo and bawl. But *not* having a girlfriend means you're a homo or a total loser or both.

Melanie Pickett was half right. I don't know whether or not I know the facts of life. You can't ask adults 'cause you can't ask adults. You can't ask kids 'cause it'd be all round school by first break. So either everybody knows everything but nobody's saying anything, or else nobody knows anything and girlfriends just sort of . . . happen.

There was a knock at the door.

———

"Jason." This young guy had a metallicky suit and a paisley tie. "Right?"

"Right."

He did a comedy finger point at his GREENLAND SUPERMARKETS badge and a James Bond voice. "The name's Lawlor . . . Danny Lawlor. Mike—your da—my boss, did I forget to mention?—sent me up to say he's really sorry but he's still being detained. The Emperor's dropped by, unannounced."

"The Emperor?"

"Emperor Craig Salt of Greenland. Best not say I called him that. Your *da*'s boss is Craig Salt. So all the managers are having to look after him in the manner to which he has become accustomed. *So*, your da's suggesting how's about you and me go in search of the ultimate fish-and-chip shop?"

"Now?"

"Unless you've got a hot dinner date?"

"No . . ."

"Grand altogether. We'll get you back in time for *Chariots of Fire*. Ah yes, my informants tell me everything. One mo, just let me unpin this absurd name badge . . . I'm a man, me, not a self-adhesive strip of letters embossed on a Dymo label printer . . ."

"Don't lean too far out!" Danny and I watched the jellyfish below our feet dangling off the end of the seawall. "If Michael Taylor's sole male heir winds up in the drink, my career prospects will most surely join him."

Sunlight on waves is drowsy tinsel.

"You'd be okay if you fell in on the harbor side." I sculpted my Mr Whippy with my tongue. "You could scramble onto one of the fishing boats. But if you fell on the sea side, you might get sucked under."

"Let's not," Danny said, rolling up his shirt sleeves, "put your theory to test."

"The ice cream's great, thanks. I've never had one with two Flakes in it. Did you pay extra?"

"No. Your man on the stall's a fellow Corkonian. We look after our own. Ah, but isn't this the life now, eh? Downright sadistic of Greenland to be holding their training conferences in a spot like this."

"What does 'sadistic' mean?"

"Unnecessarily cruel."

"Why"—I'd noticed that Danny likes questions—"is this seawall called the Cobb? Is it just in Lyme Regis?"

"Even my omniscience has its blind spots, young Jason."

(If Dad doesn't know the answer to a question, he spends ten sentences persuading himself that he *does* know.)

On the beach, well-behaved waves zipped and unzipped themselves. Mums rinsed off kids' feet with buckets. Dads folded deck chairs and issued instructions.

"Danny, do you know anyone in the IRA?"

"You ask that just because I'm Irish?"

I nodded.

"Well, Jason, *no.* Sorry to disappoint you. The Provos are busier up in Northern Ireland, the top bit. But back in Cork I do live in a turf hut with a leprechaun called Mick in my potato plot."

"Sorry, I didn't mean—"

Danny held up a peaceful palm. "Accuracy on matters Irish are not the forte of the English. Truth is, we're the friendliest people you'd wish to meet. Even north of the border. We just gun each other down occasionally, that's all."

Ice-cream drips snailed down the cone.

I don't even know what I don't know.

"Will you look at those kites now! We didn't have them when *I* was a kid!" Danny was gazing at a couple of stunt kites with snaky ribbony tails. "Aren't they something?"

We had to squint 'cause of the sun.

The tails doodlelooped red on blue, erasing themselves as they flew.

"*They,*" I agreed, "are *epic.*"

"What's Dad like to work for?"

The waitress at Cap'n Scallywag's Fish 'n' Chip Emporium arrived with our food. Danny leaned back to let the tray land. "Michael Taylor, let me see. Well regarded . . . fair, thorough . . . doesn't suffer fools gladly . . . he's put in a good word or two for *me* at timely moments, for which I'm eternally grateful . . . that do you?"

"Sure." I doused my fish with ketchup from a tomato-shaped squirter. Funny to hear Dad discussed as Michael Taylor. Along the promenade, strings of boiled-fruit lights lit up.

"Looks like you're enjoying that."

"I *love* fish and chips. Thanks."

"You're da's paying." Danny'd ordered scampi, bread, and a side salad to build a sandwich. "Remember to thank him." He turned to the first waitress and asked for a can of 7UP. A second waitress hurried over with it and asked if the food was okay.

"Oh," said Danny, "glorious."

She sort of leaned at Danny, like he was a log fire. "Would your brother like anything to drink too?"

Danny winked at me.

"Tango." Pleasure from being mistaken for Danny's brother wasn't quite wrecked by Hangman not letting me say the "Seven" in 7UP. "Please."

The first waitress fetched me one. "Here on holiday?"

"Business." Danny breathed mystery into this dull word. "Business."

More customers came in and the waitresses went.

Danny did this funny look. "We should make a double act."

Happy frying noises spat in Cap'n Scallywag's kitchen.

"One Step Beyond" by Madness came on.

"Have you got"—I chickened out of saying "a girlfriend"—"any brothers and sisters?"

"That depends"—Danny never hurries his mouthfuls—"on your mode of accountancy. I grew up in an orphanage."

God. "Like Dr. Barnardo's?"

"A Catholic equivalent, with more Jesus in the diet. Not enough to cause any lasting damage."

I chewed. "I'm sorry."

"Don't be." Danny'd handled this a billion times. "I'm not embarrassed about it. Why should you be?"

"So." Julia or Mum'd've politely changed the subject. "Did something bad happen to your mum and dad?"

"Only each other. Pass us the ketchup? They're still alive and rocking— not together—as far as I know, but, well, hey. A few experiments with foster parents did not end happily. I was what's known as a 'feisty child.' In the end the state agreed I was best off with the Jesuit brothers."

"Who're they?"

"The Jesuits? A venerable religious order. Monks."

"Monks?"

"Real live monks. They ran the orphanage. Oh, you had your usual quota of humorless bigots, but a fair share of *fierce* good educators. Lots of us got through university on scholarships alone. We were fed, clothed, cared for. Santy visited, come Christmas. Parties every birthday. *Clover* compared to growing up in a shantytown in Bangladesh or Mombasa or Lima or five hundred other locations I could name. We learned how to improvise, how to look out for ourselves, what not to take for granted. All handy business skills. Why mope around going, like, 'Woe is me'?"

"Don't you ever want to meet your real parents?"

"Not a lad to beat around the bush, are you?" Danny folded his arms behind his head. "Parents. Irish law's a little murky on this one, but my biological mother's people live up in Sligo. They own a posh hotel or some such. One time, I'd've been around your age, I took it into my head to run off to find her. I got as far as Limerick bus station."

"What happened there?"

"Thunder, lightning, hailstones, fireballs. Biggest storm in years. My connecting bus was held up by a collapsed bridge. When the sun came out again, so did my sense of reality. So I scuttled back to the Jesuits."

"Did you get into trouble?"

"The Jesuits ran an orphanage, not a prison camp."

"So . . . that was that?"

"Yup. For now." Danny balanced his fork on his thumb. "What we—orphans, I mean—miss, or lack, or want, or need are photographs of people who look like you. That never goes away. One fine day, I'll make it up to Sligo to see if I can take some. With a telephoto lens, if my nerve gives out. But these great big life . . . 'issues' . . . won't be hurried. Ripeness, young Jason, is all. Scampi butty?"

"No thanks." While Danny'd been talking, a decision'd made itself. "Will you help me buy one of those stunt kites?"

Greenland trainees'd colonized the whole lounge of the Hotel Excalibur. They'd changed out of their suits into herringbone trousers and baggy shirts. As Danny and I walked in, they smirked our way. I knew why. Looking after their boss's son was a creep's job. One called out, "Daniel the Spaniel!" and grinned the exact grin Ross Wilcox's got. "Coming to inspect the nocturnal birds of Dorset?"

"Wiggsy," Danny lobbed back, "you're a drunken sot and a reprobate and you cheat at squash. Why would anyone want to be seen *dead* in public with yourself?"

The guy look delighted.

"Want to say hello"—Danny turned to me—"to the Young Greenlanders?"

That'd be *hell*. "Is it okay if I just go upstairs and wait for Dad there?"

"Don't blame you in the least. I'll tell him where you are." Then Danny shook hands with me, like I was a colleague. "Thanks for your company. See you in the morning?"

"Sure."

"Enjoy your film."

I got the key and bounded upstairs instead of waiting for the lift. In my head I listened to the Vangelis music for *Chariots of Fire* to flush away Wiggsy and the Greenlanders. Not Danny, though. Danny's ace.

The alarm-radio said seven-fifteen but no sign of Dad yet. *Chariots of Fire* begins at seven-thirty, said the poster. I'd memorized the route to the cinema to impress Dad. Seven twenty-five came. Dad doesn't forget appointments. He'd be coming. We'd miss the adverts and Coming Soons, but a lady with a torch'd show us our seats for the film. Seven twenty-eight. Should I go downstairs and remind him? I decided not to, in case we missed each other. Then it'd all be my fault for not sticking to the plan. Seven-thirty. We'd have to spend some time working out who was who, but the film'd still be watchable. At seven thirty-five Dad's footsteps came thumping down the corridor outside. "Right!" he'd say as he burst in. "Off we go!"

The footsteps thumped past our door. They didn't come back.

The eggy daffodils on the wallpaper'd fossilized to slag-heap gray as the light faded. I hadn't turned on the light. Witchy laughter leaked into the room and music welled up from pubs all around Lyme Regis. TV'd've been pretty good 'cause it's Saturday night but Dad'd feel guiltier if he found me in silence. I wondered what Sally from the amusement arcade'd be doing now. Being kissed. A boy'd be stroking those soft bare inches between her jeans and her top. Someone like Gary Drake or Neal Brose or Duncan Priest. My memory was vague, so to pass the time I made her up. I sculpted Sally's breasts like Debby Crombie's. I gave her Amanda Turbot's hair, silking round her naked throat. I gave her a face transplant from Dawn Madden, not forgetting Dawn Madden's sadistic eyes. The teenage Madame Crommelynck's *slightly* upturned nose. Debbie Harry's full-cream lips.

Sally, the lost girl.

If Dad guessed I was trying to make him feel guilty, that'd give him the excuse to not let me. So after nine o'clock, I switched on the reading lamp and read *Watership Down*. Up to the bit where Bigwig faces up to General Woundwort. Moths kept tapping the window. Insects crawled over the glass like skaters on ice. A key turned in the lock and Dad tripped into the room. "Ah, Jason, *here* you are."

Where else*'d I be?* I dared myself to not reply to Dad.

He didn't notice I was sulking. "*Chariots of Speed*'ll have to take a rain check." Dad's voice was far too loud for the room. "Craig Salt turned up halfway through my seminar."

"Danny Lawlor told me," I said.

"Craig Salt's yacht's over in Poole, so he drove over to address the troops. Couldn't just swan off to the local fleapit with you, I'm afraid."

"Right," I said, in Mum's flattest voice.

"Danny and you had dinner, right?"

"Right."

"The world of work's about these kinds of sacrifices. Craig Salt's taking us managers out to some *place* somewhere near Charmouth, so you'll probably be asleep by the time I—" Dad saw my kite, propped up against the radiator. "What's this you've been spending your money on?"

Dad always picks faults with what I buy. If it isn't tat from Taiwan, I paid far too much for something I'll only use twice. If he can't see a problem he'll make one up, like that time I bought BMX transfers for my bike and he made a *massive* drama out of getting out insurance forms and altering the "Description" box. It's *so* unfair. I don't criticize how he spends *his* money.

"A kite."

"So I *see* . . ." Dad'd already slid my kite out of its wrapper. "What a beaut! Did Danny help you choose it?"

"Yes," I didn't *want* to be pleased he was pleased. "A bit."

"Fancy you buying yourself a kite." Dad peered down its spine. "Hey, let's get up at the crack of dawn. We'll try it out down on the beach! Just you and me, right? Before all the little tourists stake out every square inch, right?"

"Right, Dad."

"Crack of dawn!"

I cleaned my teeth without mercy.

Mum and Dad can be as ratty or sarcastic or angry as they want to me, but if I ever show a *flicker* of being pissed off then they act like I've murdered babies. I *hate* them for that. But I hate *my* guts for never standing up to Dad like Julia does. So I hate *their* guts for making me hate *my* guts. Kids can never complain about unfairness 'cause everyone knows kids *always* complain about that. "Life *isn't* fair, Jason, and the sooner you learn that, the better." So there. That's that sorted. It's fine for Mum and Dad to scrunch up any promise they make to *me* and flush it down the bog and why?

Because life *isn't* fair, Jason.

My eyes fell on Dad's electric shaver box.

I got the shaver out, just because. Snug as an unswitched-on light saber.

Plug it in, whispered Unborn Twin from the corners of the bathroom. *Dare you.*

It came to life and buzzed my entire skeleton.

Dad'd *kill* me for doing this. It's so obvious that I mustn't touch his shaver, he's never even told me not to. But Dad hadn't even bothered telling me to go to *Chariots of Fire* on my own. His shaver came closer to the bumfluff on my upper lip . . . closer . . .

It bit me!

I unplugged it.

Oh *God.* Now my bumfluff had a ridiculous patch missing.

Maggot whimpered, *What have you* done?

In the morning Dad'd see and it'd be all too *obvious* what I'd done. My one hope was to shave the whole fuzz off. Surely Dad'd notice that, too?

But I had nothing to lose. The shaver tickled. On a scale of 0 to 10, 3.

The shaver hurt a bit, too. On a scale of 0 to 10, 1¼.

I panickily examined the results. My face *did* look different, but it'd be hard to put your finger on how, exactly.

I ran my finger along where my fuzz'd been.

Not even cold milk was so smooth.

I accidentally flicked open the blade cover. Dad's gritty stubble and my almost invisible fur snowed together onto the white porcelain sink.

Lying on my chest, my front ribs pressed into my back.

Thirsty now, I needed a glass of water.

I got a glass of water. Water in Lyme Regis tastes of paper. I couldn't get to sleep on my side. My bladder'd ballooned.

I took a long piss, wondering if girls'd like me more if I had more scars. (All I've got is a nick on my thumb where I was bitten by my cousin Nigel's guinea pig when I was nine. My cousin Hugo said the guinea pig had myxamatosis and I'd die in foaming agony, thinking I was a rabbit. I believed him. I even wrote a will. The scar's nearly gone now but it bled like shook-up cherryade at the time.)

Lying on my back, my back ribs pressed into my chest.

Too hot, I took my pajama top off.

Too cool, I put my pajama top on.

The cinema'd be emptying after *Chariots of Fire* now. The lady with the torch'd be going up and down the aisles putting popcorn cones and Fruit Gum boxes and empty Malteser bags into a bin bag. Sally from Blackburn and her new boyfriend'd be stepping outside, saying what a great film it'd been, though they'd've been snogging and stroking each other all the way through. Sally's boyfriend'd be saying, "Let's go to a disco." Sally'd answer, "No. Let's go to the camper van. The others won't be back for a while."

That song by UB40 called "One in Ten" thumped up through the bones of the Hotel Excalibur.

The moon'd dissolved my eyelids.

Time'd turned to treacle.

"Oh sod soddity *sod* it and sod Craig sodding Salt too the sodding sod!"

Dad'd fallen over the carpet.

I didn't let him know he'd woken me for two reasons: (a) I wasn't ready to forgive him; (b) he was banging into things like a comedy drunk and pub fumes wafted off him and if he was going to bollock me for using his shaver, tomorrow morning'd be better. Dean Moran's right. Seeing your Dad pissed's *dead* disturbing.

Dad made his way to the bathroom like he was in zero gravity. I heard him undo his zip. He tried to piss quietly onto the porcelain.

Piss drummed onto the bathroom floor.

A wavery second later it chundered into the bog.

The piss lasted forty-three seconds. (My record's fifty-two.)

He pulled out loads of bog paper to mop up the spillage.

Then Dad switched on the shower and got in.

Maybe a minute passed before I heard a ripping noise, a dozen plastic *ping*s, a thump, and a growly *Sod it!*

I opened my eyes a slit and nearly yelled in fright.

The bathroom door'd opened by itself. Dad stood with his head in a turban of shampoo, wielding a broken shower rail. Stark raving nuddy, he was, but right where my sack-and-acorn is, Dad's got this wobbling chunky length of oxtail. Just hanging there!

His pubes're thick as a buffalo's beard! (I've only got nine.)

The *grossest* sight I *ever* saw.

Dad's snorey skonks and flobberglobbers're *impossible* to sleep through. No *wonder* my parents don't sleep in the same bedroom. The shock of seeing Dad's thing's dying down now. A bit. But will I just wake up one morning and find that rope between my legs? It horrifies me to think that about fourteen years ago the spermatozoon that turned into me shot out of *that.*

Will *I* be some kid's dad one day? Are any future people lurking deep inside mine? I've never even ejaculated, apart from in a dream of Dawn Madden. Which girl's carrying the other half of my kid, deep in those intricate loops? What's she doing right now? What's her name?

Too much to think about.

I s'pose Dad'll have a hangover tomorrow morning.

Today morning.

Chances of us flying my kite on the beach at the crack of dawn?

Big fat zero.

✳   ✳   ✳

"The wind blows north," Dad had to shout, "from Normandy, over the Channel, *smacks* into these cliffs and alley-*oop,* a thermal updraft! Perfect for kites!"

"Perfect!" I shouted too.

"Breathe this air in deep, Jason! Good for your hay fever! Sea air's chock-full of ozone!"

Dad hogged the kite spool, so I took another warm jam doughnut.

"Tonic for the troops, eh?"

I smiled back. It's *epic* being up at the crack of dawn. A red setter raced ghost-dogs through the bellyflopping waves on the shore. Shale pooed from the cliffs off toward Charmouth. Mucky clouds lidded the sunrise but today was bags windier and better for kite flying.

Dad shouted something.

"What?"

"The kite! Its background blends into the clouds! Looks like it's just the dragon flying up there! What a beaut you picked! I've worked out how to do a double loop!" Dad had that smile you never see in photos. "She rules the skies!" He edged a bit closer so he didn't have to shout so much. "When I was your age, *my* dad'd take me out on Morecambe Bay of an afternoon—Grange-over-Sands—and we'd fly kites there. Made 'em ourselves in those days . . . Bamboo, wallpaper, string and milk-bottle tops for the tail . . ."

"Will you show me"—Hangman blocked "sometime"—"one day?"

"Course I will. Hey! Know how to send a kite telegram?"

"No."

"Righto, hold her for a moment . . ." Dad passed me the spool and got a Biro from his anorak. Then he got the square of gold paper from his cigarettes. He didn't have anything to rest on, so I knelt by him like a squire being knighted so he could rest on my back. "What message shall we send up?"

" 'Mum and Julia, wish you were here.' "

"You're the boss." Dad pressed hard so I felt the Biro trace each letter through my clothes and onto my back. "Up you get." Then Dad twizzled the gold paper round the kite string like a sandwich-bag fastener. "Wobble the line. That's it. Up and down."

The telegram started sliding *up* the kite string, against gravity. Pretty soon it was out of sight. But you knew the message'd get there.

"*Lytoceras fimbriatum.*"

I blinked at Dad, not knowing what on earth he'd said. We stepped apart to let the wheezy fossil-shop owner lug a signboard outside.

"*Lytoceras fimbriatum.*" Dad nodded at the spiral fossil in my hand. "Its Latin name. Ammonite family. You can tell by these close tight ribs it's got, with these extra-fat ones every so often . . ."

"You're right!" I checked the tiny writing on the shelf. "*Ly-to-ce-ras—*"

"*Fimbriatum.* Fancy me being right."

"Since when did you know about fossils and Latin names?"

"My dad was a bit of a rock hound. He used to let me catalog his specimens. But only if I learnt them properly. I've forgotten most of them now, of course, but my dad's *Lytoceras* was *enorm*ous. It's stuck in my memory."

"What's a rock hound?"

"Amateur geologist. Most holidays, he'd find an excuse to go off fossil hunting with a little hammer he kept. I think I've still got it somewhere. Some of the fossils he got in Cyprus and India are in Lancaster Museum, last time I looked."

"I never knew." The fossil fitted into my cupped hands. "Is it rare?"

"Not especially. That one's a nice one, though."

"How old is it?"

"Hundred and fifty million years? A whippersnapper among ammonites, really. What say we buy it for you?"

"*Really?*"

"Don't you like it?"

"I *love* it."

"Your first fossil, then. An educational souvenir."

Do spirals end? Or just get so tiny your eyes can't follow anymore?

Seagulls strutted in the dustbins outside Cap'n Scallywag's. I was walking along still staring into my ammonite when an elbow swung out of nowhere and knocked my head backward on its hinge.

"Jason!" snapped Dad. "Look where you're going!"

My nose gonged with pain. I wanted to sneeze but couldn't.

The jogger rubbed his arm. "No permanent damage, Mike. The Red Cross chopper can stay on its helipad."

"Craig! Good God!"

"Out for my morning fix, Mike. This human bumper car's your handi-work, I take it?"

"Right first time, Craig. That's Jason, my youngest."

The only Craig Dad knows is Craig Salt. This tanned man matched what I'd heard. "If I'd been a truck, young fella-me-lad," he told me, "*you*'d be a pancake."

"Trucks aren't allowed down here." My crushed nose made my voice honk. "It's just for pedestrians."

"Jason." The Dad out here and the Dad in the fossil shop just weren't the same person. "Apologize to Mr. Salt! If you'd tripped him you could've caused a serious injury."

Kick the wazzock's shins, said Unborn Twin.

"I'm really sorry, Mr. Salt." *Wazzock.*

"I'll forgive you, Jason; thousands wouldn't. What's this? Bit of a fossil col-lector, are we? May I?" Craig Salt just took my ammonite. "Nice little trilo-bite, that. Bit of worm damage on this side. But not too bad."

"It's not a trilobite. It's a *Ly-to*—" Hangman blocked "*Lytoceras*" in mid-word. "It's a type of ammonite, isn't it, Dad?"

Dad wasn't meeting my eyes. "If Mr. Salt's sure, Jason—"

"Mr. Salt"—Craig Salt plopped my ammonite back—"*is* sure."

Dad just had this weedy smile.

"If anyone's sold you this fossil as anything *but* a trilobite, sue 'em. Your dad and I know a good lawyer, eh, Mike? Well. Must clock up another mile or two before breakfast. Then it's back to Poole. See if my family have sunk my yacht yet."

"Wow, have you got a yacht, Mr. Salt?"

Craig Salt'd scented my sarcasm but couldn't act on it.

I stared back, innocent, defiant, and surprised at myself.

"Only a forty-footer!" Dad said it like the Man of the Sea he isn't. "Craig, the trainees were saying what a pleasure it was yesterday to—"

"*Ah* yes, Mike. *Knew* there was something else. Would've been unprofessional of me to bring it up in front of the Great White Hopes at the hotel, Mike, but we need to talk urgently about Gloucester. Last quarter's accounts are making me *mucho depressedo.* Swindon's going straight down the bloody toilet as far as I can see."

"Absolutely, Craig. I've got some new concepts for in-store promotions we can kick about in the long grass and—"

"It's *ass* kicking we need, not *grass* kicking. Expect a call from me on Wednesday."

"Looking forward to it, Craig. I'll be in the Oxford office."

"I know where *all* my area managers are. Be more careful, Jason, or you'll cause someone an injury. Until Wednesday, Mike."

Dad and I watched Craig Salt jog down the promenade.

"What say"—Dad's jolliness was forced and feeble—"we get ourselves that bacon sandwich?"

But I couldn't speak to Dad.

"Hungry?" Dad put his hand on my shoulder. "Jason?"

I nearly biffed his hand away and flung my shitty "trilobite" into the shitty sea.

Nearly.

※　※　※

"So while *I'm* neck-deep in shipping notices, stock inventories, mailing lists, and artistic temperaments"—Mum adjusted the mirror to perfect her lipstick—"*you* get to swan around Cheltenham all morning like Lord Muck! All right for some, eh?"

"I guess so."

Mum's Datsun Cherry smells of Mint Imperials.

"Ah, you'll have a *whale* of a time! Now, Agnes says *Chariots of Fire* starts at five and twenty to two, so grab yourself a sausage roll or something for lunch and get back to the gallery by . . ." Mum checked her watch. "A quarter past one."

"Okay."

We got out of the Datsun. "Morning, Helena!" A crew-cut man marched by to where a van was docking into a delivery bay. "Proper scorcher we're in for, today's forecast says."

"About time we had a bit of summer. Alan, this is my son, Jason."

I got a crooked grin and a jokey salute. Dad wouldn't like Alan.

"Being as you're sort of on holiday, Jason, why don't I . . ." From her purse Mum unfolded a crisp five-pound note.

"Thanks!" I don't know why they're being so generous at the moment. "That's as much as Dad gave me in Lyme Regis!"

"Silly me—I meant to give you a ten . . ."

Back went the fiver and out came a tenner! That made £28.70.

"Thanks very much."

I'd need every last penny.

"Antique shops?" the woman in Tourist Information began memorizing my features in case a robbery was reported later. "Why do you want antique shops? The best bargains are in the charity shops."

"It's my mum's birthday," I lied. "She likes vases."

"Oh. For Mum? Oh! Isn't Mum lucky having *you* as a son?"

"Uh . . ." She made me nervous. "Thanks."

"Lucky, *lucky* Mum! I have a son as lovely as you, too." She flashed me a photo of a fat baby. "Twenty-six years ago, this, but he's still as adorable! Pips doesn't always remember *my* birthday, mind, but he's got a heart of gold. That's what counts, at the end of the day. Father was a waste of space, sorry to say. Pips hated the pig as much as I did. The *men*"—she made a just-swallowed-bleach face—"just fire out their snot, roll over, and that's *it*, good night. The men don't *grow* sons, feed them with their own milk, wipe their botties, powder their"—she cooed at me, but the bird of prey was back in her eyes—"little *snails*. A father will *always* turn on his son in the end. Only room for *one* cock-of-the-walk in any farmyard, *thank* you very much. But *I* showed Pippin's father the door when Pips turned ten. Yvette was fifteen. *Yvette* says Pippin's old enough to be living on his own, now, but *that* miss has forgotten who's the mother and who's the daughter since she got a pay-in-installments wedding ring on her finger. *Yvette* forgets it's thanks to *me* that *that* little Jezebel from Colwall didn't get her sharp little claws into Pippin. Seduce him into some en*tang*lement. *Yvette's* still thick as thieves with *that*"—the foamy lady nodded at the empty doorway—"*clot*. Her father. The pig. The *dolt*.

Who else put the idea into her head? Poking her pointy beak into where Pips keeps our little pick-me-ups? A mother needs a little pick-me-up occasionally, my pet. God made us mothers but he didn't make it *easy* for us to stay on top of things. *Pips* understands. *Pips* says, 'Let's call these pills *yours*, Mum. They're *our* secret, but say, if anyone asks, they're *yours*.' Pippin's not so nicely spoken as you, my pet, but his heart's twenty-four karat. But do you know what Yvette did to our pick-me-ups? Turned up uninvited one afternoon and without so much as a by-your-leave, she flushed them down the lavvy! My, Pippin turned the air *blue* when he got home and found out! Hit the *roof*! It was 'my *effing* stock' this, 'my *effing* stock' that! Never *seen* the boy in such a state! Went round to Yvette's and, well, did *he* put *her* pointy beak out of joint!" Her face clouded. "Yvette called the coppers. Shopped her *own brother*! He'd only biffed that froglet of a husband of hers a *little* bit! But Pips just disappeared after that. Days on end now, neither hide nor hair. All I want is a phone call from my son, my pet. Just to tell me he's looking after himself proper. Some nasty types keep knocking our door down. The police are just as bad. 'Where's the *effing* gear *this*? Where's the *effing* money *that*? Where's your son gone, you *effing* old bitch?' Oh *filthy* language, they've got. But even if I *had* heard from Pips, I'd rather *die* than breathe a word . . ."

I opened my mouth to remind her about the antique shops.

She shuddered out a sigh. "I'd rather *die* . . ."

"So, uh, *could* you give me a map of Cheltenham with the antique shops marked on it?"

"No, pet. I don't work here. Ask that lady behind the desk."

The first antique shop was called George Pines, out on a ring road, wedged between a betting shop and a liquor store. Cheltenham's s'posed to be posh but posh towns've got dodgy areas too. You cross a boomy rusting footbridge to get there. George Pines wasn't what you have in mind when you think "antique shop." The doors and windows had grilles. A note sellotaped to the (locked) door said, BACK IN 15 MINS but the ink'd gone ghostly and the paper'd faded. A notice said, BEST RATES FOR HOUSE CLEARAGES. Through the grimy window it was all ugly big sideboards you get in grandparents' bungalows. No clocks, no watches.

George Pines was long gone.

As I was walking back over the footbridge these two kids came toward me. They looked my own age but they'd got red-laced Docs. One wore a Quadrophenia T-shirt, the other an RAF T-shirt. Their footsteps boomed in time, *left-right, left-right.* If you look kids in the eye it means you reckon you're as hard as they are. I was carrying a fortune in cash so I kept my eyes sideways and down, on the fumy river of loud trucks and slow tankers flowing underneath us. But as the two mods approached, I knew they wouldn't go into single file to let me by. So I had to squeeze myself against the sun-hot railing.

"Got a light?" grunted the taller one at me.

I swallowed. "Me?"

"Nah, I'm talkin' to Princess *fuckin'* Diana."

"No." I gripped the rail tight. "Sorry."

The other mod grunted, "Poof."

After the nuclear war, kids like them'll rule what's left. It'll be hell.

Most of the morning'd gone before I found the second antique shop. An arch led into a cobbled square called Hythloday Mews. Wails of far-off babies spiraled round Hythloday Mews. Lacy curtains blew over window boxes. A sleek black Porsche lay waiting for its master. Sunflowers watched me from their warm wall. Here was the sign, HOUSE OF GILES. The dazzling outside hid the inside. The door was propped open by a droopy pygmy with a sign round his neck saying, YES, WE'RE OPEN! Inside smelt of brown paper and wax. Cool as stones in streams. Murky cabinets of medals, of glasses, of swords. A Welsh dresser bigger than my bedroom hid the deepest quarter from sight. From here, a scratchy noise started up. The noise unfogged itself into radio cricket.

The noise of a knife on a chopping board.

I peered round the dresser.

"If I'd known I'd end up with *this* mess," the dark American woman purred at me, "I'd have gotten the freakin' cherries." (She was sort of beautiful but too off another planet to be fanciable.) In her sticky hands dripped a greeny-red fruit the shape of a strange egg. "Cherries are the fruit. Pop 'em in, slide out the stone, masticate, swallow, *finito.* None of this . . . spatter and gore."

My first words to a real live American were "What fruit's that?"

"Know what a mango is?"

"No, sorry."

"Why apologize? You're English! You don't know real food from freakin' polystyrene. Try some?"

You can't take sweets from pervy men in parks, but exotic fruit from antique shopkeepers is probably okay. "Okay."

The woman shaved off a fat sliver into a glass bowl. She stuck a tiny silver fork into it. "Rest your feet a moment."

I sat on a wicker stool and lifted the bowl to my mouth.

The slippery fruit slid onto my tongue.

God, mango's *gorgeous* . . . perfumed peaches, bruised roses.

"So what's the verdict?"

"It's absolutely—"

The cricket commentary suddenly went crazy. "*—entire audience here at the Oval is on its feet, as Botham notches up another superb century! Geoffrey Boycott is running over to congratulate—*"

"Botham?" The woman went to red alert. "That's *Ian* Botham, right?"

I nodded.

"Shaggy like Chewbacca? Broken Roman nose? Barbarian eyes? Masculinity wrapped in cricket whites?"

"That's probably him."

"Oh." She crossed her hands over her bosomless chest like the Virgin Mary. "I would walk on burning embers." We listened to more radio applause as we finished the mango. "So." She carefully wiped her fingers on a damp flannel and switched the radio off. "Can I sell you a Jacobean four-poster bed? Or do the tax inspectors keep getting younger?"

"Uh . . . have you got an Omega Seamaster please?"

"An 'Oh*mee*ga Seamaster'? That's a boat?"

"No, it's a watch. They stopped making them years and years ago. It has to be a model called a De Ville."

"Alas, Giles doesn't do watches, honey. He doesn't want people bringing them back if they don't run."

"Oh." That was it. Nowhere else in Cheltenham.

The American woman studied me. "I *may* know a specialist dealer . . ."

"A watch dealer? Here in Cheltenham?"

"No, he operates out of South Kensington. Want me to call him?"

"*Would* you? I've got twenty-eight pounds and seventy-five pence."

"Keep your cards closer to your chest than *that*, honey. Let me see if I can find his number in this bordello Giles calls his office . . ."

"Hi Jock? Rosamund. Uh-huh. No . . . no, I'm playing shop. Giles is out vulturing somewhere. Some duchess with a big country house has died. Or a countess. Or a largesse. *I* don't know, we don't *do* queens where I come from, Jock—well, not queens who dress like they're serving life in *fashion prison* . . . what's that? Oh, Giles *did* tell me, it was someplace quaint, in the Cotswolds, English-sounding . . . Brideshead, no, that was the TV series, right? It's on the tip of my tongue, Codpiece-under-Water . . . no, Jock, I'd *tell* you if—what's that? . . . Uh-huh, I *know* there are no secrets between—uh-huh, Giles loves you like a brother, *too.* But listen up, Jock. I have a young man here in the shop . . . oh, *hilarious,* Jock, no wonder you're such a pinup with the London arthritic . . . this young man is after an Oh*meega* Seamaster—" She checked with me and I mouthed "De Ville" at her. "—De Ville . . . uh-huh, you're familiar with that model?"

The pause was somehow promising.

"Oh, you *are?*"

The moment before you win you know you've won.

"In *front* of you? Well, how fortunate I called! Uh-huh . . . *mint* condition? Oh Jock, this is getting *better* . . . so serendipitous . . . listen, Jock, about the shekels . . . we have a budgetary situation here that—uh-huh . . . yes, Jock, if they stopped making them in the fifties they *must* be hard to come by, I see that . . . I *know* you're not a registered charity . . ." She mimed me a yapping yapbird with her hand. "If you didn't breed like a buck rabbit with every she-bunny who raises her fluffy tail your way, Jock, you wouldn't *have* so many children on the brink of starvation. Just give me your best price? . . . Uh-huh . . . well, I think it might . . . uh-huh. If he does, I'll call you back."

The phone pinged in its cradle.

"He *had* one? An Omega Seamaster?"

"Uh-huh." Rosamund looked sorry. "If you can stretch to eight hundred and fifty pounds, he'll courier it to your house once your check has cleared."

Eight *hundred* and fifty pounds?

"More mango, honey?"

"So let me get this straight, Jason. You broke this freakin' watch of your grandfather's—quite by accident—in January?" I nodded. "And you've spent the last seven months scurrying around for a replacement?" I nodded. "On the resources of a thirteen-year-old?" I nodded. "By bicycle?" I nodded. "Wouldn't it be a whole load easier just to confess? Take your punishment like a man, then get on with your life?"

"My parents'd *murder* me. *Literally.*"

"*What's* that? They'd *murder* you? *Literally?*" Rosamund sealed in a mock scream with her hands. "*Kill* their own offspring? For breaking a freakin' watch? How did they dispose of your siblings when *they* broke things? Flush them down the john, joint by joint? Doesn't the plumber find their bones when he unblocks the pipes?"

"Okay, not *literally* murder me, but they'd go *mental.* It's like . . . my greatest fear."

"Uh-huh. And how long will they stay 'mental'? The term of your natural life? Twenty years? No possibility of parole?"

"Not *that* long, obviously, but—"

"Uh-huh. Eight months?"

"Several days, definitely."

"What's that? Several *days*? Holy shit, Jason."

"More than that. A week, most like. And they'd never let me forget it."

"Uh-huh. And how many weeks can you expect to remain in your mortal coil?"

"I'm—" Hangman blocked my "Sorry?" "I don't quite get you."

"Well, how many weeks are there in a year?"

"Fifty-two."

"Uh-huh. And how many years are you alive for?"

"It depends. Seventy."

"Seventy-five years, unless you worry yourself to death first. Okay. Fifty-two multiplied by seventy-five equals . . ." She tapped the sum into a calcula-tor. "Three thousand nine hundred weeks. So. You tell me your greatest fear is that Ma and Pa'll be mad at you for *one* of these almost four thousand weeks. Or two. Or three." Rosamund puffed out her cheeks, then huffed out the air. "Can I swap your greatest fear for any *one* of mine? Take two of them. No, ten. Help yourself to a cartload. *Please?*"

A low-flying Tornado rattled all of Cheltenham's windows.

"It's a *watch* you broke! Not a future. Not a life. Not a backbone."

"You don't know my parents." I sounded sulky.

"The question *here* is, 'Do you?' "

"Of course I do. We live in the same house."

"You break my heart, Jason. Oh, you break my freakin' heart."

Outside Hythloday Mews I realized I'd left my map on Rosamund's table, so I went back to get it. The blue door behind the desk'd swung open, showing a tiny bog. Rosamund was taking a thundering piss, booming *Row, Row, Row your boat gently down the stream* in a foreign language. Women had to sit down to pee, I'd always believed, but Rosamund pissed standing with her skirt hoiked up to her bum. My cousin Hugo Lamb says in America they've got these rubber willies for Women's Lib women. Maybe Rosamund had one. Her legs were hairier than dad's, mind, which is pretty unusual for women, I thought. I was dead embarrassed, so I just took my map, quietly left, and walked back toward Mum's gallery. In an unfriendly baker's I bought a sausage roll and sat down in a triangle of park. The sycamores're tatty now August's almost over. BACK TO SCHOOL posters're in the shops. These last days of freedom rattle like a nearly empty box of Tic Tacs.

Till today I thought replacing my granddad's Omega'd just be a matter of tracking one down. But now the problem's about getting hold of hundreds of pounds. I chewed my sausage roll, wondering how I could (a) lie to explain the watch's disappearance *and* (b) make it not my fault *and* (c) make the lie invulnerable to questioning.

It can't be done.

Sausage rolls start off tasting lovely but by the time you finish them they taste of peppery pig bollock. According to Julia that's exactly what sausage rolls're made of.

Mum's friend Yasmin Morton-Bagot owns La Boîte aux Mille Surprises, but Mum manages it with an assistant called Agnes. (Dad calls it "La Bot," as in "bottom," for a joke, but *boîte* means "box.") La Boîte aux Mille Surprises is half shop, half gallery. The shop part sells stuff you can't buy outside London. Fountain pens from Paris, chess sets from Iceland, atomic clocks from Austria, jewelry from Yugoslavia, masks from Burma. The back room's the gallery. Customers come from all over England 'cause Yasmin Morton-Bagot knows artists all over the world. The most expensive painting at the moment's by Volker Oldenburg. Volker Oldenburg paints modern art in a potato cellar in West Berlin. I'm not sure what *Tunnel #9* is a picture of but it costs £1,950.

Thirteen years of pocket money, is £1,950.

"We're celebrating, Jason." Agnes's got a slidey Welsh accent so I don't always know if I've heard her right. "Your mum sold a painting *just* now."

"Great. One of the expensive ones?"

"One of the very, *very* expensive ones."

"Hello, darling." Mum appeared from the gallery. "Nice morning?"

"Uh." (Hangman stopped the "Not" of "Not bad.") "Fine. Agnes says you just"—Hangman blocked "sold"—"a customer bought a picture."

"Oh, he was in the mood for a bit of a plunge."

"Helena." Agnes went stern. "You had him eating out of your *hand*. That bit about cars losing value but art always gaining. You could have sold him Gloucestershire."

Then I saw this lush girl.

All three of them were sixteen, I'd say, and rich. One sidekick had a stoaty meanness and acne not even ornate makeup could cover. The other sidekick'd been turned from a fish into a wide-eyed fat-lipped girl by some fourth-rate witch. The leader, however, who'd come into La Boîte aux Mille Surprises first, *she* could've been off a shampoo advert. Pixie ears, pixie eyes, swelling cream T-shirt, licorice miniskirt, leggings that looked sprayed onto her perfect legs, and toffee hair I'd given my soul to bury myself in. (Girls' curves never used to yank me hard like this.) Even Pixie's furry sunflower bag was from a world where nothing ugly's allowed. Not gawping at her was impossible, so I went and sat in the tiny office. Mum came in a minute later to phone Yasmin Morton-Bagot, leaving Agnes on the till. A pipeline of vision went through the door crack, between two giant candles from Palermo and under an amber lampshade from Poland. By chance, Pixie's angelic bum hovered at the end of this pipeline. It stayed there while Acne and Codgirl got Agnes to get a Chinese scroll off the wall. Their voices were posh and horsey. I was still stroking Pixie's curves with my eyes. That's why I saw her fingers flicker behind the glass display, snatch the opal earrings, and slip them into her sunflower bag.

Trouble, shouts, threats, police, whimpered Maggot. *Stammering in court when you're called to give evidence. And are you* sure *you* just *saw what you thought* you *saw?*

I whispered, "Mum!"

Mum asked me just the once. "Are you sure?" I nodded. Mum told Yasmin Morton-Bagot she'd call her back, hung up, and got out a Polaroid. "Can you shoot them when I say so?" I nodded. "Good lad."

Mum walked to the front of the shop and quietly locked the door. Agnes noticed and the atmosphere in the shop went tense and dark, like before a scrap at school. Pixie gave a sign to her sidekicks it was time to leave.

Pixie's voice was brassy. "The door's locked!"

"I'm perfectly aware the door is locked. I just locked it."

"Well you can *unlock* it again, can't you?"

"Well." Mum jangled her keys. "It's like this. A thief has just put a pair of rather valuable Australian opals in her bag. Obviously, I need to protect my stock. The thief wants to escape with her stolen goods. So we have an impasse. What would *you* do, if you were in my position?"

Acne and Codgirl were already on the verge of tears.

"What I *wouldn't* do"—Pixie sounded dangerous now—"if I were a *shop assistant*, is throw around totally pathetic accusations."

"So you won't mind proving my accusations *are* totally pathetic by emptying your bag. Imagine how stupid this shop assistant will look when there are no earrings in it!"

For one awful second I thought Pixie'd somehow put the jewelry back.

"I'm not going to let *you* or *anyone* rifle through my bag."

Pixie was tough. This battle could still go either way.

"Do *your* parents know you're thieves?" Mum turned on Acne and Codgirl. "How are they going to react when the police call?"

Acne and Codgirl even *smelt* guilty.

"We were *going* to pay." Pixie made her first mistake.

"Pay for what?" Mum smiled, sort of creepily.

"Unless you catch us walking out of your shop, you can't do a *thing*! My father has an excellent solicitor."

"Does he? So do I," Mum replied, brightly. "I have two witnesses who *saw* you trying to leave."

Pixie marched up to Mum, and I thought she was going to hit her. "GIVE ME THE KEY OR YOU'LL REGRET IT!"

"Haven't you realized by now"—I had no *idea* Mum could be so bulletproof—"you're not intimidating me in the least?"

"Please." Tears shone on Acne's face. "*Please*—I—"

"In *that* case," Pixie snapped, "suppose I just pick up one of your crappy statues and smash my way out of this—"

Mum nodded at me: *Now.*

The flash made all three girls jump.

The photo grundled out of the Polaroid. I waved it by its corner to dry it for a second or two. Then I took another photo for good measure.

"What"—Pixie was beginning to crumble—"does *he* think he's doing?"

"Next week," Mum said, "I shall visit every school in town—with a police officer and these photographs—starting with Cheltenham Girls' College." Codgirl let out a flutter of despair. "Headmistresses are always so cooperative. They'd rather expel a bad apple or two than risk their school getting into the newspapers for the wrong reasons. Who can blame them?"

"Ophelia." Acne's voice was quiet as a kitten's. "Let's just—"

" 'Ophelia'!" Mum was enjoying this. "You don't get many Ophelias to the pound."

Pixie-Ophelia's options were closing in.

"Or." Mum jangled her keys. "Turn out your bags and pockets and return my stock. Tell me your names, your schools, your addresses, and your telephone numbers. Yes, you *will* be in trouble. Yes, I *will* contact your schools. But no, I *won't* press charges or involve the police."

The three girls stared at the floor.

"But you have to choose now."

Nobody moved.

"As you wish. Agnes, telephone P.C. Morton, please. Tell him to make space in his cells for three shoplifters."

Acne put a Tibetan amulet on the counter and tears streamed down her pitted, powdery cheeks. "I've never done this before . . ."

"Choose better friends." Mum looked at Codgirl.

Codgirl's hand trembled as she produced a Danish paperweight.

"Didn't Shakespeare's Ophelia," Mum asked, turning to the real one, "come to a mad, bad end?"

"Wow." Me and Mum hurried along Regents Arcade so we'd get to the cinema before *Chariots of Fire* began. "You handled those girls amazingly."

"Fancy." Mum's shoes smacked the shiny marble. *Take that! Take that! Take that!* "An old dear like me being able to handle three spoilt Pollyannas 'amazingly.' " (Mum was dead chuffed, really.) "*You* spotted them in the first place, Jason. Old Eagle Eyes. If I was a sheriff, I'd pay you a reward."

"Popcorn and 7UP please."

"Oh, I think we can manage that."

People're a nestful of needs. Dull needs, sharp needs, bottomless-pit needs, flash-in-the-pan needs, needs for things you can't hold, needs for things you can. Adverts know this. Shops know this. Specially in arcades, shops're deafening. *I've got what you want! I've got what you want! I've got what you want!* But walking down Regents Arcade this afternoon, I noticed a new need that's normally so close-up you never know it's there. You and your mum need to like each other. Not love, but like.

"This," Mum sighed and fished out her sunglasses, "is *wonderful.*"

The queue for *Chariots of Fire* snaked down the cinema steps and along the street for eight or ten shops. The film started in thirteen minutes. Ninety or a hundred people were ahead of us. Kids, mostly, in twos, threes, and fours. A few old-age pensioners too. A few couples. The only boy queueing with his mother was me. *Wished* it wasn't so obvious I was with her.

"Jason, *don't* tell me you need the loo *after* all?"

A fat prat with floppy eyelids turned round and smirked.

I half-snapped at Mum, "No!"

(Thank *God* nobody knows me in Cheltenham. Two years ago Ross Wilcox and Gary Drake saw Floyd Chaceley queueing outside Malvern Cinema for *Gregory's Girl* with his mum. They're *still* ripping the piss out of him.)

"Don't adopt *that* tone of voice with me! I *told* you to go at the shop!"

Good moods're as fragile as eggs. "But I *don't.*"

A sick bus growled past and made the air taste of pencils.

"If you're ashamed to be seen with me, just say so." (Mum and Julia often hit bull's-eyes even I hadn't spotted.) "We can save ourselves a lot of bother."

"No!" It's not "ashamed." Well, it is sort of. But not 'cause Mum's Mum, only 'cause Mum's *a* mum. Now I'm ashamed I'm ashamed. "*No.*"

Bad moods're as fragile as bricks.

That floppy-eyelidded fat prat in front was loving this.

Miserably, I took off my sweater and knotted its arms round my waist. The queue shuffled us forward to outside a travel agent's. A girl Julia's age sat behind a desk. Lack of sunshine'd made her spotty and pale. So this is what O levels earn you. A poster Blu-Tack'd on the window roared, WIN THE HOLIDAY OF A LIFETIME WITH E-ZEE TRAVEL! Mum the Delighted, Dad the Smiley Provider, Glamourpuss Big Sister, and Tufty Brother. In front of Ayers Rock, Taj Mahal, Disneyland. "Next summer," I asked Mum, "will we *all* go on holiday again?"

"Let's just" —Mum's sunglasses hid her eyes— "wait and see."

Unborn Twin goaded me on. "Wait and see what?"

"A year's a long way off. Julia's talking about doing a Euro Rail, or whatever they're called."

"InterRail."

"How about your school skiing trip? With your friends?" (Mum hasn't noticed I'm not popular anymore.) "Julia had a lovely time in West Germany on that exchange a few years ago."

"Ulrike the Shrieker and Hans the Hands didn't sound lovely to me."

"Your sister was exaggerating, Jason, I'm sure."

"Why don't just you, Dad, and me go somewhere? Lyme Regis's nice."

"I . . ." Mum sighed. "I don't know if the problems your dad and I had this summer with time off and whatnot will be any better next year. Let's just wait and see how things turn out."

"But Dean Moran's mum works in an old folks' home and his dad's a postman but *they* always manage to—"

"Bully for Mr. and Mrs. Moran." Mum used the voice that means you're talking too loud. "But not all jobs are as flexible, Jason."

"But—"

"*E*nough, Jason!"

The cinema man has appeared. He judges who'll get in and who'll be told, "You may as well go home." The Saved and the Rejects. The cinema man's lips twitch numbers as he paces down the pavement, slow as a coffin bearer. His Biro scratches his clipboard. Queuers grin with relief when he passes, peering back to see who he'll cast off as Rejects. The Saved're such smug bastards. They've *got* a seat in the colorful kingdom in the dark. Even if it's where the screen's too close up, *Chariots of Fire*'ll run for them. Twenty people're left between the cinema man and us. *Please*, let your feet come just a *few* extra paces along the pavement, just a few more, come *on*, just a few more . . .

Please.

maggot

"Jason Taylor"—Ross Wilcox's breath smelt like a bag of ham—"goes to the pictures with *Mummy*!" A moment ago Mark Badbury'd been talking to me about how to win at Pac-Man. Now, this. I'd already missed my chance to deny it. "We *seen* yer! In Cheltenham! Queueing with yer *mummy*!"

Traffic and time in the corridor'd slowed down.

Stupidly, I tried to downgrade his attack by smiling.

"What're yer *smiling* about, yer oily fuckin' *maggot*? Touch yer mummy up in the back row, did yer?" Wilcox gave my tie a vicious yank. Just because. "Stick yer tongue in, did yer?" He pinged my nose. Just because.

"*Taylor*!" Gary Drake hunts with his cousin. "That's dis*gusting*!"

Neal Brose looked at me like you'd look at a dog taken to the vet's to be put down. Pity, but contempt, too, that it'd allowed itself to get so *weak*.

"Give Mummy a Frenchie, did yer?" Ant Little is Wilcox's latest servant. Wayne Nashend's an older one. "Slip yer finger in, did yer?"

Spectators voted with their grins.

"Answer us, then." Wilcox has a habit of holding the tip of his tongue between his teeth. (That same tongue which tastes every nook of Dawn Madden.) "Or c-c-can't y-y-yer get the w-w-words out, yer st-st-stuttery bugger?"

That shot this attack into a new dimension. A hollow pit yawned where my answer should've been.

"Ross!" Darren Croome hissed. "Flanagan's coming!"

Wilcox ground his foot on my shoe like he was putting out a cigarette. "Dicksquirt stammerstuttery mammyshagging *arse-maggot*."

Mr. Flanagan, the deputy head, breezed by, flushing the 3GL kids toward the geography room. Wilcox, Ant Little, and Wayne Nashend went but my popularity was left dying in its final spasms. Mark Badbury was going over our Maths homework with Colin Pole. I didn't approach anyone 'cause I know they wouldn't talk to me. All I could do was stare out the window till Mr. Inkberrow rolled up.

Mist's dulling the gold leaves and browning the reds.

Double Maths is ninety minutes of pure boredom on the best of days and today was the worst of the worst. *Wished* I hadn't nagged Mum to take me to *Chariots of Fire*. *Wished* I'd just gone alone and paid for myself.

Wilcox would've found some reason to deck me and put the boot in, mind. He hates me. Dogs hate foxes. Nazis hate Jews. Hate doesn't need a *why*. *Who* or even *what* is ample. This is what I was thinking when Mr. Inkberrow whacked my desk with his meter rule. I jumped in my seat and cracked my kneecap on my desk. Obviously I'd zoned out of the lesson again.

"In need of a little *focusing*, Taylor, *hmm?*"

"Uh . . . I don't know, sir."

"A quick head-to-head to sharpen your brain, Taylor. You versus Pike."

I silently groaned. Head-to-head's where Kid A solves a problem on the left of the blackboard while Kid B solves the same problem on the right, like a race. Clive Pike's the 3KM's mathematical brainbox, so I didn't stand a chance. Which was part of the fun. Even as we wrote down the dictated equation, my chalk snapped.

Half the class giggled, including some girls.

Leon Cutler muttered, "What a *loser*."

It's one thing Ross Wilcox giving you a going-over in public. Ross Wilcox's doing that to loads of kids this term. But if a Mister Average like Leon Cutler slags you off and *doesn't even care that you can hear*, your credibility is bloody bankrupt.

"Ready," called out Mr. Inkberrow from the back, "set—go!"

Clive Pike's chalk went smartly to work.

I wasn't going to solve this equation and it knew it. I don't even know what equations're *for*.

"Sir!" called out Gary Drake. "Taylor's spying on Pike. That's not very *sporting*, sir, is it?"

"I *d—*" Hangman put the boot in, too, on "didn't." "Isn't true, sir."

Mr. Inkberrow just rubbed his glasses with a handkerchief.

Tasmin Murrell risked a snickerycockery "Naughty naughty, Taylor!" Tasmin Murrell! A bloody *girl*.

"Such a sense of fair play, Gary Drake," remarked Mr. Inkberrow. "You should consider law enforcement as a career option, *hmm?*"

"Thanks, sir. Might just do that."

I'd made only a few halfhearted scratches with my chalk. Clive Pike stood back from the blackboard.

Mr. Inkberrow let some moments pass. "Excellent, Pike. Sit down."

My answer'd died in the second line of x's and y's and squareds.

Muffled giggles began breaking out.

"Silence, 3KM! I see nothing amusing about spending a week of my life teaching *anyone* quadratic equations when the result is this . . . dog's dinner. Sit down, Taylor. Everyone, page eighteen. Let us see if your woeful ignorance is shared by the rest of the form."

"*Spazzo*," hissed Gary Drake, as I stepped over the foot he'd stuck out to trip me. "*Maggot*."

Carl Norrest didn't say a word when I sat back down at our desk. He knows how it feels. But I knew this was just the beginning. I've memorized our new third-year timetable and I knew what was coming up in the third and fourth periods.

Mr. Carver, our usual P.E. teacher, had taken the fifth-year rugby team to Malvern Boys' College, so this student teacher, Mr. McNamara, was taking us juniors on his own. This was good news 'cause if Carver scents you're unpopular, he joins in. Like the showers after winter football when Carver sits on the gym horse calling out, "Off with your cacks, Floyd Chaceley, or are we de*formed*?" and "Backs to wall, lads, Nicholas Briar's coming through!" Of course, most of us laughed like this was the funniest thing on earth.

The bad news was, my form (3KM) and Ross Wilcox's form (3GL) do P.E. together and Mr. McNamara can't discipline a class of boys to save his life. Or mine.

The changing room stinks of armpits and soil. It's divided into zones. The hard kids' zone's farthest from the door. The lepers' zone's nearest the door. Everyone else's is in between. Normally that's me, but today all the pegs there'd gone. The traditional lepers, Carl Norrest, Floyd Chaceley, and Nicholas Briar, acted like I'm one of them now and made space. Gary Drake,

Neal Brose, and Wilcox's lot were busy with a bum-flick battle so I changed quickly and hurried out into the cold morning. Mr. McNamara got us doing warm-up exercises before starting us on laps. I jogged at a careful pace that kept Ross Wilcox's lot on the far side of the track from me.

Autumn's turning miserable, rotting and foggy. The next field along from our sports field was burnt flapjack brown. The field after that was the color paintbrush water goes. The Malvern Hills were rubbed out by the season. Gilbert Swinyard says our school and the Maze prison were built by the same architect. The Maze prison's in Northern Ireland where Bobby Sands and the IRA hunger strikers died by degrees.

On days like today, I believe Gilbert Swinyard.

"So you reckon you've got what it takes to be center forward for Liverpool? For Man. U.? For England?" Mr. McNamara paced to and fro in his black-and-orange Wolverhampton Wanderers tracksuit. "So you reckon you've got the guts? The grit?" Mr. McNamara's Kevin Keegan perm bounced. "Clue-less! Look at you! Want to know what Loughborough University taught *me* about sweat and success? Well, I'm gonna tell you anyway! Success in sport—and in life, lads, yeah, in *life*—equals SWEAT! Sweat and success"—Darren Croome belted out a loud fart—"equals success and sweat! So when you get out there on that pitch today, lads, show me some *sweat*! I wanna see *three hundred percent* sweat! We're not gonna *nancy about* choosing teams today! It's 3KM stick 3GL! Brain versus brawn! Real men can go up front, ponces in midfield, cripples in defense, nutters in goal—only joking, I *don't* think! Move it!" Mr. McNamara blasted his whistle. "Come on, lads, keep it flowing!"

Maybe the sabotage'd been planned in advance, or maybe it just happened. Once you're a leper you're not let in on things. But pretty soon, I realized 3KM kids and 3GL kids were switching teams at random. Paul White (3GL) banged a long-distance shot at his own goal. Gavin Coley did a spectacular dive, the wrong way. When Ross Wilcox fouled Oswald Wyre (his team) in our penalty area, it was Neal Brose (our team) who took it and scored. Mr. McNamara must've guessed liters of piss was being taken. Perhaps he didn't want to turn his first solo lesson into a bollocking parade.

Then the fouling began.

Wayne Nashend and Christopher Twyford pogoed onto each of Carl Norrest's shoulders. Carl Norrest cried out as he buckled under their weight. "Sir!" Wayne Nashend sprang up first. "Norrest took my legs from under me! Red card, sir!"

McNamara looked at trampled, muddy Carl Norrest. "Keep it flowing."

I spent the game near enough to the ball to not get done for malingering, but far enough to avoid having to touch it. I heard the feet come thudding up but before I'd time to turn, a rugby tackle knocked me flat. My face was smeared into the mud.

"Eat as much as yer want, Taylor!" Ross Wilcox, sure enough.

"Maggots *love* this stuff!" Gary Drake, sure enough.

I tried to roll over but they had all their weight on my back.

"Oy!" McNamara's whistle blew. "You!"

They got off me. I got to my feet, trembling with victimhood.

Ross Wilcox prodded his heart. "Me, sir?"

"Both of you!" McNamara pounded up. (Everyone'd abandoned the football to watch this new sport.) "What in *hell* d'you think you're playing at?"

"Bit of late tackle, sir." Gary Drake smiled. "I admit."

"The ball was up the other end!"

"Honest, sir," said Ross Wilcox. "I thought he had the ball. Blind as a bat without my glasses."

(Wilcox doesn't wear glasses.)

"So you knocked this boy to the ground with a rugby tackle?"

"I thought rugby's what we're playing, sir."

(The spectators cackled.)

"Oh, a comedian, are we?"

"No, sir! *Now* I've remembered it's football. But when I *made* the tackle, I thought it was rugby."

"Me too." Gary Drake began jogging on the spot like a cartoon Sport Billy. "Too much competitive spirit, sir. Clean forgot. Sweat equals success."

"Right! Run to the bridge, the pair of you, to jog your memories!"

"*He* made us do it, sir." Ross Wilcox pointed at Darren Croome. "If you don't punish him too you're letting the ringleader off scot-free."

Bone-thick Darren Croome gooned back.

"All three of you!" Mr. McNamara's inexperience showed itself again. "The bridge and back! Go! And who told the rest of you the game's over? Keep it flowing!"

The bridge's just a footbridge that connects the far end of the school playing field to a country lane that goes down to Upton-on-Severn. "Run to the bridge!" is a standard Mr. Carver punishment. There's a clear view so the teacher can check they've run all the way. Mr. McNamara got back to refer-

McNamara must've recognized me as the kid trodden into the mud. He figured I'd be the likeliest to grass. *"Names."*

I shrank as the Devil turned eighty eyes on me.

There's this iron rule. It says, *You don't get people into trouble by naming them, even if they deserve it.* Teachers don't understand this rule.

McNamara folded his arms. "I'm *waiting.*"

My voice was a tiny spider's. "I didn't see, sir."

"I said, *'Names'*!" McNamara's fingers'd balled into a fist and his arm was twitching. He was on the very *edge* of belting me one. But then all light drained from the room, like a solar eclipse.

Mr. Nixon, our headmaster, materialized in the doorway.

"Mr. McNamara, is this child your main offender, your chief suspect, or a recalcitrant informer?"

(In ten seconds I'd be sandwich spread or relatively free.)

"He"—Mr. McNamara swallowed hard, not sure if his teaching career was minutes away from amputation—"says he 'didn't see,' Headmaster."

"There are none so blind, Mr. McNamara." Mr. Nixon advanced a few steps, hands hidden behind his back. Boys shrank against the benches. "One minute ago I was speaking on the telephone to a colleague in Droitwich. Abruptly, I was obliged to apologize, and terminate the conversation. Now. Who can guess the reason?" (Every kid in the room stared *very* hard at the dirty floor. Even Mr. McNamara. Mr. Nixon's stare'd've vaporized you if you met it.) "I ended my conversation due to the *infantile braying* coming from this room. Literally, I could *no longer hear myself think.* Now. I am not concerned about the identity of the ringleader. I do not care who roared, who hummed, who remained mute. What I *care* about is that Mr. McNamara, a guest in our school, will report to his peers—with just cause—that *I* am the headmaster of a zoo of hooligans. For this affront to my reputation, I shall punish *every one of you.*" Mr. Nixon lifted his chin one quarter inch. We flinched. " 'Please, Mr. Nixon! *I* didn't join in! It's not *fair* if you punish *me!*' " He dared anyone to agree, but nobody was stupid enough. "Oh, but I am not paid my strato*spheric* salary to be *fair.* I am paid my stratospheric salary to uphold standards. Standards which *you*"—he knit his hands together and cracked the knuckles, sickeningly—"just trampled into the *dirt.* In a more enlightened age, a sound thrashing would have taught you a sense of decorum. But as our masters at Westminster have deprived us of this tool, other, more onerous techniques must be found." Mr. Nixon reached the door. "The Old Gym. A quarter past twelve. Latecomers will receive a week's detention. Absentees will be expelled. That is all."

Old school dinners've been replaced this September by a cafeteria. A sign saying RITZ CAFETERIA OPERATED BY KWALITY KWISINE is bolted over the dining room, though the reek of vinegar and frying hits you in the cloakrooms. Under the writing's a smiley pig in a chef's hat carrying a platter of sausages. The menu's chips, beans, hamburgers, sausages, and fried egg. Pudding's ice cream with tinned pears or ice cream with tinned peaches. To drink there's fizzless Pepsi, sicky orange, or warmish water. Last week, Clive Pike found half a millipede in his hamburger, still wriggling. Even worse, he never found the other half.

As I queued up, people kept glancing at me. A pair of first years weren't trying too hard not to laugh. Everyone's heard it's Get Taylor Day. Even dinner ladies witched at me from behind the shiny counters. Something was going on. I didn't know till I sat down with my tray next to Dean Moran at the lepers' table.

"Um . . . someone's put some stickers on your back, Jace."

As I took off my blazer an earthquake of laughter rocked the Ritz Cafeteria. Ten sticky labels'd been put on my back. On each was written MAGGOT in a different pen by a different hand. I *just* stopped myself running out. That'd make their victory even more perfect. As the earthquake calmed down, I peeled off the stickers and tore them to shreds under the table.

"Ignore the wankers," Dean Moran told me. A fat chip slapped his cheek. "Funny!" he shouted in the direction it'd flown from.

"Yeah," Ant Little called from Wilcox's table, "we thought so." Three or four more were lobbed over. Miss Ronkswood came into the hall, stopping the chip bombardment.

"Hey." Unlike me, Dean Moran's able to ignore stuff. "Heard the news?"

Miserably, I picked specks of dried-on food off my fork. "What?"

"Debby Crombie."

"What about Debby Crombie?"

"She's only in the club, ain't she?"

"Netball?"

"*The* club!" Dean hissed. "Preggers!"

"Pregnant? Debby Crombie? A baby?"

"Keep yer voice down! Looks that way. Tracy Swinyard's best mates with the secretary at Upton Doctors. They went on the piss at the Black Swan two nights ago. After a drink or five she told Tracy Swinyard to cross her heart and hope to die, and told her. Tracy Swinyard told my sister. Kelly told me at breakfast this morning. Made me swear not to tell on our nan's grave."

(Moran's nan's grave's *littered* with shredded oaths.)

"Who's the father?"

"Don't have to be Sherlock Holmes. Debby Crombie ain't been out with no one since Tom Yew, has she?"

"But Tom Yew was killed back in June."

"Aye, but he were in Black Swan Green in April, weren't he? On leave. Must've pumped his tadpoles up her back then."

"So Debby Crombie's baby's dad's dead, even before it's born?"

"Cryin' shame or what? Isaac Pye said he'd get an abortion if he was her, but Dawn Madden's mum said abortion's murder. Anyhow, Debby Crombie told the doctor she's havin' the baby, no matter what. The Yews'll help raise it, Kelly reckons. Bring Tom back to life, in a way, I s'pose."

These jokes the world plays, they're not funny at all.

I've never heard anything, said Unborn Twin, *so hilarious*.

I bolted my egg and chips to get to the Old Gym by 12:15.

Most of our school's built in the last thirty years, but one part's an old grammar school from Victorian times and the Old Gym's in that. It's not used much. Tiles get blown off on stormy days. One missed Lucy Sneads by inches last January, but no one's been killed yet. One first year kid *did* die in the Old Gym, though. Bullied so badly, he hanged himself with his tie. Up where the gym ropes hang down. Pete Redmarley *swears* he saw the kid hanging there, one stormy afternoon three years ago, not quite dead. The kid's head flip-flopped 'cause of his snapped neck and his feet spasmed, twenty feet off the ground. Pale as chalk, he was, 'cept for the red welt where his tie'd burnt. But his *eyes* were watching Pete Redmarley. Pete Redmarley never's set foot in the Old Gym since. Not once.

So anyway, our form and 3GL were waiting in the quad. I'd sort of attached myself to Christopher Twyford, Neal Brose, and David Ockeridge talking about *Dirty Harry*. *Dirty Harry* was on TV on Saturday. Near the start there's a scene where Clint Eastwood doesn't know if he has a bullet left in his gun to shoot the baddie.

"Yeah," I chipped in, "that bit was *epic*."

Christopher Twyford and David Ockeridge's stare said, *Who gives a toss what* you *think?*

"Only total space cadets," Neal Brose told me, "say 'epic' anymore, Taylor."

Mr. Nixon, Mr. Kempsey, and Miss Glynch walked across the quad. A major bollocking was coming. Inside, seats'd been arranged in exam rows; 3KM sat on the left, 3GL on the right. "Does anyone," Mr. Nixon began, "believe he shouldn't be here?" Our headmaster may as well've said, "Does anyone wish to shoot their own kneecaps?" Nobody fell for it. Miss Glynch spoke mainly to 3GL. "You've let your teachers down, you've let your school down, and you've let yourself down . . ." Mr. Kempsey did us after. "I do not recall, in twenty-six years of teaching, feeling this *sickened*. You have behaved like a pack of hooligans . . ."

This took till 12:30.

Grimy windows rectangled misty gloom.

The exact color of boredom.

"You shall remain in your seats," announced Mr. Nixon, "until the one o'clock bell. You shall not move. You shall not speak. 'But sir! What if I need the lavatory?' Humiliate yourself, as you sought to humiliate a member of my staff. You shall fetch a mop *after* the bell. Your detention shall be repeated every lunchtime this week." (Nobody dared groan.) " 'But sir! What is the *point* of this static punishment?' The point *is*, that the victimization of the few—or even the one—by the many has no place in our school."

Our head then left. Mr. Kempsey and Miss Glynch had books to mark. Only their scratching pens, kids' stomachs, flies entombed in the strip lights, and distant cries of free kids ruckled the silence. The unfriendly clock's second hand shuddered, *shuddered*, shuddered, *shuddered*. That clock was more than likely the last thing in the world the kid who hanged himself saw.

Thanks to these detentions, Ross Wilcox won't get me in the next few lunchtimes. Any normal kid'd be nervous if they'd got two classes of boys sentenced to a week of detention. Might Mr. Nixon be banking on us doing his job punishing the ringleaders ourselves? I sneaked a glance at Ross Wilcox.

Ross Wilcox must've been staring at me. He flashed me a *fuck you* V and mouthed, "*Maggot.*"

" '*I got the conch—*' *Jack turned fiercely. 'You shut up!'* " Shit. The word "circle" was coming up. "*Piggy wilted. Ralph took the conch from him and looked round the—*" Desperately, I used the Trip Method, where you set up the stammer letter (S) but sort of trip over it into the vowel to get the word out. "Sss-*ircle of boys.*" Cased in sweat now, I glanced at Mr. Monk, our student teacher for English. Miss Lippetts *never* makes me read aloud but Miss Lippetts'd gone to the staff room. Obviously she hadn't told Mr. Monk about our arrangement.

"Good." Patience strained Mr. Monk's voice. "Go on."

" '*We've got to have special people for looking after the fire.*' " (S-consonant words're easier than S-vowel words, I don't know why.) " '*Any day there,*' " I read, swallowing, " 'there *m-may be a ship out there*'—*he waved his arm at the taut wire of the horizon*—'*and if we have a signal going they'll come and take us off.*' " (Hangman let me say "signal" like a superior boxer lets the loser land a punch or two, for fun.) " '*And another thing. We ought to have more rules. Where the conch is, that's a meeting. The sssame up here as down there.*' *They*—" Oh shit shit shit. Now I couldn't say "assented." Normally it's only words *beginning* with S. "Erm . . ."

" '*Assented,*' " said Mr. Monk, surprised that a kid in the top form couldn't read such a simple word.

I wasn't stupid enough to try to repeat it, like Mr. Monk expected. "*Piggy opened his mouth to ssspeak, caught Jack's eye and shut it again.*" There's no *way* I was hiding my stammer now. Hangman knew he was on to a major victory. I'd just had to use the Punch Method *again* for "speak." Using brute force to punch the word out's a last resort 'cause your face goes spaz. And if Hangman punches back harder the word gets stuck and *that's* when you turn into the classic stuttering flid. "*Jack held out his hands for the conch and*"—suffocating in plastic—"*ssstood up, holding the delicate thing carefully in his*"—my earlobes *buzzed* with stress—"*sssooty hands. 'I agree with Ralph. We've got to have these rules and obey them. After all, we're not—we're not—*'—Sorry sir . . ." I had no choice. "What's that word?"

" '*Savages*'?"

"Thankssir." (Wished I had the guts to press my two Biros against my eyeballs and head-slam the desk. *Anything* to get away.) " '*We're English, and the English are best at everything.*' Er . . . '*Ssso we've got to do the right things.*' "

Miss Lippetts walked in and saw what'd happened. "Thank you, Jason."

No "How come *he* gets off so lightly?" rippled round the class.

"Please, miss?" Gary Drake stuck up his hand.

"Gary?"

"This part's *brill.* Honest, I'm on the edge of my seat. Mind if *I* read?"

"Glad you're enjoying it, Gary. Go ahead."

Gary Drake cleared his throat. " '*Ralph—I'll split up the choir—my hunters, that is—into groups, and we'll be responsible for keeping the fire going—*' " Gary Drake read with exaggerated polish, just to contrast with how he read next. "*This generosssity brought a ssss-SSS-patter—*" (He got me. Boys were sniggering. Girls were looking round at me. My head burst into flames of shame.) "*—of applause from the boys, s-s-s-s-s-s-s-so—*"

"Gary Drake!"

He was all innocent. "Miss Lippetts?"

Kids turned round to stare at Gary Drake, then me. *Is Taylor the School Stutterer going to cry?* A label'd been stuck on me that I'll *never* peel off.

"Do you believe you are being amusing, Gary Drake?"

"Sorry, miss." Gary Drake smiled without smiling. "Must've picked up a nasty stutter from somewhere . . ."

Christopher Twyford and Leon Cutler shook with stifled laughter.

"You two can shut up!" They did. Miss Lippetts's no idiot. Sending Gary Drake to Mr. Nixon'd've turned his joke into today's main headline. If it isn't already. "That is despicably, fatuously, *ignorantly* weak of you, Gary Drake." The rest of the words on page 41 of *Lord of the Flies* swarmed off the page and buried my face in bees.

Seventh and eighth periods were Music with Mr. Kempsey, our form teacher. Alastair Nurton'd taken my usual seat next to Mark Badbury so without a word I sat with Carl Norrest, Lord of Lepers. Nicholas Briar and Floyd Chaceley've been lepers together so long they're almost married. Mr. Kempsey was still furious with us for the McNamara Affair. After we'd chanted, "Good afternoon, Mr. Kempsey," he just wanged us our exercise books like Oddjob throwing his hat in *Goldfinger*. "I quite fail to see what is 'good' about *this* afternoon, when you have rubbished the founding principle of the comprehensive school. Namely, that the putative crème de la crème impart their enriching essence to the milkier orders. Avril Bredon, distribute the textbooks. Chapter three. It is Ludwig van Beethoven's turn to be hanged, drawn, and quartered." (We don't actually make music in Music. All we've done this term is copy out chunks from *The Lives of the Great Composers*. While we're doing this, Mr. Kempsey unlocks the record player and puts on an L.P. of that week's composer. The poshest voice on earth introduces that composer's greatest hits.) "Remember," warned Mr. Kempsey, "to rewrite the biography *in your own words."* Teachers're always using that "in your own words." I hate that. Authors knit their sentences tight. It's their job. Why make us unpick them, just to put it back together more shonkily? How're you s'posed to say *Kapellmeister* if you can't say *Kapellmeister*?

Nobody messes about much in Mr. Kempsey's class, but today the mood was like somebody'd died. The only minor distraction was Holly Deblin, the new girl, asking if she could go to the sick bay for a bit. Mr. Kempsey just pointed at the door and mouthed, "Go." Third-year girls're allowed to go to the sick bay or toilets much more freely than boys. Duncan Priest says it's to do with periods. Periods're pretty mysterious. Girls don't talk about them when boys're around. Boys don't joke about them much, in case we give away how little we know.

Beethoven going deaf was the high point of his chapter in *The Lives of the Great Composers.* Composers spent half their lives walking across Germany to work for different archbishops and archdukes. The other half must've been lost in church. (Bach's choirboys used his original manuscripts to wrap their sandwiches in for years after he'd died. That's the only other thing I've learnt in Music this term.) I polished Beethoven off in forty minutes, long before the rest of the class.

"*Moonlight Sonata,"* the poshest voice on earth told us, *is one of the best-loved pieces in any pianist's repertoire. Composed in 1782, the sonata evokes the moon over calm, peaceful waters after the passing of a storm.*

A poem nagged as "Moonlight Sonata" played. Its title's "Souvenirs." Wished I could've netted the lines in my rough book, but I daredn't, not in class, not on a day like today. (And now it's all gone 'cept for "Sunlight on waves, drowsy tinsel." Don't write it down and you're doomed.)

"Jason Taylor." Mr. Kempsey'd noticed that my attention'd left the text-book. "An errand for you."

School corridors're sort of sinister during classtime. The noisiest spaces're now the silentest. Like a neutron bomb's vaporized human life but left all the buildings standing. These drowned voices you hear aren't coming from class-rooms, but through the partitions between life and death. The shortest route to the staff room was the quad, but I took the longer way, via the Old Gym. Teachers' errands're in-between times where no one can hassle you, like Free Parking in Monopoly. I wanted to spin this space out. My feet clomped over the same worn boards boys did somersaults on before they went off to the

First World War to be gassed. Stacked chairs block off one wall of the Old Gym, but the other wall's got a wooden frame you can climb. For some reason, I wanted to peer out through the window at the top. It was a minor risk. If I heard footsteps I'd just jump down.

Once you're up there, mind, it's higher than it looks.

Years of muck'd grayed the glass.

The afternoon'd turned to heavy gray.

Too heavy and too gray to not turn into rain. "Moonlight Sonata" orbited out past the tenth planet. Rooks huddled on a drainpipe, watching the school buses lumber into the big front yard. Bolshy, bored, and bargey, like the Upton Punks hanging out by their war memorial.

Once a Maggot, mocked Unborn Twin, *always a Maggot*.

Points behind my eyes ached with the coming rain.

Friday'd come round, sure. But the moment I get home, the weekend'll begin to die and Monday'll creep nearer, minute by minute. Then it'll be back to five more days like today, worse than today, far worse than today.

Hang yourself.

"Lucky for *you*," a girl's voice said and I nearly fell fifteen feet to a nest of fractured bones, "I'm not a teacher on patrol, Taylor."

I peered down at Holly Deblin peering up. "S'pose so."

"What're *you* doing out of class, Taylor?"

"Kempsey sent me to get his whistle." I clambered down. Holly Deblin's only a girl but she's as tall as me. She throws the javelin farther than anyone. "He's doing the bus queues today. Are you feeling better?"

"Just needed to lie down for a bit. How about *you*? Giving you a hard time, aren't they? Wilcox, Drake, and Brose and them."

No point denying it, but admitting it made it realler.

"They're dickheads, Taylor."

Darkness in the Old Gym smoothed away Holly Deblin's edges.

"Yeah." They *are* dickheads, but how does that help me?

Was it then that I heard the first tappings of rain?

"You're not a maggot. Don't let dickheads decide what you are."

Past the clock where semi-bad kids're made to stand, past the secretary's office where form captains fetch the registers, past the storeroom, a long passageway leads to the staff room. My footsteps got slower as I got nearer. Its steel door was half open today. Low chairs, I saw. Mr. Whitlock's black Wellingtons.

Cigarette smoke billowed out like fog in Jack the Ripper's London. But just this side of the door, there's a hive of cubbyholes where the more important teachers've got their own desks.

"Yes?" Mr. Dunwoody blinked at me, dragonishly. A going-brown chrysanthemum leaned over his shoulder. The art teacher's scarlet book was called *The Story of the Eye* by Georges Bataille. "As the title suggests," Mr. Dunwoody said, seeing that the book'd caught my attention, "*it's* about the history of opticians. What are *you* about?"

"Mr. Kempsey asked me to come and get his whistle, sir."

"As in, '*Whistle, and I'll come to you, my lad*'?"

"I s'pose so, sir. He told me it's on his desk. On a paper of interest."

"Or perhaps"—Mr. Dunwoody stuck a Vicks nasal inhaler up his large red nose and took an almighty sniff—"Mr. Kempsey's getting out of teaching while his ticker is not yet dicky. Off to Snowdonia, to herd sheep? With Shep, his border collie? 'Oh Give Me a Cot in the Land of the Mountains'? Could *this* be why he sent you for his whistle?"

"I think he's just doing the bus queues, sir."

"End cell. Under the tender gaze of the Holy Lamb." Mr. Dunwoody got back to *The Story of the Eye* without a word.

I walked down the empty hive. Desks come to resemble their owners, the way dogs do. Mr. Inkberrow's desk's all neat stacks and piles. Mr. Whitlock's is grubby with seed trays and copies of *Sporting Life*. Mr. Kempsey's cubbyhole has a leather chair, an Anglepoise reading lamp like my dad's, and a picture of Jesus holding a lantern by an ivy door. On his desk was *Plain Prayers for a Complicated World*, *Roget's Thesaurus* (Dean Moran's dad calls it "Roger's Brontosaurus"), and *Delius as I Knew Him*. Mr. Kempsey's whistle was exactly where he'd told me. Under the whistle was a thin stack of Xeroxes of Xeroxes.

Contrary to popular wisdom, bullies are rarely cowards.

Bullies come in various shapes and sizes. Observe yours. Gather intelligence.

Shunning one hopeless battle is not an act of cowardice.

Hankering for security or popularity makes you weak and vulnerable.

Which is worse: Scorn earned by informers? Misery endured by victims?

The brutal may have been molded by a brutality you cannot exceed.

Let guile be your ally.

Respect earned by integrity cannot be lost without your consent.

Don't laugh at what you don't find funny.

Don't support an opinion you don't hold.

The independent befriend the independent.

Adolescence dies in its fourth year. You live to be eighty.

I folded the top Xerox up and slipped it into my blazer pocket. Just because.

"Hunting for a needle in the ocean?" Mr. Dunwoody's head appeared round his partition. "As the Asiatics might say? In lieu of a haystack?"

I thought he'd seen me nick the sheet. "Sir?"

"Pearls before swine? Or a whistle on a desk?"

I dangled the whistle at Mr. Dunwoody. "Just found it, sir . . ."

"Wherefore dalliest thou? With the speed of a wingéd monkey, convey it presently to its rightful owner. Huzzah!"

First years were playing conkers in the queue for the Black Swan Green bus. At Miss Throckmorton's I was skill at conkers. Us third years can't play conkers, though, 'cause it's too gay. It's maimball or nothing. But at least the conkers was something to watch. Wilcox'd made it risky even to talk to Jason Maggot, School Stutterkid. After Mr. Kempsey'd herded the Birtsmorton lot onto their bus, he blew his whistle for the Black Swan Green kids. I wonder if he meant for me to take that sheet. When you decide Mr. Kempsey's all right, he acts like a prat. When you decide Mr. Kempsey's a prat, he acts all right.

Three rows from the front's too girly a seat for a third-year boy, but sitting near Wilcox's squad at the back'd've been *asking* for it. Middle-ranking kids trooped past the spare seat next to me. Robin South, Gavin Coley, Lee Biggs didn't even look at me. Oswald Wyre shot a *"Maggot!"* at me. Across the playground a bunch of kids by the bike sheds'd turned to puppet shadows in the mist.

"*Christ!*" Dean Moran sat by me. "What a day!"

"All right, Dean." I felt miserable I felt so grateful.

"Tell yer what, Jace, that Murcot's a bloody *nutter*! In Woodwork just now, right, a plane flew over and what does Murcot yell at the top of his lungs? 'Hit the deck, boys! It's the goddamn Jerries!' Honest to God, we all had to get down on our hands and knees! D'yer reckon he's going senile?"

"Could be."

Norman Bates, the driver, started the engine and our bus moved off. Dawn Madden, Andrea Bozard, and some other girls started singing "The Lion Sleeps Tonight." By the time the bus got to Welland Cross, fog was closing in thick.

"I was going to invite yer over this Saturday," said Moran. "Dad got a video recorder off this bloke in a pub in Tewkesbury."

Despite my problems, I was impressed. "VHS or Betamax?"

"Betamax, of course! VHS's going extinct. Problem is, when we got the video out of its box yesterday, half its insides was missing."

"What did your dad do?"

"Drove straight over to Tewkesbury to have it out with the bloke who'd sold it to him. Problem is, the man'd vanished."

"Could anyone at the pub help?"

"No. The pub'd vanished an' all."

"Vanished? How can a pub vanish?"

"Sign in the window. 'We have ceased trading.' Padlocks on the doors and windows. For Sale sign. That's how a pub vanishes."

"Bloody hell."

Some trailers were parked in the Danemoor Farm lay-by, despite the hill of gravel left there to ward off Gypsies. They hadn't been there this morning. But this morning belonged to a different age.

"Come over on Saturday anyway, if yer want. Mum'll cook yer lunch. It'll be a right laugh."

Tuesday, Wednesday, Thursday, and Friday had to be got through first. "Thanks."

Ross Wilcox and his lot'd streamed off the bus first without even a glance at me. I crossed the village green thinking the worst of this turd of a day was over.

"Where d'*you* think you're going, Maggot?" Ross Wilcox, under the oak tree with Gary Drake, Ant Little, Wayne Nashend, and Darren Croome. They'd've loved me to make a run for it. I didn't. Planet Earth'd shrunk to a bubble five paces wide.

"Home," I said.

Wilcox flobbed. "Ain't yer go-go-go-going to t-t-talk to us?"

"No thanks."

"Well yer ain't *goin'* to yer poncy fuckin' home down poncy fuckin' King-fisher Meadows yet, yer poncy fuckin' *Maggot.*"

I let Wilcox make the next move.

He didn't. It came from behind. Wayne Nashend pinned me in a full Nelson. My Adidas bag was ripped out of my hand. No point in shouting, "That's my bag!" We all knew that. The *crucial* thing was to not cry.

"Where's yer bumfluff, Taylor?" Ant Little peered at my upper lip. "Ain't yer got any bumfluff left?"

"I shaved it off."

" 'I shaved it off.' " Gary Drake mimicked me. "That s'posed to impress us?"

"There's this joke going round, Taylor," said Wilcox. "Have yer heard it? 'D'yer know Jason Taylor?' "

" 'N-n-n-o,' " replied Gary Drake. " 'B-b-but I t-trod in s-s-some once!' "

"Yer a *laughingstock*, Taylor," spat Ant Little. "A piss-flaps toss-pot *laughingstock*!"

"Going to the pictures with your *mummy*!" said Gary Drake. "You don't deserve to *live*. We should *hang* you from this tree."

"Say somethin' then." Ross Wilcox came right up close. "*Maggot.*"

"Your breath smells really bad, Ross."

"*What?*" Wilcox's face arseholed up. "*WHAT?*"

"I'm not trying to be insulting, honest. But your breath reeks. Like a bag of ham. Nobody tells you 'cause they're scared of you. But you should clean your teeth more often or eat mints 'cause it's *chronic.*"

Wilcox let a moment drag by.

A double-handed slap whacked my jaw.

"Oh and you're saying yer *not* scared of me?"

Pain is a good focuser. "It could be halitosis. The chemist in Upton could give you something for it, if it is."

"I could kick your *head in,* you dickless *twat*!"

"Yeah, you could. All five of you."

"*On my fuckin' own!*"

"I'm not doubting it. I saw you fight Grant Burch, remember."

The school bus was still by the Black Swan. Norman Bates sometimes gives a bundle to Isaac Pye and Isaac Pye gives Norman Bates a brown envelope. Not that I was expecting any help.

"This—oily—spacko—*Maggot*"—Ross Wilcox jabbed my chest with each word—"needs—a—GRUNDY!" A grundy's where a bunch of kids yank you up, hard, by your underpants. Your feet leave the ground and the crotch of your pants is forced up your bum-crack so your balls and dick get crushed.

So a grundying's exactly what I got.

But grundies're only much fun if the victim squeals and tries to fight. I steadied myself on Ant Little's head and sort of rode it out. Grundies humiliate rather than hurt. My attackers pretended to find it funny, but it was heavy, unrewarding work. Wilcox and Nashend trampolined me up and down. My pants just burnt my crotch rather than split me in two. I was dropped onto the soaking grass.

"That," promised Ross Wilcox, panting, "is just for *starters.*"

"Maaaaaaggot!" Gary Drake sang out of the mist by the Black Swan. "Where's your bag?"

"Yeah." Wayne Nashend booted my arse as I got up. "Better find it."

I sort of hobbled toward Gary Drake, my bumbone smarting.

The school bus revved up. Its gears cranked.

Grinning this sadistic grin, Gary Drake swung my Adidas bag.

Now I saw what was coming and broke into a run.

Tracing a perfect arc, my Adidas bag landed on the roof of the bus.

The bus jerked into motion, off to the crossroads by Mr. Rhydd's.

Changing course, I sprinted through the long wet grass, *prayed* the bag'd slide off.

Laughter *acker-ack-ack*ed after me, like machine guns.

One halfpence of luck rolled my way. A combine harvester'd made a slow traffic jam from Malvern Wells. I managed to reach the school bus while it waited at the crossroads by Mr. Rhydd's shop.

"*What,*" snarled Norman Bates as the door opened, "d'you think you're *playing* at?"

"Some boys"—I fought for breath—"chucked my bag on the roof."

The kids still on the bus lit up with excitement.

"*What* roof?"

"The roof of your bus."

Norman Bates gave me a look like I'd shat in his burger. But he swung down, nearly knocking me over, jumped down, marched to the end of the bus, climbed up the back-end monkey ladder, grabbed my Adidas bag, lobbed it at me, and climbed back down to the road. "Yer mates're bunch o'wankers, sunbeam."

"They're not my mates."

"Then why let 'em push you around?"

"I don't *let* them. There's five of them. Ten of them. More."

Norman Bates sniffed. "But only one King Turd. Right?"

"One or two."

"One'll do. What yer need is one of these little beauties." A *lethal* Bowie knife suddenly rotated in front of my eyes. "Sneak up on King Turd." Norman Bates's voice softened. "And *slice—his—tendons*. One slit, two slit, tickle him under there. If he fucks around with you after that, just puncture the tires on his wheelchair." Norman Bates's knife disappeared into thin air. "Army and navy surplus stores. Best tenner you'll ever spend."

"But if I sliced Wilcox's tendons, I'd get sent to Borstal."

"Well wakey *fucking* wakey, sunbeam! *Life's* a Borstal!"

you just said. Don't answer, and it's like you're admitting it's okay for Wilcox to be ripping into you. "S-s-so d-d-d-do girls find your s-s-s-stutter s-s-s-sexy, T-T-Taylor?" Oswald Wyre and Ant Little do this jackal laughter like their master's all six Monty Pythons rolled into one comedy thug. Wilcox's power is that you think it's not him speaking but Public Opinion judging you through him. "B-b-b-bet it m-m-m-makes 'em fizz in their p-p-p-p-per-per-pah-pah-pi-pi-poo-poo-poo-panties!"

Two rows in front, Squelch suddenly vommed a party-sized tube of Smarties he'd drunk to win a go on Ant Little's Space Invaders calculator. A tide of multicolored vomit advancing down the aisle was enough to distract Wilcox. I got off at Druggers End and went round the back of the village hall and over the glebe, alone. It takes a while. Over by Saint Gabriel's some way-too-early fireworks streaked spoon-silver against the Etch A Sketch gray sky. Someone's older brother must've bought them from Mr. Rhydd's. I was still too poisoned by Wilcox to taste the last watery blackberries of 1982.

Was it the same poison that spoilt Dad's incredible present? *John Craven's Newsround* was about the *Mary Rose*. The *Mary Rose* was Henry VIII's flagship that sank in a storm four centuries ago. It was lifted out of the sea bottom recently. All England was watching. But the silty, drippy, turdy timbers lugged up by the floating cranes look nothing like the shining galleon in the paintings. People're now saying the money should've been spent on hospital beds.

The doorbell rang.

"Chilly day," rasped an old man in a tweed cap. "Nip in the air." The man was today's second surprise. His suit had no obvious color. He had no obvious color, come to that. I'd put on the the door chain 'cause Dad says not even Black Swan Green's safe from perverts and maniacs. The chain amused the old man. "Crown jewels you've got stashed away in there then, is it, eh?"

"Erm . . . no."

"Ain't goin' to huff and puff and blow yer house down, yer know. Lady of the house at home, by any chance?"

"Mum? No. She's working in Cheltenham."

"A shame that is. Year back, I grinded her knives sharp as *razors* but no doubt they'll be blunt again by now. A blunt knife is the most dangerous knife, yer know that? Any doctor'll tell yer as much." His accent skimmed and skittered. "Blunt blades slip fierce easy. She'll be back soon, will she?"

"Not till seven."

"Pity, pity, don't know when I'll be passin' here again. How 'bout yer fetchin' them knives now, and I'll make 'em nice and sharp anyway, eh? To surprise her, like. Got my stones and my tools." He thumped a lumpy kit bag. "Shan't take no more'n a second. Yer mam'll be *that* pleased. The best son in the Three Counties, she'll call yer."

I doubted that very much. But I don't know how you get rid of knife grinders. One rule says you mustn't be rude. Just shutting the door on him'd've been rude. But another rule says Never Talk to Strangers, which I was breaking. Rules should get their stories straight. "I've only got my pocket money, so I couldn't afford—"

"Cut yer a deal, my chavvo. I like a lad who keeps his manners about him. 'Manners do maketh the man.' A proper clever haggler, yer mam'll call yer. Tell us how much pocket money's in yer piggy bank, and I'll tell yer how many knives I can do for what yer got."

"Sorry." This was getting worse. "I'd best ask Mum first."

The knife grinder's look was friendly on the surface. "*Never* cross the womenfolk! Still, I'll see if I can't call this way in a day or two after all. Unless the *squire* o' the manor's at home, that is, by any chance?"

"Dad?"

"Aye, Dad."

"He won't be back till . . ." You never know these days. Often he calls to say he's stuck in a motel somewhere. "Late."

"If he isn't fierce worried about his driveway"—the knife grinder tilted his head and sucked air—"he needs to be. Tarmac's cracked serious like. Pack of tinkers laid it originally, that's my guess. Rain'll freeze inside them cracks come winter, prize the tarmac up, see, and by spring it'll be like the moon! Needs tearin' up and relayin' *proper*. Me and my brother'll get it done faster than—" His finger click was as loud as the popper in Frustration. "Tell yer Dad from me, will yer do that?"

"Okay."

"Promise?"

"I promise. I could take your phone number."

"Telephones? *Liar*phones, I call 'em. Eye to eye's the only way."

Knife Grinder heaved up his kit bag and walked down the drive. "Tell yer dad!" He knew I was watching. "A promise is a promise, *mush*!"

"How generous of him" was what Mum said when I told her about the TV. But how she said it was sort of chilling. When I heard Dad's Rover get home

I went out to the garage to thank him. But instead of looking pleased he just mumbled, a bit embarrassed—no, almost like he was sorry about something—"Glad it meets with your approval, Jason." Only when Mum dished up the stew did I even remember the Knife Grinder's visit.

"Knife grinding?" Dad forked off some gristle to one side. "That's a Gypsy scam, old as the hills. Surprised he didn't get his tarot cards out, there on the porch. Or start scavving for scrap metal. If he comes back, Jason, shut the door on him. *Never* encourage those people. Worse than Jehovah's Witnesses."

"He said he might"—now *I* felt guilty for making that promise—"come back to talk about the driveway."

"What *about* the driveway?"

"It needs retarmacking. He said."

Dad's face'd turned thundery. "And that makes it true, does it?"

"Michael," Mum said, "Jason's just reporting a conversation."

Beef gristle tastes like deep-sea phlegm. The only real live Gypsy I ever met was a quiet kid at Miss Throckmorton's. His name's gone now. He must've skived off most days 'cause his empty desk became a sort of school joke. He wore a black sweater instead of green and a gray shirt instead of white, but Miss Throckmorton never once did him up for it. A Bedford truck used to drop him off at the school gates. In my memory that Bedford truck's as large as the whole school. The Gypsy kid'd jump down from the cabin. His dad looked like Giant Haystacks the wrestler, with tattoos snaking up his arms. Those tattoos and the glance he shot round the playground made sure *no one*, not Pete Redmarley, not even Pluto Noak, *thought* about picking on the Gypsy kid. For his part, the Gypsy kid sat under the cedar sending out *Piss off* waves. He didn't give a toss about Kick the Can or Stuck in the Mud. One time, he was at school for a rounders match and he whacked the ball clean over the hedge and into the glebe. He just strolled round the posts with his hands in his pockets. Miss Throckmorton had to put him in charge of scoring 'cause we ran out of rounders balls. But when we next looked at the scoreboard he'd gone.

I blobbed HP sauce into my stew. "Who *are* Gypsies, Dad?"

"How do you mean?"

"Well . . . where did they live originally?"

"Where do you think the word 'Gypsy' is from? E*gyp*tian."

"So Gypsies're African?"

"Not now, no. They migrated centuries ago."

"Why don't people like them?"

"Why *should* decent-minded citizens like layabouts who pay nothing to the state and flout every planning regulation in the book?"

"*I* think"—Mum sprinkled pepper—"that's a harsh assessment, Michael."

"You wouldn't if you'd ever met one, Helena."

"This Knife Grinder chap made an *excellent* job of the scissors and knives last year."

"Don't tell me"—Dad's fork stopped in midair—"you *know* this man?"

"Well *a* knife grinder's been coming to Black Swan Green every October for years. Couldn't be *sure* if it's the same one without seeing him, but I'd imagine he probably is."

"You've actually given this beggar *money*?"

"Do *you* work for nothing, Michael?"

(Questions aren't questions. Questions're bullets.)

Dad's cutlery clinked as he put it down. "You kept this . . . *transaction* hushed up for a whole year?"

" 'Hushed up'?" Mum did a silent *huh* of strategic shock. "You're accusing me of 'hushing up'?" (That made my guts quease. Dad flashed Mum this *Not in front of Jason* look. That made my guts quease and shudder.) "Doubtless I didn't want to clutter your executive day with trivial housewifery."

"And how much"—Dad wasn't backing off—"did this vagrant rip you off for?"

"He asked for one pound and I paid it. For sharpening *all* the knives, and a jolly good job he made of them. One pound. A penny more than one of your frozen Greenland pizzas."

"I can't believe you fell for this Gypsy-shire-horses-painted-wagons-Jolly-Old-England hokum. For God's sakes, Helena. If you want a knife sharpener, buy one from an ironmonger's. Gypsies *are* work-shy hustlers and once you give them an *inch*, a horde of his cousins'll be beating a path back to your door till the year two thousand. Knives, crystal balls, and tarmacking today, and car stripping, raids on garden sheds, flogging stolen goods tomorrow."

Their arguments're speed chess these days.

I'd finished. "Can I get down now please?"

It's Thursday so I watched *Top of the Pops* and *Tomorrow's World* up in my room. I heard kitchen cupboards being slammed. I put on a cassette Julia'd made for me from Ewan's L.P.s. The first song's "Words (Between the Lines of Age)" by Neil Young. Neil Young sings like a barn collapsing but his music's epic. A poem called "Maggot" about why kids who get picked on get picked on nagged at me. Poems are lenses, mirrors, and X-ray machines. I doodled for a bit (if you pretend not to look for words they come out of the thickets) but my Biro died so I unzipped my pencil case to get a new one.

Inside the third surprise was waiting for me.

The scalpeled-off head of a real live dead mouse.

Tiny teeth, shut eyes, Beatrix Potter whiskers, French-mustardy fur, maroon scab, nubby spinal bone. Whiffs of bleach, Spam, and pencil shavings.

Go on, they'd've said. *Put it in Taylor's pencil case. It'll be an ace laugh.* It'd've come from Mr. Whitlock's Biology dissection class. Mr. Whitlock threatens to dismember anyone nicking mouse parts, but after a flask of his special coffee he gets drowsy and careless.

Go on, Taylor, get out yer pencil case. Ross Wilcox probably sneaked it in there himself. Dawn Madden must've known too. *G-g-get out your p-p-p-P-P-PENcil case*—Wilcox's eyeballs popped—*T-T-Ta-T-T-TTT-Taylor.*

I got a wad of bog paper to wrap the head in. Downstairs Dad was reading the *Daily Mail* on the sofa. Mum was doing her accounts on the kitchen table. "Where're you off to?"

"To the garage. To play darts."

"What's that tissue you're holding?"

"Nothing. Just blew my nose." I stuffed it in my jeans pocket. Mum was about to demand an inspection but, thank *God,* she changed her mind. Under cover of darkness I sneaked down to the rockery and tossed the head into the glebe. Ants and weasels'll eat it, I s'pose.

Those kids must *hate* me.

After one game of Round the Clock later I put my darts away and came back inside. Dad was watching a debate about whether or not Britain should have American cruise missiles on its soil. Mrs. Thatcher says yes, so it'll happen. Since the Falklands no one can tell her no. The doorbell rang, which is odd, on an October evening. Dad must've thought the Gypsy was back. "I'll deal with this," he announced, and folded his paper with a jarky snap. Mum let out this tiny *Pah!* of disgust. I sneaked up to my spy position on the landing in time for Dad unchaining the door.

"Samuel Swinyard's the name." (Gilbert Swinyard's dad.) "My farm's up Druggers End. Would you have a minute or two?"

"Certainly. I used to buy our Christmas trees from you. Michael Taylor. What can I do for you, Mr. Swinyard?"

"Sam's fine. I'm collectin' signatures for a petition, see. You might not know this but Malvern Council're plannin' to build a site for Gypsies right *here* in Black Swan Green. Not temp'ry. *Perm'*nant like."

"This *is* disturbing news. When was this announced?"

"Exactly, Michael. Never *was* announced! Tryin' to sneak it through on the sly they are, so no 'un catches on till it's done and dusted! They're plannin' on puttin' the site down Hake's Lane, by the incinerator. Oh, they're all craft that Malvern Council lot are. Don't want the gyppoes in their *own* backyard, no thank you very much. *Forty* caravans, they've earmarked land for. Forty *they say* but there'll be hundreds of 'em once it's built, once you add on their relatives an' hangers-onners. Proper Calcutta it'll turn into. Count on it."

"Where do I sign?" Dad took the clipboard and scribbled his name. "As a matter of fact, one of those Gypsy—blighters—called here this afternoon. Around four o'clock, when housewives and children are likeliest to be at home, unprotected."

"Don't surprise me one *bit*. Been duckerin' all round Wellington Gardens too, they was. Older houses've got more precious junk to scav, see, that's their reck'nin'. But if this camp goes ahead, it'll be more o' the same every *day*! And once scavvin' stops workin' for Gypsies, they try more direct ways to cross their palms with our silver, if you catch my meanin'.'"

"I hope," Dad said, returning the clipboard, "you're getting a positive response to your efforts, Sam?"

"Only three refusals, who're half-gyppo 'emselves if you ask me. The vicar said he can't get involved in '*party-zan politics*' but his missus nudged him fast enough, sayin' *she* ain't no clergyman. Every'un else—as quick to sign as yourself, Michael. There'll be an emergency meetin' in the village hall Wednesday comin' to discuss how best to stuff them pillocks up in Malvern Council. Can I count on yer bein' there?"

Wish I'd said yes. *Wish* I'd said, "Here's my pocket money, sharpen what you can, please, right now." The Knife Grinder'd've got his gear out, there, on our doorstep. His metal files, stones, his (what?) flint flywheel. Crouched over it, his face glowing and creased like a goblin, eyes burning dangerous. One claw making the flywheel spin, faster, blurrier, one claw bringing the blunt blades closer, slowly, *closer*, till the stone touches the metal and buzz-sawing sparks gush, furious blue, dribble, spurt into the drizzly Coke-dark dusk. I'd've *smelt* the hot metal. Heard it shriek itself sharp. One by one, he'd work through the dull knives. One by one, old blades'd be made newer than new and whistlier than Norman Bates's Bowie knife and sharp enough to pass through muscle, bone, hours, dread, through "Those kids must *hate* me." Sharp enough to slice *What'll they do to me tomorrow?* into wafers.

God, I *wish* I'd said yes.

*   *   *

Being seen with either of your parents in public is pretty gay. But tonight loads of kids were walking to the village hall with their parents too, so that rule didn't apply. The windows of Black Swan Green Village Hall (erected 1952) glowed buttery yellow. It's only a three-minute walk from Kingfisher Meadows, slap bang by Miss Throckmorton's. Primary school seemed so *huge* then. How can you be sure anything is *ever* its real size?

The village hall smells of cigarettes, wax, dust, cauliflower, and paint. If Mr. and Mrs. Woolmere hadn't saved us chairs up front, Dad and I'd've had to've stood at the back. The last time it was as full as tonight was on the Christmas nativity play night when I'd been a Scruffy Urchin of Bethlehem. The audience's eyes reflected the stage lights like cat's eyes at night. Hangman made me have to half-fudge a few key lines, to Miss Throckmorton's disgust. But I'd played the xylophone okay and sung *White or black or yellow or red, Come see Jesus in his shed* okay too. You don't stammer when you sing. Julia had braces for her teeth then, like Jaws in *The Spy Who Loved Me.* She told me I was a natural. That wasn't true but was so nice of her I've never forgotten.

So anyway, tonight the audience was hysterical, like a war was about to break out. Cigarette fug blurred the lines. Mr. Yew was here, Collette Turbot's mum, Mr. and Mrs. Rhydd, Leon Cutler's mum and dad, Ant Little's dad, the baker (who's always at war with the hygiene people). All yackering yackerly to be heard over the yackering yacker. Grant Burch's dad was saying how Gypsies steal dogs for fighting and then eat the evidence. "It happens on Anglesey!" Andrea Bozard's mum agreed. "It'll happen here!" Ross Wilcox sat between his dad, the mechanic, and his new stepmother. His dad's a bigger, bonier, redder-eyed version of his son. Wilcox's stepmother couldn't stop sneezing. I tried to avoid looking at them, the way you try not to be sick by ignoring the fact that you're about to be. But I couldn't help it. Up on the stage with Gilbert Swinyard's dad were Gwendolin Bendincks, the vicar's wife, and Kit Harris, the Borstal teacher, who lives up the bridleway with his dogs. (Nobody'd try to steal *his* dogs.) Kit Harris's nickname's Badger 'cause of his white streak in his hair. Our neighbor Mr. Castle walked on from the wings to take the last chair. He gave Dad and Mr. Woolmere a heroic nod. Dad and Mr. Woolmere returned the nod. Mr. Woolmere muttered to Dad, "Didn't take old Gerry long to get in on the action . . ." Taped to the front of the trestles was a length of wallpaper. On it was painted VILLAGE CAMP CRISIS COMMIT-TEE. The V, C, C, and C were blood-red. All the other letters were black.

Mr. Castle got up to his feet and the hushers began hushing the yackers. Last year Dean Moran and Robin South and me were playing footy and Moran wellied his ball into the Castles' garden but when he asked for it back Mr. Castle said it'd crushed a hybrid rose worth £35 and he wouldn't give Moran's ball back till we'd paid for his rose, which means never, 'cause you don't have £35 when you're thirteen.

"Ladies, gentlemen, fellow Black Swans. That so many of you have braved this frosty evening is in it*self* proof of the strength of feeling in our community about our elected council's shameful—shame*less*—attempt to meet its obligations under the"—he cleared his throat—"1968 Caravan Sites Act, by turning our village—*home*, to all of us—into a dump for so-called Travelers, Gypsies, Romanies, or whatever the correct 'liberal'—with a *very* small *l*—phrase is in vogue this week. That not a *single* councilor bothered to appear this evening is less than edifying proof"—Isaac Pye, the landlord of the Black Swan, yelled, "We'd've *lynched* the buggers out on the green, that's why!" and Mr. Castle smiled like a patient uncle till the laughter'd died away—"is less than edifying proof of their duplicity, cowardice, and the weakness of their case." (Applause. Mr. Woolmere shouted, "Well said, Gerry!") "Before we begin, the committee wishes to welcome Mr. Hughes of the *Malvern Gazetteer*"—a man in the front row with a notepad nodded—"for slotting us into his busy diary. We trust his report of the *outrage* being perpetrated by those criminals at Malvern Council will reflect his newspaper's reputation for fair play." (That sounded more of a threat than a welcome.) "Now. *Apologists* for Gypsies will in*evitably* drone, 'What do you have against these people?' *I* say, 'How much time have you got? Vagrancy. Theft. Sanitation. Tuberculosis . . .' " I missed what he said next, thinking how the villagers *wanted* the Gyspies to be gross, so the grossness of what they're not acts as a stencil for what they are.

"Nobody *denies* that the Romany people need a permanent place of abode." Gwendolin Bendincks's hands shielded her heart. "Romanies are mothers and fathers, just like us. Romanies want what they *believe* is best for their children, just like us. Heaven *knows* I'm not prejudiced against *any* group of people, however 'way out' their color *or* creed, and I'm sure no one in this hall is either? We are all Christians. Indeed, without a permanent site, how will Romanies ever be taught the responsibilities of citizenship? How *else* will they be taught that law and order guarantees their children a brighter future than begging, horse dealing, and petty crime? Or that eating *hedgehogs* is simply *not* a civilized act?" Dramatic pause. (I thought how all leaders have the knack of turning what people're afraid of into bows and arrows and muskets and grenades and nukes. That knack is power.) "But *why* oh *why* do the Powers That Be believe that Black Swan Green is an appropriate location for their 'project'? Our village is a finely balanced community! A horde of outsiders, *especially* one of, shall we say, 'problem families,' swamping our school and our surgery would tip us into *chaos! Misery! Anarchy!* No, a permanent site *has* to be near a city big enough to mop them up. Cities, with infrastructure. Worcester, or better still—Birmingham! The message *we* send to Malvern Council is united and strong. 'Don't you *dare* fob *your* responsibilities off onto *us*. Country people we may be, but by golly *yokels* that you can *hoodwink* we are jolly well not!' " Gwendolin Bendincks smiled at her standing ovation like a cold man smiling into a bonfire.

"I'm a patient man." Samuel Swinyard stood, feet planted apart. "Patient and tol'rant. I'm a farmer, I'm proud of it, an' farmers ain't people to get a bee in their bonnets about nothin'." (A rash of good-humored mutterings broke out.) "I ain't sayin' I'd be objectin' to a *perm*'nant 'campment 'n' all for Gypsies if they *was* pure Gypsies. My dad, Abe, used to employ a few *pure* Gypsies come harvesttime. When they put their minds to it they was hard 'nough workers. Dark as niggers, teeth strong as horses', their people'd wintered'n all in the Chilterns since the Flood. Had to keep an eye on 'em. Slipp'ry as the Devil they could be. Like in the war and they all dressed up as women or buggered off to Ireland to avoid goin' off to Normandy. But at least with *pure* Gypsies yer knew what they was an' where you stood. Now why I'm on this stage tonight is, most of these characters driftin' round *callin'* 'emselves Gypsies're chancers an' bankrupts an' crim'nals who wouldn't know a *pure* Gypsy if one flew up his"—Isaac Pye shouted, "Arse, Sam, *arse*!" and a giant fart of laughter erupted from the back of the hall—"nose, Isaac Pye, *nose*! Beatniks an' hippies an' tinkers 'n' all who tag 'emselves 'Gypsies' so they can qualify for handouts! Unedyercated scroungers after '*social security*.' Oooh, it's all flush-toilet campsites they're wantin' now! Social workers flappin' round at their every beck and call! Why don't I call myself a Gypsy and get all this loot 'n' all for free, eh? Beats workin' for a livin'! 'Cause if I wanted to—"

The fire alarm blared out.

Samuel Swinyard frowned, annoyed. Not scared, 'cause there's no such thing as a real fire alarm, only fire drills. We had one at school just last week. We had to walk out of French in an orderly fashion and line up in the playground. Mr. Whitlock stormed round yelling, "Burnt to toast! The lot of you! TOAST!"

But the village hall alarm went on, and on, and on.

People round us began saying, "Ridiculous!" and "Can't some Einstein turn the bloody thing off?" Gwendolin Bendincks said something to Mr. Castle, who cupped his ear to say, *What?* Gwendolin Bendincks repeated it. *What?* A few people'd stood up now and were looking round, anxiously.

Fifty shouts exploded at the back. "*FIRE!*"

The village hall was a churn of panic.

Boiling hollers and fried shrieks swarmed over our heads. Chairs went flying and actually bounced. "*Gypsies've gone and torched the place!*" Then the lights went out. "*Get out! Get out!*" In that awful darkness Dad'd pulled me into him (the zip of his coat gouged my nose) like I was a baby. We stayed put right there, right in the middle of the row. I could smell his underarm deoderant. A shoe whacked my shin. One flickery emergency light came on. By its light I saw Mrs. Rhydd hammering on the fire exit. "Locked! *The ruddy thing's locked!*" Wilcox's dad was breaststroking people out of his way. "*Smash the windows! Smash the sodding windows!*" Only Kit Fletcher was calm. He contemplated the crowd like a hermit contemplating some quiet forest. Diana Turbot's mum screamed as a string of whopping pearls unstringed themselves and bounced under hundreds of feet. "*You're crushing my hand!*" Walls of villagers skittled over, down, around, over. A headless crowd's the most dangerous animal.

"It's all right, Jason!" Dad was squeezing me so tight I could hardly breathe. "I've got you!"

* * *

Dean Moran's place is actually two tumbly cottages knocked together and it's so old it's still got an outside bog. Pissing into the next door field's fresher so I usually do that. Today I got off the school bus with Dean at Druggers End 'cause we were going to play on his Sinclair ZX Spectrum 16k. But Dean's sister Kelly'd sat on the tape recorder that morning so it couldn't load any games. Kelly does the Pick 'n' Mix at Woolworth's in Malvern and what Kelly sits on isn't ever the same again. So Dean suggested we customize Operation in his bedroom. Dean's bedroom wall's papered with posters of West Bromwich Albion. West Brom're always getting relegated, but Dean and his dad've always supported West Brom and that's that. Operation's this game where you take out bones from a patient's body. If you touch the sides with the tweezers his nose buzzer buzzes and you don't collect your surgeon's fee. We tried to rewire Operation with a giant battery so you'd get electrocuted if you touched the sides. We killed Operation and the patient forever, but Dean says he got bored of it yonks ago. Outside we made a crazy golf course with planks, pipes, and old horseshoes from the choked orchard where Dean's garden stops. Evil frilly toadstools'd broken out of the rotted stump. A moon-gray cat watched us from the roof of the outdoors bog. We found two clubs but couldn't find a single ball, not even in the bottomless shed. We *did* find a broken loom and the bones of a motorbike. "How *about*," suggested Dean, "we have a looksy down our well?"

The well's covered by a dustbin lid under a stack of bricks to stop Dean's sister Maxine falling in. We took the bricks off, one by one. "Yer can hear a drownin' girl's voice, some nights when there's no wind an' no moon."

"Yeah, sure you do, Dean."

"Swear on me nan's grave! A little girl drowned in this well. Her petticoats an' that pulled her under before they could rescue her."

This was all too detailed to be bullshit. "When?"

Dean dumped the last brick. "Olden times."

We peered down. Our heads were tombed in the quiverless mirror. Hush of a tomb, and chillier.

"How deep does it go?"

"Dunno." The well elastics words down, then catapults echoes up. "One time me and Kelly tied a fishing lead to a line and lowered it down, right, and after fifty meters it were *still* goin' down."

Just the thought of falling down sent my balls ferreting up.

Damp October dusk gathered round the well.

"Ma*ma!*" A kitteny voice blasted us away. "I CAN'T SWIM!"

Shat myself, I *shat* myself.

Mr. Moran had hy*sterics*.

"Dad!" Dean groaned.

"Sorry, lads, couldn't resist it!" Mr. Moran wiped his eyes. "Just came out to plant next year's daffodillies, heard what you were talking about, and I could *not* resist!"

"Well, I don't half wish"—Dean replaced the lid—"you had of!"

Dean's dad set up table-tennis by balancing a wall of spine-up books across the kitchen table. Our bats were Ladybird books. (Mine was *The Elves and the Shoemaker* and Dean played with *Rumpelstiltskin*. Right spazzers we must've looked, specially Mr. Moran, who played cradling a can of Dr Pepper. (Dr Pepper's fizzy Benylin.) Brill laugh it was, mind. More fun than my portable TV, any day. Dean's little sister Maxine kept score. The whole family calls her Mini Max. We played Winner Stays On. Dean's mum got home from the old folks home on the Malvern road. She just took one look at us, said, "Frank Moran," and lit a fire that smelt of dry-roasted peanuts. My dad says real fires are more faff than they're worth, but Dean's dad says in a Tavish McTavish voice, "*Neeever* buy ye a hoose wi'oot a chimberly pot." Mrs. Moran pinned her hair back with a knitting needle and thrashed me, 21–7, but instead of staying on Mrs. Moran read aloud from the *Malvern Gazetteer*: BURNT CRUMPETS UNLEASH ANARCHY AT VILLAGE HALL! " 'Black Swan Green villagers learnt you can have smoke without fire on Thursday. The inaugural meeting of the Village Camp Crisis Committee, set up by residents to fight a proposed Gypsy site in Hake's Lane, Black Swan Green, was interrupted by a fire alarm, which triggerered a frantic stampede . . .' Well, dearie *dearie* me." (The article itself wasn't funny, but Mrs. Moran read it in this yokel news voice that made us *pee* ourselves.) " 'Emergency services rushed to the scene, only to discover the alarm had been triggered by smoke from a toaster. Four people were treated for injuries caused by the stampede. Eyewitness Gerald Castle, of Kingfisher Meadows, Black Swan Green'—that's your neighbor ain't it, Jason?—'told the *Gazetteer*, "It's a minor miracle nobody was maimed for life." ' Oh, sorry, I shouldn't be laughin'. It's not funny at all, really. Did you actually see this stampede, Jason?"

"Yes, Dad took me. The village hall was *packed*. Weren't you there?"

Mr. Moran'd gone sort of stony. "Sam Swinyard came sniffin' round for my signature but I politely declined him." The conversation'd taken a wrong turn. "Impressed by the level of debate, were you?"

"People were pretty much against the camp."

"Oh, doubtless they were! Folks'll do bugger all while the unions their grandfathers *died* for get dismantled by that creature in Downing Street! But once they smell a threat to their house prices they're up in arms faster'n *any* revolutionary!"

"Frank," Mrs. Moran said, like a hand brake.

"*I* ain't ashamed of Jason knowing I've got Gypsy blood in my veins! My grandfather was one, Jason, see. *That's* why we didn't go to the meeting. Gypsies ain't angels but they ain't devils neither. No more an' no less than farmers or postmen or landlords, anyhow. Folks ought to just leave 'em be."

I didn't know what I should say, so I just nodded.

"Nattering won't get supper on the table." Mrs. Moran got up. Mr. Moran got out his *Word Puzzler's Weekly. Word Puzzler's Weekly*'s got ladies in bikinis on the cover but nothing nudier inside. Maxine, Dean, and I put the Ladybird books away till the smell of gammon and mushrooms filled the small kitchen. I helped Dean lay the table to postpone going home. The Morans' cutlery drawer isn't scientifically divided like ours. It's all higgledy-piggledy. "You'll be stayin' for a bite, Jason?" Dean's mum peeled potatoes. "Milady Kelly phoned me at work. They're all off for pie and chips after work 'cause it's somebody's birthday, so we've got room for one more."

"Go on," urged Dean's dad. "Ring your mum on our jellybone."

"Better not." Actually I'd've *loved* to stay, but Mum throws an eppy if I don't book meals at other kids' houses weeks in advance. Dad goes all policemanlike too, as if the offense is too serious to merely get cross at. *Dad* eats dinner in Oxford more often than he eats at home these days, mind. "Thanks for having me."

Dusk'd sucked mist from the ground. The clocks're going back next weekend. Mum'd be home from Cheltenham soon but I wasn't in any hurry. So I went the long way via Mr. Rhydd's shop. Less chance of running across Ross Wilcox's lot if I avoided the mouth of Wellington Gardens, I thought. But just as I passed the lych-gate of Saint Gabriel's, kids' shouts spilt out of Diana Turbot's garden. Not good.

Not good at all. Up ahead were Ross Wilcox himself, Gary Drake, and ten or fifteen kids. Older kids, too, like Pete Redmarley and the Tookey brothers. War'd broken out. Conkers for bullets, crab apples and windfallen pears for heavy artillery. Spare ammo was carried in pouches made of turned-up sweaters. A stray acorn whistled by my ear. Once I'd've just picked the side with the most popular kids on it and joined in, but "once" isn't now. Chances are the cry'd go up, *"G-g-g-get T-T-T-TTTaylor!"* and both armies'd turn their fire on me. If I tried to leg it, there'd be a foxhunt through the village with Wilcox as the hunt master and me as the fox.

So I slipped into the ivy-choked bus shelter before anyone spotted me. The buses to Malvern and Upton and Tewkesbury once stopped here, but they've mostly been canceled now 'cause of cuts. Snoggers and graffitiers've taken it over. Fruit bounced past the doorway. I realized I'd just trapped myself. Pete Redmarley's army was falling back this way with Gary Drake and Ross Wilcox's lot war-crying after them. I peered out. A cooking apple spectacularly exploded on Squelch's head, ten feet away. In seconds the defenders'd draw level and I'd be found hiding. Being found hiding's worse than just being found.

Squelch rubbed apple from his eye, then looked at me.

Shit-scared he'd give me away, I put my finger on my lip.

Squelch's gurn turned to a grin. He put his finger on his lip.

I darted out of the shelter, across the Malvern road. I had no time to find a path so I just jumped into the denseness. Holly. Just my luck. I sank down through prickly leaves. My neck and bum got scratched but scratches don't hurt like humiliation hurts. Miracle of miracles, no one trumpeted out my name. The battle spilt this way and that, so close to my hiding place I heard Simon Sinton mumble instructions to himself. The bus shelter I'd left twenty seconds ago was requisitioned as a bunker.

"That *hurt*, Croome, you *tosser!*"

"Oh did it hurt, poor little Robin South, I'm *so* sorry!"

"C'mon you lot! Show 'em who *this* village belongs to!"

"Kill 'em! Massacre 'em! Dump 'em in a pit! Bury 'em!"

Pete Redmarley's forces rallied. The battle stayed vicious but stalemated. The air thickened with missiles and the cries of the hit. Wayne Nashend foraged for ammo just feet from my hiding place. It looked like the war'd spilled into the woods. My only way out was deeper in.

The wood invited me on, curtain after curtain, like sleep. Ferns stroked my forehead and picked my pockets. *Nobody knows you're here,* murmured the trees, anchoring down for the winter.

Picked-on kids act invisible to reduce the chances of being noticed and picked on. Stammerers act invisible to reduce the chances of being made to say something we can't. Kids whose parents argue act invisible in case we trig-

ger another skirmish. The Triple Invisible Boy, that's Jason Taylor. Even *I*
don't see the real Jason Taylor much these days, 'cept for when we're writing
a poem, or occasionally in a mirror, or *just* before sleep. But he comes out in
the woods. Ankley branches, knuckly roots, paths that only might be, earth-
works by badgers or Romans, a pond that'll ice over come January, a wooden
cigar box nailed behind the ear of a secret sycamore where we once planned
a treehouse, birdstuffedtwigsnapped silence, toothy bracken, and places you
can't find if you're not alone. Time in the woods's older than time in clocks,
and truer. Ghosts of Might Be run riot in the woods, and stationery shops and
messes of stars. Woods don't bother with fences or borders. Woods *are* fences
and borders. *Don't be afraid. You see better in the dark.* I'd love to work with
trees. Druids don't exist nowadays, but foresters do. A forester in France.
What tree cares if you can't spit your words out?

This druid feeling I get in the woods's so thrilling it makes me want to crap,
so I dug a hole with a flat stone inside a clump of mitten-leafed shrubs. I
pulled down my cacks and squatted. It's ace shitting outside like a caveman.
Let go, thud, subtle crinkle on dry leaves. Squatted craps come out smoother
than craps in bogs. Crap's peatier and steamier in open air, too. (My one fear
is bluebottles flying up my arsehole and laying eggs in my lower intestine.
Larvae'd hatch and get to my brain. My cousin Hugo told me it actually happened to an American kid called Akron Ohio.) "Am I normal," I said aloud
just to hear my voice, "talking to myself in a wood like this?" A bird *so* near it
might've perched on a curl of my ear musicked a flute in a jar. I *quivered* to
own such an unownable thing. If I could've climbed into that moment, that
jar, and never *ever* left, I would've done. But my squatting calves were aching,
so I moved. The unownable bird took fright and vanished down its tunnel of
twigs and *nows*.
    I'd just wiped my ass with mitten leaves when this *massive* dog big as a
bear, this brown-and-white wolf, padded out of the murky bracken.
    I thought I was going to die.
    But the wolf calmly picked up my Adidas bag in its teeth and trotted off
down the path.
    Only a dog. Maggot trembled. *It's gone, it's okay, we're safe.*
    A dead man's groan unwound itself from deep inside me. Six exercise
books, including Mr. Whitlock's, plus three textbooks. Gone! What'd I say to
the teachers? "I can't hand in my homework, sir. A dog ran off with it." Mr.
Nixon'd bring back the cane just to punish my lack of originality.

Far too late I jumped up to give chase, but my snake-clasp belt twanged undone, my trousers unhoiked, and I flew head over arse like Laurel and Hardy. Leaf mold in my underpants, a twig up my nose.

Nothing for it but follow the way the dog might've gone, scanning the clotted woods for patches of trotting white. Whitlock's sarcasm'd be everlasting. Mrs. Coscombe's fury'd be hot as ovens. Mr. Inkberrow's disbelief'd be as unbendy as his blackboard ruler. *Shit, shit, shit.* First every kid labels me as a tragic case, now half the teachers'll think I'm a waste of space. "What were you doing traipsing through the woods at that hour?"

An owl? Here was a bent glade I knew from when us village kids used to fight war games in the woods. Pretty seriously we took it, with prisoners of war, cease-fires, flags one side had to steal (footy socks on a stick), and rules of combat that were half tag, half judo. More sophisticated than those Passchendaeles back on the Malvern road, anyhow. When field marshals picked their men I was snapped up 'cause I was an ace dodger and tree climber. Those war games were ace. Sport at school isn't the same. Sport doesn't let you be someone you're not. War games're extinct now. Us lot were the last ones. Apart from the lake where people walk dogs, every season chokes up more and more paths in the woods. Ways in've been wired off or walled up by brambles and farmers. Things get dense and thorny if they're left on their own. People're getting edgy about kids running around after dark like we used to. A newspaperboy called Carl Bridgewater was murdered not long ago, in Gloucestershire. Gloucestershire's only next door. The police found his body in a wood like this.

Thinking about Carl Bridgewater made me a bit scared. A bit. A murderer might *dump* a body in a wood but it'd be an idiotic place to wait for victims. Black Swan Green Wood isn't Sherwood Forest or Vietnam. All I had to do to get home was backtrack, or keep going till I reached fields.

Yeah, without my Adidas schoolbag.

Twice I saw a patch of white and thought, *The dog!*

One time it was just a silver birch. The second time, a placky bag.

This was hopeless.

The lip of the old quarry reared up. I'd forgotten it since the war games stopped. Not a big drop, but you wouldn't want to tumble down it. The bottom was a sort of three-sided basin with a track going out that led to Hake's Lane. Or is it Pig Lane? I was surprised to see there were lights and voices on the quarry floor. Five or six caravans, I counted, plus motor homes and a truck, a horsebox, a Hillman van, and a motorbike and sidecar. A generator was chugging. *Gypsies,* I thought. *Has to be.* At the foot of the scree below my overhang about seven or eight figures sat round a dirty fire. Dogs, too.

No sign of the wolf who'd robbed me, and no sign of my Adidas bag. But, surely, it was likelier my bag'd be here than anywhere else in the wood. Problem was, how does a kid from a four-bedroom house down Kingfisher Meadows with Everest Double Glazing go up to Gypsies and accuse their dogs of nicking stuff?

I *had* to.

How *could* I? I went to that Village Camp Crisis Committee meeting. But my *bag.* At the very least, I figured, I should come into their camp by the main track, so they didn't think I was spying on them.

"Gonna stay spyin' on us all evenin', are yer?"

If Dean Moran's dad'd put five shits up me, this rammed home *ten.* A broken-nosed face appeared in the clotted dark behind me. Fierce. "No." I might've begun pleading. "I just thought—" But I didn't finish 'cause I'd taken a step back.

Empty air.

Stones, soil sliding, me sliding with it, down and round and (*You'll be lucky if you only break a leg,* said Unborn Twin) round and down and ("*Feck!*" and "*Mind it!*" and "*MIND IT!*" shouted real humans) down and round and (dice in a tumbler) round and down and (caravans campfire collarbones) breath *whacked* out of my lungs as I came to a dead stop.

Dogs were going wild, inches away.

"GERROUT O' HERE YER GERT DAFT BUGGERS!"

My wakes of pebbles and dirt caught up with me.

"Well," the voice rasped, "where in bugger did *he* drop from?"

It was like when someone on TV wakes in hospital and faces swim up, but spookier 'cause of the dark. My body ached in twenty places. Scraper pain, not axed pain, so I reckoned I'd be able to walk. My vision spun like a washing machine at the end of its cycle. "A kid's skidded down the quarry!" Voices rang out. "A kid's skidded down the quarry!" More people appeared in the firelight. Suspicious if not hostile.

An old man spoke in a foreign language.

"Don't have to bury him *yet!* 'Tain't a cliff he dropped!"

"It's okay." Grit clogged my mouth. "I'm okay."

A near one asked, "Can yer stand up, boy?"

I tried but the ground hadn't stopped tumbling yet.

"Wobbly on his trotters," the raspy voice decided. "Park yer arse a mo, *mush*, round the fire. Help us, one of yer . . ."

Two arms supported me the few steps to the fire. An aproned mother and daughter stepped from a caravan where *Midlands Today* was on. Both women looked hard as hammers. One held a baby. Kids jostled to get a better look. Wilder and way harder than *any* kid in my year, even Ross Wilcox. Rain, colds, scraps, bullies, handing in homework on time, such things didn't worry these kids.

One teenager was whittling at a lump and not paying me the blindest bit of notice. Firelight flashed off his sure knife. A mop of hair hid half his face.

The raspy man turned into the knife grinder. This reassured me, but only a bit. Him on my doorstep was one thing, but me crashing down here wasn't the same. "Sorry to . . . thanks, but I'd best be off."

"*I* caught him, Bax!" The Bust-Nosed Boy came bum-skiing down the scree. "But the *divvy* fell off himself! I never pushed him! But I should of! Spyin', he was, the spyin' bugger!"

Knife Grinder looked at me. "You ain't ready to leave yet, chavvo."

"This'll, er"—Hangman blocked "sound"—"appear weird, but I was in the woods over by Saint Gabriel's—the church—and I'd just"—Hangman blocked "sat"—"I'd just rested when this dog"—God, this sounded *so* pathetic—"this *massive* dog came up and grabbed my bag and ran off with it." (Not one flicker of sympathy on not one face.) "It's got all my exercise books and textbooks in." Hangman was making me duck words like a liar does. "Then I followed the dog, well, I tried to, but it got dark, and the path, well, kind of path, just led me to . . ." I pointed up behind me. "Up there. I saw you down here but I *wasn't* spying on you." (Even the baby looked dubious.) "Honest, I just wanted my bag back."

The whittler still whittled.

A woman asked, "Why was yer in the wood in the first place?"

"Hiding." Only the unpretty truth'd do.

"Hiding?" her daughter demanded. "Who from?"

"A bunch of kids. Village kids."

"What yer do to 'em?" asked Bust-Nosed Boy.

"Nothing. They just don't like me."

"Why not?"

"How should I know?"

"*Course* yer know!"

Of course I do. "I'm not one of them. That's it. That's enough."

Warmth slimed my palm and a fangy lurcher looked back up. A man with greased-back hair and sideburns snorted at an older one. "Should o' seen yer face, Bax! When the boy came tumbling down out of nowhere!"

"Frit as sin I was!" The old man chucked a beer can into the fire. "An' I don't mind ownin' it, Clem Ostler. Thought he was a mulo up from the graveyard. Or gorgios chuckin' stoves or fridges down like that time up Pershore way. Nah, I never got a good feelin' about this atchin-sen." (Either Gypsies bend words out of shape, or they have new words for things.) "This 'un"—I got a suspicious nod—"a-creepin' up on us jus' proves it."

"Ain't it more polite," Knife Grinder said, turning to me, "just to *ask* 'bout yer bag, if yer thought we had it?"

"Reckon we'd skewer yer an' roast yer alive, didn't yer?" The woman's folded forearms were thick as cables. "Everyone knows us Gypsies're *all* partial for a bit o' gorgio in the pot, ain't that right?"

I shrugged, miserable. The whittler still whittled. Wood smoke and oil fumes, bodies and cigarettes, bangers and beans, sweet and sour manure. These peoples' lives're freer than mine, but mine's ten times more comfortable and'll probably be longer.

"S'pose, now," a short man said from a throne of stacked-up tires, "we help yer look for this bag o' yours? What'd yer give us back?"

"*Have* you got my bag?"

Bust-Nosed Boy shot back, "What you accusin' my uncle of?"

"Steady, Al." Knife Grinder yawned. "He ain't harmed us so far as I can see. But how he might earn a bit o' goodwill is tellin' us if that carry-on at the village hall Wednesday last was over that 'perm'nant site' the council're after building down Hake's Lane. Half the bones o' Black Swan Green was sardined in there. Never seen the like."

Honesty and confessing're so often the same. "It was."

Knife Grinder leaned back, pleased, as if he'd won a bet.

"*You* went along, did yer?" asked the one called Clem Ostler.

I'd already hesitated too long. "My dad took me. But the meeting was interrupted halfway because—"

"Find out everything about us," demanded the daughter, "did yer?"

"Not a lot" was the safest thing to say.

"Gorgios"—Clem Ostler's eyes were slits—"don't know one fat rat squeak about us. Yer 'experts' know even less."

Bax, the old man, nodded. "Mercy Watts's family got moved onto one o' them 'official sites' down Sevenoaks way. Rents, queues, lists, wardens. Council houses on wheels, they are."

"That's the dumbfool joke of it!" Knife Grinder poked the fire. "We don't want 'em built any more'n yer locals. That new law, that's what this whole blue-arsed carry-on's about."

Bust-Nosed Boy said, "What new law's that then, Uncle?"

"Goes like this. If the council ain't built their quota o' perm'nant sites, the law says we can atch wherever we please. But a council what *has* got the quota can get the gavvas to move us on if we're atchin' anywhere what *ain't* a perm'nent site. This is what this place down Hake's Lane's about. Ain't 'bout kindness."

"Learn *that* at yer meetin' "—the mother scowled at me—"did yer?"

Clem Ostler didn't let me reply. "Once they get us tied down, then they'll be crammin' our chavvies into their schools, turnin' us all into *Yessirs, Nosirs, Three bags full Sirs.* Turn us into a bunch o' didikois an' kennicks, stuffed up in brick houses. Wipe us off the earth, like Adolf Hitler tried to. Oh more gradual like, much gentler, but get rid of us all the same."

" 'Assimilation.' " Bust-Nosed Boy glared my way. "That's what social workers call it, ain't it?"

"I"—I shrugged—"don't know."

"S'prised a gyppo knows a big word like that? Yer don't know who I am, do yer? Oh, I remember *you* all right. These yots don't forgets a face. We was both at the littl'uns school in the village. Frogmartin, Figmortin, the teacher's name was, summat like that. Yer was stuttery then, too, wasn't yer? We was playin' that game, that Hangman game."

My memory passed me the Gypsy kid's name. "Alan Wall."

"That's my name, Stuttery, don't wear it out."

"Stuttery" was an improvement on "Spy."

"What"—the mother lit a cigarette—"gets *my* goat about gorgios is how they call *us* dirty when they have toilets in the same room they wash in! *And* all use the same spoons and cups and bathwater and don't throw their rubbish for the wind an' rain to sort out natural, no, they *keep* their muck to go rotten in *boxes*!" She shuddered. "Inside their houses!"

"Sleepin' with their pets an' all." Clem Ostler poked the fire. "Dogs're mucky enough but *cats*. Fleas, dirt, fur, all in the same bed. Ain't that right? Oy, Stuttery!"

I'd been thinking how Gypsies *wanted* the rest of us to be gross, so the grossness of what they're not acts as a stencil for what they are. "Some people let their pets sleep *on* their bed, sure, but—"

"'Nother thing." Bax spat into the fire. "*Gorgios* don't just marry one girl and stick with her, not nowadays. They'll get divorced quick as changin' cars, despite their fancy weddin' vows." (Tuts and nods all round the fire, 'cept for the whittler. By now I'd guessed he was deaf or dumb.) "Like that butcher in Worcester who divorced Becky Smith when she got too saggy."

"Gorgios'll rut *anythin'*, married or no, livin' or no," Clem Ostler went on. "Dogs on heat. Anywhere, anytime, in cars, down alleys, in skips, *anywhere*. And they call *us* 'antisocial.' "

Everyone chose the same moment to look at me.

"Please." I had nothing to lose. "Has anyone seen my school bag?"

"A 'school bag' is it now?" Tire Man sort of teased. "A 'school bag'?"

"Oh, put the boy out of his misery," muttered Knife Grinder.

Tire Man lifted up my Adidas bag. "A bag like this?" (I choked down an *Oh* of relief.) "Yer welcome to it, Stuttery! Books never taught a man to mong or ducker." A circle of hands passed the bag to me.

Thanks, blurted out Maggot. "Thanks."

"Fritz ain't too picky 'bout what he brings back." Tire Man whistled. The wolf who'd robbed me lolloped out of the dark. "My brother's juk, ain't yer, Fritz? Stayin' with me till he's let out of his lodgings in Kiddyminster. Greyhound legs, collie brains, ain't yer, Fritz? I'll miss yer. Drop Fritz over a gate an' he'll get yer a fat old pheasant or a hare without you settin' foot past that farmer's No Trespassin' sign. Won't yer, Fritz, eh?"

The whittling kid stood up. Everyone round the fire watched.

He tossed me a heavy lump. I caught it.

The lump was rubber, once part of a tractor tire, maybe. He'd carved it into a head the size of a grapefruit. Sort of voodooish, but amazing. A gallery like my mum's would snap it up, I reckon. Its eyes're spacey and sockety. Its mouth's this gaping scar. Its nostrils're flared, like a terrified horse's. If fear was a thing and not a feeling, it'd be this head.

"Jimmy," Alan Wall said, studying it, "yer best ever."

Jimmy the Whittler made a pleased noise.

"Quite an honor," the woman told me. "Jimmy don't make them for every gorgio who falls into our camp, yer know."

"Thanks," I told Jimmy. "I'll keep it."

Jimmy hid behind his mop of hair.

"Is it *him*, Jimmy?" Clem Ostler meant me. "When he came a-tumblin' down? This is what he looked like when he fell?"

But Jimmy'd walked off behind the trailer.

I looked at Knife Grinder. "Can I go?"

Knife Grinder held up his palms. "Y'ain't a prisoner."

"But you just tell *them*," Alan Wall said, pointing toward the village, "we ain't all the thieves an' that they say we are."

"The boy could preach till he's purple," the daughter told him. "They'd not believe him. They'd not *want* to believe him."

The Gypsies turned at me, as if Jason Taylor is the ambassador of the land of brick houses and mesh fences and estate agents. "They're scared of you. They don't understand you, you're right. If they could just . . . Or . . . it'd be a start if they could just sit here. Get warm, round your fire, and just listen to you. That'd be a start."

The fire spat fat sparks up at pines lining the quarry, up at the moon.

"Know what fire is?" Knife Grinder's cough's a dying man's cough. "Fire's the sun, unwindin' itself out o' the wood."

goose fair

That *ace* song "Olive's Salami" by Elvis Costello and the Attractions drowned out whatever Dean yelled at me, so I yelled back, "*What* was that?" Dean yelled back, "Can't *hear* a word yer sayin'!" but then the fairground man tapped him on his shoulder for his 10p. That's when I saw a matt square on the scratched rink, right by my dodgem.

The matt square was a wallet. I'd've handed it in to the fairground man but it flipped open to show a photo of Ross Wilcox and Dawn Madden. Posed like John Travolta and Olivia Neutron-Bomb on the *Grease* poster. (Instead of Sunny America, mind, it was a cloudy back garden down Wellington Gardens.)

Ross Wilcox's wallet was *stuffed* with notes. There *had* to be fifty quid in there. This was serious. More money than I've ever had. Putting the wallet between my knees, I looked round to check nobody'd seen. Dean was yelling whatever it was at Floyd Chaceley now. None of the kids in the queue was paying me any attention.

The prosecution (a) pointed out it wasn't my money and (b) considered the *panic* Ross Wilcox'd feel when he'd lost all this money. The defense produced (a) the dissected mouse head in my pencil case, (b) the drawings of me eating my dick on blackboards, and (c) the never-ending *Hey, Maggot? How's the s-s-s-sssssssspeech therapy going, Maggot?*

The judge arrived at his verdict in seconds. I stuffed Ross Wilcox's wallet in my pocket. I'd count my money later.

The dodgem man waved at his slave in a booth, who pulled a lever, and every kid in the bumper rink went, *At last!* Sparks blossomed off the tops of the poles as the dodgem cars wheezed into electric life and Elvis Costello turned into "Every Little Thing She Does Is Magic" and dazzling oranges, lemons, and limes lit up. Moran banged me a beaut from the side, howling like the Green Goblin decking Spider-Man. I twisted my wheel to get him back, but I bumped Clive Pike instead. Clive Pike tried to get *me* back, and it went on like that, swerving, eddying, and ramming for five minutes of heaven. *Just* as the power died and every kid in the bumper rink went *Not Already!* a Wonder Woman dodgem bashed into me. "Oops," laughed Holly Deblin, at its wheel. "I'll get you back for that," I called to her. "Oh," Holly Deblin shouted back, "poor me." Wilcox's wallet was snug against my thigh. Bumper cars're ace, just *ace*.

"Yer *know* why yer barred!" By the out gate, the fairground man was snarling at Ross Wilcox by the in gate. With him was Dawn Madden in lizard jeans and a furry neck thing. She crumpled a stick of Wrigley's Spearmint into her bitter-cherry mouth. "So *drop* the '*What've* I *done?*' bollocks!"

"It's *got* to be on the rink!" Ross Wilcox in despair was a glorious sight. "It's *got* to be!"

"If yer jump from car to car stuff's *gonna* fall out! Not that *I* give a toss if yer 'lectrocute yerself but I *do* give a toss about my licence!"

"Just let us *look!*" Dawn Madden tried. "His dad'll *murder* him!"

"Oh and I *care*, do I?"

"Thirty seconds!" Wilcox was hysterical. "That's all I'm askin'!"

"An' I'm *tellin'* yer I ain't fannyin' about fer the likes o' *you* when I got a business to run!"

The fairground man's slave'd counted in another bunch of kids by now. His master clanged the gate shut, missing Wilcox's fingers by a tenth of a second. "Whoops!" Black Swan Green's hardest third year looked round for allies in his hour of need. There was nobody he knew. The Goose Fair brings people from Tewkesbury and Malvern and Pershore, from *miles* around.

Dawn Madden touched Ross Wilcox's arm.

Wilcox slapped her hand off and turned away.

Hurt Dawn Madden said something to Wilcox.

Wilcox snapped, "Yes it *is* the end of the world, yer dozy cow!"

You just don't talk to Dawn Madden like that. She looked away for a moment, scalded. Then she gave Wilcox a crushing whack on the eye. Just watching, me and Dean jumped.

"*Ouch!*" said Dean, delighted.

Ross Wilcox sort of crumpled in shock.

"I *warned* yer, yer knobhead!" Dawn Madden was fangs and claws and screaming fury. "I *warned* yer! Yer can find yerself a *real* dozy cow!"

Ross Wilcox's hesitant fingers went to his pounded eye.

"I'm *chuckin'* yer!" Dawn Madden turned and walked.

Ross Wilcox cried after her, "DAWN!," like a man in a film.

Dawn Madden turned round, fired Wilcox a twenty-thousand-volt "*Fuck off!*" Then the crowds swallowed her up.

"That'll be one *doozy* of a shiner," Dean remarked, "will that."

Wilcox looked at us, and his wallet in my pocket shrieked at its master to rescue it, but he didn't even see us. He ran after his ex-girlfriend for a few frantic paces. Stopped. Turned. Checked his eye, for blood, I s'pose. Turned. Then a black hole between Captain Ecstatic's Zero Gravity Dome and the Win-A-Smurf stall sucked Ross Wilcox in.

"Oh, my heart's bleedin'," sighed Dean, happily. "Gospel. Let's go find Kelly. I promised we'd look after Maxine for a bit."

Passing the Score-Less-Than-20-with-3-Darts-and-Pick-Any-Prize! darts stall someone called out, "Oy! Oy, *deaf-aid!*" It was Alan Wall. "Remember *me*? And my Uncle Clem?"

"Course I do. What're you doing here?"

"Who d'you *think* runs fairs?"

"Gypsies?"

"Mercy Watts's people own *all* of this. Have for years."

Dean was pretty impressed.

"This is Dean and his little sister Maxine."

Alan Wall just nodded at Dean. Clem Ostler solemnly presented Maxine with a shiny windmill. Dean told her, "Say *Thank you*, then." Maxine did, and blew on her windmill. Alan Wall asked, "Fancy yerself as a bit of an Eric Bristow, then, eh?"

"Mr. One Hundred and Eighty," said Dean, "that's what they call me." He slid two 10ps from his pocket over the counter. "One for me, one for Jace."

But Clem Ostler slid the coins back. "Never refuse a gift off of a Gypsy, boys. Or yer balls'll shrivel up. Ain't jokin'. Drop off, in the worst cases."

Dean got an 8 on his first throw, a 10 on his second. His third throw blew it with a double 16. I was *just* about to take my throw when a voice stopped me. "Aw, looking after baby sister, are we?"

Gary Drake, with Ant Little and Darren Croome.

Moran sort of flinched. Maxine sort of wilted.

Stick your darts, urged Unborn Twin, *into their eyeballs.*

"Yeah. We are. What the *fuck* is it to you?"

Gary Drake wasn't expecting that. (Words are *what* you fight with but what you fight *about* is whether or not you're afraid of them.) "Go on, then." Gary Drake recovered quick. "Throw. Amaze us."

If I threw it'd look like I was obeying him. If I didn't I'd just look like a total wally. All I could do was try to blank Gary Drake out. My strategy was to aim at treble 20 *so* carefully that I'd end up missing a fraction and getting a 1 or 5. My first dart got a 5. Quickly, before Gary Drake could put me off, I threw again and got a double 5.

My last dart was a clean 1.

Clem Ostler did a fairground shout, "A winner!"

"Oh right!" Ant Little jeered. "A *born* winner!"

"Born *laughingstock*." Darren Croome snorted his sinuses clear.

"*You* lot had *five* goes yerselves earlier," Clem Ostler told him. "Cacked it up every single time, didn't yer?"

Gary Drake didn't quite dare tell a man who works in a fair to piss off. Fairground-worker laws aren't quite the same.

"You choose the prize, Max," I told Dean's sister. "If you want."

Maxine looked at Dean. Dean nodded back. "If Jace says so."

"Shame you can't win any *friends* here, Taylor." Gary Drake couldn't walk off without the last insult.

"I don't need many."

"Many?" His sarcasm's thick as toilet bleach. "*Any*."

"No, I've got enough."

"Oh, yeah," snided Ant Little, "like *who* exactly? Apart from Moron Bum-Chum?"

If your words're true, they're armed. "No one you'd know."

"Y-y-yeah, T-T-T-Taylor." Gary Drake resorted to a stutter joke. "That's 'cos *your* m-m-m-mates are all in your f-f-f-fuckin' head!"

Ant Little and Darren Croome dutifully snorked.

If I got into a scrap with Gary Drake I'd probably lose it.

If I retreated I'd lose too.

But sometimes an outside force just shows up. "A kid who does *speed-wankin'* contests"—Alan Wall looked sort of sideways at Gary Drake—"in Strensham's barn up the bridleway ain't got no business labelin' *anyone* 'bum-chum.' Don't yer think?"

All of us, even Maxine, stared at Gary Drake.

"*You*," Gary Drake shot back, "*whoever* you are, are *so* full of shit!"

Skinny Clem Ostler cackled like a fat old woman.

" 'Full of shit'?" Alan Wall was only one year older than us, but *he* could beat Gary Drake into a Gary Drake omelette. "Come here and say that."

"You were *seeing* things! I've never *been* to Strensham's barn!"

"Oh, yer dead *right*, these yots've been seein' things!" Alan Wall tapped his temples. "I seen *you* an' that lanky git from Birtsmorton one evenin' two weeks ago, sittin' in the hayloft above the Herefordshire milkers—"

"We were *drunk*! It was just for a *laugh*! *I'm* not listening"—Gary Drake backed off—"to some fucking *gyppo*—"

Alan Wall leapt over the stall. Before his feet hit the turf Gary Drake'd fled. "You two his mates?" Alan Wall advanced on Ant Little and Darren Croome. "Are yer?"

Ant Little and Darren Croome stepped back, like you'd back away from a trotting leopard. "Not specially . . ."

"The cuddly E.T.?" Maxine stood on her tiptoes and pointed. "Can I have the cuddly E.T.?"

"My dad," said Clem Ostler, "called himself 'Red Rex' in prizefightin' circles. Weren't red-haired, weren't polit'cal, he just liked the sound of it. Red Rex was the Goose Fair's fighter. The bones o' more than forty years ago, this'd be. Things was rougher an' leaner back then. My family'd follow Mercy Watt's old man gaff-catchin' round the Vale of Evesham, down the Severn Valley, tradin' horses with other Romanies an' farmers an' breeders an' that. Usually a bit o' money floatin' round the fairs, so the men'd feel flush 'nough for a punt or two on a fight. A nearby barn'd be found, lookouts posted for gavvas if we couldn't pay 'em off, an' my dad'd challenge all comers. Dad weren't the beefiest of his six brothers, but that was why, see, men'd bet *stupid* vonga, *wads* of it, on deckin' him or on gettin' first blood. Dad weren't much to look at. But I'm tellin' yer, Red Rex soaked up punches like a *boulder*! Slipp'rier than shit through a goose. No gloves in them days, mind! Bare-knuckle fightin', it were. My first memories was of watchin' Dad fight. These days those prizefighters'd be professional heavyweights or riot police or somethin', but times was diff'rent. Now, one winter"—fresh screams from the Flying Tea Cups ride drowned Clem Ostler out for a moment—"one winter, word reached us 'bout this *gigantic* Welsh bastard. Monster of a man, serious, six foot eight, six-nine, from Anglesey. That was his name in all. Say 'Anglesey' that year, an' everyone'd knew who yer meant. Fightin' his way east, they said, *rakin'* it in, just by smashin' prizefighters' skulls to eggshells. One blacksmith, name of McMahon, in Cheshire, *died* after half a round with Anglesey. 'Nother needed iron plates put in his skull, three or four climbed into the ring fit men an' were carried out cripples for life. Anglesey'd been mouthin' on how he'd hunt down Red Rex at the Goose Fair, right here, in Black Swan Green. Pulp him, skin him, string him up, smoke him, sell him to the pig farmers. Sure 'nough, when we got to our old atchin'-sen down Pig Lane, Anglesey's people was there. Wouldn't budge till after the fight. *Twenty* guineas was the prize money! Last man standin'd scoop the lot. Unheard of, back then, that sort o' money."

"What did yer dad do?" asked Dean.

"No prizefighter can turn an' run an' no Gypsy can either. Reputation's everythin'. My uncles clubbed round for the stake money, but Dad weren't havin' it. Instead, he arranged with Anglesey to gamble every last stick we owned. *Everythin'!* Trailer—*our home,* remember?—the Crown Derby, the beds, the dogs, the fleas on the dogs, the *lot.* Lose that fight an' we'd be on our arses. Nowhere to go, nowhere to sleep, nothin' to eat."

I asked, "What happened?"

"Anglesey couldn't resist it! Floorin' Red Rex *and* cleanin' him out! The night o' the fight the barn was packed. Gypsies'd come from Dorset, Kent, half of Wales. What a fight that was! Tellin' yer. *What* a fight. Bax an' us older uns, we still remember it, blow by blow. Dad an' Anglesey pounded each other to jam. Them clowns yer get boxin' on the telly, with their *gloves* an' their *doctors* an' their *referees*, they'd've run *screamin'* from the punishment Anglesey an' Dad dealt each other. Bits was hangin' off Dad, there was. He could hardly *see*. But I'm tellin' yer. Dad gave as good as he got. Floor o' that barn was redder'n a *slaughterhouse.* Right at the end, the punches'd stopped. It was all they could do just to *stand.* At last, Dad swayed up to Anglesey, raised his left hand 'cause his right was so busted, and did this . . ." Clem Ostler placed his forefinger between my eyes and pushed me, so gently I hardly felt it. "*Down* that Welsh juk went! Like a tree. Wham! *That* was the state they was in. Dad quit fightin' that night. He had to. Too badly busted up. Took his vonga an' bought a carnival ride. By an' by he became the Goose

Fair's chief toberman, so he did all right. Last time we spoke was down Chepstow way, in the crocus-tan, in hospital. Just a couple o' days b'fore he died. Lungs'd flooded out so bad he kept coughin' up bits. So I asked Dad why'd he done it? Why'd he bet his family's trailer instead o' just money?"

Dean and I stared back, waiting for the answer.

" 'Son, if I'd just been fightin' for the *vonga*, for the *money*,' he told me, 'that Welsh bastard'd've beat me.' Fightin' just for money weren't enough. Dad knew it. Only by fightin' for *everythin' he loved*, see, me, my mum, his family, our home, the *lot*, only *then* could Dad take the pain. So yer see what that says? Yer see what I'm sayin'?"

The sea of people washed me and Dean up outside the Black Swan, where Mr. Broadwas and two pissed wurzels with black teeth and a grinning disease were perched on four stone mushrooms. Dean looked at his dad's cup a bit nervously.

"Coffee, son!" Dean's dad held his cup so Dean could see in it. "From my flask! Good an' hot, for a night like this." He turned to Mr. Broadwas. "The missus's got him well trained."

"Good" — Mr. Broadwas speaks as slowly as plants — "for both of you."

"So how long," asked Isaac Pye, lugging a crate of beers, "we staying on the wagon this time, then, Frank Moran?"

"Ain't gettin' off of it." Dean's dad didn't smile back.

"Leopards changing their spots, is it?"

"I ain't *talkin'* 'bout spots, Isaac Pye. Talkin' about *drink*. For them as're all well and good with alcohol, alcohol's all well and good. But for me, it's an illness. Doctor just told me what I already knowed. Ain't had a drop since April."

"Oh aye? Since *April*, this time, is it?"

"Yeah." Dean scowled at the publican. "April."

"If yer say so." Isaac Pye edged past into his pub. "If yer say so. But yer can't bring beverages from outside onto my premises."

"No fear of that, Isaac Pye!" Dean's dad yelled, as if the louder he yelled it, the truer it'd be. "No *fear* of that!"

Halls of Mirrors're usually crummy affairs with only Fattypuffs and Thinifers mirrors. But *these* mirrors melted you to self-mutants. Spotlights brightened and blackened the room. I was alone. Alone as you can be, that is, in a Hall of Mirrors. I got out Wilcox's wallet to count the money, but decided to wait till I was somewhere safer. "Maxine?" I called out. "You here?"

I left to carry on the search, but as I moved an African tribesman with a neck giraffed by iron rings waded toward me from the depths of the first mirror. His ears were droopy and dripping. It was a dreamish sight. *Can a person change*, asked the tribesman, *into another person?*

"You're right. That's the question."

I *thought* I heard a scuffle.

"Maxine? Come out, Maxine! This isn't funny!"

In the second mirror was a Gelatinous Cube. All face, no body, just twiggy limbs waving at its corners. By puffing out my cheeks I nearly doubled its size. *No*, answered the Cube. *You can only change superficial features. An Inside-You must stay unaltered to change the Outside-You. To change Inside-You you'd need an Even-More-Inside-You, who'd need an Inside-the-Even-More-Inside-You to change it. And on and on. You with me?*

"I'm with you."

An invisible bird brushed my ear.

"Maxine? This isn't funny, Maxine."

In the third mirror was Maggot. My waist and legs got squidged into a tail. My chest and head flared up into a big shimmering glob. *Don't listen to them. Ross Wilcox and Gary Drake and Neal Brose pick on us because you don't blend in. If you had the right hair and clothes and spoke the right way and hung out with the right people, things'd be fine. Popularity's about following weather forecasts.*

"I've always wondered what you looked like."

Mirror Four held Upside-down Jason Taylor. *What good's Maggot ever done you?* At Miss Throckmorton's I used to imagine people in the Southern Hemisphere walking round like this. A jerk of my leg moved my mirror arm. Flap my arm, my mirror leg flapped. *How about an Outside-You*, suggested Upside-Down Me, *who is your Inside-You too? A One-You? If people like your One-You, great. If they don't, tough. Trying to win approval for your Outside-You is a drag, Jason. That's what makes you weak. It's boring.*

"Boring," I agreed with Upside-Down Me. "Boring. Boring."

"*I'm* not bored!" a furry E.T. leapt out at me.

I experienced cardiac arrest in the Hall of Mirrors.

"Loonies talk to themselves." Maxine frowned. "Are *you* a loony?"

Kelly Moran chatted to Debby Crombie by the toffee-apple stall. As, surely, the richest kid in the Three Counties, I bought one for me, Dean, and Maxine. Biting into toffee-armored apples requires technique. Your teeth bounce off. Bash the hard toffee against your fangs, that's the only way. Then sink your incisors in to prize off the crust of toffee.

Debby Crombie looks like she's got a rugby ball up her sweater. The whole village knows she's pregnant with Tom Yew's baby. "That E.T.'s never real," she said to Maxine, "is it?"

"It *is* real," said Maxine. "It's name's Geoffrey."

"Geoffrey the E.T. *Stylish.*"

"Thanks."

"Bit o' news to warm the cockles of yer hearts." Kelly turned to Dean and me. "Angela Bullock heard from Dawn Madden *herself* that she's not only chucked your old mate Loverboy Wilcox—"

Dean clucked, "We saw 'em have a *massive* barney earlier!"

"But listen, this is even better." A squeak of pleasure escaped Kelly. "Wilcox's lost his wallet, right, with *hundreds* of quid in it!"

(A mile-long neon Chinese dragon wove through the Goose Fair and bit my jeans pocket. Luckily, no one else saw it.)

"Hundreds of quid?" Dean gaped, literally. "Where'd he lose it?"

"*Here! Now!* In the Goose Fair! Of course Diana Turbot couldn't keep a secret to save her *life*, so half the village're truffling round looking for it right *now*. Probably been found already. But who's goin' to hand all that money back to an arsey turd like Ross Wilcox?"

"Half of Black Swan Green," Dean answered, "is in his gang."

"That doesn't mean they *like* him."

"How come"—my voice felt wobbly—"Wilcox was walking about with hundreds of pounds on him?"

"Well, *isn't* that a tale o' *woe*! *Apparently* your mate Ross was at his old man's garage after school when this car pulls up, right. Knock, knock, it's the Inland Revenue. Gordon Wilcox's years behind on his tax. Last time they visited he chased 'em off with a blowtorch, but this time they'd brought a copper from Upton. But before they can knock on his office, right, Gordon Wilcox whips open the safe and hands Wilcox Junior everythin' in it to spirit off home. Out of sight, out of accounts, like. Big mistake! Wilcox hung on to it, didn't he? Thought he'd impress his girlfriend with, shall we say, eh, Debs, the thickness of his *wad*? Maybe he meant to siphon a bit off. Maybe he didn't. We'll never know, 'cause it's vanished."

"So what's Wilcox doin' now?"

"He was sitting smoking in the bus shack, last Angela Bullock heard."

"Must be shittin' bricks," said Debby Crombie. "Gordon Wilcox's sick in the head, that man. Vicious."

"How d'you mean?" I'd never spoken to Debby Crombie till tonight. " 'Vicious'?"

"You *do* know," Kelly put in, "why Ross Wilcox's mum left?"

She realized her son was pure evil? "Why?"

"She lost a strip of postage stamps."

"Postage stamps?"

"One strip of five second-class postage stamps. They was the straw what broke the camel's back. Honest to *God*, Jason, Gordon Wilcox beat that woman *so* black and blue, the hospital had to feed her through a tube for a week."

A black hole just got bigger. "Why didn't he get sent to prison?"

"No witnesses, a crafty lawyer who said she'd chucked herself downstairs over and over, plus his wife conveniently going mental. 'Unsound mind,' the judge in Worcester decided."

"So if he'd do *that*"—Debby Crombie clutched her rugby ball—"over a strip of stamps, imagine what he'll do over hundreds of pounds! Sure, Ross Wilcox is a nasty piece of work, but you wouldn't wish a maulin' off of Gordon Wilcox on your worst enemy."

Dean'd gone yahooooooooooooooooing down Ali Baba's Helter Skelter ahead of me. Just as I got my mat ready fireworks erupted in the sky over toward Welland. Guy Fawkes Night's not till tomorrow, but they can't wait in Welland. Stalks climbed, then popblossomed into slow-slow-*slow* . . . motion Michaelmas daisies. Raining-silvers, purples, phoenix golds. Crunkly *booms* arrived a second late . . . *boom* . . . *boom* . . . Fireworkpetals fell away and faded to ash. Only five or six big ones went off, but what beauts they were.

No footsteps were clomping up the stairs of the tower.

Still perched on the lip of the slide, I got out Wilcox's wallet to count Wilcox's money. My money. The notes weren't fivers, nor tenners; they were *all* twenty-pound notes. I've never even *touched* a twenty. Five of them, I counted, ten of them, fifteen of them . . .

Thirty Queen Elizabeths. Starlight-pale.

SIX—I screamed—*HUNDRED*—silently—*POUNDS*.

If anyone found out, *anyone*, things'd get grimmer than I dared imagine. I'd wrap the notes in polyethylene, put it in a sandwich box, and stash it away.

Somewhere in the wood'd be safest. And it'd be safest to wang the wallet into the Severn. Shame. All I have in the way of a wallet is a zippy pouch thing. I sniffed Wilcox's wallet so atoms from *his* wallet'll turn into me. If only I could breathe in Dawn Madden atoms.

The Goose Fair's literally magic, I thought, sitting there. It turns my weakness into power. It turns our village green into this underwater kingdom. "Ghost Town" by the Specials bubbled up from the Magic Mountain, "Waterloo" by ABBA from the Flying Tea Cups, the *Pink Panther* music from the Chair-o-Plane. The Black Swan was so full its innards were spilling out. Farther off, villages floated on empty spaces, where wide fields were. Hanley Castle, Blackmore End, Brotheridge Green. Worcester was a galaxy squashed flat.

Best of all? *I'd* be pounding Wilcox into a pulp. Me. Via his dad. Why should I feel bad about that? After what Wilcox's done to me. Neither of them'd ever know it. It's the perfect revenge. Besides, Kelly exaggerates. No father'd beat up his own son *that* badly.

Footsteps came up the tower. I hastily stuffed my fortune into my pocket, repositioned myself on the scratchy mat, and a wonderful thought slid into my head as I slid off the lip. Six hundred pounds *could* buy an Omega Seamaster.

Grand Master of the Helter Skelter, tonight I leaned into the curves.

"Hey," said Dean, as the crowds swept us by Fryer Tuck's Chip Emporium. "That's never yer dad, is it?"

Can't be, I thought, but it was. Still in his overcoat and suit from the office. He had this ironed-in frown and I thought how he needs a very long holiday. Dad was eating chips with a wooden fork from a cone of newspaper. There're dreams where right people appear in wrong places, and this was like that. Dad spotted us before I could work out why I wanted to dodge off. "Hullo, you two."

"Evening"—Dean sounded nervous—"Mr. Taylor." They hadn't met since the Mr. Blake Affair back in June.

"Good to see you, Dean. How's your arm?"

"Right as rain, thanks." Dean wiggled his arm.

"I'm very pleased to hear it."

"Hi Dad." I don't know why *I* was nervous too. "What're you doing here?"

"Didn't know I needed your permission to come, Jason?"

"No, no, I didn't mean that . . ."

Dad tried to smile but he just looked pained. "I know, I know. What *am* I doing here?" Dad forked a chip and blew on it. "Well, I was driving home. Saw all the hullaballoo." Dad's voice was somehow different. Softer. "Couldn't very well miss the Goose Fair, could I? 'I'll have a little wander,' I thought. Smelt these." Dad waggled his cone. "Y'know, after *eleven years* in Black Swan Green this is my *first time* at the Goose Fair? I kept meaning to bring you and Julia when you were little. But something important always got in the way. So important, I've got no idea what those things were."

"Oh. Mum phoned, from Cheltenham. To tell me to tell you there's a cold quiche in the fridge. I left you a note on the kitchen table."

"Very thoughtful of you. Thanks." Dad gazed inside his cone as if answers might be written there. "Hey, have *you* eaten? Dean? Fancy anything from Fryer Tuck's Chip Emporium?"

"I ate a sandwich and a black cherry yogurt." I didn't mention the toffee apple in case it counted as throwing money away. "Before I came."

"I had three o' Fryer Tuck's All-American Taste-Tastic Hot Dogs." Dean patted his stomach. "Recommend 'em highly, I do."

"Good." Dad squeezed his head like he had a headache. "Good. Oh. Let me give you a little, uh . . ." Dad slipped two new pound coins into my hand. (One hour before, two pounds'd've been loads. Now it's less than one three-hundredth of my entire estate.)

"Thanks Dad. Would you like to . . . uh . . . ?"

"I'd *love* to, but I have paperwork coming out of my paperwork. Plans to plan. No rest for the wicked. Good seeing you, Dean. Jason's got a telly in his room, doubtless he hasn't shut up about it. Come over and watch it! No point in it just . . . y'know . . . sitting there . . ."

"Thanks very much, Mr. Taylor."

Dad dropped the cone into an oil drum full of rubbish and walked off.

Suppose, prompted Unborn Twin, *you never see him again?*

"Dad!"

I ran up to him and looked him square in the eye. Suddenly, I'm nearly as tall as he is. "I want to be a forester when I'm older." I hadn't meant to tell him. Dad always finds problems with plans.

"A forester?"

"Yeah." I nodded. "Someone who looks after forests."

"Mmm." That was the closest he came to smiling. "There's kind of a big clue in the word, Jason."

"Well. Yeah. One of those. In France. Maybe."

"You'll have to study hard." Dad made a *could do worse* face. "You'll need the sciences."

"Then I'll get the sciences."

"I know."

I'll *always* remember meeting Dad tonight. I know I will. Will Dad? Or will, for Dad, tonight's Goose Fair just be one more of the trillion things you even forget forgetting?

"What's all this," asked Moran, "about a portable TV?"

"It only works if you hold its aerial, which means you're too close to watch it. Wait here a mo, will you? Just off to the wood for a waz."

As I jogged over the village green, the Goose Fair slid off and fell away. Six hundred pounds. Six thousand Mars bars. One hundred and ten L.P.s. Twelve hundred paperbacks. Five Raleigh Grifters. One-quarter of a Mini. Three Atari Home Entertainment Systems. Clothes that'll make Dawn Madden dance with me at the Christmas Village Hall Disco. Docs and denim jackets. Thin leather ties with pianos on them. Salmon-pink shirts. An Omega Seamaster De Ville made by snowy-haired Swiss craftsmen in 1950.

The old bus shack was just a box of black.

I told you, said Maggot. *He's not here. Go back now. You tried.*

The black smelt of fresh cigarettes. "Wilcox?"

"Fuck off." Wilcox struck a match and his face hovered there for one flickery second. The marks under his nose might've been cleaned-up blood.

"Just found something."

"And why d'yer s'pose"—Wilcox didn't get it—"I give a flying fuck?"

"'Cause it's yours."

His voice lurched like a dog on its lead. "*What?*"

I dug out his wallet and held it toward him.

Wilcox leapt up and snatched it off me. "*Where?*"

"Dodgems."

Wilcox thought about ripping my throat out. "*When?*"

"Few minutes ago. Sort of wedged down the edge of the rink."

"If yer've taken *any* of this money, Taylor"—Wilcox's fingers trembled as he took out the wodge of twenty-pound notes—"yer fuckin' dead!"

"No, really, don't mention it, Ross. No, honest, you'd've done the same for me, I know you would." Ross Wilcox was too busy counting to really listen. "Look, if I *was* going to steal any of it, I'd hardly be here giving it *back* to you, would I?"

Wilcox got to thirty. He took a deep breath, then remembered me, witnessing his *utter* relief. "So now I'm s'posed to kiss yer arse, am I?" His face snarled up. "Tell yer how *grateful* I am?"

As usual, I didn't know how to reply to him.

The poor kid.

The fairground man on the Great Silvestro's Flying Tea-Cups locked the padded bars that'd stop me, Dean, Floyd Chaceley, and Clive Pike from being flung halfway to Orion. "So are you," Dean asked him, a bit sarkily, "the Great Silvestro?"

"Nah. Silvestro died last month. His other ride, Flying Saucers, went and collapsed on him. Made all the newspapers up in Derby, where it happened. Nine lads about your age, plus Silvestro—crushed, mangled, pitted, juiced." The fairground man shook his head, wincing. "The only way the police could sort out who was what was calling in a team of dentists. Dentists with ladles and buckets. Guess why the ride collapsed. You'll never guess. *One single bolt* hadn't been tightened proper. *One bolt.* Casual labor, see. Pay peanuts, get monkeys. Right. That's the last of you done."

He waved at an assistant, who pulled a big lever. A song that went, "Hey! (HEY!) You! (YOU!) Get off of my cloud!" blasted out and hydraulic tentacles lifted our giant teacups higher than houses. Floyd Chaceley, Clive Pike, and Dean Moran and me did a rising *Oooooohhhhh!*

My hand touched my flat pocket. Apart from £28 in my Trustees Saving Bank account, all the money I had left in the world was the two pounds Dad'd given me. Perhaps giving Wilcox back his wallet *had* been idiotic, but at least now I could stop worrying about whether I should or not.

The Great Silvestro's Tea-Cups swung into motion and an orchestra of screams tuned up. My memories're all sloshed out of order. The Goose Fair was sluiced from a bowl of starry dark. Clive Pike, to my left, eyes beetling bigger than humanly possible, g-force ribbling his face. ("HEY! *HEY!*") Starry dark, sluiced from a bowl of the Goose Fair. Floyd Chaceley, who *never* smiles, on my right, laughing like Lord Satan in a mushroom cloud. Screams chasing their tails fast as the melting tigers in *Little Black Sambo.* ("YOU! YOU!") Goose Fair and November night propellering one into another. *Courage is being scared shitless but doing it anyway.* Dean Moran, opposite, eyes clenched, lips valving open as a cobra slithers out, a shiny cobra of half-digested toffee apple, candy floss, and three of Fryer Tuck's All-American Taste-Tastic Hot Dogs, highly recommended, writhing longer. ("GET OFF

OF MY CLOUD!") That such a volume of food could *still* be uncoiling from Dean's stomach is supernaturally peculiar, missing my face by inches, climbing higher, till it *lunges* and turns into a billion globs of puke, bulleting passengers of the Late Great Silvestro's Flying Tea-Cups (*now they've* really *got something to scream about*) and a thousand and one innocent civilians milling at the wrong time in the wrong part of the Goose Fair.

The giant machine groaned like the Iron Man as our Tea-Cup sank earthward. Our heads slowed slower. All the screams and commotion were the by-products of Dean Moran, Vomit Fountain, I still assumed.

"Gonads," stated the fairground man, seeing the state of our Tea-Cup. "Shriveled, syphilitic gonads. Ern!" He yelled at his assistant. "Ern! Bring the mop! We've got a puker!"

It took a few seconds to realize that the screams weren't coming from nearby, but farther off. By the crossroads, over by Mr. Rhydd's.

Ross Wilcox must've marched back to the Goose Fair to find Dawn Madden right after I'd left him. (Dean's sister Kelly filled in these missing pieces. She heard this bit from Andrea Bozard, who'd nearly got mown down by Wilcox as he passed by.) Ross Wilcox must've felt as saved as he'd just felt damned, I s'pose. Like Jesus, rolling the stone from his tomb when everyone'd thought that he was a goner. "Sure, Dad," he'd be able to say, "here's yer money. I kept it on me in case the pigs raided our house, like." First he'd find Dawn Madden, agree he'd been a dickhead, seal his apology with a fondling snog, and his world'd be the right way up again. Round the time me and Dean were being fastened into Silvestro's Tea-Cup, Wilcox asked Lucy Sneads if she'd seen Dawn Madden. Lucy Sneads, who can be a nasty piece of work if the mood takes her, and who has some portion of responsibility for what happened next, helpfully told him. "Over there. In that Land Rover. Under the oak." Only two people'd've seen Ross Wilcox's face, lit bright by Mary Poppins's merry-go-round, when he unpopped the flap on the back. One was Dawn Madden herself, her legs wrapped round the other witness. Grant Burch. Ross Wilcox, I imagine, gawped at the couple like a seal gawping at a seal clubber. Ruth Redmarley told Kelly she saw Wilcox slam the Land Rover flap shut, howling "BITCH!" over and over and banging the Land Rover with his fist. It must've hurt. Ruth Redmarley watched him then jump on Grant Burch's brother's Suzuki (the same scrambler that used to be Tom Yew's), turn the keys, keys which Grant Burch'd left in the ignition 'cause it was right by the jeep (nobody'd steal it from under his nose, right?), and kick it into life.

If Ross Wilcox hadn't grown up around motorbikes 'cause of his dad and brother, it probably wouldn't've occurred to him to nick the Suzuki. If it hadn't started first time, even on a cold November night, Grant Burch might've managed to get his trousers on in time to stop what happened. Robin South reckons he saw Tom Yew on the back of the Suzuki as Wilcox fraped it over the village green, but Robin South's so full of crap it's untrue. Avril Bredon says she saw the Suzuki hit the muddy bit by the main road at about fifty miles per hour, and you can believe Avril Bredon. The police believed her. The bike slid round so the back faced front, clipped the Boer War Memorial, and Ross Wilcox got cartwheeled over the crossroads. Two girls from the Chase Comprehensive were phoning their dads from the phone box by Mr. Rhydd's. We won't know their names till next week's *Malvern Gazetteer*'s out. But the last person to see Ross Wilcox was Arthur Evesham's widow, on her way home from bingo at the village hall. Ross Wilcox came bowling by and missed her by inches. She's the one who knelt down by Ross Wilcox to see if he was dead or alive, the one who heard him grunt, "I think I lost a trainer," sputter out a bagful of blood and teeth, and garble, "Make sure no one nicks my trainer." Arthur Evesham's widow's the one who first saw Wilcox's right leg stopped at his knee, looked back, and saw gobby smears streaking the road. She's being helped into the second ambulance right now. See her face? Stony hollow in the flashing blue light?

disco

Rule One is *Blank out the consequences.* Ignore this rule and you'll hesitate, botch it, and be caught like Steve McQueen on barbed wire in *The Great Escape.* That's why, in Metalwork this morning, I focused on Mr. Murcot's birthmarks like my life depended on it. He's got two long ones on his throat in the shape of New Zealand. "Top of the morning, boys!" Our teacher crashed his cymbals. "God save the queen!"

"The top of the morning, Mr. Murcot," we chanted, then turned toward Buckingham Palace and saluted. "And God save the queen!"

Neal Brose, standing by the vise he shares with Gary Drake, stared back at me. *Don't think I've forgotten,* his eyes told me, *Maggot.*

"Projectwards, boys." Half the class're girls but Mr. Murcot always calls us "boys" unless he's bollocking us. Then we're all "girls." "Today's the final class of 1982. Fail to finish your projects today, and it's transportation to the colonies for the terms of your natural lives." Our project this term was to design and make some sort of a scraper. Mine's to clean between the studs on my football boots.

I let about ten minutes go by, till Neal Brose was busy on the drill.

My heart pumped fast, but I'd made up my mind.

From Neal Brose's black Slazenger bag I took out his Casio College Solar-Powered Mathematical Calculator. It's the most expensive calculator in W. H. Smiths. A dark suction pulled me on, almost reassuringly, like a canoeist paddling straight at Niagara Falls instead of trying to fight the current. I took the prized calculator out of its special case.

Holly Deblin noticed me. She was tying back her hair to prevent it from getting caught in the lathe. (Mr. Murcot enjoys going over the hideous face-first deaths he's witnessed over the years.) *I think she likes us,* whispered Unborn Twin. *Blow her a kiss.*

I put Neal Brose's calculator into the vise. Leon Cutler noticed too but just stared, not believing it. *Blank out the consequences.* I gave the rod-handle-thing a strong turn. Tiny pleas snapped in the calculator's casing. Then I put *all* my weight on the rod thing. Gary Drake's skeleton, Neal Brose's skull, Wayne Nashend's backbone, their futures, their souls. *Harder.* The casing shattered, circuitry crunched, shrapnel tittered on the floor as the fifteen millimeter-thick calculator turned into a three millimeter-thick calculator. *There.* Powderized. Shouting'd broken out all over the metalwork room.

Rule Two is *Do it till it's undoable.*

Those're the only two rules you need to remember.

Giddy glorious waterfalls, down I went.

"Mr. Kempsey informs me"—Nixon laced his fingers into a mace—"that your father recently lost his job."

"Lost." Like a job's a wallet you'll lose if you're careless. *I* hadn't breathed a word at school. But yes, it's true. Dad'd got to his office in Oxford at 8:55 A.M., and by 9:15 A.M. a security guard was escorting him off the premises. "We must tighten our belts," says Margaret Thatcher, though *she* isn't, not personally. "There is no alternative." Greenland Supermarkets sacked Dad 'cause an expense account was £20 short. After eleven years. This way, Mum'd told Aunt Alice on the phone, they don't have to pay Dad a penny in redundancy money. Danny Lawlor'd helped Craig Salt to stitch him up, she added. The Danny Lawlor I met in August was dead nice. But niceness isn't goodness, I s'pose. Now he's driving Dad's company Rover 3200.

"Jason!" barked Mr. Kempsey.

"Oh." Yes, I was in a silo of shit. "Sir?"

"Mr. Nixon asked you a question."

"Yes. Dad was sacked on Goose Fair day. Uh . . . some weeks ago."

"A misfortune." Mr. Nixon has a vivisector's eyes. "But misfortunes are commonplace, Taylor, and relative. Look at the misfortune Nick Yew has endured this year. Or Ross Wilcox. How is destroying your classmate's property going to help your father?"

"It won't, sir." The bad-kid chair was so low Mr. Nixon might just as well saw off its legs completely. "Destroying Brose's calculator hasn't got a thing to do with my dad getting sacked, sir."

"Then what," Mr. Nixon asked, reangling his head, *"was* it to do with?"

Do it till it's undoable.

"Brose's 'popularity lessons,' sir."

Mr. Nixon looked at Mr. Kempsey for an explanation.

"Neal Brose?" Mr. Kempsey cleared his throat, at a loss. " 'Popularity lessons'?"

"Brose"—Hangman blocked "Neal," but that was okay—"ordered me, Floyd Chaceley, Nicholas Briar, and Clive Pike to pay him a pound a week for popularity lessons. I said no. So he got Wayne Nashend and Ant Little to persuade me what'll happen if I don't get more 'popularity.' "

"What manner"—Mr. Nixon's voice hardened, a good sign—"of persuasion do you claim these boys employed?"

There was no need to exaggerate. "Monday they emptied my bag down the stairs by the chemistry lab. Tuesday I got pelted with clumps of soil in Mr. Carver's P.E. lesson. In the cloakroom this morning Brose and Little and Wayne Nashend told me that I'll get my face kicked in on my way home tonight."

"You're saying"—Mr. Kempsey's temperature rose nicely—"that *Neal Brose* is running some sort of extortion racket? Under my very nose?"

"Does 'extortion' mean," I asked, although I knew perfectly well, "beating someone up if they don't give you money, sir?"

Mr. Kempsey thought the sun, moon, and stars shone out of Neal Brose's arse. "That would be one definition." *All* the teachers do. "Do you have evidence for this?"

Let guile be your ally. "What sort of evidence do you have in mind, sir?" Things were running in favor enough to add, with a straight face, "Hidden microphones?"

"Well . . ."

Mr. Nixon took over. "If we interview Chaceley and Pike and Briar, will they confirm your story?"

"It depends on who they're most afraid of, sir. You or Brose."

"I *promise* you, Taylor, they will be most afraid of *me.*"

"Casting aspersions on a boy's character is a very serious act, Taylor." Mr. Kempsey wasn't yet convinced.

"I'm glad to hear you say so, sir."

"What I am *not* glad about"—Mr. Nixon wasn't letting an interrogation get pally—"is that you brought this matter to my attention not by knocking on my door and telling me, but by attacking the property of your alleged persecutor."

That "alleged" warned me the jury was still out.

"Involving a teacher means you're a grass, sir"

"*Not* involving a teacher means you're an *ass*, Taylor."

Maggot'd've buckled under the unfairness of it all.

"I hadn't thought this far ahead." Just find what's true, hold it up, and take the consequences without whining. "I had to show Brose I'm not afraid of him. That's all I thought of."

If boredom had a smell, it'd be the stationery storeroom. Dust, paper, warm pipes, all day, all winter. Blank exercise books on metal shelves. Piles of *To Kill a Mockingbird*, of *Romeo and Juliet*, of *Moonfleet*. The storeroom's also an isolation cell in drawn-out cases like mine. Apart from a square of frosted glass in the door, the only light's a brown bulb. Mr. Kempsey'd told me, curtly, to get on with my homework till I was sent for, but for once I was up to date. A poem inside kicked my belly. Since I was in so much shit already, I nicked a nice exercise book with stiff covers off a shelf to write in. But after the first line I realized it wasn't a poem. More of a . . . what? A confession, I s'pose. It began,

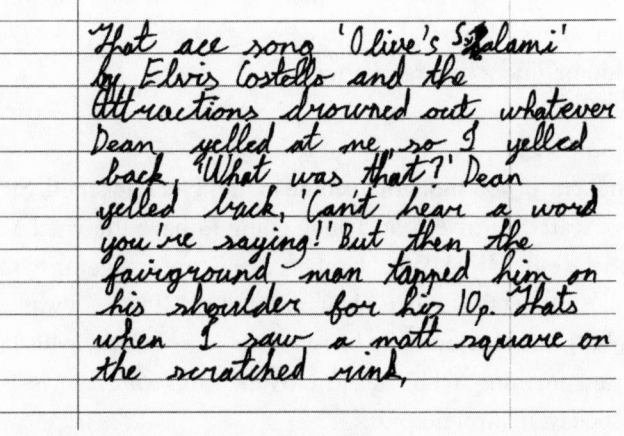

and on it went. When the bell went for morning break I found I'd filled three sides. Fitting words together makes time go through narrower pipes but faster.

Shadows passed the frosted-glass window as teachers rushed to the staff room to smoke and drink coffee. Joking, moaning shadows. Nobody came into the storeroom to get me. The entire third year'd be talking about what I'd done in Metalwork, I knew. The whole school. People say your ears burn when people're talking about you, but I get a hum in the cellar of my stomach. *Jason Taylor, he didn't, Jason Taylor, he did, oh my God really he grassed* who *off?* Writing buries this hum. The bell went for the end of break and the shadows passed by in the other direction. Still nobody came. In the outside world Mr. Nixon'd be summoning my parents. He wouldn't have much luck till tonight. Dad'd gone to Oxford to meet "contacts" about a new job. Even Dad's reel-to-reel answering machine's been sent back to Greenland. Through the wall the school Xerox machine was droning, droning, droning.

A twitch of fear lunged when the door opened but I trampled it dead. It was just a pair of second-year squirts, sent to get a pile of *Cider with Rosie.* (We read it last year too. One scene gave every boy in the classroom boners you could actually *hear* growing.) "Is it *true*, Taylor?" The larger squirt addressed me like I was still in my Maggot Period.

"What the fuck is *that*," I replied, after a pause, "to *you?*"

I managed to say it so evilly the second-year spilt his books. The smaller squirt spilt his books too as he bent down to help.

I clapped, dead slow.

"What *appalls* me, 3KM"—Mr. Kempsey's nickname may be "Polly," but he's dangerous when he's this angry—"is that these acts of intimidation have been going on for weeks. *Weeks.*"

3KM hid behind a funeral silence.

"WEEKS!"

3KM jumped.

"And not *one* of you thought to come to me! I feel sickened. Sickened and scared. Yes, scared. In five years you're going to have the vote! You are supposed to be the elite, 3KM. What kind of citizens are you going to make? What kind of police officers? Teachers? Lawyers? Judges? 'I knew it was wrong but it wasn't my business, sir.' 'Better to let someone else blow the whistle, sir.' 'I was afraid if I said anything, I'd be next, sir.' Well, if this *spinelessness* is the future of British society, heaven help us."

I, Jason Taylor, am a grass.

"Now I strongly disapprove of *how* Taylor brought this woeful business to my attention, but at least he *did*. Less impressive are Chaceley, Pike, and

Briar, who only spoke up under duress. What is to your collective *shame* is that it took Taylor's rash act this morning to force events to a head."

Every kid in front'd turned round to look at me, but it was Gary Drake I went for. "What *is* it, *Gary?*" (Hangman'd handed me a free pass for the afternoon. I sometimes think Hangman wants to come to one of Mrs. de Roo's "working accommodations," too.) "Don't you *know* what I look like after three years?"

The eyes switched to Gary Drake. Then to Mr. Kempsey. Our form teacher *should* open fire on me for talking while he was talking. But he didn't. "Well, Drake?"

"Sir?"

"Feigned incomprehension is the last resort of the fool, Drake."

Gary Drake actually looked awkward. "Sir?"

"You're doing it again, Drake."

Gary Drake nicely stamped on. Wayne Nashend and Ant Little suspended. Chances are, Mr. Nixon's going to expel Neal Brose.

Now they'll *really* want to kick my face in.

Neal Brose normally sits up front in English, slap bang in the middle. *Go on*, said Unborn Twin, *take the bastard's seat. You owe it to him.* So I did. David Ockeridge, who sits next to Neal Brose, chose a seat farther back. But Clive Pike, of all people, put his bag next to me. "Anyone sitting here?" Clive Pike's breath smells of cheese'n'onion Outer Spacers, but who cares?

I made a *Go ahead* face.

Miss Lippetts shot me a look as we chanted, "Good afternoon, Miss Lippetts." So swift and crafty it was almost not there, but it was. "Sit down, 3KM. Pencil cases out, please. Today, we'll exercise our supple young minds with a composition, on *this* theme . . ." As we got our stuff out, Miss Lippetts wrote on the board.

A SECRET

The slap and slide of chalk's a reassuring sound.

"Tamsin, do me the honor, please."

Tamsin Murrell read, " 'A secret,' miss."

"Thank you. But what *is* a secret?"

It takes everyone a bit of time to get going after lunch.

"Well, say, is a secret a thing you can see? Touch?"

Avril Bredon put her hand up.

"Avril?"

"A secret's a piece of information that not everybody knows."

"Good. A piece of information that not everyone knows. Information about . . . who? You? Somebody else? Some*thing*? All of these?"

After a gap, a few kids murmured, "All of these."

"Yes, I'd say so too. But ask yourselves this. Is a secret a secret if it isn't true?"

That was a tight knot of a question. Miss Lippetts wrote,

MISS LIPPETTS IS NANCY REAGAN.

Most of the girls laughed.

"If I asked you to stay behind after class, waited till we were alone, and then whispered, in all seriousness, this statement, would you go 'No! Really! Wow! What a secret!' Duncan?"

Duncan Priest had his hand up. "I'd phone Little Malvern Loonybin, miss. Book you a room with a nice mattress. On all the walls." Duncan Priest's small fan club laughed. "That's not a secret, miss! It's just the gibberish of an utter nutter."

"A pithy *and* rhyming assessment, thank you. As Duncan says, so-called secrets that are palpably false cannot be considered as secrets. If enough people *believed* I was Nancy Reagan, that might cause me problems, but we still couldn't really think of it as a 'secret,' could we? More of a mass delusion. Can anyone tell me what a mass delusion is? Alastair?"

"I heard loads of Americans think Elvis Presley is still alive."

"Fine example. However, I'm now going to let you in on a secret about myself which *is* true. It's a *touch* embarrassing, so please don't spread it around at breaktime . . ."

MISS LIPPETTS IS AN AXE MURDERER.

Now half the boys laughed too.

"*Shhh!* I buried my victims under the M50. So there's no evidence. No suspicion. But is *this* secret still a secret? If it's one that nobody, and I mean *nobody*, has the faintest suspicion about?"

An interested silence played itself out.

"Yes . . ." muttered a few kids as a few kids muttered, "No . . ."

"You'd know, miss." Clive Pike raised his hand. "If you really were an axe murderer. So you can't say nobody knows it."

"Not if miss was a schizo*phrenic* axe murderer," Duncan Priest told him. "She might just . . . *turn*, like that, chop you to bits for forgetting your homework, *whack splurt splatter*, flush the remains down the sewers, black out, then wake up again as mild-mannered Miss Lippetts, English teacher, go, 'Gosh, blood on my clothes again? How odd that this keeps happening whenever there's a full moon. Oh well. Into the washing machine.' Then it *would* be a secret nobody knew, right?"

"Delicious imagery, Duncan, thank you. But imagine *all* the murders to have *ever* occurred in the Severn Valley, since, say Roman times. All those victims, all those murderers, dead and turned to dust. Can *those* violent acts, which no one, remember, has thought about for a thousand years, also be called 'secrets'? Holly?"

"Not secrets, miss," said Holly Deblin. "Just . . . lost information."

"Sure. So can we agree, a secret needs a human agency to *know* it, or at least write it down? A holder. A keeper. Emma Ramping! What are you whispering to Abigail?"

"Miss?"

"Stand up, please, Emma."

Worried, lanky Emma Ramping stood up.

"I'm conducting a lesson here. What are you telling Abigail?"

Emma Ramping hid behind a very sorry face.

"Is it a piece of information that not everybody knows?"

"Yes, miss."

"Speak up, Emma, so the groundlings can hear you!"

"Yes, miss."

"Aha. So you were confiding a secret to Abigail?"

Emma Ramping reluctantly nodded.

"How topical. Well, why not share this secret with us? Now. In a nice loud voice."

Emma Ramping began blushing, miserably.

"I'll do you a deal, Emma. I'll let you off the hook if you just explain why you're happy sharing your secret with Abigail but not the rest of us."

"Because . . . I don't want everyone to know, miss."

"Emma is telling us something about secrets, 3KM. Thank you, Emma, be seated and sin no more. How do you *kill* a secret?"

Leon Cutler stuck up his hand. "Tell people."

"Yes, Leon. But how many people? Emma told Abigail her secret, but that didn't kill it, did it? How many people have to be in the know before the secret's an ex-secret?"

"Enough," Duncan Priest said, "to get you sent to the electric chair, miss. For being an axe murderer, I mean."

"Who can reconstruct Duncan's glorious wit into a general principle? How many people does it take to kill a secret? David?"

"As many"—David Ockeridge thought about it—"as it takes, miss."

"As it takes to do *what*? Avril?"

Avril Bredon frowned. "As it takes to change whatever it *is* the secret's about. Miss."

"Solid reasoning, 3KM. Maybe the future is in safe hands, after all. If Emma told us what she told Abigail, *that* secret would be dead. If my murders are exposed in the *Malvern Gazetteer*, I'm—well, dead, if Duncan's on the jury, anyway. The scale is different, but the principle is the same. Now, my next question is the one that truly intrigues me, because I'm not sure what the answer is. Which secrets *should* be made public? And which *shouldn't*?"

That question had no quick takers.

For the fiftieth or hundredth time that day I thought of Ross Wilcox.

"Who can tell me what this word means?"

ETHICS

Chalk mist falls in the wakes of words.

I'd looked "ethics" up once. It crops up in the *Chronicles of Thomas Covenant* books. It means Morality. Mark Badbury already had his hand up.

"Mark?"

"The answer's in what you just said, miss. Ethics is to do with what you should and shouldn't do."

"Very smart answer, Mark. In Socrates' Greece they would have considered you a fine rhetorician. Is it *ethical* to get *every* secret out in the open?"

Duncan Priest cleared his throat. "Seems pretty ethical to get *your* secret out in the open, miss. To stop innocent schoolkids being chopped up."

"Spot on, Duncan. But would you spill the beans on *this* one?"

BATMAN'S REAL NAME IS BRUCE WAYNE

Most of the boys in the class let out murmurs of admiration.

"If *this* secret gets out, what is every master criminal in the world going to do? Christopher?"

"Blow Bruce Wayne's mansion to smithereens, miss." Christopher Twyford sighed. "No more Caped Crusader."

"Which would be a loss to society at large, yes? So sometimes it's ethical *not* to reveal a secret. Nicholas?"

"Like the Official Secrets Act." Nicholas Briar usually doesn't say a word in class. "When the Falklands War was on."

"Just so, Nicholas. Loose lips sink ships. Now. Think about your *own* secrets." (The connection between Ross Wilcox's wallet and his lost leg. My grandfather's smashed-up Omega Seamaster. Madame Crommelynck.) "How quiet it has suddenly become. Right, are *all* your secrets of the 'Yes, I should tell' or 'No, I shouldn't tell' varieties? Or is there a third category that, ethically speaking, is *not* so clear-cut? Personal secrets that don't affect anyone else? Trivial ones? Complex ones, with uncertain consequences if you tell them?"

Mumbled yeses, growing in strength.

Miss Lippetts got a fresh stick from a box of chalk. "You acquire more of these ambiguous secrets as you age, 3KM. Not less. Get used to them. Who can guess why I'm writing this word . . ."

REPUTATION

"Jason?"

3KM turned into a radiotelescope and tuned in on the class grass.

"Reputation is what gets damaged, miss, once a secret's out. Your reputation as a teacher'd be shot to bits, once it's proved you *are* an axe murderer. Bruce Wayne's reputation as this wouldn't-say-boo-to-a-goose Mr. Nobody'd be done for. It's like Neal Brose, too, isn't it?" (If I can grind a solar-powered calculator to bits, then stuff this rule that I should be ashamed for grassing on a kid and getting him expelled. In fact, stuff all rules.) "*He* had quite a secret going, didn't he? Wayne Nashend knew, Anthony Little knew. A few others." Gary Drake, over to my left, stared straight ahead. "But once his secret is out, his *reputation* as this . . ."

To everyone's surprise, Miss Lippetts suggested, "Golden boy?"

"Golden boy. *Excellent* word, Miss Lippetts." (For the first time in God knows how long I earned some class laughs.) "That reputation's wrecked. His *reputation* with kids as this . . . hard-knock you don't mess with is wrecked too. Without a reputation to hide *his* secret behind, Neal Brose is . . . totally . . . completely . . ."

Say it, nudged Unborn Twin, *I dare you to.*

". . . buggered. Miss. Screwed and buggered."

That appalled silence was *my* handiwork. Words made it. Just words.

Miss Lippetts *loves* her job, on good days.

My mind was scratching itself raw over how Mum and Dad'll react to what I did today, so I got the Christmas tree out of its cupboard as a distraction. The Quality Street tin of decorations too. December 20's here and Mum and Dad've hardly *mentioned* Christmas. Mum's at the gallery seven days a week and Dad keeps going off for interviews that only lead to more interviews. I put the tree together, and strung its fairy lights. When I was a kid Dad'd buy real trees from Gilbert Swinyard's dad. Mum got this artificial one from Debenhams in Worcester two years ago. I whinged that it didn't smell of anything, but she pointed out *I* wasn't the one who had to hoover and unpick the needles from the carpet. Which I s'pose's fair enough. Most of the decorations are older than me. Even the tissue paper they're wrapped in's ancient. Frosted baubles Mum and Dad bought for their first (and last) Christmas alone together, without Julia or me. A tin choirboy hitting a high note, his mouth a perfect O. A wooden family of jolly snowmen. (Everything wasn't made of plastic in those days.) The fattest Father Christmas in Lapland. Precious Angel, from Mum's mum's mum. Precious Angel's made of blown glass; she was a gift to my great-grandmother from a one-eyed Hungarian prince, so the story goes, at a ball in Vienna, just before the First World War.

Step on her, said Unborn Twin. *She'd crunch like a Crunchie.*

No bloody way, I told Unborn Twin.

The phone rang.

"Hello?"

Clunks and grundlings. "Jace? Julia. Long time no speak."

"You sound like you're in a blizzard."

"Call me back. I'm out of coins."

I dialed the number. The line was better.

"Cheers. No blizzards yet, but it's *freezing* up here. Is Mum there?"

"No. She's still at the gallery."

"Oh . . ."

Joy Division throbbed in the background.

"What is it?"

"Absolutely nothing."

"Absolutely nothing" is always something. "*What*, Julia?"

"Nah . . . nothing. When I got back to Halls this morning, there was a message from Mum, that's all. Did she phone me yesterday evening?"

"Could've done. What was the message?"

"Phone home immediately, it said. But our avuncular super-efficient porter—in our *dreams*—didn't write the time of the call. I phoned the gallery at lunchtime, but Agnes told me Mum's gone to her solicitors. Phoned *again*, but she hadn't got back. So I thought I'd phone you. But there's no need to worry."

"Solicitors?"

"Just be business stuff. Is Dad in?"

"He's doing interviews in Oxford."

"Right. Good. Sure. He's . . . y'know, keeping up okay?"

"Oh . . . okay. He's not locked himself in his office again, anyway. Last weekend he made a bonfire of Greenland files in the garden. Dean and me helped. Poured petrol on! It was like the *Towering Inferno*. Then this week Craig Salt's lawyer phoned Dad to say a delivery man was coming that afternoon to collect all the computer gear, and that if Dad didn't cooperate they'd sue."

"What did Dad do?"

"When the van pulled up, Dad dropped the hard drive out of my bedroom window."

"But that's upstairs."

"I know, and you should've heard the *monitor* smash! He told the delivery bloke, 'Give Craig Salt my compliments!' "

"Jesus! Worm turns, or what?"

"He's been decorating, too. Your bedroom was first on the hit list."

"Yeah, Mum said."

"Do you mind?"

"Well, no. It's not like I wanted them to preserve it forever like a Shrine to Julia or anything. Brings it home to you sharpish, though. 'Right, you're eighteen years old, off you go. Drop by the care home in about thirty years, if you're passing.' Oh ignore me, Jace, I'm being morbid."

"You're still coming home for Christmas, right?"

"Day after tomorrow. Stian's driving me down. His family owns this mansion in darkest Dorset."

"Stan?"

"No, *Stian*. He's Norwegian, Ph.D. in dolphin language? Didn't I mention him in my last letter?"

Julia knows *exactly* what she "mentions" in her letters.

"*Wow*. So he speaks in dolphin with you?"

"He programs computers that might, one day soon."

"What happened to Ewan?"

"Ewan's a *dear*, but he's in Durham and I'm up here and . . . well, I knocked it on the head. In the long run, it's for the best."

"Oh." But Ewan had a Silver MG. "I liked Ewan."

"Cheer up. Stian's got a Porsche."

"*God*, Julia. What sort? A GT?"

"*I* don't know! A black one. So what're *we* getting for Christmas?"

"Tube of Smarties." Dusty family joke. "Actually, I haven't looked."

"*Right!* You *always* go on prezzie hunts."

"Honest, I haven't. Record tokens and book tokens, most like. I haven't asked for anything. 'Cause of . . . y'know, Dad's job. And they haven't asked me. Anyway, who used to play your Christmas L.P.s in *November* and make me stand sentry in case they came back from shopping?"

"Remember that time you didn't? They caught me and Kate dressed in Mum's old wedding gear dancing to 'Knowing Me, Knowing You.' Speaking of which, has the Accept-No-Imitations Black Swan Green Grand Christmas Village Hall Disco already come and gone?"

"Starts in about an hour."

"Going with anyone?"

"Dean Moran's going. A few kids from my class."

"Oy! I told you about *my* love life."

Talking about girls with Julia's still pretty new. "That's 'cause you *have* a love life. I *did* sort of fancy this one girl, but she's . . ." *Helping the love of her life learn to walk with a plastic leg.* ". . . she's not interested."

"Her loss. Poor you."

"Odd thing is, I saw her at school last week, and, it's weird, but . . ."

"Your crush had evaporated?"

"Yeah. Into thin air. How does *that* happen?"

"Ah, search me, little brother. Search Aristophanes. Search Dante. Search Shakespeare. Search Burt Bacharach."

"Actually, I might not even go to the disco."

"Why not?"

Because I got Ant Little and Wayne Nashend suspended and Neal Brose expelled today and chances are they'll be there.

"I'm not feeling that Christmassy this year."

"Nonsense! Go! Shoes, not trainers. *Polish* them. Those black jeans we bought you in Regents Arcade. And that V-necked mustard sweater, if it's clean. Plain white T-shirt underneath. Logos are naff. Nothing pastel, nothing sporty. *Definitely* not that *yucko* piano tie. *Tiny* bit of Dad's Givenchy round your gills. Not Brut. Brut's as sexy as Fairy Liquid. Nick some of Mum's mousse and stick your fringe up a bit so you don't look like a Cub Scout. Dance your socks off, and may the bluebird of happiness fly up your nose."

"Okay." *Brose and Little and Nashend'll win if I don't.* "Bossy."

"What use is an unbossy lawyer? Look, there's a queue for the phone. Tell Mum I called. Say I'll keep checking the message board this evening. Till late."

The bruising cold wind shoved me along, every step bringing the class grass nearer to Brose, Nashend, and Little. Past Miss Throckmorton's, the village hall floated in the arctic dark, a lit-up ark. Its windows were stained disco colors. Michael Fish said the area of low pressure moving over the British Isles is coming from the Urals. The Urals're the USSR's Colorado Rockies. Intercontinental missile silos and fallout shelters're sunk deep in the roots of the mountains. There're research cities so secret they've got no names and don't appear on maps. Strange to think of a Red Army sentry on a barbed-wire watchtower shivering in this very same icy wind. Oxygen he'd breathed out might be oxygen I breathed in.

Julia'd spun out that conversation to distract me from something.

Pluto Noak, Gilbert Swinyard, and Pete Redmarley stood in the hallway. I'm really not their favorite person since that time they chucked me out of Spooks. They don't pick on me, they just act like I don't exist. Which is normally fine. But tonight this even older kid was with them. Stubbly, grim, brown leather jacket, All Blacks rugby shirt. Pluto Noak tapped him and pointed at me. A flock of girls behind me blocked off my escape route but the rugby kid'd already plowed right up to me. "*This* is him?"

"Aye!" Pluto Noak caught up. "That's him."

The hallway went very quiet.

"News for *you*." He gripped my coat so tight seams ripped. He throbbed with loathing. "*You* picked on the wrong kid today." His front teeth didn't part as he spoke; only his lips twitched. "You knobless, gobless, gutless, spineless, brainless, arseless, dickless, shitless, witless, pissless, bollockless piece of—"

"Josh." Pluto Noak clutched the kid's arm. "Josh! *This* ain't Neal Brose. This is *Taylor*."

This kid Josh glared at Pluto Noak. "This isn't Neal Brose?"

"No. Taylor."

Leaning against the door of the bogs, Pete Redmarley flicked a Minstrel into the air and caught it in his mouth.

"*This*"—Josh glared at Pete Redmarley—"is *that* Taylor?"

Pete Redmarley crunched his Minstrel. "Uh-huh."

"*You're* the Taylor"—Josh let go of my coat—"who grassed on those little midget Kray Twins who were squeezing *my* brother for money?"

"Who's—" My voice cracked. "Who's your brother?"

"Floyd Chaceley."

Mild Floyd Chaceley has one holy *ghost* of a big brother.

"Then, I'm *that* Taylor, yeah."

"Well." Josh patted my coat smooth. "Well done *you*, *that* Taylor. But if anyone of *you* lot"—everyone in the hallway shrank under his evil eye—"*knows* this Brose or Little or Nashend, tell 'em I'm *here*. Tell 'em I'm waiting, *now*. Tell them I want *words*."

Inside the village hall proper, a few kids were already dancing to "Video Killed the Radio Star." Most of the boys'd drifted to one side, too cool to dance. Most of the girls'd drifted to the other, too cool to dance too. Discos're tricky. You look a total wally if you dance too early, but after one crucial song tips the disco over, you look a sad saddo if you don't. Dean was talking to Floyd Chaceley by the hatch where they sell sweets and cans of drink. "Just met your brother," I told him. "Jesus. Wouldn't want to get on the wrong side of *him*."

"Stepbrother." Thanks to me, Floyd'd spent the morning in Nixon's office giving evidence against Neal Brose. For all I knew Floyd hated me. "Yeah, he's all right. Should've seen him earlier. Threatening to set Brose's *house* on fire."

I envied Floyd, having already squared the day with his mum and dad.

"Don't reckon Nashend or Little'll be showing up tonight, neither." Dean appeared by my side and offered me his Twirly Whirly to bite a bit off of.

Floyd bought me a Pepsi. "*Look* at Andrea Bozard!" Dean pointed at the same girl who used to pretend to be a pony at Miss Throckmorton's and make nests using acorns as eggs. "In that ra-ra skirt."

Floyd asked, "What about her?"

"*Lush?*" Dean did a panting doggy face. "Or what?"

"Friggin' in the Rigging" by the Sex Pistols came on and the Upton Punks pogoed up the front. Oswald Wyre's older brother Steve head-butted the wall, so Philip Phelps's dad drove him to Worcester Hospital in case he fell into a coma. But it got some of the boys dancing (sort of), so next the D.J. put on "Stand and Deliver" by Adam and the Ants. "Stand and Deliver" has this special dance that Adam Ant does in the video. You all line up and make an X with your wrists in the air as you pace along to the music. But everyone wanted to be Adam Ant, who does it one step ahead of his pack, so the line got faster and faster up and down the village hall till kids were virtually sprinting. Next was "The Lunatics (Have Taken Over the Asylum)" by Fun Boy Three. It's undanceable to, unless you're Squelch. Maybe Squelch heard a secret rhythm nobody else heard.

Robin South called out, "Squelch, yer spazzer!"

Squelch didn't even notice that nobody else was dancing.

Secrets affect you more than you'd think. You lie to keep them hidden. You steer talk away from them. You worry someone'll discover yours and tell the world. You think *you* are in charge of the secret, but isn't it the *secret* who's actually using *you*? S'pose lunatics mold their doctors more than doctors mold their lunatics?

In the bogs was Gary Drake.

Once I'd've frozen, but not after a day like today.

"All right?" Gary Drake said. Once he'd've sneered a comment about me not being able to find my dick. But suddenly I'm popular enough for Gary Drake to give an "All right?" to?

December cold streamed in through the window.

The boredest tilt of my head told Gary Drake, *Yeah.*

Cigarette butts bobbed in the Yellow River of steaming piss.

"Locomotion" got all the girls doing this choo-choo dance in a snaky line. Then there was "Oops Upside Your Head," which's got a sort of rowing-boat dance to it. It's not a dance for boys. "House of Fun" by Madness is, though.

"House of Fun" is about buying condoms but the BBC didn't ban it soon enough 'cause the BBC only spots secret meanings weeks after the dimmest duh-brain in Duffershire's got it. Squelch did this electrocuted dance that more kids copied to take the piss at first, but actually it worked. (There's a Squelch hiding in all great inventors.) Then "Once in a Lifetime" by Talking Heads came on. *That* was *the* crucial song that made it more bonzoish not to dance than to dance, so now me and Dean and Floyd did. The D.J. switched the strobe light on. Only for short bursts, 'cause strobes make your brain blow up. Dancing's like walking down a busy high street or millions of other things. You're absolutely fine as long as you don't think about it. During the strobe storm, through a stormy night forest of necks and arms, I saw Holly Deblin. Holly Deblin's got a sort of Indian goddess dance, swaying but sort of flicking her hands. Holly Deblin *might*'ve seen me through her stormy night forest, 'cause she *might*'ve smiled. (*Might* isn't as good as *did* but it's miles better than *didn't*.) Next was "I Feel Love" by Donna Summer. John Tookey showed off this new New York craze called break dancing but went spinning out of control into a group of girls, who toppled like skittles. John Tookey had to be rescued by his mates from stabbing female heels. During Bryan Ferry's "Jealous Guy" Lee Biggs got off with Angela Bullock. They snogged in the corner and Duncan Priest stood right by them and did his imitation of a cow giving birth. But the laughers were envious too. Angela Bullock wears black bras. *Then*, during "To Cut a Long Story Short" by Spandau Ballet, Alastair Nurton got off with Tracey Impney, this giant goth from Brotheridge Green. Gary Numan and Tubeway Army's "Are 'Friends' Electric?" came on and Colin Pole and Mark Badbury did this glazed robot dance. "This song's *ace!*" Dean yelled in my ear. "It's so *futuristic*. Gary Numan's got a friend named 'Five'! Is that brill or *what*?" Dancing's a brain the dancers're only cells of. Dancers think *they*'re in charge but they're obeying ancient orders. "Three Times a Lady" by the Commodores cleared the floor 'cept for boyfriends and girlfriends who smooched, enjoying being looked at, and snoggers who just snogged and forgot they were being looked at. Second choices were going for the third choices now. Paul White got off with Lucy Sneads. Next on was "Come on Eileen" by Dexy's Midnight Runners. A disco's a zoo too. Some of the animals're wilder than they are by day, some funnier, some posier, some shyer, some sexier. Holly Deblin'd obviously gone home.

"I thought you'd gone home."

An EXIT sign glowed alien-green in the dark.

"*I* thought *you*'d gone home."

The disco vibrated the plywood floor. Behind the stage there's this narrow back room stacked with stacks of chairs. It's got a sort of big shelf too, ten foot up and as wide as the back room. The table-tennis tabletops're kept up there and I know where the ladder's hidden.

"No. I was just dancing with Dean Moran."

"Oh yeah?" Holly Deblin did this funny jealous voice. "What's Dean Moran got that I haven't? Is he a good *kisser*?"

"*Moran*? That's re*volting*!"

"Revolting" was the last word I ever spoke as someone who'd never kissed a girl. I'd always worried but kissing's not so tricky. Your lips *know* what to do, just like sea anenomes know what to do. Kissing spins you, like Flying Tea-Cups. Oxygen the girl breathes out, you breathe in.

But your teeth can clunk, something chronic.

"Whoops." Holly Deblin drew back. "Sorry!"

"That's okay. I can glue them back in."

Holly Deblin twizzled my moussed hair. The skin round her neck's the softest thing I've *ever* stroked. And she let me. That's the amazing bit. She *let* me. Perfume counters in department stores, Holly Deblin smells of, the middle of July, and cinnamon Tic Tacs. My cousin Hugo reckons he's kissed *thirty* girls (and not only kissed) and he's probably up to fifty by now, but you can only have one first one.

"Oh," she said. "I nicked some mistletoe. Look."

"It's all squashy and—"

During my second ever kiss Holly Deblin's tongue visited my mouth, like a shy vole. You'd think that'd be disgustingsville too but it's wet and secret and mine wanted to visit hers back so I let it. *That* kiss ended 'cause I'd forgotten to breathe. "This song"—I was actually panting—"that's on right now. Sort of hippieish, but it's *beautiful*."

Words like "beautiful" you can't use with boys you can with girls.

" 'Number Nine Dream.' John Lennon. *Walls and Bridges* L.P., 1974."

"If that's s'posed to impress me, it *really* does."

"My brother works at Revolver Records. His L.P. collection stretches to Mars and back. So how d'you know about *this* little hidey-hole?"

"This back room? Used to come to youth club here, to play table tennis. I thought it'd be locked tonight. But I was wrong, obviously."

"Obviously." Holly Deblin's hands slid under my sweater. Years of hearing Julia and Kate Alfrick talk about wandering hands warned me off doing the same. Then Holly Deblin sort of shivered. I thought she might be cold, but she sort of giggled.

"What?" I was scared I'd done something wrong. "What?"

"Neal Brose's face, in Metalwork, this morning."

"Oh. That. This morning's one big blur. The whole day is."

"Gary Drake got him off the drill, right, and pointed at what you were doing. Brose didn't get it at first. That *thing* you were annihilating in the vice was actually his *calculator*. Then, *then*, he got it. He's a smarmy bastard but he's not stupid. He saw what'd happen next, and next, and next. He knew he was stuffed. Right at that moment, he knew."

I toyed with Holly Deblin's clacky beads.

She said, "I was pretty surprised, too."

I didn't hurry her.

"I mean, I *liked* you, Taylor, but I thought you were . . ." She didn't want to say anything that might hurt my feelings.

"A human punchbag?"

Holly Deblin propped her chin on my chest. "Yeah." Her chin dug in a bit. "What happened, Taylor? To you, I mean."

"Stuff." *Her* calling me "Taylor" feels closer than "Jason." I'm still too shy to call her anything. "The year. Look, I don't want to talk about Neal Brose. Another time?" I slipped off this woven band she wore round her wrist and slipped it over mine.

"Thief. Get your *own* top-of-the-range fashion accessories."

"I *am* doing. This one's the first in my collection."

Holly Deblin gripped my *slightly* big ears in her fingers and thumbs and steered my mouth to hers. Our third kiss lasted the *whole* of "Planet Earth" by Duran Duran. Holly Deblin guided my hand to where it could feel her fourteen-year-old heart beating against its palm.

"Hello, Jason." The lounge, lit by the Christmas-tree lights and the gas fire, reminded me of Santa's Grotto. The TV was off. Dad was just sitting there, so far as I could see, in the fruity dark. But the tone of his voice told me he knew all about Neal Brose and the wafered Casio. "Enjoy the disco?"

"Not bad." (He didn't care about the disco.) "How was Oxford?"

"Oxford was Oxford. Jason, we need to have a little chat."

I hung up my black parka on the coat stand, knowing I was a condemned man. "A little chat" means I sit down and Dad lays into me, but Holly Deblin must've rewired my head. "Dad, can I start?"

"All right." Dad looked calm, but volcanoes are calm just before they blow half a mountain away. "Go ahead."

"I've got two things to tell you. Big things, really."

"I can guess what one is. You had an exciting day at school, by all accounts."

"That's one of them, yes."

"Mr. Kempsey telephoned earlier. About that expelled boy."

"Neal Brose. Yeah. I—I'll pay for a new calculator."

"No need." Dad was too drained to throw an eppy. "I'll post his father a check in the morning. *He* telephoned too. Neal Brose's father, I mean. He apologized to *me*, actually." (*That* surprised me.) "Asked me to forget the calculator. I'll send the check anyway. If he chooses not to cash it, that's his lookout. But I think it'll draw a line under the affair."

"So . . ."

"Your mother might want to put in her sixpence ha'penny, but . . ." Dad shrugged. "Mr. Kempsey told me some bullying's been going on. I'm sorry you didn't feel you could tell us about it, but I can hardly get angry with you for that. Can I?"

Now I remembered Julia's phone call. "Is Mum home?"

"Mum's"—Dad's eyes went uneasy—"staying at Agnes's tonight."

"In Cheltenham?" (That didn't make sense. Mum never stays at anyone's 'cept Aunt Alice's.)

"There was a private view that went on late."

"She didn't mention it at breakfast."

"What's the second thing you wanted to tell me?"

This moment'd taken twelve months to whoosh here.

"Go on, Jason. I doubt it's as bad as you think."

Oh yes it is. "I was out"—Hangman stopped "skating"—"er . . . last January, when the pond in the woods froze over. Messing about with some other kids. I had Granddad's watch on. His Omega—" Hangman blocked "Seamaster." Saying this in reality was more dreamlike than the dozen bad dreams I've had about saying it. "The watch he bought when he was in the"—*God,* now I couldn't say "navy"—"stationed in Aden. But I fell over"—I couldn't turn back now—"and smashed it to pieces. Honest, I've spent all year trying to find a new one. But the only one I heard about cost eight hundred and fifty pounds. And I don't have that much money. Obviously."

Dad's face hadn't twitched. Not one muscle.

"I'm really sorry. I was an idiot to take it out."

Any *second* that calm'd crack and Dad'd an*nihil*ate me.

"Ah, it doesn't matter." (But grown-ups often say exactly that exactly when it matters most.) "It was only a watch. Nobody got hurt, not like that poor Ross Wilcox lad. Nobody died. Be more careful with fragile things in the future, that's all. Is there *anything* left of the watch?"

"Only the strap and the casing, really."

"Hang on to those. Some craftsmen might be able to graft parts of another Seamaster into Granddad's. You never know. When you're running thousand-acre nature reserves in the Loire Valley."

"So you're not going to . . . *do* anything? To me, I mean."

Dad shrugged. "You've put yourself through the mill already."

I'd *never* dared hope it'd go *this* well. "You were going to tell me something big too, Dad."

Dad swallowed. "You did a lovely job of decorating the tree."

"Thanks."

"Thank *you*." Dad took a sip of his coffee and grimaced. "I forgot to put in the NutraSweet. Would you mind getting it for me from the kitchen, love?"

"Love"? Dad hasn't called me that in *aeons*. "Sure." I went into the kitchen. It was freezing in there. Relief'd made gravity a bit weaker. I got Dad's NutraSweet, a teaspoon, and a saucer and went back to the lounge.

"Thanks. Sit down again."

Dad clicked a tiny capsule into his whirlpool of Nescafé, stirred it in, and picked up the cup and saucer. "Sometimes . . ." The awkwardness after his "sometimes" grew, and grew, and grew. "Sometimes, you can love *two* people in different ways at the same time." Just speaking, I saw, was a super*human* effort. "Do you understand?"

I shook my head. Dad's eyes might've given me a clue, but now he's staring down at his coffee. He's leaning forward. His elbows are resting on the coffee table. "Your mother and I . . ." Dad's voice's gone *horrible*, like some *shite* actor in some *shite* TV soap. "Your mother and I . . ." Dad's trembling. Dad doesn't tremble! The cup and saucer begin to clatter so he has to put them down, but he's hiding his eyes. "Your mother and I . . ."

january man

"Ap*parently*, he even took out *loans* for her!"

Guess who Gwendolin Bendincks was talking about?

"*Loans?*" Mrs. Rhydd actually squealed. "*Loans?*"

Why should *I* scurry off in shame? I've done nothing wrong. Was it *my* fault they hadn't noticed me, browsing through *Smash Hits* behind a pyramid of Pedigree Chum cans?

"Loans. To the tune of twenty—*thousand*—pounds."

"You could buy a small house with that! What does she need twenty thousand pounds for?"

"Polly Nurton says she has an office-equipment firm or some such in Oxford which supplies Greenland—the supermarkets, that is, not the country. Now isn't *that* a cozy little arrangement?"

Mrs. Rhydd didn't get it.

"Mrs. Rhydd, he works for Greenland as an area manager. Well, he did. He was sacked two months ago. Wouldn't surprise me to learn there's a connection between *that* and *this* whole . . . carry-on. Polly Nurton isn't one to beat around the bush, as you know. She said, What respectable organization wants an adulterer at the wheel? Doubtless he got her the contract with Greenland years ago, back when their . . . li*ai*son began."

"You mean they've been . . . for some time?"

"Oh yes! They committed their first . . . indiscretion *years* ago. He confessed to Helena at the time and swore to cut her off. Helena forgave him. For the sake of the family. One would. I mean" — people tend to whisper the word in case it brings them bad luck — "Divorce. It's a drastic step. Perhaps they didn't meet in the intervening years, perhaps they did. Polly Nurton didn't say and I'm no snoop. But once a lemon meringue's cut, no *amount* of tears can make it whole."

"*True*, Mrs. Bendincks. So *very* true."

"But Polly does know this much. When her business foundered last year — shortly after her husband'd upped sticks and left her with their baby — doubtless having scented something rotten in the state of Sweden, as it were — she turned to her former beau."

"The *brass* neck!"

"Last January, this was. Polly said she had some sort of a breakdown. Maybe she did, maybe she didn't. But she made nuisance calls to his house at all hours, *that* sort of carry-on. So, he borrowed a *hill* of money without so much as breathing a *word* to his own wife, using her family home as collateral."

"Your heart goes out to poor Mrs. Taylor, doesn't it?"

"Well ex*act*ly! She didn't know a *dickie bird* until she went through his bank statements. What a *way* to learn your *own home* is in hock! Can you ima*gine* how *duped* you'd feel? How be*trayed*? Ironic thing is, Helena's gallery in Cheltenham has people queueing round the block — *Home and Country* is doing a feature on it next month."

"If you ask me," steamed Mrs. Rhydd, "*she's* behaved no better than a common strump — "

Mrs. Rhydd sort of pufferfished as she caught sight of me. I put down *Smash Hits* and walked up to the counter. I'm getting lots of practice at acting like nothing's wrong.

"He*llo*! Jason, isn't it?" Gwendolin Bendincks switched on her smile at full beam. "You won't remember a wrinkly like me, but we met at the vicarage, this past summer."

"I remember you."

"I bet he says that to *all* the girls!" (Mrs. Rhydd had the decency to look mortified.) "So the weatherman says we're in for a good dumping of snow tonight. You'd *love* that, wouldn't you? Sledging, igloo building, snowball fights."

"How are" — Mrs. Rhydd fiddled with a price gun — "*things*, my pet? You're moving out today, aren't you?"

"The removal men're loading up the heavy stuff now. Mum, my sister,

Kate Alfrick, and Mum's boss are packing the last bits and pieces, so they told me to go off for a couple of hours to—" Hangman blocked "say good-bye."

"To bid Black Swan Green au revoir." Gwendolin Bendincks jumped in with a knowing smile. "You'll visit us *soon*, won't you? Cheltenham's hardly the ends of the earth, is it?"

"I guess not."

"You're putting a jolly brave face on it, Jason." She clasped her hands like she'd trapped a grasshopper. "But I want to say, if Francis—the vicar, I mean—and I can be any help whatso*ever*, our door's always open. Will you tell your mother that?"

"Sure." *I know a well you can drown yourself in.* "Sure."

"Hullo, Blue," Mr. Rhydd came from the back. "What'll it be?"

"One quarter of rhubarb and custards, and one of crystallized ginger." Crystallized ginger makes my gums sweat but it turns out that Mum loves it. "Please."

"Right you are, Blue." Mr. Rhydd climbed his ladder to the jars.

"Cheltenham's divine." Gwendolin Bendincks got back to work on me. "Old spa towns have such character. Is it a *large* place your mother's renting, Jason?"

"Haven't seen it yet."

"And your father's going to be based in Oxford?" (I nodded.) "No luck with a new job, yet, I hear?" (I shook my head.) "Firms only just back from the Christmas hols, that's why. Still, Oxford's hardly the ends of the earth, is it, Mrs. Rhydd? Be going up to see Dad soon, will we?"

"We . . . haven't talked about it much, yet."

"One thing at a time, very wise. But you'll be looking forward to a brand-new school! Like I *always* say. A stranger is just a friend you haven't met yet." (Bollocks. I've never met the Yorkshire Ripper, but he wouldn't be a friend.) "So, is your old house in Kingfisher Meadows officially on the market yet?"

"Soon, I s'pose."

"Reason I ask is, our vicarage moved to a bungalow on the Upton road, but that was only a stopgap. Tell Mum to have her agent give Francis a tinkle before it's advertised anywhere. Mum'd rather do business with a friend than with some outsider she wouldn't know from Adam. Remember those ghastly Crommelynck characters who foisted themselves onto us? So you'll tell her? Promise me, Jason? Scout's honor?"

"Sure, I promise." *In about forty years.* "Scout's honor."

"Right you are, Blue," said Mr. Rhydd, twirling the bags closed.

an evil-eyed witch. She's frumpier than Mum, *any* day, and mousier. Brown hair in a bob, brown eyes. She doesn't look a *thing* like a stepmother. Which is what she'll be, by and by.

"Hello, Jason." The woman Dad'd rather spend the rest of his life with than Mum looked at me like I had a gun pointed at her. "I'm Cynthia."

"Hi. I'm Jason." This was very very *very* weird. Neither of us tried to shake hands. In the back of her car was a BABY ON BOARD sticker. "You've got a baby?"

"Well, Milly's more of a toddler now." If you just heard her voice next to Mum's you'd say Mum's posher. "Camilla. Milly. Milly's father—my ex-husband—we're already . . . I mean, he's not on the scene. As they say."

"Right."

Dad watched his future wife and his only son from his ex-garage.

"Well." Cynthia smiled unhappily. "Come and visit whenever you want, Jason. Trains go to Oxford from Cheltenham, direct." Cynthia's voice is less than half the volume of Mum's. "Your dad would like you to. He *really* would. So would I. It's a big old house we're in. There's a stream at the end of the garden. You could even have your—" She was about to say, "your own bedroom." "Well, you're welcome, anytime."

All I could do was nod.

"Whenever it suits." Cynthia looked at Dad.

"So how—" I began, suddenly scared of having nothing to say.

"If you—" she began in the same second.

"After you—"

"No, after you. Really. You go ahead."

"How long . . ." No grown-up's ever made me go first. ". . . have you known Dad?" I'd meant the question to sound breezy but it came out all Gestapo.

"Since we were growing up." Cynthia was working hard to iron out any extra meanings. "In Derbyshire."

Longer than Mum, then. If Dad'd married this Cynthia in the first place, instead of Mum, and if they'd had a son, would it have been me? Or a totally different kid? Or a kid who's half me?

All those Unborn Twins're a numbing prospect.

I got to the lake in the woods and remembered the game of British Bulldogs we'd played here when the lake froze last January. Twenty or thirty kids, skimming and shrieking, all *over* the shop. Tom Yew'd interrupted the game, scrambling down the path I'd just taken, on his Suzuki. He'd sat on the exact same bench I was sitting on, remembering him. Now Tom Yew's in a cemetery on a treeless hill on a bunch of islands we'd never even *heard* of last January. What's left of Tom Yew's Suzuki's being picked apart to repair other Suzukis. The world won't leave things be. It's always injecting endings into beginnings. Leaves tweezer themselves from these weeping willows. Leaves fall into the lake and dissolve into slime. Where's the sense in that? Mum and Dad fell in love, had Julia, had me. They fall *out* of love, Julia moves off to Edinburgh, Mum to Cheltenham, and Dad to Oxford with Cynthia. The world never stops unmaking what the world never stops making.

But who says the world has to make sense?

In my dream a fishing float'd appeared in the water, orange on glossy dark, just a few feet out. Holding the rod was Squelch, sitting on the other end of my bench. This dream Squelch was so realistic in every detail, even his smell, I realized I must be awake. "Oh. All right, Mervyn? God, I was dreaming about . . ."

"Wakey wakey stiffy shakey."

". . . something. Been here long?"

"Wakey wakey stiffy shakey."

My Casio said I'd only been asleep for ten minutes. "Must've . . ."

"It'll snow soon. It'll stick an' all. School bus'll get stuck."

My joints clunked as I stretched. "Aren't you watching *Moonraker*?" My joints unclunked.

Squelch gave me this tragic look like *I* was the certified village idiot. "Ain't no TV here. I'm fishin', I am. Come to see the swan."

"Black Swan Green hasn't got any swans. That's the village joke."

"Crotch rot." Squelch shoved one hand down his pants and gave his grollies a good scratching. "Crotch rot."

A robin landed on the holly bush, as if posing for a Christmas card.

"So . . . what's the biggest thing you've caught in this lake, Merv?"

"Ain't never caught bugger all. Not down this end. I fishes up the narrer end, up by the island, don't I?"

"So what's the biggest thing you've caught up the narrow end?"

"Ain't never caught bugger all up the narrer end, neither."

"Oh."

Mum lugged a last box into Mum's Datsun. Dad called Yasmin Morton-Bagot a Hooray Henrietta once, and maybe she is one, but Hooray Henriettas can be as tough as Hell's Angels. Julia fitted a laundry basket, a wound-up washing line, and a bag of pegs into Yasmin Morton-Bagot's Alfa Romeo.

T minus five minutes, I reckoned.

The net curtain in Mr. Castle's bedroom twitched. Mrs. Castle came close to the glass like a drowned face. She peered down at Mum, Julia, and Yasmin Morton-Bagot.

What big eyes Mrs. Castle has.

She felt me watching her and our eyes met. Quick as a minnow, the net curtain twitched back.

Julia received my telepathic signal and looked up at me.

I half-waved.

"I've been sent to get you." My sister's footsteps clopped into my room. "Dead or alive. Could start snowing any minute. The radio said ice sheets and woolly mammoths are moving down the M5, so we'd better get going."

"Okay." I didn't move off my windowsill perch.

"Much louder without carpets and curtains, isn't it?"

"Yeah." Like the house hasn't got any clothes on. "Much." Our quiet voices boomed, and even daylight was a notch whiter.

"I always envied you your room." Julia leaned on my windowsill. Her new hair suits her, once you get used to it. "You can keep an eye on the neighbors from here. Spy on the Woolmeres and the Castles."

"*I* envied you *yours*."

"What? Up in the attic like a Victorian pot scrubber?"

"You can see right up the bridle path to the Malverns."

"When a storm was on I thought the whole roof was going to lift off, like in *The Wizard of Oz*. Used to petrify me."

"That's difficult to imagine."

Julia toyed with the platinum dolphin necklace Stian'd given her. "What's difficult to imagine?"

"Difficult to imagine anything *ever* petrifying you."

"Well, *behind* my fearless facade, little brother, I am regularly scared *witless* by all manner of things. But how stupid of us. Why on earth didn't we just swap rooms?"

The echoey house asked its far corners but no answer rebounded back.

Our right to be here is weaker by the minute.

Some snowdrops'd come out in the boggy spot, by Dad's greenhouse. By Dad's ex-greenhouse.

"What was the name of that game," Julia asked, staring down, "when we were kids? I described it to Stian. Where we'd chased each other round and round the house and the first one to catch up with the other won?"

"Round and Round the House."

"*That* was it! Apt title." Julia was trying to cheer me up again.

"Yeah." I let her think it was working. "And *you* hid behind the oil tank one time and watched me sprint past for thirty minutes like a total prat."

"Not thirty minutes. You caught on after twenty, at most."

But it's okay for Julia. On Monday her cool boyfriend will land in Cheltenham in his black Porsche, she'll just hop in, and off they'll zoom to Edinburgh. On Monday *I've* got to go to a new school in a new town and be the New Kid Whose Parents by the way Are Getting Divorced. I don't even have a proper uniform yet.

"Jason?"

"Yeah?"

"Any idea why Eliot Bolivar stopped writing poems for the parish magazine?"

Just six months ago Julia saying that'd've mortified me, but my sister'd asked it seriously. Was she bluffing, to draw me out? No. How long'd she known? But who cares?

"He smuggled his poems into that bonfire Dad lit for his Greenland paperwork. He told me the fire turned all his poems into masterpieces."

"I hope"—Julia bit at a spike of fingernail—"he hasn't given up writing altogether. He's got literary promise. When you next run into him, tell him from me to stick at it, will you?"

"Okay."

Yasmin Morton-Bagot fumbled through her glove compartment and got out a map.

"The weirdest thing," I said, my fingers drumming the Oxo tin, "is leaving the house without Dad. I mean, he ought to be running around now, turning off the boiler, the water, the gas . . ." This divorce's like in a disaster film when a crack zigzags along the street and a chasm opens up under someone's feet. I'm that someone. Mum's on one side with Julia, Dad's on the other with Cynthia. If I don't jump one way or the other I'm going to fall into bottomless blackness. "Checking windows, one last time, checking the 'lecky. Like when we went on holidays up to Oban or the Peak District or somewhere."

I haven't cried about the divorce once. I'm not going to now.

No *bloody* way am I crying! I'll be fourteen in a few days.

"It'll be all right." Julia's gentleness makes it worse. "In the end, Jace."

"It doesn't *feel* very all right."

"That's because it's not the end."

acknowledgments

Thank you to Nadeem Aslam, Eleanor Bailey, Jocasta Brownlee, Amber Burlinson, Evan Camfield, Lynn Cannici, Tadhg Casey, Stuart Coughlan, Louise Dennys, Walter Donohue, Maveeda Duncan and her daughter, David Ebershoff, Keith Gray, Rodney Hall, Ian Jack, Henry Jeffreys, Sharon Klein, Kerr's Bookshop in Clonakilty, Hari Kunzru, Morag and Tim Joss, Toby Litt, Jynne Martin, Jan Montefiore, Lawrence Norfolk, Jonathan Pegg, Nic Rowley, Shaheeda Sabir, Michael Schellenberg, Eleanor Simmons, Rory and Diane Snookes, Doug Stewart, Carole Welch, and the White-Haired Lady of Hay-on-Wye who advised me to keep the rabbit, which nonetheless escaped from the final manuscript.

Special thanks to my parents and Keiko.

A distant ancestor of the first chapter appeared in *Granta* 81. A recent ancestor of the second chapter appeared in *New Writing 13* (Picador). The fifth chapter was researched with reference to *The Battle for the Falklands* by Max Hastings and Simon Jenkins (Pan Books, 1997). The eighth chapter quotes from *Le Grand Meaulnes* by Alain-Fournier (Librairie Fayard, 1971). The novel owes debts of detail to Andrew Collins's memoir *Where Did It All Go Right?* (Ebury Press, 2003).

DAVID MITCHELL was born in northwestern England in 1969. He wrote his first two novels, *Ghostwritten* and *Number9Dream*, while living in Japan, and his third, *Cloud Atlas*, on his return to England. His novels have received several awards and been translated into twenty languages. David Mitchell now lives in Ireland with his family.

about the type

This book was set in Electra, a typeface designed for Linotype by W. A. Dwiggins, the renowned type designer (1880-1956). Electra is a fluid typeface, avoiding the contrasts of thick and thin strokes that are prevalent in most modern typefaces.